Julian Rathbone is the author of ma[...]
acclaimed *The Last English King*, K[...]
shortlisted *Joseph*. He lives in Hampsh[...]

Praise for Julian Rathbone

A Very English Agent

'There is a wealth of solid research underpinning this light-hearted romp through the first half of the nineteenth century. Scene after scene is both outrageously over the top and oddly convincing ... For rollicking period fiction, with a razor-sharp mind behind it, the book would be hard to better' David Robson, *Sunday Telegraph*

'The photograph of Julian Rathbone on the dust jacket shows a man with a twinkling eye and a mischievous smile and both adjectives are more than applicable to his new novel ... Never less than invigorating and entertaining' *Observer*

The Last English King

'Gripping ... a rattling good story, told in strong, clear prose ... unforgettable' *Spectator*

'A triumph ... echoes of *I Claudius*' *Independent*

Kings of Albion

'The War of the Roses never seemed so strange – or so real ... a historical novel of charm and intelligence' *Sunday Telegraph*

'A superb adventure story' *Independent*

Joseph

'A delight ... an inventive, comic, parodic romp through bloody battles, brothels, witchcraft, torture and philosophising' A. S. Byatt, *Literary Review*

'Glittering entertainment' Michael Ratcliffe, *New Statesman*

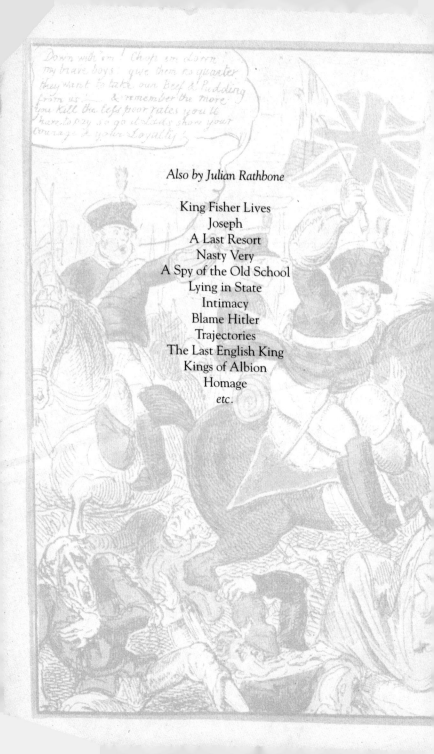

Down with 'em! Chop 'em down! my brave boys! give them no quarter they want to take our Beef & Pudding from us. & remember the more you kill the less poor rates you'll have to pay so go it Lads show your courage & your Loyalty!

Also by Julian Rathbone

King Fisher Lives
Joseph
A Last Resort
Nasty Very
A Spy of the Old School
Lying in State
Intimacy
Blame Hitler
Trajectories
The Last English King
Kings of Albion
Homage
etc.

A Very English
Agent

Julian Rathbone

ABACUS

An *Abacus* Book

First published in Great Britain by Little, Brown in 2002
This edition published by Abacus in 2003

Copyright © Julian Rathbone 2002

The moral right of the author has been asserted.

A CIP catalogue record for this book is
available from the British Library.

ISBN 0 349 11508 7

Typeset in Goudy by M Rules
Printed and bound in Great Britain
by Clays Ltd, St Ives plc

Abacus
An imprint of
Time Warner Books UK
Brettenham House
Lancaster Place
London WC2E 7EN

www.TimeWarnerBooks.co.uk

This book is for all at Little, Brown who have done
so much for me as an author over the last six years,
particularly Richard Beswick, Philippa Harrison,
Viv Redman (who was previously my editor at
Gollancz), Joanna Thurman, Andy Hine and,
of course, their wonderful sales force.

Acknowledgements

I should like to thank the following (and this list is by no means complete): the first Duke of Wellington, William Wordsworth, William Cobbett, Jane Austen, John Keats, Percy Bysshe Shelley, Lord Byron, Mary Shelley, Lord Tennyson, Henry Mayhew, Frederick Engels, Karl Marx, Charles Dickens, Wilkie Collins, Mrs Beeton, Thomas Hardy, Joseph Conrad, Sir James Frazer, James Joyce and F. R. Leavis, all of whom I have fictionalised or from whom I have borrowed characters, and occasionally actual phrases, sentences or even a paragraph or two.

I am a novelist, not an historian. I do not go to primary sources. While preparing and writing *A Very English Agent*, I have dipped into what seems like hundreds of books and articles and I have surfed the net. I have not kept a list of everything I have looked at, but the following were indispensable: *The Duke* by Philip Guedalla, *Wellington: Pillar of State* by Elizabeth Longford, *Waterloo: New Perspectives* by David Hamilton-Williams, *Captain Swing* by E. J. Hobsbawm and George Rudé, *The Making of the English Working Class* by E. P. Thompson, *The Great Exhibition* by John R. Davis (which I plundered as it was the only detailed source I could find), *Karl Marx* by Francis Wheen, *Darwin* by Adrian Desmond and James Moore, *Records of the Rathbone Family*, edited by Emily A. Rathbone, *The Annals of London* by John Richardson, and *Shelley: The Pursuit* by Richard Holmes. Invidious to single one volume from the rest but the last named gave me more pleasure than any of the others and is surely one of the very best literary biographies ever written.

Of all the many web sites I visited spartacus.schoolnet.co.uk was the one I used far more often and usefully than any other. Again, the 1911 edition of the *Encyclopædia Britannica* was always my first resort and often the only one I needed. Finally, a special thank you to Margaret Olive, Head of History at Ringwood (Comprehensive) School, whose extensive file on Peterloo virtually wrote a chapter for me, though, there, and elsewhere, I must admit to much embroidery beyond what the sources tell us.

Part I

WAR

Nothing except a battle lost can be half so melancholy as a battle won.

ARTHUR WELLESLEY, DUKE OF WELLINGTON

1

I was fifteen years old, or was it twenty, when I was thrust on to the stage of world history.* I remember it well. The thing of it is I don't remember anything before – just tall dark shapes walking across muddy deserts out of darkness. So my earliest memory is of a woman, a girl. No, I tell a lie. My first memory is of a butterfly, a fritillary perhaps, slowly opening and closing its wings, cinnamon coloured with intricately patterned black spots and smudges and dots, cut as with scissors into a swallow-tail, and occasionally wiping its eyes and its watch-spring proboscis with its front legs. It was sitting on a rounded mound of white skin, just inches from my eyes, a shoulder of perfect marble but for a mole or two which rose and fell almost imperceptibly as the woman beneath me breathed in and out – more easily than I, since my waist was being squeezed by arms that threatened to crush the life out of me.

Maribel was a big girl. And therefore far bigger than I. She

* In fact, if you'll forgive the word in a comment on a work of fiction, and if you believe what we later learn about Charlie, he was probably twenty-five. J. R.

3

was naturally gap-toothed, had a snub-nose, and ebony eyes that grinned a lot. Her dark hair, crudely cut, was shortish and largely hidden by the only garment she was wearing – a red scarf with white polka dots, that covered most of her head and was knotted behind her neck. Moments before she had shed a short ochre shift, a coarse black skirt and wooden sabots, after first undressing me.

A prolonged rattle of musketry about half a mile away caused her to move more sharply than before and the butterfly took off. Its weaving, dithering flight took it to a bramble in flower where it settled once more, this time to feed on blackberry-flavoured nectar extracted from the centre of a corolla made by the five pearly petals of a tiny bramble flower. Maribel lifted her head, a curiosity tinged with concern tightening her lips and creasing her brow. Then she smiled up at me, murmured in her coarse dialect, and wriggled a little, repositioning herself so my tautly stiff member could penetrate yet further.

I wriggled too and my knees squelched in the mud, cow-shit and chalky grit between her noble thighs.

The musketry which had distracted Maribel was the British army clearing its throat: that is, in order to clean the barrels of their Brown Besses each soldier had discharged his piece into the air.

Presently I discharged my piece into Maribel, but too soon for her. It did not matter. Such is the potency of youth I suffered only a momentary and partial weakening of flesh and desire and she quickly resumed her approach to ecstasy.

This was a long time coming. The problem was, she was large and I so small, my whole physique I mean, not my member, and the mounds and slopes of her thighs and pubis were such that even though he was, and is, large in terms of the rest of me, he could do little more than cross the threshold of the door she had opened so wide.

She reversed our positions. Large and huge, she was also strong and healthy. With both hands clasped about my waist she hoisted me above her, much as if I were a pet cat or puppy,

4

and rolling with the slight incline into the bottom of the sunken ditch or track, got me on to my back and herself over me, knees planted in the wet loam on either side of my body, hands way beyond my head, her breasts now slapping my cheeks, obscuring what I might have seen of the sky through the branches of elder and plates of elderflower above us. Positioned thus she attempted to lower her pudenda on to my gallant and manly prick which still stood to attention as straight as any bear-skinned Imperial Guardsman. Holly leaves dug into my back like a thorny penitential shirt.

A hundred thousand feet beat the ground and bands played, but not close enough to distract my Maribel. More troublesome to her were the flies, those bright brown ones that bite voraciously. A yard from her left knee there was a large wet cowpat that had attracted them initially to sup from the yellowish liquor that lay pooled in its shallow crater, but now, thirst satisfied, they sought meatier sustenance. She took a moment from what she was attempting to slap one that had settled on the shoulder that had been beneath my gaze and was now above it. She smeared its corpse from her hand and on to my stomach and then thrust it, her hand I mean, back between us, searching him out, feeding him in so I thought she'd swallow him whole, balls and all, and the rest of me behind them.

Harness jangled, a lot of harness, above a clipping and clopping of hooves, many many hooves; we heard the squelch and rattle as the six-foot rye beyond the hedge of holly, hawthorn and elder was pushed aside and trampled. Moving my head as far as I could to the left and peering up through a triangle of light fringed by the hair in her armpit, I could see pennants on the ends of steely lances briskly rise and fall with the motion of the trotting chargers beneath them. A bugle call and all as one wheeled away from the ditch and were gone. But not before the sun had flashed from the rear piece of a cuirass, as bright as a mirror.

There was a down beyond our ditch, a long, low snaking rise above rolling fields of rye tall enough to hide a man, bluey green, more blue than green when the breeze ran its fingers through. Deep ditches like the one we were in, overhung with double canopies of elder, alder in the deeper dips, holly, hawthorn and banked with dock, sorrel, nettles, cranesbill, bugloss, and Solomon's seal, ran down its slope. There were foxgloves too, and clouds of butterflies, small and blue, white, scarlet and black, as well as jet and cinnamon. A distant cock crowed, a blackbird sang above our heads, and a mile away the wheels of half a thousand cannon, limber carts and fourgons squealed in unharmonious discords.

Maribel snorted or sighed, hoisted one dimpled knee and milk-white thigh over my body as if dismounting a diminutive hobby horse and exposed for a moment the darkness in her heavy bush, clogged with slime. Then, sitting up on her huge buttocks, she slewed herself round, pushing up a little gelid wave of brackish mud, so we were next to each other, side by side. For a moment she sat forward, arms spread across her raised knees, turned her head and shook it again so her black hair streaked with russet mud moved lankly beneath her polka-dot scarf and across her massive alabaster shoulders. She frowned, pouted, adjusted the scarf and thought. Then she curled her heavy arm about my waist and, pushing a little and mumbling imprecations until I caught on what she wanted, had me astride her once-again recumbent torso but with my back to her face and my head between her thighs.

Her odours were magnificent. Farmyard shit behind sweet, musky hawthorn blossom. I suffocated. I gasped, pulled back. Heaved in the foetid air and plunged back in. I went to work, the earth shook, the thunder roared in my ears. I flattened my shoulders and chest across her rounded stomach, reached under and between and got two fingers up her bum. That did it – she spasmed and so did I.

The rolling thunder went on, and the earth continued to shake.

She rolled me off her, squelch into the mud, and sat up facing me. Her head was framed by an oval of light at the end

6

of the green tunnel we sat in. She smiled at me, a silly smile, part shy, part triumphant, making twin moons of her apple cheeks. She panted a little, then spoke, head up and on one side, searching the dappled leaves, blossom and sunlight. I can't be sure what she said, but I'd guess, Englished, it went like this.

'What the fuck is going on?'

'A battle?' said I.

A sphere, iron, a foot or more in diameter, fused with a spluttering string, dropped through the canopy twenty feet behind her, trundled down the slope towards her, the fuse hissed and disappeared and the shell exploded. Fragments of casing and several pounds' weight of musket balls screamed through the air, tearing down leaves, twigs and elder blossom. A piece of casing nearly severed her head and four balls smashed their way into her back. She fell forward, over her knees, on to her face.

I owe her much. Had she not sheltered me from the blast, albeit unwittingly, I should have been blown to bits.

2

In such moments one acts rationally. Lightning, they say, does not strike in the same place twice. However, a shell fired from a howitzer with the same charge, in the same direction, with the muzzle at the same elevation, might. I ran up the ditch away from poor Maribel, avoiding the still smoking pieces of jagged iron, as fast as my bare feet slithering in cow-shit and snared with brambles would let me, and found a sort of tiny cave, more like a foxhole really but not as deep, where the mossy roots of an overarching hazel, growing in the bank, had been partly washed away leaving a nest like a loosely woven basket. I crawled into this hole – it would not have been big enough to shelter a normal lad of my age – and half on my side pulled my knees up to my chin. I put my thumb into my mouth, breaking off only to brush away the flies that wanted to make a meal of Maribel's blood, still smeared across my neck and shoulder and in my hair.

The noise receded somewhat, came and went, a jumble of bugle calls, shouts, marching feet, trotting hooves, jangling accoutrements near by, distant sounds of intermittent music as bands played and bagpipes wailed, and the steady almost unbroken rumbling roar of distant artillery. That a battle was in progress I was now certain, but, it seemed to me, in spite of the shell that had killed Maribel, its epicentre was way off to the west: only occasionally did a gun bang away near by, or musketry briefly rattle.

I thought of my clothes: a shirt, a blue coat and white trousers cut down to fit me, albeit loosely. They had belonged to Maribel's brother, a fusilier in the Grande Armée, who lay up in the farm nursing the stumps of his foot and hand, fallen off on account, they said, of the cold coming back from Moscow, wherever that was. Anyway his clothes, uniform really, were where I had left them, bundled up in the ditch five paces beyond Maribel's torn body.

I racked my brains trying to work out where I was in relation to the farm buildings Maribel had led me away from. Her father had said the cattle were to be kept stabled that day, on account of the quantity of soldiers in the area. Her normal occupation was to herd these huge kine, uddered like barrels, with stalactites of green saliva drooling from their mouths, along the double-hedged ditch and up on to the pasture on the ridge they called the mount of St John where she watched over them until evening milking time. But that day he had sent her, with me as her helper, with a fardel of hazel branches on her back, to block off gaps that the soldiers in the area had made in the hedges.

Clearly I could go back the way I had come, but this I was loth to do. First, Maribel's torn remains lay in my path, and secondly I did not feel I wanted to venture along that winding tunnel of bushes and trees until I had gained some knowledge of what now lay at the end of it. Consequently, naked as I still was, I grasped the smooth trunk of my hazel and hoisted myself up through its leafy twigs to the level of the field above.

Having climbed for a hundred yards or so in that first fright I was now almost at the point where the floor rose to the level of the land around it; I was therefore in something of a vantage point, having a long view along the rise to my right, while to my left the rye-covered slopes rolled down to a shallow and wide bottom before climbing again to a similar rise whose crest was a thousand yards or so to the south. The immense amphitheatre that lay spread before me was so filled with animation, movement, death and glory that it quite seized my breath and for a time held me, driving from my mind almost all thoughts of self-preservation.

On my side of the wide shallow valley I could see a line of capped or shakoed heads behind a hedge of muskets, the muzzles of cannon and a fluttering flag or two. Small groups of mounted officers hacked along the path or track in front of them, occasionally reining in to point their telescopes and spyglasses across the valley to the further side. Occasionally round shot hit the wet earth and grass in front of them, spewing up a little storm of mud or bouncing on into the lines beyond.

A solitary tree, an elm not full grown, stood on the ridge about halfway along the rise, marking a crossroads where a proper road, a paved *chaussée*, cut right down the southern slope and up the side of the northern one. Under its branches was a larger group of horsemen, a dozen or so, some uniformed, some in riding clothes such as gentlemen might wear for a day following hounds. In their centre and a little to the front of the rest was a man in a small fore and aft cocked hat wearing a dark blue coat, white breeches and black boots that came midway up his calves.

Thus the rise to my right. It compared ill with that to my left. Here was a mighty army, formed up in oblong blocks of men, a couple of hundred across, eighty or so deep, each uniformed in its own way, many in blue, but black, yellow, brown and orange featured too. I don't know how many, maybe eighty thousand men all told, with batteries of cannon between them and on the rise above them. And even as my gaze swept along all these pieces flashed as one, white smoke billowed from every muzzle, the report of their powder seemed to bend the air which was filled with screaming shot, a terrible storm of it that lasted twenty minutes or more and seemed to drive the redcoats back from their rise, leaving no doubt hundreds of dead, dying, mutilated and broken bodies behind them.

Drums began to beat, hundreds of them, trumpets brayed, bands played the 'Revolutionary Hymn' and one by one those solid blocks of men began to move down into the bottom, trampling what rye still stood in just such a way as I expected they would soon be trampling what was left of the raggle-taggle army that had all but disappeared behind the ridge on my side. Several things now seemed to happen almost at once. Though I shall take them in due order you must believe one followed another as quickly as one swallow might track the flight of another in an evening sky.

First, the ridge that had seemed deserted suddenly filled with men, marshalled in double ranks, each rank a couple of hundred strong, then a gap into which cannon were trundled with remarkable speed, the gunners heaving and hauling on the spokes to drag them through the mud, then two more ranks, and so forth for a distance along the ridge of five hundred paces or more. Most wore uniforms of orange and buff and for a moment or two stood firm, firing volley after volley into the massed columns before them. The progress of these seemed to stammer but those behind pressed those in front, their officers capered and hallooed, waving their plumed hats and swords. They surged up the last ten or twenty paces, closing with the men who faced them and driving them back to a low and now much damaged hedge that ran along the side of the road.

All circumstances favoured the attackers who had no more slope to contend with and saw for the most part only the backs of their opponents. Keeping line and station they poured on to the ridge which flattened into a plateau, so their foremost ranks were almost beyond my sight, when suddenly all seemed to stop, and a shudder, such as a bull in a bullfight might make when the picador's pike finds its withers, ran through all, and through the bedlam I heard bugles call, bagpipes play, and above the caps of the Frenchmen I could see, here and there, along the line, three Union flags, billowing in the breeze though already torn with shot. Volleys rang out in terrible unison and then a sudden glitter of bayonets ran along the

11

ridge and the hedge that were the limit of my view and over they came like a crest of breaking surf, thundering out of the ocean on to a windswept beach, a double line of redcoats.

Out near the front of them a thickset man of some years, dressed in a shabby grey greatcoat, beneath a high top hat, whirled a furled umbrella from the back of his horse, but for a moment only: a ball took him in the head and hurled him backwards into the mêlée.

But now it was steel against steel, bayonet against bayonet, and I doubt many of his men saw him go so fiercely were they engaged. The columns staggered, here and there fell back, but again the press of men behind was too great, and slowly their sheer weight pushed their wounded and dying in front of them and even under their boots as they went on back again over the ridge. Especially those in the third column I could see had reached the hedge whence they poured shot across the road into the thin lines in front of them. Almost along the whole ridge now it seemed the French would push through and by sheer weight of numbers, at least two to one, push back their opponents, even cause them to break and run. But now that straight figure with the short fore and aft cocked hat appeared on his chestnut charger, rallied a line of men, made them form up and in the nick of time waved his hat in a circle above his short-cropped hair and, through the smoke that billowed about him, directed a volley at point-blank range at the horde that was on the point of overwhelming them.

And then, even nearer my hazel tree, where the fourth column of French was just clambering on to the flat at about the place where my sunken path levelled up and formed a junction with the road on the ridge, came a sudden wailing of bagpipes and a double line of kilted Scotsmen came over the rise and hurled themselves with claymores and bayonets into the mass in front of them, many of whom, so sudden and fierce was the onslaught upon them, began to wheel away from the crest, in a movement across the slope rather than up it, and many broke ranks and fled.

12

But in spite of these two successes the battle was clearly lost, they were no more than boulders in a flood, enough to cause an eddy and break the flow where they were but not enough to stem or dam the tide. Or so I thought. By now I had myself been caught up in the horror and fury of the contest, had climbed my hazel tree, though keeping as much of its thin branches as I could between me and the battle, and naked as I still was found myself hallooing on the gallant men who had carried all before them and driven the British and their allies out of their position and were on the point of finally crushing them. This seemed to me, young and ignorant as I was, the most desirable outcome, if for no other reason than that the only clothes I had, still on the sunken path behind me, were those of a French fusilier.

However, three single notes, high and piercing, blown from a single bugle, cut through the pandemonium like a cheese wire. The call was taken up. In response to it I could see how many of the redcoats and kilted Scots attempted to disengage from the French and form discrete squares or columns with gaps between them. For a moment or two some French did indeed flood into these gaps but then paused and turned, and ran helter-skelter back through the hedge, some pausing to seek its shelter but most crashing pell-mell into the host that still toiled up the slope behind them.

The cause of this turnabout became immediately apparent. All along the front a mass of horsemen appeared, big men on big horses with very big swords. The mêlée was now so dense and confused and filled with smoke that I could only mark those nearest to me. It was a sight of such terror, savagery, magnificence and horror that it even now haunts me some thirty-seven years later as I write.

The horses were all greys, white or dappled, but all huge. Their eyes rolled white, spume flew from their bits, their snorting nostrils flared, cavernous and red, their club-like hooves shod with steel hurled clods of mud behind them, crushing flesh and bone beneath them. And the men. Giants, in black cockaded bonnets, heavily moustached, eyes furious and red, red as their tunics, and those swords . . . three feet long, six inches broad, weighty as axes, with brass basket hilts adding yet more, they inflicted damage as savage as that caused by a cannon shot fired at point-blank range into a man's chest. I saw one man's head sliced like a loaf so his face dropped clean off and he kicked it with his own feet before he fell; another took a blow on his shoulder that went at a slant clean through and across his chest, right down to his waist on the other side so one half of his body fell away and his heart and liver plopped out on a cascade of blood.

The French columns became a seething, milling crowd. Some flung down their arms and ran at the British infantry which just moments before they were about to overwhelm, shouting 'prisonnier, s'il vous plaît, prisonnier', or turned and ran, or threw themselves on the ground with arms pulled over their heads.

These cavalry were madmen. The bloodlust of their Viking ancestors, for these were Scots as well, had them in its grip, and on they went, cutting and hewing and trampling, down into the bottom of the valley and then labouring against the slope and mud up the other side. They charged the guns. They actually charged the guns, and here their savagery was at its worst for these gunners had taken dreadful toll of the ranks on the ridge, and all were smashed, cut to pieces, or ridden down by those terrible hooves, the cannon overturned and tumbled.

They had gone too far. Their horses were blown, they no longer presented serried ranks, it was each for each, and as they milled about in reckless disorder, many not knowing now what was expected of them, more bugles sounded, distantly to my ears for now they were some thousand paces away and cohorts of lancers, Polish I believe they were, came over the hill and down upon them, skewering riders and horses alike with weapons not as dreadful as those swords but just as deadly and held, of course, so the lancers themselves were beyond the reach of those mighty sabres.

The Scots were reluctant to go, but eventually a few hundred perhaps hacked back across the field of corpses and more than one horse that I saw carried two men: it seemed that, big though the men were, there was room on their backs for two.* The lancers having achieved their object held back, more disciplined than their opponents, ready to fight again if needed, while the British cavalry was now all but spent.

The battle was neither won nor lost. It would go on. I had watched much of it, had been moved by elation, a wild excitement that had me hollering at times. But now, as I clung still to the hedge I was in, high enough to see across what was left of the rye, it was horror that swept over me, horror and the cold, relentless grip of abject terror. I had seen men, enormous numbers of men, die in the foulest ways imaginable, and others reduced to a sort of purity of spirit that turned them into killing engines, a purity that denied all the complexity and subtlety that makes a man a human, that purity of spirit that characterises the bigot, the rabid dog, the focused tiger, the strike of an eagle, all savage claws and tearing beak. In front of me men still screamed and moaned, nursing shattered bones that stuck out of their clothes, hopelessly shoving knapsacks or blankets into the holes from which their lifeblood pumped, staring at spilled intestines, hoping perhaps they belonged to someone else. In the spaces where no men lay the very soil and trampled corn had changed colour – the dun darkness of clay was streaked and pooled with blood. But it was the smell that finally made me retch and vomit and drove me away – men shit and wet themselves when they are mutilated or die. Blood itself carries a heavy iron tang. And most of the men, dead, dying or picking their way back up the hill, were drunk on the cheapest of spirits whose fumes added their poison to the rest. The acrid smell of burnt powder drifted in the miasma of smoke that settled in the hollows untouched by what little wind there now was. In short, and to make no more of a meal of it, it seemed best to me to be out of it and off.

* Rolf Harris has said how he discovered an old man singing a version of 'Two Little Boys' in a bar in the outback. No doubt the singer was a descendant of a nineteenth-century transportee who had in mind the battle of Waterloo. J. R.

3

I let myself slip down through the branches until my toes could search out and find a hold on the roots, then I twisted my torso and let myself go the rest of the way. I landed, crouched over my bare knees on the floor of the sunken path, facing downhill. I came to poor Maribel. She was still on her knees, broken ribs thrusting through the fat-edged holes in her back, bum in the air, smashed head resting on one arm in front of her, the other flung out in what must have been a final and instinctive attempt to break her fall. Ten yards beyond her lay my clothes, and hers, heaped beneath a holly bush. I pulled on her brother's cutdown jacket and trousers. The coarse material chafed against the scratches my back and legs had sustained, some from Maribel's squared off and grubby nails, and the trousers rasped on genitals that still felt the effect of her less than subtle handling. My glans especially was so swollen that it resembled a peeled shallot.

The track I was on ran down to the floor of the valley, took a dog leg half-left, passed the gates to a larger farm then almost immediately the wicker fence of her father's which was a more humble affair of cob walls and thatched roofs. I hurried on

16

beneath the branches of a gnarled and lichened apple tree, indeed slunk past not wishing to be the bearer of melancholy tidings regarding the daughter of the house.

A little further on the path met a brook or ditch which it followed into a small hamlet. I realised that if I were spotted by any of the people in these places, I would be called in, I would be questioned as to the whereabouts and fate of Maribel, and almost certainly constrained to remain among them. This I did not want. A battle was raging. By dusk it would be decided one way or another. These places would at the very least be commandeered as field hospitals. In all probability they would be ransacked, pillaged, the women raped, the men slaughtered. I had seen enough of war to know how soldiers behave after a battle whether won or lost. I decided I needed to be further off yet. A sudden swelling in the awful roar of guns behind me told me I was right. A horse or even a donkey would have helped, but my feet would have to do.

I took a right turn out of the hamlet and climbed a gentle rise through orchards and copses, glancing over my shoulder every now and then back to the clouds of smoke that seemed to merge with the low grey rain clouds that drifted intermittently above them. The concatenated cacophony of battle, already at this distance melded into a relentless roar like continuous thunder, rolled on, prompting unremitting urgency, panic even, to my none too clean heels which soon carried me along a track that threaded dense and extensive woodland.

At last I began to feel safe, at least temporarily out of harm's way. My jogging run slowed to a brisk walk, I struggled to breathe less quick and noisy, even pulled a leafy switch off a birch branch to chase off the flies that pursued me. An orange squirrel flashed up the smooth grey trunk of a giant beech, and an enamelled cock pheasant scampered across my path. Imagine my horror then when a bend in the track showed me the edge of the wood thinning out. Light and sky appeared in front of me and I found I was looking at the backs, a hundred

17

paces away, of a hundred horsemen, some mounted, some standing at their horses' heads.

They wore brass helmets with black plumes, green uniforms with red facings, and carried small muskets and curved sabres scabbarded in silver. Among them were some six pieces of cannon with heavier horses tethered behind them, cropping the short grass on the edge of the wood. I had no idea what nationality they were, nor whose side they were on.

I was faced, I calculated, with three courses of action. I could go back the way I had come, I could hide under a bush in the undergrowth which was thicker near the edge of the forest, I could climb a tree. I chose the last option. I often feel there is a lot of cat in me, and it is what a cat would have done. The lowest branches of the bigger trees were beyond my reach, but a glance around me revealed a silver birch that had rotted the way they sometimes do, and fallen against a sturdier beech. The former provided a stairway into the beechen green heaven of the latter, and in moments I was perched in the fork of a forest giant some twelve feet above the path I had been on. By pushing aside a swag of leaves I could see the troops at the end of it.

Within moments there was a sudden commotion among them: the hussars formed up in two triple lines on both sides of the guns, the gunners rammed home cartridges of powder, shot and wadding, officers checked the sighting of each, a sabre flashed and boomaboomboom they all went off almost together, briefly veiling their crews in white smoke which quickly dispersed as they swabbed out the barrels and reloaded. A battle in miniature now developed, and, though I could only sense what was happening, it was not difficult to guess how it was proceeding.

First the guns continued their salvos for a further ten minutes or so, then a bugle call sent the first three files of horsemen over the ridge and out of sight. Presently they returned, but some wounded, some dying, filtering through the ranks which had remained behind and forming up again. The guns resumed for a shorter space, and then the second three files went over. This time the fighting was nearer; I could hear the pop of muskets, the clash of swords, the neighing and indeed screaming of horses. In short my friends, if indeed they were my friends, were being driven in, a perception confirmed as the guns were suddenly and briskly limbered up, their horses harnessed and, a moment or two later, with whips cracking and much hallooing their teams drove them along the path and under my perch, the men's red faces streaked black with powder, their lips snarling in their hurry to get away. What was left of the hussars followed, but in better order, squadrons in line abreast facing the way they had come until those behind had passed between them, and so on, horse and foot, turn and turn about, past my tree and into the dim fastnesses of the forest through which I had come.

Several were wounded and some dying; indeed one young officer, almost the last of the pack, who held his reins in his mouth and contrived to prevent his left arm from falling off by holding it in place with his right, keeled over as his horse ambled beneath me. He landed face up, his countenance contorted in the grim rictus of a painful death.

Almost he was my undoing.

I could not help but see a large gold locket on a gold chain that had been cut by the blow that killed him, causing the locket to flop through the bloody slash that had sliced his breast as well as his arm. He also had a silver-handled pistol holstered at his side. Now I was very conscious that I had no means of support or survival about me. I was yet more hungry than before, and it occurred to me that if I could not buy food with the gold, I might obtain it by resorting to the methods of the footpad or highwayman by using the pistol. Consequently I slid down my angled birch trunk and began to rummage about the body of the dead hussar.

'*Siesprechenmitmeinoberfuehrerderwinkelmittoffenbachgoethe-undhummelichhabenderschmalz.*'

Confused by the sounds of the retreating hussars and their

19

artillery, with the rumble of the greater battle still in my ears which in any case were somewhat numbed by all they had already been battered with, I had failed to notice the approach of yet another hussar but differently uniformed, this time in blue with white frogging, different that is from the one whose body I was attempting to plunder. I may not have transliterated his words with any exactness since they were strained through an enormous moustache, and I have very little German, which was the language I supposed him to be using, but I believe I understood the gist.

I froze with terror as his sabre rasped out of its scabbard, and, kneeling as I was, waited for the stroke which I was sure would take off my head. Well, froze is not quite right. Actually I shitted myself.

However, his execution of my execution was postponed *sine die* by the arrival of several more like him, one of whom was openly weeping.

'*Countwilhelmvonschwerinmiteinrondschottinbitztodist*,' he wailed, in so far as his moustache allowed. They all had moustaches, big hairy affairs, spiked with grease at the ends.

'*Gottinhimmelweristderkommandant?*'

'*Vonbulowsichisthierbereits.*'

'*Achso.*'

Following their gaze in the direction from which they had come I could now see a considerable body of horse fanning out from the track across the edge of the wood, and hear too the squeal of cannon wheels which preceded their appearance. Behind them, not yet visible but clearly audible, an oompapa-pah brass band played a Bohemian march to the tune Papa Haydn filched for his ploughman's whistle in *The Seasons*. The troopers' attention shifted back to me.

'*Weristdis?*'

'*Einfranzisker?*'

Well, I won't bother you with any more of my cod German, suffice it to say that I managed to persuade them that I was no Frenchman at all, but rather an Englishman sent to spy on the

French, how otherwise would it be that I was trying to get at documents the French hussar no doubt had pocketed inside his tunic?

The second of the Germans, who wore a sergeant's chevrons on his shoulder, had enough English to understand most of what I said and he escorted me to a man I took to be a staff officer from the sash he wore over his shoulder. And so, stage by stage, I was passed down the line and up the hierarchy, and down the hill, until I reached a huge fat old man with the biggest moustache of all, and a load of bullion on his shoulders. He had a red face, was sweating a lot, and seemed to be in some pain, a condition he alleviated by quaffing liquor from a crystal jug with a pewter lid. Nevertheless, two of his aides rode beside him and frequently reached out supporting hands to keep him from falling off his big black horse. His name I misheard as Marshal Belchum. Remember, especially while you read the next page or so, my ears were still both ringing and numbed by the sound of battle.

Using an interpreter whose English was less than adequate he asked me where he might find his kamerad Willingdone. How the fuck should I know? I thought.

'Hedgehog Willingdone,' they insisted.

'Hedgehog?' I asked. 'Is it his first name?'

'*Nein, nein.* His given name is Achtour. Herzog Achtour Willingdone. The Kommandant of the Dutch and Belgian army. Al zo the Inglanders.'

'Ah,' I said, the light beginning to dawn, 'you mean Arthur Wellington. But he's not a hedgehog.'

'*Nein* hedgehog. Herzog.'

'Not a Herzog either. As far as I know.'

At this the interpreter, a tall man with a long square jaw, hitherto pale but now reddening up nicely, stamped his foot, so his spurs jingled.

'He is *ein* Herzog, *ein Prinz, ein erzherzog*, a duck. A Superduck.'

'Ah,' I said again. 'I'm with you. The Duck, Duke of

21

Wellington, is over there,' I waved a hand up the hill, 'losing a battle.'

'How far?'

I thought. The hill, the forest, the village, the farms, and that was only the outer edge of it all. 'Four, five miles,' I hazarded.

'Show us the way.'

Not bloody likely. I'd just spent the last hour or so getting as much distance between myself and the killing fields as time and a feeble frame allowed.

'Just follow the path,' I said, 'straight through the forest.' Inspiration came. 'March towards the sound of the guns.'

Marshal Belcher, or whoever, shouted a reply, had a coughing fit, another dose of schnapps, and barked again while one of his aides sponged down his sashed, starred and medalled stomach with a dirty napkin. The gist relayed through the interpreter was that I was to be taken back to the front of the column and that I was to be nailed to a tree the moment the kapitan in charge of me surmised I was failing to do my duty. In short, I was to be their guide.

He concluded his order with his favourite word of command, bellowed even louder than the rest: '*Vorwärts!*' which doesn't mean 'four warts' but 'forwards'.

On the way back up the hill, with a larger escort than before, we passed a burial party shovelling the remains of a cavalry officer into a couple of farmer's hay bags, the hay, freshly mown so you could see the daisies and immortelles still amongst the grass, had been tipped out of them and a solitary riderless horse was making a meal of it. He, the horse that is, had a lot of blood on his neck and back, and one booted leg still dragged from one of his stirrups. The gentlemen with me crossed themselves as we passed. I guessed this was the count, whatever, reported knocked to *bitz* by the French round shot.

On the plateau at the top, with the forest stretched in front of us, a brigade of horse and a few guns were already deployed in front of the woods, making a line some two to three hundred paces across the path. I managed to cast a glance back over the valleys and downs below. Winding through a village and all the way up the hill was a very considerable army, or corps at any rate, infantry on the road, and ammunition waggons, guns, and so forth, with cavalry out in the fields on either side, flags and a couple of bands playing. A brave sight, though I noticed some of the flags were already holed and tattered, and many of the men wore bandages or slings. Clearly they had already been knocked about a bit and I rather hoped, for their sakes, that they would be spared a further drubbing at the end of their march. In short, it occurred to me, I'd be doing them a favour if I got them lost in the forest.

However, I felt the threat to nail me to a tree was not an idle one and I resolved after all to do the best I could. This was not as easy as it may sound. Most forests, and this was no exception, are crissed and crossed by numerous paths and tracks – some the frequented paths of deer and such like, others marking the shortest or most manageable route between habitations, as well as those left by foresters themselves marking where timber has been cut and dragged or carted to sawmills and charcoal burners. Nor was the noise of battle much help since it seemed to stretch right across the westerly semicircle in front of us.

Fortunately the army's progress was slow, very slow, since its commanders, fearing an ambush, insisted on maintaining the extended line on both sides of the path, a line which had to push its way through thickets and plantations sometimes so close that a horse could not squeeze between the trunks nor its rider get his head low enough beneath its boughs. Thus I was given time at the many junctions to make a judgement as to which path to follow, and for the most part I got it right.

Nevertheless, an hour or more followed during which we covered scarcely as much as a mile and a half towards the roar of guns, while the noise we made, as of undergrowth crushed, branches snapping, horses snorting, gun wheels screeching, soldiers cursing and crows cackling as we passed beneath them, mingled with the sounds of battle. A heavy closeness settled on

23

us as spells of hot sunlight penetrated the canopy and gnats and midges came in clouds about our heads. Still, the inevitable arrived, the trees thinned to an orchard and then, at last, the rolling plain opened again before us.

Thus it was that the Prussian army arrived, guided by me, on to the field of a battle which would have been lost without them. This was neither the first nor the last occasion on which I saved Europe from barbarism. I trust this consideration will be borne in mind should my affairs be brought to judgement.

4

The battle had shrunk in the time I had been away. Nothing much was happening in the ground nearest to us. In so far as the hollow or bottom between the ridges was a hollow, though it appeared, from the slight eminence we were on, to roll and rise and drop in such gentle undulations you would not call it a valley, it was filled with the dead and dying, a square mile or so of them, not lying at ease, but twisted and wrenched, broken and butchered, smashed to pieces by sabre and shot. Many lay in discernible formations, parts of a column, a square of redcoats, a troop of gunners with their engine a mangled wreck amongst them, and so on. And all of it seemed to no purpose, for on our left the shrunken columns of mainly blue were still formed up where they had been, while along the ridge to our right, but with far wider gaps between them, short lines of redcoats could be seen.

But further off, almost two miles away, the battle raged on along the northern ridge and just below it. The farm on the Brussels road, beneath the elm tree, was the centre of it. Beneath clouds of smoke, cannon flashed, volleys sparkled along the crest and in the buildings themselves an inferno of steel and shot continued to rage between ever decreasing numbers of men. And those with telescopes or whatever could make out how, along the thousand paces beyond the elm, the French were launching wave after wave of cavalry charges, interspersed with prolonged bombardments from the cannon that still blazed away from the southern rise. Clearly it was only a matter of time before the red lines would break, the squares give in, the last cannon manned by the British overturned or unmanned by the slaying of its crew.

Indeed, even as we debouched out of the thicker woods into the orchards and smaller copses below, mounted couriers arrived to tell us so, pleading that the relief we brought should be immediately deployed. Yet, the rules of war must be observed, and all must be done in due order and in the proper fashion. First the Prussian cavalry formed up on the lower slopes, then the light troops in open order who would skirmish ahead of us, and finally the heavy infantry drawn up in the lines prescribed half a century earlier by Frederick, the Great Sodomist, himself.

This delay also had the advantage of allowing Marshal Blusher, or whatever, to lollop up among us, still supported by his aides. He handed his crystal mug to one aide, took a spyglass from the other, wiped his eye with the linen napkin and slowly, very slowly, surveyed the whole scene. The purple bruised clouds were gathering again to the west and from time to time obscuring the sun which was by now almost in his eyes where the cloud allowed it, though, it being almost the summer solstice, sunset was four, even five, hours off.

His glass swung from the small farm on the south side to the one still contested on the north and back again to a largish village with a church, in front of the road and in a slight dip to our left. Swinging thus he could see that the main body of French, not then engaged, lay well in front of this village and so he took it into his head that to march on it would initiate a circling movement bringing him to the rear flank of the enemy, possibly, if they committed themselves even further to their attack

26

on the British and Dutch, permitting him even to get behind them.

He snapped up his glass and bellowed again: '*Vorwärts!*' and off we all went.

I am no strategist, tactician or master of the arts of war, but one thing was clear. By setting off thus obliquely in a south-westerly direction he was doing nothing to bring immediate aid to his allies, the hard-pressed Dutch and Belgians on his right. Though perhaps he thought that since they had held the line all day he could leave them to continue to do so. Moreover, by withdrawing into the village itself, Plancenoit it was called, the French were giving themselves a highly defensible redoubt from which they would not be easily shifted.

And so it turned out. It took four hours, until sunset and the very end of the battle, and three-quarters of the Prussian army, to get the French out of Plancenoit, and the space between the Prussians and the Dutch and Belgians was continually threatened for three of them until the final Prussian corps came up and plugged the gap – but all this you will have read, as indeed have I, in the dispatches, memoirs and history books that have poured from all the presses of Europe these last four decades.

What, meanwhile, was I doing?

Not a lot. Having brought Marshal Bulcher to the field, my usefulness was expended. I was now ignored, a state of being that I have learned to relish. It has always been my inclination to stand by and observe. I have not been a doer. Out of the way, yes, but nevertheless on the lookout, the *qui vive*, a watcher. And, when paid, a recorder of events.

However, my desire to be out of it was frustrated. Behind me were some eight thousand men drawn up in solid lines several files deep and marching relentlessly to the beat of drums. There was, in brief, no way back. They trod on my heels and pushed me *vorwärts* with bayonets and butts. Once I simulated a stumble over a wretchedly screaming voltigeur who had lost an ear and the side of his cheek below it, being prepared to be trampled rather than face the shot and shell that were thudding into

27

the ranks around me, but the officious sergeant hauled me up by the collar and pushed me on.

On we went over trampled rye littered with bodies, dead horses, smashed cannon and so on, beneath billowing smoke and occasional squalls of rain, through churned-up mud and blood, heading always more downhill than up towards the steeple of the church in Plancenoit, the French defending every yard of the way with cavalry charges, bombardment and fusillades but rarely coming close enough to contest the ground with bayonets. After nearly two hours of this, during which we covered a bare two thousand paces, we came to a rise a few feet or so higher than the village and achieved a sort of lull while the artillery came up and proceeded to bombard the houses that clustered round the church, now thickly garrisoned. On our right, I could make out a line of bushes still apparent though much shattered, winding back across the ground, and I realised that it must mark another sunken track much like the one I had left poor Maribel in so many hours before.

All in all I felt the whole business had become too much like the playing fields of Eton, and I decided to do what I could to get out of it.

Taking advantage of a shell that exploded some twenty yards away and whose blast of broken metal took off the head of the officious sergeant, I contrived partly to run and partly crawl the hundred or so yards that took me to it. I pushed my way through brambles and elder and rolled down into it. Once thus below the general level that was swept with lead and iron, I crawled on my stomach over and round a dead horse and into a pool, an inch or two deep, of mud and blood, edged by a clump of bedraggled and shell-shocked alder.

For a moment or two I considered my situation, in a somewhat wild and delirious way. It seemed to me that however incompetently led they might be by the ancient, drunken and possibly wounded Bloocher, the result of the battle could no longer be expected to favour the armies of the Emperor Mapoleum and the Frenchness of my jacket and trousers might count against me at the end of the day. Therefore I wriggled out of them, and, naked as I was again, assumed the posture and contours of a corpse and, exhausted by stress, fear, physical exertion, hunger and even the after-effects of spending myself twice for Maribel so many hours earlier, passed out into a sort of half-waking, half-unconscious coma. Oddly, I felt freshened by my nakedness, cleaner though filthy, more myself somehow, divested of all pretence.

I came properly to in a sort of stillness and the fading light of a falling dusk. My ears sang as if my head had been battered by a malevolent schoolteacher, but the roar cleared as I half sat and shook my head. I looked around. The scene had changed. The hedge and alder and so forth had been flattened, though a trunk or two still poked up out of the mud, white shards and shredded bark, like shattered teeth. A dead horse and a further five dead men had joined me while I slept, in uniforms of various hues, contorted by the wounds that had killed them: one smashed by a cannon ball he had taken in his chest, one sabre-slashed with a blow that had typically gone diagonally through collarbone and scapula, through his chest and into his stomach so one half of his torso and his left arm had flopped to one side of the rest, exposing the spongy lungs inside. Worst of all was a pair of bonneted Scotsmen, skewered together by a single lance, the rear one still clutching his one-time saviour round the waist, chest pressed into his mucker's back. 'Did you think I would leave you dying?' I imagined the rider saying as he allowed his mate to climb aboard behind him.

And so on. The tiny pool and its streams had been churned up so as to be indistinguishable from the mud by hundreds of horseshoes and boots. Such liquid as now settled in the prints, running down the slopes from above, was made up of human blood rather than water.

Gradually my humming ears attuned themselves to the buzz of noise around and distant. Gunfire still rumbled, but a mile or more away and only intermittently. Nearer at hand a chorus of tuneless, disharmonious moans and groans was pierced by occasional screams that cut through the rest like a hot knife through butter. I breathed in, making the mistake of using my nose. Again the smell was appalling. Burnt powder cut with the sour iron smell of spilled blood, worse than the stench of any abattoir or shambles. Shit and urine too, and the bily smell of vomit. I looked up, my eyes drawn by the cackling of a hundred or more large crows that suddenly filled the portion of sky I could see above me, disturbed perhaps from eating at one spot, and seeking another.

One let drop a gobbet of fresh meat which fell, splat, in the mud a yard from me and slightly behind, leading me to look over my shoulder, and then up. On the rise above me, silhouetted against angry clouds taking on the tinges of a summer sunset, two men stood. Their cutaway jackets of red and white, their white soft chamois leather breeches and shin-high boots, were splattered with mud and blood, but they appeared to be unharmed, though one supported his left hand in the fastenings of his jacket.

'I say. It's young Charlie, I'm sure. Has to be. Can't be two like him.'

'Damnme, George, has to be. Can't be two like him.'

'Where's his togs then? When he turned up he was wearing an ensign's uniform. Eighty-eighth. Connaughts.'

'Damnme George. You're right. Lost his togs.'

'Must be dead meat and some bastard has had 'm off him.'

'Damnme George, poor Charlie, eh? Miss him though he was a cunning little bugger. Still . . . press on, what?'

They picked their way through the corpses, along the ridge above me, and presently were gone.

Clothes? I knelt up, straightening my torso, and looked around, knuckles still in the mud, saw the tunnel of bushes forming the double hedge and the rising banks of the ditch I had crawled down, all smashed and churned and littered like the rest with the twisted bodies of men and horses which had fallen into it. I heaved myself into an upright position, my joints cracking and prodding me with pain as I did so, and looked about for the clothes I had taken off.

They were gone or so muddied, bloodied and maybe covered by a corpse that I could not see them. However, something of what I had just heard filtered into my confused mind and I recollected that they were not the clothes of a British ensign but of a French fusilier.

'Charles,' I said to myself, using the name I had just been given, sounding the 'ch' of Charles as if it were a 'sh', and failing to sound the s, '*si tu es français tu es foutê*'. Then in English, which came with equal fluency, 'Charles, if you're French, you're fucked'.

I walked, or rather stumbled, back to my churned-up puddle and looked around for a suitable red coat, but one so arranged that I could with some ease take it off its present incumbent. For this reason I rejected a poor fellow who still looked with clouded surprise at the haft of the lance that had fastened his coat more or less permanently to his chest and back and presently found another, a young lad only a foot or so taller than I, clearly, from the broken instrument at his side, a drummer-boy, propped sitting against a fence post looking with equal puzzlement at the stumps where his legs had been and through which his life had bled away. It was a struggle, and I was tired and sick, but I managed it. I put this new coat on. Its tails trailed the ground, and its cuffs, turned up and buttoned with regimental brass, flopped below my hands if I let them, but I wrapped it round my hairy body and relished the warmth it brought with it.

I am more than averagely hirsute, as well as only four feet and eight inches high, but apart from a barrel of a chest, and only slightly bowed legs, more or less perfectly formed. Back then, nearly forty years ago, my chest and legs were more like other men's than they are now.

Thus clad I began to pick my way up the slopes and across the ditches towards the southern ridge, arguing to myself that clearly the redcoats who had begun the battle on the northern ridge had won, and therefore they would have moved across the wide valley. What was I looking for? I am not sure. Food perhaps, something drinkable to slake an importunate thirst certainly, means by which I could identify myself with and perhaps join the company of the victors. From the clothes I had discovered, and stirrings of memory, a readiness in the first instance to speak French and so forth, it seemed to me that possibly I had been on the wrong side at the outset of the engagement and prior to it as well. It seemed prudent to re-establish myself as an Englishman.

The landscape I walked through was a picture of hell. Smoke drifted across it from patches of rye that smouldered listlessly from the cartridge papers of discharged muskets. Bodies lay broken, those still alive moaned and shrieked. The living searched for friends among the dead or brought them succour. Some struggled down the hill and back up the other side, carrying the wounded on greatcoats slung between two muskets, though in fact most of the wounded and dead on these slopes were French and the victors were content to leave them where they lay. Some indeed turned corpses over and ransacked their pockets, pulled rings from fingers, sought what might be more useful to the living than the dead. And all across the field the crows gathered where they could, hopping and gouging with their heavy grey beaks, or, sated or frightened, cruising away on listless wings.

Without thought or plan I was drawing a diagonal across the ground and presently, near the top of the rise, came upon the paved road I had noted much earlier in the day. There was more movement here. Tired men hurried up and down in both directions, a herd of Frenchmen with only four redcoats in charge were chivvied as if by dogs down the slope. Their heads hung like those of weary sheep, while the redcoats caroused from a bottle they passed between them, occasionally prodding the defeated in the buttocks with a bayonet to keep them moving. I passed through a shallow cutting and as I came out the other side heard a slow trotting of tired horses behind me.

Six mounted men passed me, led by that now familiar figure in a small cocked hat on a chestnut charger whose shoulders were lathered with sweat. Willingdone. Hedgehog Willingdone.

They reined in on the crest and just as I came up with them were joined from the other side by a similar group, but different in so far as the centre of this one was none other than that same fat old man with a huge moustache, still supported on his tired black horse by his faithful aides.

They embraced each other. Belchum and Willingdone. It was an awkward business since both were mounted. The chestnut, albeit tired and hanging his head, felt the uneasiness of the movement and kicked out behind him, so an aide's horse shied back from him.

'*Mein lieber Kamerad.*' The old fat man's expostulation was hoarse and guttural. '*Quelle affaire!*'

This seemed to exhaust all the French he knew and each resorted to his own language – an aide who understood both languages spoke for each in turn; then the Englishman with the large nose and cocked hat briefly shook the fat old man's hand again, turned his chestnut's head back down the slope in the direction from which he had come and tapped him with his short crop into a slow trot. As he hacked past me his deep-set but tired and wild eyes caught and held mine. They were eyes that never missed a detail and the sight of a midget lost in a red coat too large for him held him for less than a second but did not connect on this occasion with his noble but preoccupied mind. A spatter of rain crackled out of the overcast sky. He reined in again and an aide passed him a dark blue cloak which he fastened over his shoulders. He feared, it seemed, the effect of a wetting more than the shot and shell that had been flying about him all day. He resumed his progress not at a trot but a slow, meditative, funereal walk, his horse's weary head sunk almost to its knees, his own now slumped forward with the pointed brim of his hat pulled low, almost as if he could not bear to survey the horrors around him.

33

The German who had translated for them called after them: 'Where will his grace lodge tonight?'

'He has a room in a village three miles back,' came the answer.

'What's the name of it?'

'Waterloo.'

Part II

PEACE

Mark! Where his carnage and his conquests cease!
He makes a solitude, and calls it – peace!

LORD BYRON, *The Bride of Abydos*

5

It is January 1853. Two men sit at a large polished table in a high-ceilinged room. There is a marble fireplace, carved in severe neo-classical design, with bright fire-irons and furniture made out of bluish steel. Coals burning in the grate and boiling water, pumped through a huge cast-iron radiator with a back ridged like a dinosaur's, make the room warm, even hot, though the iron grey sky outside is filling with large snowflakes.

On the wall above the fireplace there is a large and finely engraved double portrait, washed with aquatint, framed in ebony. The woman in it exhibits the first flush of mature womanhood, and is dressed in an off-the-shoulder gown with a pointed bodice and a full, probably panniered skirt. Her hair is bunched over her ears beneath a tiara. A very tall man with a fine forehead and moustache stands behind her but in an attitude that suggests support. Over his military uniform he wears the star and sash of the Garter, as indeed does the woman.

The two gentlemen at the table are dressed in civilian but formal clothes – black cutaway coats with abbreviated tails worn over matching trousers, white shirts and cravats, waistcoats. Their top hats have been left on a spare chair in a corner

37

by the door beneath their topcoats which hang on the stylised horns of an antlered stand. One of these gentlemen is middle-aged, his companion elderly, perhaps sixty.

In front of them there is a small pile of paper, a couple of quires or so, neatly stacked. The younger of the two is still holding the last sheet which he now places, face down, on top of the rest, before moving to the window. The old man stays sitting, his grey face pale, the muscles in his cheeks clenched so the tendons show. He won't weep, he says to himself, he will not weep.

The younger man turns from the window.

'You were there, weren't you?' he asks, not so much to confirm what he already knows but rather seeking to build a bridge to further discourse. 'With your own company, I believe?'

'Yes. Poor old Wilfrid Smith took a ball in the eye in the wood at Quatre Bras two days before. Which he died of. I was made brevet captain on the spot.' He speaks the clipped English of the gentry, not moving his upper lip. He is lean, hair short-cropped and white, a slight stoop. His companion, tubbier as well as younger, rubicund complexion, dark thinning hair smoothed over a domed forehead to compensate for incipient baldness, waits for more but does not get it. The older man needs prompting.

'The officers who saw him in his ditch mentioned the Connaughts.'

'Yes. And you see they weren't at Waterloo. The Connaughts. In Canada by then, fighting the Yankees.'

'Did he desert from them, do you think?'

'Possibly. There were desertions from regiments that had been in the Peninsula once they knew they were off to America. His story as I recollect was that he was separated from the army in the south-west of France, in the back end of 'thirteen, and made his way north to join the Allies when he heard about Buonaparte coming out of Elba. No idea what he was up to in the eighteen months between.'

The younger man knows when to wait.

38

'There must,' the older man suggests after a pause, 'there must be someone from the regiment who will know better than I whether or not this man you've got is the real Boylan.'

'Maybe. But they're deuced thin on the ground.'

'I suppose so. We lost three-quarters of the men in that damned gravel pit. Freddie and I were the only two to come out unscathed. Well, apart from my arm. Spent ball broke it. Never set properly.'

The younger man has already noticed how the older's left hand is withered and held awkwardly.

'But our Charlie wasn't one of them.'

'Evidently not. In fact, when Freddie and I came across him, as we thought dead and stripped, after the battle, just below La Belle Alliance, it was the first we'd seen of him since Quatre Bras, two days before.'

'Could he have deserted a second time?'

'After Quatre Bras? Possibly. If he knew what had happened to Blücher at Ligny, it would have seemed a rational thing to do. We believed he was part French, you know. He spoke the lingo remarkably well. That I do remember.'

The older man falls quiet, his grey eyes misty now, remembering.

The younger man sighs, decides to press on.

'Anyway. Whatever. The thing is, the young man you knew as Charlie Boylan was not with the regiment at Waterloo.'

'I didn't see him there. But that's not to say he wasn't. The last time I can say for certain that I saw him was just before we came into the line at Quatre Bras. On the sixteenth. Two days earlier.'

The balding but younger man takes a turn round the space he is in, chewing his thumb knuckle as he does so.

'As you know,' he eventually says, 'we are trying to establish whether or not the misshapen troll we have locked up in a cell at Pentonville, scribbling these somewhat distasteful memoirs, is the person he says he is, and to what extent we can attribute a reasonable level of veracity to them.'

'I rather gathered that was your purpose.' There is now a certain withdrawal in the older man's tone, not far off disgust. The younger man believes this is prompted by the nature of what he has just read. In fact the older man's problem is that he suspects the Charlie who is now locked up in Pentonville could possibly be the very same Charlie who impregnated Lady Danby some twenty-two years earlier during his, Danby's, absence serving King and Empire in India. And the idea of Pentonville disturbs him too. Modern prisons with one man to one cell, like a hotel or inn, replacing the hulks and transportation. He blames continental ways of thinking, Prince Albert and nonconformist do-gooders, all very much what he thinks they had been fighting to preserve the British from at that awful battle they are now remembering. He takes a turn away from the table to the fire, and, in spite of the heat, stretches out his hands, the withered left one supported in the palm of the right, before turning back into the room. He clears his throat, trying at least to be as helpful as he can. This rather awful young man is after all, he supposes, trying to do his job and deserves that much.

'Clearly your man, if he is Boylan, has something to hide. He avoids the lie direct. His assertion that he cannot remember what happened before the battle is a poor subterfuge.' The old man pulls a handkerchief from his trouser pocket and wipes first his face, then his left hand. The motion suggests an attempt at cleansing rather than mere removal of excessive perspiration. 'The stuff about the French girl was disgusting. Or was she Walloon? Belgian I suppose she'd be now if she had survived. I trust you will not ask me to read any more in the same vein.'

'I will spare you that, I promise you.' The Civil Servant comes round the table and perches his bottom on the edge, facing him. 'Perhaps I should explain the situation more fully.'

'I wish you would.'

'The man, mannikin, call it what you will, we hold in Pentonville, was arrested a month ago, shortly after the Duke's funeral, attempting to enter the Palace of Westminster with a loaded pistol in his pocket. He claimed to be owed a substantial sum by a government department that employed him for some years, but dismissed him a long time ago. The department in question, which is part of the Home Office, has disowned him.'

'If you are talking about the people I think you are talking about, none of this surprises me.'

This time the disdain is that which most Englishmen share for a government department that operates clandestinely, with a secret budget, and not always within the law.

'Our friend then asserted that he could prove what he claimed, and called for pen and paper. My superiors granted his request.'

'Good Lord. Why?'

The Civil Servant shrugs dismissively and goes on.

'The outline of his memoirs, presented to us verbally during interrogation, suggests that his full written memoirs will be . . . shall I say . . . interesting? Some of it, if true, and if published, would impugn previous governments and individuals over the last forty years, and would cause very severe embarrassment to individuals still living and the relicts of those dead, and also, ah, institutions. Even, um, royalty could be involved. The duty that has been placed on me is to establish to what extent his account is veracious and to what extent a pack of lies. It begins with Waterloo. You were at Waterloo. I could find no other survivors from the Donegal Rifles in town.'

'I'll do what I can.'

At last we're getting somewhere is the hope that crosses the Civil Servant's mind. Again he deploys a patience he does not feel while the old man shifts his station to a position at the tall window from which he can see the snow scurrying up Whitehall to swirl around the Nelson Column. A grandiose monument, only ten years old and forty years late, he muses. The Duke deserves and surely will get something better. George Danby clears his throat.

'I had a friend, Freddie, like me a captain in the Donegals. I believe the two officers who are mentioned in that account,' he

41

gestures towards the table without turning away from the window, 'may well be he and I, Freddie and me that is. Freddie was, indeed still is, a fool. As much may be guessed from the brief exchange recorded there. If it's not verbatim it must be deuced close to it. Anyway, the point is, Freddie, who is, of course, Sir Frederick Tarrant St Giles, Baronet, took a minor post as equerry, attaché, whatever, at the Paris Peace Conference. He needed a manservant and picked up Boylan after the battle . . .'

He rubs his hand over his face, shudders briefly, looks up at the man who has become his interrogator.

'Do you think I could have a glass of water?'

'Of course. Malvern all right?'

Danby nods, waits. The Civil Servant pulls a bell sash, a clerk puts his head round the door and is sent for a bottle of Malvern. The whole interruption lasts nearly three minutes, during which the Civil Servant takes a walk round the room, and Danby continues to fidget, though his slightly opaque blue eyes seem fixed on the room's high cornice. A coal falls an inch or two in the fire.

He drinks a little water and goes on.

'It's all so long ago. Battles long ago and far off things.' He shakes his head, clears his throat and approaches his subject warily, as if he is stalking it, from another angle.

'Freddy, as I have said, was a fool, a likeable chap, but a fool. He tended to be the butt of the people he worked with, was ignored when he was not teased. I think he believed that having a more or less perfectly formed midget as his body servant would give him a certain cachet. Something like that, anyway.'

He turns abruptly from the window and faces the Civil Servant.

'Can I go now?' There is an uncharacteristic hint of pleading in his voice.

'Of course. Just one or two more questions though, if you don't mind, sir. First, let me be sure I have got this right. I

42

gather from what you have said that the author of these pages may well be the person he says he is. Charles Boylan.'

'It's certainly possible.'

'And one other thing. I have read much further into these . . . memoirs . . . than you have and I should like you to substantiate a couple of points that occur later. There is no need for you to read them. First, I am right, I think, in saying that Sir Frederick Tarrant St Giles married your sister Sophie before removing to Paris . . . ?'

'Yes. Just after Waterloo.'

'And that Sir Frederick's older but unmarried sister Poppea went with them, as a companion for Lady Tarrant St Giles.'

'That is so. And it did not need my presence here to establish that.' Old George Danby's voice is suddenly very frosty indeed. He takes a slim gold hunter from his waistcoat pocket, springs the gold lid, checks what he sees against the enamel-faced ormolu clock on the mantelpiece beneath the ebony-framed picture of his Queen and her Consort. 'I have an engagement at my club. I will bid you good afternoon, sir.'

Sir George Danby's complexion is now the pasty white that only suppressed but Jovian anger can produce. He begins to put on his coat and shrugs the Civil Servant away when the latter moves in to help him. Then he picks up his hat and stick. The Civil Servant opens the door for him.

'You may be sure, sir, there is absolutely no question of these papers being published.'

'Sir. If you do publish them, then most certainly you will be damned.'

6

The Civil Servant, whose name is Thomas Cargill, follows George Danby out into Whitehall, which for once is living up to its name. Huge flakes of snow float like swan's down into the penumbras of the gaslights and out again, rendering almost invisible Gwydyr House and the Banqueting Hall on the other side of the thoroughfare, lying as they do beyond the turning into Downing Street. In the other direction the vast site where the rebuilding of the Houses of Parliament is almost complete looks shadowy and insubstantial since the part he can see is still curtained with wooden scaffolding, like net. He swings himself up the springy step of a Hansom Patent Safety Cab parked at the front of the more or less permanent rank that serves the Ministries' functionaries.

'Waw-erloo, sir?' the cabbie calls out hopefully.

'Pentonville. The prison.'

'Bugger that for a laugh,' the cabbie mumbles to himself, then louder: 'Caust yer, sir. This time o' night, not to mention the wevver.'

'Come, sir. It's not yet five o'clock.'

The cabbie blows snow off his moustache with an upward

push of air propelled across his protruding lower lip, but makes no move to draw the handle of his whip from the holder at his side.

'Waw-erloo I can do. Pen-unville, no.'

Cargill gives it a moment's thought. He'll get a receipt out of the man, and, under the new system, a refund from the Treasury, though it may take months.

'Listen, my man. My business at the prison won't occupy me for more than a half-hour. Wait for me to conclude it, then you may take me back to Waterloo.'

'Spoke like a gen-ulmun. Done.' And cabbie releases his whip, shakes up the reins and stirs his dappled, blinkered grey into a steady trot.

I *am* a gentleman; does he mean to imply I am not? But Cargill keeps the thought to himself.

The irregular circle round the Nelson Column is solid with cabs and omnibuses and even though the cab has only to cut across one corner to go down Strand it takes nearly five minutes to clear it.

The department stores in Strand, in spite of recent competition from the new ones in Regent Street and Oxford Street, are still busy, their gaslit gilded windows filled with the winter fashions, all feathers and velvets, contrasting here and there with odd scraps of black bunting, ragged and torn now, that still cling to the higher cornices, sad remnants of the funeral two months ago. They pass the six pillars of the Lyceum, already more than ten years old, and at present deserted though theatre-goers and their cabbies will begin to gather in the next hour or so, and finally the Law Courts. Cabbie won't strike north until they reach the Farringdon Road, since Bloomsbury and the warrens north of Covent Garden are still virtual no-go areas on a dirty night, even though the rookeries have been cleared from St Giles.

Finally there's the long trek up the Caledonian Road with the awesome castellated gates of the prison looming above the squat terraces, steepled churches and gaunt chapels. The snow is whirling now on a strong breeze sulphurous with coal smoke – it's grey before it lands, and forms a muddy slush yellowed with straw and droppings. The big rear wheels of the cab crunch and slosh through it. Hatted, cloaked and shawled figures scurry from pool to pool of lamplight, not wanting to linger in the dark patches between, where men in battered top hats rescued from refuse heaps lean against railings, smoking and poking with their sticks at the more respectable citizens who lift their skirts or step high to avoid the muck as they hurry along.

Cabbie, at his own insistence, is allowed to wait in the first courtyard.

'It aint a neighbourhood I'd choose to park in, not unprotected like.'

Turnkeys, with huge bunches of the commodity hanging from their broad leather belts, take charge of Cargill, check his Home Office pass and usher him, always in pairs at least with him between them, through three double gates, each double locked. They cross yards and negotiate more cage-like gates, enter the central block, climb clanging stairs, walk along galleries of cast and wrought iron down one of the arms that thrust out into the yards from the centre like spokes on a wheel. His destination is on the top floor and almost at the furthest end of the gallery. Their steps echo like cracked bells, their shadows, thrown by gas mantles set high beyond normal reach, shrink in front of them, then, lengthening, chase them to the next pool of light. They are greeted by howls at various points and a banging of tin plates on the insides of the studded doors they pass – signs of anger or madness or both perhaps, Cargill cannot decide. Although the prison is not yet ten years old, and much of the paintwork, at least that above reach, is still clean and bright and the blacking on the ironwork glossy, the stones and bricks already sweat out the smells of urine, faeces, semen, coal gas and mashed turnip.

Turnkey One pushes open the square judas and peeps in.

'E's awake right enough. And still at his scribblin'.'

46

He bends his knee to the lock without stooping while Turnkey Two, drawn truncheon raised, stands to the side of the door.

'Scribble, scribble, scratch, scratch, like a bleeding little squirrel, aint you, nibblin hon huh hacorn.' Turnkey One derisive, perhaps revealing a past as a sergeant in Her Majesty's army, then back to Cargill. 'We locks you in wiv 'im, sir, haccordin to Governor's standin' regs, but we be just outside and hat your call if need be.' He peeps round the doorjamb. 'But e's a armless little runt has'll give you no trouble, I'm sure.'

Indeed the comparison with an arboreal rodent is apt. The figure in front of Cargill is small and hunched with a shock of white hair streaked with the ebony it once was, looking up from big dark eyes, above high cheekbones, but he has only one large incisor, the other is missing. In profile his nose is slightly hooked, a touch larger than you would expect. He is wearing a torn frock coat green with mildew, over an etiolated frame, breeches that must have been ten years old or more and slippers made from carpet offcuts which do not reach the flagged floor below him. He is seated on a three-legged stool at a small deal table, just large enough to support a large pile of unused quarto, a smaller pile covered in tiny spidery writing and an inkwell. By the light of one tallow candle whose fumes recall sour mutton, its guttering flame almost dying in a pool of grease, he rushes on, the patent steel nib of his pen scratching and squealing over the paper, to the end of a sentence which he marks with a downright stab, leaving a splatter of ink for a full stop. He leans back, spreads his bird-like shoulders, arms at his sides, palms stretched out.

'Cargill! Good chap! Good to see you!'

Though his accent is toney, his voice rattles, and he ends on a phlegmy cough. He spits an oyster on to the floor, slips half off his stool so his foot can reach it and rubs the sputum with the sole of his carpet-clad foot.

'Bloody damp in here, fog gets in, doncherknow? And that fuckin' candle poisons what air there is. Be the death of me.'

47

Elbows come up on to the table, chin perches in his palms, head cocked cockily on one side, while a grin that is clearly meant to express knowingness creases his thin lips, lights his bloodshot eyes.

The furnishings of the cell stretch to a wooden shelf a couple of feet wide and a couple of feet from the ground supporting a thin mattress and a threadbare blanket, all of which do for a bed, and a chipped enamel lidded slop bucket. Cargill sits on the edge of the bed, having first pushed away a corner of the mattress to reveal the deal boards. Lice or bedbugs are what he fears.

'Right, Boylan—' he begins.

'Charles, dear boy. Please. Or Charlie if you like.'

'Charlie Boylan. Or shall we say . . . Bosham?'

For a second, no more, the small rodent reacts, his face suddenly without expression except for his eyes which seem to flash, revealing a hidden understanding, then they too go blank and then enquiring.

'Whatever name you care to choose, squire. But that aint one I've ever used. And there have been a few.'

'You still maintain you have no recollection of any event in your life preceding the battle of Waterloo?'

'That is correct.'

'So how do you know your name was Boylan? Charles Boylan?'

'Because that was the name they gave me, the name they said they knew me by before the battle.'

'All right. After the battle you were taken up by then Captain Sir Frederick Tarrant St Giles of the Donegal Rifles as his personal body servant.'

There is something shifty now in Charlie's attitude; his head sinks a little between his shoulders, his eyes wander to the corner where two walls meet beneath the ceiling.

Cargill pretends a sudden thought has struck him with a blinding Damascene certainty.

'By Jove I've got it.' He stands up, clicks his fingers. 'After the engagement at Quatre Bras, and having heard of the defeat of the Prussians on the same day, you absconded. You changed sides. You thought Boney was bound to win and you changed sides. Was that it? If that really is the case it would not stand you in good stead should it come out during an inquiry into your claim against the Home Office based on services rendered but not paid for. No, indeed it would not.'

Squirrelly rodent runs, as it were, to the top of his tree, from which he chatters angrily.

'That is a foul slander, Mr Cargill. If I was of an age and in a state of health that would permit it, I'd call you out for that, sir. By God I would.' Then the voice becomes shriller yet, before dying into a whine. 'Believe me, sir, I have always held at the forefront of my mind the fact that I am an Englishman; this has been the guiding principle of my life. Always I have sought to serve my country, put what my employers believed were the best interests of my country before anything else. Believe me, sir, I am an honest man and whatever deceptions I have been party to have always been in the interests . . .' The whine dies away on a tide of spittle and suppressed coughs.

Cargill watches, his breast filled with a sudden surge of feelings of superiority and disdain. He feels sure he is right. However, he must press on.

'Believe me, Boylan, I shall follow this up. In the meantime there is a gap to fill in before we reach the year 1816, when certain officials at the Home Office gave you employment. Fifteen months? I'd like to know how they passed for you, what brought you to Whitehall.'

For a moment Charlie Boylan, if that indeed is his name, chews on the already splintered end of his wooden nib holder, then puts it down, leans back as much as his ungrounded feet and backless stool will allow. Presently the bluster he had indulged in drifts back to the wary grin which is, in company, his most habitual expression.

'Not your business really, is it, Mr Cargill? The point atissue' – he elides the two words into a sneeze – 'is whether or not

I have a just claim against your employers for a substantial pension, now they no longer wish to employ me. What I done, did, during the infrequent periods when I was not in their employ, is not relevant, has no relevance.'

'Nevertheless—'

'My lips are sealed.' Charlie touches the side of his red but thin nose with a grubby finger, then picks it assiduously. Through the process he continues: 'Repootation of a lady at stake, Mr Cargill. Noblesse obleedge, doncher know?'

He attempts to flick free the outcome of his excavations, but it adheres to the ball of his index finger, which he rubs and smears on the corner of the table.

Cargill sighs.

'You were, I believe, for most of that time, in the employ of Sir Frederick Tarrant St Giles who was employed as ADC to a military attaché at the Conference of Paris.'

'I moved about, but yes, you can say that.'

'You don't care to elaborate.'

'Like I said. Not relevant.'

'What I am trying to establish is what or who recommended you to the notice of and subsequent employment by the ... government agency that employed you towards the end of 1816. Whether or not I accept your story and recommend my superiors to countenance your claim either in whole or in part may well depend on your answer to this question.'

Cargill's impatience infuses this speech. The dank cold is seeping into him, he wonders if his cabbie has stuck to his bargain, his wife in Clapham will be wondering where he is, he is tired. Charlie's grin, without becoming any less of a grin, hardens into a sardonic mask.

'Oh dearie dear. Quite the madame now, aren't we?' Then the grin goes. 'Don't come the madame wiv me, Mr Cargill. Take what I written here, which goes from September 1816, and forget the interim.'

'Mr Boylan, I must—'

'Cargill? Go fuck yourself.'

50

And he picks up thirty or so sheets covered with his spidery hand, chivvies their edges into uniformity, hands them across. Then ostentatiously he pulls a blank sheet off the other pile, dips his pen and writes, scratchily.

Cargill pushes the papers he has been given into his bag, finds his hat and cane, and taps the nail-studded plank door with its judas.

7

Cabbie, grumbling wheezily at the wait he has suffered, but in the weaselly, blackmailing way of his tribe, flicks his old grey mare into a trot.

'Fort you was never comin' out, guvnor. Crawsed my mind to scarper but could well see they was no cabs nearer than King's Craws an I thought this fare I ave is a reel genelman, e woan let me down, so it's not for me to let im down nyver. Wa'erloo, you said, squire, am I right?'

Waterloo.

Filled with smoke, the Portland stone and bright red brickwork of the façade are already streaked with greasy coal stains, but retain an elegance later generations will ignore. There are, as yet, only three platforms behind the Wellington Arch. He catches the next train to Clapham. It is late, the train, one of the last of the day, is not crowded and he has a corner on the bench from which he can look down from the embanked railway on the new crowded terraces of artisans', clerks' and tradesmen's cottages in Lambeth and Vauxhall, sparsely lit with gas, slowly filling with freezing mustard coloured fog, the London Particular.

He reflects on Charlie Boy, Charlie Boylan. Such a chameleon, such a Proteus, now, with old age approaching, assuming different shapes in order to escape questioning, trial, punishment, or, on the other hand, to claim or blackmail a pension for undercover services rendered . . . the same Protean skills that indeed served him and his country (countries?) throughout his long career. He can assume the accent and manners of a gentleman, not well enough to deceive a gentleman but well enough to fool a member of the humbler classes, and vice versa. A country bumpkin would accept him as a mill-worker, a mill-worker as a soldier, a soldier as a seaman and so on. No wonder he has spent, or so Charlie said, much of his life as a spy – almost it can be said he has been called to the trade, has a vocation. But where has he come from? Does it matter?

Cargill suddenly slaps his forehead, to the mild consternation of the pen-pusher with ink-stained fingers on the opposite bench. Had there not been a spy, who, the day after Quatre Bras, two days before Waterloo, got into Napoleon's headquarters, had even perhaps approached the Tyrant Himself, with details of the Duke's and, especially, the Prussians' strength following their defeat at Ligny, and their dispositions? Could not that spy have been Charlie? Might he not, having seen the strength of the French, their pomp and grandeur, the day after they had won one battle and drawn a second, have decided to change sides and hidden himself away in the farmhouse at Papelotte?

Well, maybe. But the last person to admit it would be Charlie himself.

The little suburban train pulls into Clapham, not yet the junction it will later become. Outside the station a cab-horse steams and stamps and Cargill, wary though not really frightened of the footpads and beggars who still haunt the common (a Peeler or two are always on the beat near by, and as a Home Office official he carries a police whistle which will summon them if need be) takes the cab again. Partly he is mindful of the new system of reimbursement. Pools of dim gaslight beneath

53

the trees illuminate the smutty snow on the common and lend it an orange glow. A solitary shepherd, known to be mad, blows on his nails and guards his flock of five emaciated ewes, asserting commoners' rights that disappeared long ago.

At home, in a terrace of new red- and yellow-brick villas which borrow some cachet from the few Queen Anne houses that remain bordering the south side of the common, his wife, some ten years younger than him, takes his coat, brushes his jacket with her palm and his cheeks with her lips.

He takes these little ministrations as signs of affection – but in fact her eyes are searching the interstices of his garments, and her nostrils flare, to catch any hint or sign that the two hours during which she has been expecting him were spent in a public house, or, worse still, a brothel. Before her marriage she was governess in a house that laid claim to distant aristocratic connections: she left when the oldest son, a pupil at Dulwich College, contracted syphilis. Such a household was not for her. Now, she detects the dank staleness of prison still on him which she cannot identify but, strangely, even ineptly, she does not associate with sin.

Satisfied that he is clean, she takes him to their tiny dining room, the rear-facing room on the ground floor, where they have a light supper of beef broth, cold mutton, pickles and cheddar cheese, served by a skivvy, an Irish woman called Deirdre, who frequently wonders, but not aloud, whether she might do better on the street. Or even in Canada, where she has a cousin working on the railroads. Meanwhile Cargill looks round with quiet pride and pleasure at the very modern furniture, heavy and grand, dark, solid and simple, chosen from Heal's in Tottenham Court Road and carted all the way from their warehouses. They are, according to a new system of deferred payment, not yet paid for. For a middle-of-the-range civil servant with prospects in the Home Office Heal's has been happy to give credit, or, as they put it, open an account, a privilege until recently only extended to the landed gentry.

Presently the maid-of-all-work clears the table and Cargill

and his wife move through folding doors into the front room where the maid has already drawn the dun-coloured velveret curtains and stirred up the small coal fire. Here the furniture is more comfortable (though still very upright), upholstered in beige plush velveteen with newly washed and starched anti-macassars, the very latest thing. For an hour he reads *The Times*, delivered after his morning departure, and now freshly pressed and mounted on a pearwood baton, while Mrs Cargill sews – first embroidering a sampler, then almost surreptitiously darning the heels of his socks. Surreptitiously because Cargill believes this is menial work and should be left to the maid.

Meanwhile, back in Pentonville, the supply of gas is turned off, the light from the gas mantles quickly fades from incandescent white to ruby red and dies with a brief breath of half-burnt coal gas. Charlie pees, for the most part accurately, into his enamel bucket, then snuffs his greasy tallow candle and feels his way to his tiny bed. Years that have as often as not seen him living in similar deprivation or worse have trained him to cope. He knows how to roll himself in the thin blanket in such a way that his weight will keep the edges from coming loose; he knows that a foetal position creates a little globe of warmth between his thighs and stomach and that if he keeps one hand beneath his ear and the other close to his genitals, neither will get frostbite. Not that frostbite is a likely danger: there will no doubt be a skin of ice on the sweating walls beneath the tiny panes of the high-barred window before dawn but it will not be cold enough to freeze the urine in his bucket. The Donner Pass through the Sierra Nevada five years earlier had been a bloody sight colder. Except, of course, it was not then known by that name.

And it always helps to think of warmth, remember heat.

Paris, in the winter of 1815, was hot.

8

If you could afford it. Fires blazed in huge grates, newish central heating wheezed and grumbled, many rooms still had the big ceramic, closed-in stoves, often wonderfully decorated, in each corner, relics of the days when a Viennese Queen and then, more recently, a Viennese Empress held court here. And Charlie's employer was rich enough.

Captain Sir Frederick Tarrant St Giles Bt, ADC to His Britannic Majesty's Military Attaché at the Court of the restored (for the second time) Louis XVIII of France, was the possessor of a fortune of some four thousand pounds a year derived from estates in Dorset and Jamaica. He was therefore able to keep an establishment in Paris larger and grander than was appropriate for the lowliness of his position in the diplomatic hierarchy. He rented a not insubstantial apartment occupying two floors of a large house a mere quarter of a mile from the British Embassy. There he was meant to work at a desk when he was not out in the countryside unravelling such mysteries as the semaphore telegraph system Napoleon had introduced, or the means whereby the Great Man had managed to move such huge numbers of cannon so quickly over such vast distances. The embassy itself, the Hôtel de Charost, in the rue Faubourg St Honoré, once the palace of Napoleon's sister Pauline Borghese, bored him with its flamboyant decorations, and inadequate accommodation for the army of pen-pushers that had descended on it, and he got out as much and as often as he could.

Freddie kept a carriage, several horses, and, once the initial raptures of his newly acquired marital state had worn off, spent as much time as he could spare from his duties both public and domestic, drag-hunting in the Bois de Boulogne. Taking actual foxes was frowned on – unless the Duke himself was riding out to hounds – there were not enough. Damned Frenchies shot them.

Freddie's wife, Sophie, née Danby, was porcelain: cold and fragile, and happy to leave the running of the household to Poppea, his older and unmarried sister.

Poppea was resigned to remaining unmarried. Not that she lacked suitors. In her own right she had an income of fifteen hundred a year and her brother was prepared to give her husband, whenever he materialised, the prosperous living of Tarrant Withering in the Wold, or, if the cloth proved unattractive, would buy him a commission in the Donegal Rifles. Or even a rotten borough in Parliament, a step which could expose him to the patronage of greater men than he. In short, Frederick found his sister an embarrassment and was prepared to pay to get her off his hands.

Why? She was eight years older. Nearly thirty-one. From her first attempt to suffocate him in his cradle she had bullied him mercilessly, and even more so once sibling rivalry was compounded with the knowledge that as a male their father's baronetcy and substantial fortune would pass to him and not to her. Moreover, she contracted smallpox at the age of twelve and was left with skin, not just her face, pitted, dry and grey like pumice. By the time she was eighteen she was six feet tall and large boned, with red knees and red elbows and a hard thin body. Nevertheless, such are the attractions to younger

57

sons of a reasonable income and a respectable position, there were suitors. However, having a healthy respect for her own character and gifts, she had decided it was beneath her to buy a husband, and indeed had no real desire for one.

Sex was another matter. Not only did she desire sex, she was prepared to pay for it. Uncircumscribed by marital vows, she ranged freely and widely. Nor, once a clandestine reputation was established among rakes, pugilists, circus strong men, butchers, market porters and the like, did she often have to resort to the chinks to get what she wanted. She developed an expertise in the cruder arts of love and a freedom of approach to them that excited both the curious and the jaded.

Poppea's sexual proclivities had hitherto been for large men, the larger the better. Less than conventional in most things, she yet followed the conventional wisdom that women are naturally both more frail and smaller than men: she felt obliged to cast about for men who could physically dominate her. Some months passed therefore before she began to look speculatively at the urchin (as she took him to be) that her brother kept as a body servant. Charlie went about the place quietly performing his duties: clothed in livery, he brushed and pressed Sir Freddie's clothes, filled his bath and scrubbed his back, helped him to dress in the morning, fetched the farrier when his mare slipped a shoe, uncorked champagne, replenished his snuffbox or trimmed and lit his cigarillo. He also carried excuses on Sir Freddie's behalf to his porcelain wife when he was detained at the embassy beyond dinner time.

An urchin? At just over four feet and six inches tall with a fresh face and a sprightly way of walking, it was easy to underestimate Charlie's age. Fifteen at the most, you'd say at first glance, but then you took in the coat of fine black hair, fur almost, on the back of his hands, the way the shadow on his cheeks darkened with sunset, and a nose that was fully formed, large, and with a slight droop that gave character to, or spoilt, depending on your taste, an otherwise good-looking face. And you wondered: twenty? Five and twenty?

One afternoon in January 1816 she sat at her mirror and gazed sadly through one good eye at the puffy, deep purple mess that was the other. The evening before she had enjoyed an evening of cards at Lady Beckinsale's and at the end begged the loan of an escort. 'That big fellow at the door will do. I'm only a step away and it's not worth getting the carriage out for it.'

They had been playing whist and Poppea had won six guineas and a louis d'or. And after that they, that is her hostess and two other haute monde gossips, had taken advantage of the absence of their menfolk on manoeuvres to drink a bottle each of champagne.

At her own door she had made an improper suggestion to the 'big fellow', supported by an offer of the louis d'or. He turned out not to be an honest Christian but a Quaker with principles and a tendency to delusive hallucinations. Convinced she had turned into or been possessed by the devil (and indeed in the dim Parisian gaslight, with her white face taking on a greenish tinge and draining the brown colour from her cloak so it seemed black, he had some excuse) he had first struggled to free himself from her embrace, and then, when she got her hand under the flap of his breeches and took hold of his privates, he had soundly thumped her before making his escape.

So here she was, sitting up in bed, with her hand-held silver mirror, a hangover (Lady Beckinsale served an inferior champagne and, when that ran out, Calvados) which carried with it the warm but irritable longings for sex hangovers often induce, and . . . a shiner. Moreover, in three hours' time she had engaged to appear in public at a charity tea for the Orphans of Waterloo. A married woman with a black eye never excites comment – everyone knows how she came by it. But a spinster, and a plain one at that, thus disfigured, was sure to inspire gossip.

'What,' she asked her maid, Marie-Claude, 'am I to do about this?'

Marie-Claude suggested Goulard Lotion – a drachm of sugar of lead, two pints of rainwater, two teaspoonfuls of spirits of wine. Or a warm bread poultice.

'Get them,' grunted Poppea. 'Both of them.'

A twenty-minute wait, during which the Miss Tarrant St Giles had a pee in the chamber pot and then returned to her large old-fashioned, pre-Revolution curtained bed where she contemplated the shifting shadows on its silky canopy and the pleasant coolness of a light reflected from the snow-covered roofs opposite.

A discreet knock on the white door.

'Come.'

The pinchbeck handle turned.

Charlie. On one spread hand a plate covered with muslin. He remained hidden from her by the satin bed curtain which was embroidered with crimson roses.

'Madame—' he began.

'Miss Tarrant, if you please.'

'Miss Tarrant. Marie-Claude has gone to the apothecary for Goulard Lotion. But first she asked me to prepare a bread poultice. I asked her what the poultice was for. She told me. I recollected that a more sovereign remedy for your ladyship's condition is thought to be a slice of raw beefsteak. I have taken the liberty of bringing one since Marie-Claude was under the apprehension that a state of emergency existed.'

'Charlie, is it?'

'Yes, Miss Tarrant.'

'I am not a ladyship.'

'No, Miss Tarrant. But I am sure you should be.'

Was this insolence? Or sincere if naive appreciation of her real worth? She had to find out. She sat up, pulled back the curtain. Although she was on a bed and he was standing, because of the difference in their statures their heads were at a level and only a foot or so apart.

60

She saw brown eyes as soulful as mountain tarns (she knew her Wordsworth), sensuous lips (she knew her Byron), the long nose (personal experience had not yet confirmed the superstition that the size of that organ betokens the size of another, but she lived in hope). She did not see, or at any rate take note of, his simian aspect, his barrel chest, his black hair that stood up in a crest like a hoopoe's.

He saw one pale blue eye like an aquamarine, a wide if thin mouth, straw-coloured tresses tied up loosely, one might say wantonly, above shoulders as thin and fragile as a bird's. He did not remark how the craters and fissures in her skin were filled with cracked white paste, how her stature was similar to a heron's, nor how the lid of her second eye, the left one, which she kept as angled from him as was possible without removing him from her field of vision, was puffy and coloured like a thundercloud at sunrise.

She patted the side of the bed.

'Sit.'

He sat, holding the plate on his knees. She lifted the muslin, looked at the tongue-shaped slab of bleeding meat.

'I'm not puttin' that on m'face,' she said.

He covered it again and reached across her to put the offending plate on her bedside cabinet. She caught his hand as he straightened, and held it, running the fingers of her other hand across its back.

She sighed.

'Are you hairy like this . . . all over?' she murmured, and when he nodded assent, added: 'Show me.'

'Show you? How?'

'Take your shirt off.'

He was, just so. Across his shoulders, down his arms, over his chest, a thick pelt, not as thick as a dog's, but rich, silky, shiny, each hair an inch or so long, lay in whorls occasionally matted with moisture, thinner where clothes were closer: on his elbows, around his brick-coloured nipples.

'Turn around.'

61

He shifted, pushing his knees the other way, in the direction of the foot of the bed. At the back of his head his hair, coarser and darker than his body hair, and of course thicker, was tied into a short ponytail beneath the upstanding crest. And from the nape of his neck down, his pelt swooped and turned towards his buttocks, the groove of which just showed above the top of his tight breeches.

'Lock the door.' Her voice cracked. To compensate she injected into it an imperial note. This was to be a command not a request, and certainly no plea. 'And take off everything you still have on.'

Charlie did as he was told, but all with his back to the bed. When he turned, the curtain was again drawn shut. He uttered a tiny cough.

'Ready? Then, you may come to bed with me.'

He opened the curtain and found he could not see his seductress. She had burrowed into a fortress of pillows, ribbons and quilts and only one hand remained visible. The thin fingers made a crook, and indicated he should make a breach and enter. He did so and found that she had removed her night gown and released her abundant hair while he was undressing, and, in the close perfumed warm darkness of the large bed he discovered, not for the first time, what many many men know well, that in darkness the delights a woman can offer depend not at all on how they look *à plein jour*.

For once the nose turned out to be a valid predictor. Lost beneath feather-bedding, somewhere between her diaphragm and her bony knees, he gasped for air and thrashed about while her long fingers dragged up his sides and back against the lie of all that hair and then smoothed it down again as her nails plunged towards his buttocks.

But it was, in the end, the aftermath that brought them both the deepest satisfaction. Poppea remained on her back, cradled his head between her long, wide-spaced but not abundant breasts, let him pull up his knees so the soles of his feet rested against her raised thighs, and folded her arms about his shoulders.

After so many partners weighing in at a minimum of fifteen stones, his lightness was a new-found delight and she felt as if she were floating on air. They lay like that for an hour, and then another, occasionally shifting to ease an incipient cramp or parting skin and hair where heat had induced a sweat. Sometimes she stroked his head, occasionally he put a hand on her nipple and after a time she shifted his head so his mouth closed over it instead. Marie-Claude tried the door handle, but finding the door locked returned below stairs where, being a girl of some brains, she penned an apology to the Orphans of Waterloo, adding that Miss Tarrant St Giles was indisposed.

Meanwhile, Charlie remained the child Poppea had never had, and she the mother he had never known and that was why, nearly thirty-seven years later, Charlie Boy comforted and warmed himself with the memory in his hard cold bed in Pentonville jail.

9

'I *will* marry him.'

Almost she stamped her foot, but shod in silk and soft kid as it was, and placed on a thick Turkey carpet, there would be no point.

'Damnme, Poppy, you'll do no such thing.'

'Pray, sir, how will you prevent me? I have my own money, and I am of an age.'

He looked up at her from behind the huge ormolu and rose-wood Louis something desk that went with the apartment, and which stood like a bastion between them. With a slight lifting of his head he indicated the three men who stood in the shadows behind him. It was indeed a gloomy sort of a place, this study Sir Frederick had requisitioned for his own, hung with crimson damask wallpaper, and filled with furniture too dark and heavy.

'Damnme Poppy, it's a matter of principle, don't you see? Noblesse oblige, eh? That sort of thing.'

'Explain yourself more fully.'

'Damnme, Poppy, you can't marry a servant. You can't marry a freak, a dwarf.'

He did not sound the 'w' in the last word, made a 'dawf' out of it.

'He's not a dwarf. He's a mannikin. A miniature.'

Well, not entirely, she thought to herself, and the corner of her mouth lifted. Her brother took the shift in her expression for a sneer.

'It's not a laughing matter, Poppy. Not a laughing matter at all.'

'Indeed not, sir.'

She waited. Outside a February icicle, loosened by the temporary afternoon thaw, dropped from a gutter and clattered on the sill below. Her brother fiddled with a cut-down quill, began to pick his teeth with it. She realised that the immediate situation was impossible: although by eight years her junior he was treating her like a naughty girl, or a servant caught in some peccadillo. She broke the silence.

'Come to the point, Freddie. Who are these persons you have brought me here to meet?'

'Ah, ah yes, indeed.'

His high-backed, winged, studded leather chair squeaked a mouse fart beneath him as he reached forward to pick up a paper from the marquetry surface of the desk. Holding the paper at a distance, for he was already afflicted with long sight, he began to read.

'Um. First we have Doctor Edouard de Brillancourt from the faculty of medicine in the Ecole Supérieure . . .' – a thin lantern-faced man wearing a wig ribboned in the nape of his turkey neck took a step forward and inclined his head.

'Next to him I should like you to meet Professor Boris de Tocqueville who lectures on feminine hysteria and related diseases of the weaker sex to students who attend the Charenton Hop . . . Hospital for mental defectives.'

This one was plump, pink-faced, held a small top-hat in front of his stomach.

'And Herr Doktor Franz Hoessler from the University of Heidelberg at present attached to the Prussian army of occupation.'

65

Dr Hoessler wore a braided uniform. Poor Poppea wondered if its significance was military or academic. She rather thought these Prussians went in for uniforms – a trait which betokened a certain lack of confidence in themselves or their abilities, that they had to be thus advertised. He clicked his heels and jerked his head at her. She felt a wave of dizziness as the significance of their presence began to dawn.

She addressed herself to the Prussian.

'And you too, sir, specialise in the treatment of mental defectives?'

Again the bullet-shaped head jerked as if activated by a puppeteer's string.

Freddie cleared his throat and lifted a second sheet of paper. She could see the writing, some of it printed pro forma, the rest in minuscule copperplate, was dense. It looked legal, could have been medical, was possibly both. But before he could speak Herr Doktor Hoessler intervened.

'The three of us, Mizz Tarrant St Giles, are united in our opinion that you are suffering from an advanced form of erotomania, characterised by obsessive behaviour of an inappropriately sexual nature. A course of treatment at the Charenton Hospital for the Mentally Infirm has been prescribed by my colleague Professeur de Tocqueville. It only needs your guardian's signature on the paper he is holding for us to be empowered to conduct you to Charenton.'

Poppea took a deep breath, drew herself up to her full height which was more than that of any of the gentlemen in front of her, though de Brillancourt came close.

'By what right, Freddie, do you call yourself my guardian?'

A shadow of despair, hopelessness and confusion anyway, passed across her brother's face. God, she thought, he's put on weight in the last eight months, since the battle; he'll have an apoplexy before long. But not soon enough. Meanwhile he glanced over his shoulder for help. Hoessler came to his rescue.

'The right of guardianship passes to the nearest male adult relative in all cases where three medical practitioners in the disciplines associated with mental disorder have signed a certificate warranting a female person to be no longer capable of sound judgement by reason of mental derangement.'

'And you have signed such a certificate.'

'Following the accounts we have been given of your recent behaviour, Mizz Tarrant St Giles, we had no choice.'

Poppea took a deep breath.

'Fuck off, then,' she said, and with one sweeping movement of her arm sent every object on her brother's desk, inkwells, a cylindrical ebony rule, papers, scales, sealing wax and seals, and a silver sand-shaker cascading to the floor, and stormed out.

Behind her the four men looked at one another with expressions that mixed smug self-satisfaction at this proof that their diagnosis had been accurate with Tartuffian sympathy. They shrugged and nodded, smiled ruefully at each other.

'What can you say?' murmured one.

'What can you do?'

Poppea avoided Charenton by allowing her brother to rent a villa for her on Ischia where, on the anniversary of the battle, she attempted to give birth to twin boys, both weighing a few ounces more than fourteen pounds and neither bearing any resemblance at all to Charlie. All three, mother and babes, died.

Charlie himself was summarily dismissed. He hung on in Paris for six months through a cold spring and into an appalling summer, when the rain never stopped. He starved, but so did half Paris. At last he risked the whipping he had been promised if he set foot again in Sir Frederick and Lady Tarrant St Giles's residence and begged an audience with his erstwhile employer, promising news of an important nature if his request was accepted. Brought before Sir Frederick, in dripping clothes, the remains of his old livery, and with a steady downpour drumming on the pavement outside, he came straight to the point.

'I desire gainful employment, sir,' he said. 'Not less than a pound a week, and preferably in England.'

'Damnme Boylan, get out before I get the servants to give you the thrashing you deserve.'

Charlie, trying to appear less frightened than he was, hurried on.

'I have here, sir,' and he drew from his waistcoat pocket a small notebook bound between board covers, 'a copy I have made of a diary which is in my possession.'

'Damnme, Charles. If you've blackmail in mind I'll have them pull your balls off first.'

'In it the late Miss Tarrant, who has gone where no terrestrial revelation can harm her, recorded in detail her encounters with numerous lovers, all, apart from your humble servant, large men with rough tastes. She modelled her style, and her attention to detail, on the writings of le Comte de Sade. A printer in Brussels has expressed an interest, but the feelings I still have for your family suggested to me I should seek your permission before . . .'

Sir Frederick, grateful that Charlie's demands went no further than a plea for employment, promised that he would see what he could do. In the meantime perhaps a purse of five guineas would alleviate any distress he might be in?

Charlie dreams on. Back in Clapham Mrs Cargill yawns discreetly behind her palm, withdraws her darning mushroom from the last of her husband's socks, and begins to pack all away in her basketwork sewing box. Mr Cargill looks up from *The Times*, flaps the pages like a swan's wings, until they are in order again, and rolls it round its pearwood staff.

'Bed then, my dear?'

'I think so. Don't you?'

'I have a file or two to glance through. Prepare myself for tomorrow, you know?'

'Of course, dear.' With a swish of silk over crinoline she heads for the door to the tiny hall and narrow stairs. Since their honeymoon this has been their normal routine. Not having a dressing room it allows her to get into her nightgown and cap, and into bed, without the impropriety of allowing him to see her undress. Meanwhile, he can enjoy one of the small cigars he allows himself and a small brandy to settle his stomach. And, indeed, prepare himself for the next day's work.

'You will turn out the gas, and put the guard in front of the fire?'

'Yes, dear.'

As soon as he has heard her footstep on the fifth stair, the one that squeaks, he fetches himself a cigar from the drawer of his new roll-top desk (as displayed at the Great Exhibition), lights it with a taper from the fire, pours himself the brandy in a plain glass (the crystal is kept for special occasions of which there have been none since their marriage), withdraws a file of Treasury paper from his case and undoes the red tape that holds the leaves together without disturbing the binding.

'Confidential. Strictly Restricted.

'In the matter of the man who calls himself Charles Boylan,' he reads, and then with his finger traces on: 'Said Boylan was first employed by the Department in September, 1816, on the recommendation of Philip Tarrant St Giles, MP. It was objected at the time that on account of the said Boylan's conspicuous physique (he is close to being a dwarf) he would prove to be a poor asset in the trade to which he was to be assigned. Nor was the Board impressed by his manner or his apparent intellectual capacity. However, it appeared that the Minister himself was concerned that the man should be found employment, in part apparently to avoid embarrassment to the Tarrant St Giles family, to whom the Minister was under some sort of unspecified obligation. The Board consequently agreed to take on the said Boylan for a period of probation not exceeding nine months, at the end of which his record in the Department's service would be assessed. See addendum 1 . . .'

Cargill dutifully folds back the dry hard pages and finds addendum 1.

'Philip Tarrant St Giles was the member for The Tarrants in

the County of Dorset from 1809 to 1819, sitting on the government benches. He was the uncle of Captain Sir Frederick Tarrant St Giles from whose employ said Boylan had recently been discharged. The nature of the obligation to the Tarrant St Giles family the Minister acknowledged has not been recorded, nor is the nature of the embarrassment the family was anxious to avoid . . .'

Cargill sighs. Puffs a little, sups a little. Clearly it is not going to be easy to extract from the official verbiage anything of real substance from this earlier report, dated 1831. He wonders . . . will Charlie Boy have been more forthcoming in his own accounts? Will they be as fanciful, corrupt, and corrupting, as his account of the battle of Waterloo? But it's too late to think of reading the papers he has brought from Pentonville, that dark blotched and spidery scrawl, especially by gaslight. He'd tackle them by daylight, back at the office.

Stimulated in part by his recollection of Boylan's account of his coupling with Maribel, he takes himself up to the already darkened room above him.

Being Welsh by birth, Mrs Cargill thinks of Wales.

10

I left Paris in the Paris–Calais diligence on the eighth of September 1816, being the Virgin's birthday. We were hardly out of the suburbs before the ravages caused by the terrible weather and aborted harvest became apparent, not to mention the late revolutions and wars so recently ended. The wheat rotted in the fields, water lay in sheets on the meadows, and at every stop the people flocked around us begging not for money but for scraps of food we might have brought with us. What use was cash when what they needed to buy was not to be had for love nor money?

The situation was no better on the other side of the Channel, once we were clear of Dover and ensconced in the post chaise, except of course for the fact that the people who waylaid us in the first village out of Dover were more phlegmatic, more stoical, more *manly* than the French: instead of expostulating, crying, throwing their arms about, shrugging their shoulders and puffing out their lips they merely threatened to beat us to a pulp if we did not pass over what bread and other provisions we might have with us. Our coachman and his sidekick kept them at bay with their blunderbusses but never-theless we gave them some crusts.

Once clear of them we partook of a good meal of oysters, cheese, fine Kentish ale and white bread made from flour a Dover baker had bought illegally from a Swedish merchantman making a fine profit exporting his country's surplus to those in need. These had all been wrapped in sacking and tied in a bundle on the roof of our coach where they looked like the rest of the baggage. Had we left our provisions open to view I am sure the villagers of Buckland would have braved our escorts' firearms for the sake of a meal.

A young but fat man, already prematurely balding as we saw when he removed the low crowned hat he was wearing, enter-tained us with a knowledgeable account of why so many summers had been so bad in recent years.

'They are,' he told us, us being a gentleman of the cloth, two lady schoolteachers returning to Sidcup after enjoying a holi-day at Folkestone, and three soldiers, a sergeant and two corporals, on their way home to Newcastle from France, having been laid off by the Army of Occupation as being of no further use. 'They are, these bad summers, the sure conse-quence of a general warming of the climate in the northern hemisphere . . .'

'Don' feel warm to me,' grumbled one of the soldiers, looking up from the tinder box he was scraping away at, preparatory to getting a glow on a wick he could then light his clay with. 'Fucking cold if you ask me. For September.'

'But why, sir,' said the clergyman, putting aside the book of Wesleyite sermons he had been pretending to read, 'is the gen-eral atmosphere becoming warmer? If indeed it is.'

'On account,' said our plump friend, 'of the vastly increased number of manufactories in the middle parts of England, many of them burning coal to make steam power in the first place, and in the second, these late wars which have seen such a vast increase in the expenditure of powder, the burning of cities, the explosion of magazines and so forth.'

72

'They do say,' one of the teaching ladies offered, 'the noise of cannon fire causes thunder—'

'If the manufactories in the middle shires and the North are to blame,' a thin grey man who had hitherto sat silent in the corner furthest from me, hiding behind his newspaper, chipped in, 'then surely we may expect some improvement. For they are all shut down and the hands laid off, on account that none have money to spare to buy what the mills produce, the price of wheat being one hundred and three shillings.'

'Ay, there's great hunger in the North,' the second and older of the ladies added. 'Did you hear of the unemployed weaver's wife, carrying her child she was, dropped dead of hunger right in front of the overseers?'

At which all fell silent for a moment and the coach swayed and thumped on over the broken surface of the road or splashed through the deeper pools that lay in the dips. Then quite suddenly the clouds cleared a little and the sun shone, and all looked green and pleasant again, old England as she was meant to be, though much of the sparkle came from where the beams fell on water still held in the leaves of the elms we were passing under.

'There. What did I say?' the younger teacher chirped. 'Weather's on the mend. All will be well, you'll see.'

Which was a lie. She'd said no such thing.

This is all by the way. Where was I? It is the fucking cold in this place makes my mind wander when I try to write. It would be a kindness, a service indeed that would save Mr Cargill much labour in reading my scrawl, and also time wading through the waffle my frozen brain leads me into, if he were to persuade the Governor of this place to allow me a small bowl of charcoal, such as Iberian peasants place beneath their tables in winter as the most economical way of keeping themselves from freezing to death, or, at the very least a pair of cut-down woollen gloves known to the poorer sort as 'mittens'. Poor little kittens they have lost their mittens and don't know where to find them. And so have I. So have I.

Seventeenth of September 1816. The first day I set foot inside the gloomy portals of His Majesty's Government's Home Office. Not strictly true. On that occasion, and indeed every other, I was redirected by the officious functionary on the steps, a retired colour sergeant from the Brigade of Guards, judging by the combination of a Peninsular War medal and a Waterloo medal, clanging together below the multiple capes of his capacious topcoat, to the mews behind the main building, and a small door, not much bigger than a coal-hole, at the foot of a short flight of steps, that led to the basements below. The portals were not for mortals.

I should like to describe for you the scene on that gusty autumn day, but it is all now confused in my mind, and, I daresay, in the mind of almost anyone whose memory stretches back, all too inaccurately, a full third of a century and more. The thing of it is this piece of London, indeed almost every piece of London you care to think of, has so changed and continues to change during these decades my story wanders through, that I cannot be sure what building, what street, what neighbourhood was pulled down by a particular point in time, rebuilt, pulled down again and built again. I therefore must trust Mr Cargill to forgive any errors of a topographical or architectural nature that may creep into my narrative, and beg him, and any reader who may follow where his eyes have gone before, not to attribute substantive error to my tale merely on the grounds that I have prematurely razed a church or ministry in one place or raised a department store or vast estate of dwellings in another.

You will not believe this, but I think I am right when I say that at the time I am speaking of, the Great Wen or Carbuncle which even then seemed large enough to be a universe in its own right, concluded on the western side with some newish buildings round the village of Kensington, while to the north there were still market gardens between Islington and

Hampstead. Regent Street had only got as far north as its junction with Piccadilly, the money having run out in those hard times, and Nash's great curving terrace remained a dream on paper. Although building, of a sort, was indeed continuous from the eastern boundary of Hyde Park to the docks at Wapping, and took in first Hanover and Berkeley Squares from a hundred years ago, there then lay a hideous no-man's land of squalor, disease and deprivation, known collectively as 'The Rookeries', between Soho and the Inns of Court, bounded to the north by Holborn and Covent Garden to the south.

Westminster was an enclave of government containing some notable buildings that dwarfed the rest – the Abbey, of course, the Palaces of Westminster and St James (the former palace later destroyed by fire nearly twenty years ago as I write this, and the new one still not completely finished), the Whitehall, the ministries of state, and the houses of the grandees who ruled us, vying in splendour and surpassing in newness those of the King (or was he still Regent in 1816? – I forget) who wanted a palace built but could not afford it, together with the gaming houses, hostelries, coffee-houses, assembly rooms, a handful of theatres, pleasure gardens, livery stables and the rest that sought to satisfy their immediate needs.

For the most part the roads that served these establishments were rutted lanes, only the major arteries being metalled or cobbled and lit with the very new invention of gas-lighting, while the interstices remained dark alleys, the haunts of footpads, beggars, whores and men mutilated in the late wars.

Yet, crossing Westminster Bridge on my way from lodgings in Lambeth I recall there was a brightness, a glittering in air that was, in those days, still largely smokeless, at least in the earlyish hours of a morning in September, and one could remark how ships, towers, domes and temples lay open to fields, yes fields, and to the sky. *Eheu fugaces sunt.*

Enough. I have a story to tell.

I knocked on the area door, which was presently opened by

75

a fair-haired lad dressed seemly enough in white shirt, dark breeches, green apron and buckled shoes.

'Who pays the piper?' said he.

'He who calls the tune,' I replied, giving the answer I had been enjoined to offer.

The lad stuck his head over my shoulder and checked out the narrow yard, assuring himself that I was alone, then: 'Step this vay, sir,' and he stood aside.

He insisted on remaining behind me as we threaded our way through a maze of vaulted corridors, whitewashed to be sure, with red-tiled floors and black oak doors every five paces or so. On these were painted, very small, in white paint, Roman numerals and lower case letters of the alphabet, separated into small groupings by dashes, colons, commas and slashes. Sam, for that, on a later visit, I learned was his name, carried a wax taper held above his head which threw my shadow ahead of us and 'Take a right here, sir', 'The left this time if you please', he called out, until we came to a crossroads at what I took to be the centre of the great building we were under.

Although dark the air was cool but not dank and only very slightly musty which argued perhaps the presence somewhere of ventilation. Only once did we come upon any clue as to the purposes to which this vast cellarage had been put, and that in the shape of an old man, attired like my guide, only with spectacles on the end of his pointed nose, who pushed along over the flags so it made a trundling noise, like truck wheels on rails, a large trolley with three shelves and a lanterned candle on its prow. It was piled high with sheaf upon sheaf of papers, neatly bound and tied with scarlet ribbon, some laid flat to make rectangular towers, others rolled into tubular shapes and placed in leather buckets. No doubt, I surmised, but not aloud, we were finding our way through some vast and inclusive archive.

At about this point I was startled to hear the report of a pistol shot, somewhat muffled by thick walls but close enough.

'Pay no attention,' said Sam. 'It's just our Captain Quex a-trying out one of his new toys.'

76

The crossroads was in fact a roundabout though not, of course, a carousel, and out of it, circling its cylindrical wall, rose a cast-iron spiral stair, dimly lit by a glazed circular lantern or dome some six or seven storeys above us. Four turns of this stair took us past two doors and on to a third which Sam, who had now extinguished his taper, told me to open.

'Take the fifth door on the left,' he said. 'They are vaiting for you.'

The corridor I was now in was high-ceilinged with moulded plaster above a dado of darkened oak carved in linenfold patterns. Above the dado hung portraits of presumably notable men, and the whole was lit by a chain of small chandeliers, each with four lit candles among the crystal droplets, although there was adequate enough lighting at each end provided by tall windows at least eight feet high set between crimson drapes.

I tapped as discreetly as I might on the panel of what I calculated to be the fifth door but was later pointed out to me as the fourth, and was answered by a braying laugh that came clattering down two octaves, like a horse's. Not wishing to sound peremptory and already advised that I was expected, I turned the large brass door handle and eased the big door open. I was confronted, a bare yard or so in front of me, by a figure I had last seen, mounted on his chestnut horse, less than a year before, cantering through the Bois de Boulogne in pursuit of a fox. He was shorter than I remembered, only five feet and three-quarters (which of course still made him very considerably taller than I by a clear foot), wore a blue short-tailed coat over white trousers strapped down over his insteps. His complexion was between bronzed and ruddy, still carrying the effects of campaigning for seven years in all weathers, his eyes a vivid greenish hue, made more startling by his high colour. His hair was abundant, a rich brown but greying at the temples. His large arched and boney nose was all the weapon he had and all he needed to make him the most formidable man on earth.

'Who the divel are you?' he barked, then turned his head

over his right shoulder to the man behind him who wore a black coat and knee breeches, somewhat old-fashioned. 'Why, Sidmouth, I think this is one of those worms of yours you were talking about, come to tell you what plots the Jacobins are hatching up in Golden Square or out in Camden Town. Is that it, young feller me lad?'

He put his hands on his thighs and bent his knees a little to bring his face nearer to mine.

I managed to stammer out that I was Charles Boylan, and that I was there to undertake any employment, however worm-like, his grace or his lordship might care to invite me to.

'Don't be ashamed of your trade, me lad. You serve a good cause, the maintenance of order, decency and so forth in the realm. Many a battle I won through people of your sort coming with news of what was happening on the other side of the hill. Here's a sixpence for you . . .' and he delved in his trouser pocket. 'Damnit Sidmouth, got nothing but French coppers in me pocket. Give him a sixpence for me, there's a good chap. Must be off, get the Dover packet back to Paris before they realise I'm not there . . .' and then, with his hand on the door, he turned.

'Harry, take my word for it. And it is after all what you have brought me all this way to tell you. Get the ringleaders. Show no mercy. String 'em up just as soon as the due proprieties of law have been observed. Make sure as many of the mob as can, see it done. Nothing like a good hanging in public to make ordinary people respect the law. Learnt that in the Peninsula. Catch the scum looting they soon desisted when they saw their colleagues swinging from an oak or olive tree. Snuff it out now, I say. Or at best we'll have a rebellion like the American one, at worst a storming of the Bastille and all that followed on from that.'

'Arthur, we don't have a Bastille.'

'Then the scum will find one. The Tower like as not. May not have prisoners in it, but then neither did the Bastille, but there's a handy lot of muskets stacked away there. Now, I really must be off. Give us your hand again.'

He came back a pace or two and shook hands with this man Henry Sidmouth, whom I later took to be Henry Addington, first Viscount Sidmouth, Minister of State for Home Affairs.

The Great Man gave me another glance as he went by for the second time.

'By God, you've the look of a rogue about you! Seen you before, of course. Never forget a face, and certainly not one like yours. I'm sure you'll do the business for us to a T.' Then he turned back to Sidmouth. 'Don't look all that English though, does he?'

'I'm sure he'll make a very English agent.'

'Maybe, maybe.' He turned back to me, tweaked my ear. 'Make sure his lordship here gives you that, whatd'y'call it? The Tanner.'

With that he was gone and the laugh echoed down the corridor behind him. Worth ten thousand men in a battle, they said, and the space and silence he left behind him made you believe it.

The man who remained stood with his back to the window, another tall one which looked down into a courtyard with the towers of the Abbey visible beyond the further wing. In his sixties, with the pale complexion and deep lines of a drudge or fanatic, his build was thin, beneath a high-domed forehead, bushy eyebrows, narrow eyes and a long nose. A slight jowly presence above his high collar gave weight to looks that were in no way striking. He wore an air of authority like a cloak. And I mean like a cloak: son of a country doctor I later learnt, and no grandee, he put it on and off as required – it did not come to him natural, like the Duke's.

The Minister scrutinised me for a moment or two with a cold eye. Then he reached round and found a small silver bell on his desk, which he rang.

'What in creation,' he said, as if to himself, but meaning me to hear, 'was young Freddie up to when he employed you?'

A side door opened and a figure I was to get to know well over the years appeared. I must attempt a description, but, apart

79

from two characteristics I shall dwell on in a moment, I find it almost impossible to do so. He was, precisely, nondescript. He was of middling height, not fat nor thin. He was middle-aged and one felt he always had been, always would be. His clothes were sombre, clean but not immaculate, pressed, but yesterday perhaps not today. In short, neither slovenly nor dandyish. A moment after he was gone you would not be able to swear to the colour of his eyes, nor even whether his sideburns were short or long, trimmed or shaggy.

And those two characteristics? His hair was darker than brown but not black, yet had one long thin white streak running from his forehead and across his crown. And the other was his manner, and particularly the way he moved. It was not until our third meeting that I found the word for it. Feline. That was it. He moved with the slow fluent dignity of a cat confident of the safety of its surroundings.

'Mr Stafford,' his lordship said, 'this is Charles Boylan, about whom I have spoken to you. Take him away and instruct him in his duties.'

Mr Stafford gestured acquiescence by inclining his head.

'Mr Boylan. Be so good as to follow me.'

I waited. They both looked at me. I looked at his lordship.

'His grace's sixpence?'

A closing down of his considerable eyebrows signified Sidmouth's impatience.

'Give him sixpence, John. I'll see you get it back.'

Whether Stafford got it or not I don't know. If he did, he was in pocket, for he never gave it to me.

11

There were many consequences flowed from what any reader of this memoir, this claim, this plea will acknowledge was a momentous moment on a par with the battle of Hastings, the Magna Carta, the Bill of Rights, nay the very battle of Waterloo itself, for historic significance. On it depended the very survival of the British State, thus allowing the steady and healthy *organic* growth towards moderate and well-considered reform instead of violent and bloody revolution ending in the execution of kings and, who knows, votes for women, that were very much on the cards.

The most immediate consequence was that I was employed as potboy in the Three Tuns, north-east of King's Cross and south-west of the commons south of Islington village, known as Spa Fields. I was paid a shilling a day and what I could eat in the way of bread and cheese and drink in the way of mild ale. Mr Stafford paid the landlord, an Irishman whose name was MacKillop, five pounds down for what he called my 'insertion' and to myself a further two shillings a day. My duties were, on the one hand, to collect pewter mugs, and, from the snug, glasses, as and when they were left, dirty plates and knives from the tables, occasionally wipe down the latter, and serve behind the counter or bar at busy times – all that for my one shilling; for my two shillings on the other hand, I was to listen out for talk of treason and revolution, reporting the identity not of those who were particularly outspoken or fervent, for that would have meant listing the whole shoal the Three Tuns habitually caught in its net, nor those who paid their tuppence for Cobbett's *Political Register* and another penny to join the Hampden Club that met on Thursday nights in the upstairs room to talk up universal suffrage and annual parliaments; but those who passed on messages concealed in a palm or slipped in a pocket, or spoke of caches of powder and arms and so forth. All this was to be coded in a tedious number cipher and left in a hollow oak tree on Primrose Hill, which Stafford designated my 'drop'.

Dear old Stafford. He had many similar wrinkles and conceits for running what he called 'The Firm'. For instance, after three meetings, which he attended himself and which served as training in my new profession, I was not to see him except by appointment in the Home Office, nor, if I met him in the street, address him or acknowledge our acquaintance. Between us he set a gentleman called Guy de Bourgeois, an erstwhile Cambridge scholar, from St John's College, sent down, it was said, for neglecting his theological studies in preference for scientific pursuits, though actually his misdemeanour was, in his own words, buggering a boy in the choir with an arse like a jelly on springs.

Anyway, this man de Bourgeois, a thin, rakish cove who laughed a lot but like a donkey 'ee-aw' rather than a stallion among the trumpets, was to be thought of, Stafford said, as my 'control'. Via the oak on Primrose Hill my messages went to him, and via the same oak his, or rather Stafford's, commands came to me.

Stafford himself, after developing the analogy of a spider whose web stretches not just across the metropolis but the whole country, referred to himself as . . . 'The Web-Master'.

And, in precisely the way that I had a 'cover', that of a potboy, so too did he. He was Chief Clerk at the Bow Street Magistrates' Court.

As a wet and wretched autumn deepened into an early winter, with some snow, it was indeed plain, once one was away from Westminster and the clerks' and artisans' cottages just south of the river, who served Westminster, that the ordinary people did have cause for complaint. Successive poor harvests and the totally ruined one of the previous summer had raised the price of wheat (much of it imported and only, according to the Corn Laws, to be sold at the same rate as English wheat) to heights which left the ordinary labourer, if he had work at all, with nothing left in his pocket . . . once he had provided himself and his family with the staple of life. The consequence was he bought nothing but bread, and all those who weaved and span and made clothes and shoes, and furniture, and pots and pans, and carriages, and ships, the croppers and stockingers and all the rest could not shift the products of their trades and soon lacked, the poorer less well-paid sort at any rate with nothing put by for the very real and unmetaphorical rainy day, the wherewithal to buy bread. And you can add to this seething mass of discontent the paid-off soldiers and sailors of the wars, many of whom would have found work beyond them anyway, supposing any became available, since most lacked a hand or a foot, an arm or a leg.

Bread may have been in short supply, but, as is usually the case, ale and beer and gin, it seemed, did remain within reach of the pockets of the poor, and tobacco too, and no doubt put words in their mouths which, in sobriety, they would deny.

Thus, as I passed among these horny-handed sons without toil with mugs of ale and occasionally pasties and buns, or stood behind the counter scooping farthings and halfpennies out of the pools of liquor, with the air filled with tobacco smoke cut with hempen rope to make it go further, these are the sorts of conversation that filled my ears . . .

'Six thousand men'll turn out on Spa Fields before the month's out.'

'Sure to. And we'll march 'em down to Westminster and blow the Parliament House, see if we don't.'

'That's right. Us labouring folk can't stand it no longer.'

'Damn all such rogues as governs England. Come the revolution then all these great men's heads goes off . . .'

And so forth. Yes, I thought to myself, maybe, but not until this pub closes . . .

The attentive reader will have noted a significant conjunction in the above vis-à-vis my personal situation and the price of wheat: 'as much bread and cheese as I could eat' was a settled clause in my contract with MacKillop. It led to an acquaintance of some importance in my life.

Although the Three Tuns remained open for twenty hours in every twenty-four, and even though serving of victuals and drink stopped between midnight and four in the morning, there were generally a few who hid under the settles, or sat knees up in the darker corners on a tiled floor awash with beer spillage, pastry crusts and dog-shit, hoping for a little warmth if not sleep through the worst part of the night. At four it was my duty to come down from where I slept in the tiny hayloft over the lean-to stable where MacKillop kept a spavined mare and, armed with a broom, chase these flotsam of life back out into the street, forbidding their return until they had gathered together a day's supplies of coppers enough to feed at our counters without begging off the regular customers. This they generally managed as early as four o'clock in the afternoon during winter, by when they were back with their pennies and occasionally a silver thrummer.

So there I was, about the beginning of November 1816, I reckon, leaning on my broom handle, which came above my head, watching the five or six rag-pickers, mudlarks, and so forth, and a Highlander in the tatters of the uniform of a sergeant of the 92nd with a bagpipe under his arm, slithering over the frosty cobbles by the light of a setting waning moon, as they made their way downhill, towards the City and the river. It was odd the Highlander should be among them. He had a room not far away, which he shared with his young daughter. He had, however, I remembered, been boisterously bad-tempered the night before, drinking gin as well as the beer he normally stuck to, and had, I supposed, simply passed out before rather than after he could get home.

A moment or two later I turned back in, unlocked the tiny kitchen behind the bar, hoiked half a stale loaf out of the bread bin, lifted the cheese net and sliced a neat triangle out of the still fresh Suffolk Hard that we'd started the day before, and thus began a breakfast before moving on to my next task which was the sweeping out of the now uninhabited floor of the two main rooms, the snug and the public. Uninhabited as I thought.

'Gi' us a bite.'

Well, not often I look down on a face, but I did this time. Just.

'Gi' us a bite. I'm that starved.'

Eyes blue with a violet tinge in certain lights, such as that given off by the one tallow candle I'd set going on the wooden board that drained into the lead sink. Long, straggled, greasy hair with some straw stuck in it, which I knew in daylight could lead you to suspect, in spite of the filth, was yellowy red. Freckles. Baby nose, rosebud mouth with gaps where she'd lost her front milk teeth, cheeks high and plump enough to make you think she wasn't as starved as she cracked on. Arms, legs and bony knees that thin and stick-like they made you think she was telling the truth after all. Cotton dress, with a lace edging coming adrift and a burn mark in the skirt which was why some toff's bint had binned it, a woollen shawl pulled off an old woman who'd frozen stiff and dead the winter before in the portico of St Paul's, Covent Garden. Shoes, buckled and pointed toes, satin covered, three sizes too big, which she took off to dance barefoot to the Highland sergeant's bagpipe. I knew her, everyone knew her, as Maggie-May. Not the name she goes by these days, eh?

How old in 1816? Eight? Nine? Not more than ten. She wouldn't know. I doubt anybody did.

Without thinking, I carved off another doorstep from the big loaf, came fresher than mine had, and another wedge of cheese and thereby made a friend for life. It was, she said years later, the fact I just did it. I didn't grumble or question, let alone push her out, I just did it. If any question at all was in my mind it was answered by 'as much bread and cheese as I can eat', so why not?

Anyway, I drew a half of small beer to wash down what I'd eaten, and a horn cup of water from the pitcher for her, and we got to talking, which we went on with while I went out into the rooms with my broom and began sweeping, she putting the stools on the tables for me, and bundling up the rubbish and chucking it out in the street for the dustmen.

'So why aren't you out with your dad?' I asked. 'He just left here. He'll be looking for you.'

For I knew she danced to his pipes round Smithfield or Covent Garden until the markets closed up about seven then went on to do the same outside the new shops in Strand, ending up with the clubs in St James's, a full sixteen-hour stint.

'Macpherson's no dad o' mine,' she said, very brusquely. Her accent was Scottish but not purely so – I guess she'd picked it up from being in the company of Highlanders, getting on for three years she reckoned. She went on to tell me how her mother was a laundry lady with the 92nd, one of the hundred allowed for the whole regiment, but not from Scotland herself, though maybe Ireland, Maggie-May didn't really know. She wasn't actually that sure of the difference between Ireland and Scotland, thought of both as places where the 'sojers' come from. They'd been in Spain and the south-west of France the year before Waterloo. Maggie-May had no idea who her father was and very little recollection of any life before Spain, or so she said.

'Anyway, me mam got her legs broke on the road between Brussels and Waterloo, run over by a gun carriage going lickerty-split to get to the battle on time, and she died not long after.

An' I like had an older sister, Annie, an' she took up with a corporal and together they passed me on to Macpherson when the fighting was done. I already danced flings an' such like, and especially the sword dance. An' I've worked the streets, and markets and such like wiv 'im ever since but never gone further out of London than Islington. But I'm through wiv 'im now. So there.'

This last said with a flash of venom that quite took my breath away. Such hate from a tiny slip of a girl.

'Why? What's he done?'

'Taint dacent to tell you.'

But I knew she would. By now I'd set the broom aside and was behind the counter giving the mugs that had been draining in the kitchen overnight a rub before hanging them on their hooks. Maggie-May went down on one knee, scooped up the last of the rubbish between two short lengths of broken plank and took it outside. She came back, stood in the doorway, and, low though it was, the top of her head only came halfway up the door jamb, with the orange three-quarter moon dying behind it.

'Down Drury Lane, last night, we was playing the Theatre Royal crowd as they come out, and a genelman offers Macpherson a guinea if he'll let him have me for the rest of the night. I told 'em to fuck orff and ran all the way back here and hid. Macpherson followed me and nearly caught me but he couldna find me, an' he passed out under that bench, he was that pissed by chuckin' out time.'

I was almost as shocked by the words she used as by the suggestion she should be prostituted so young. I mean fourteen yes, even twelve, but ten! or less! But another thought had crossed my mind.

'Where was you hiding then?'

Notice my attempt to share her vernacular. It's a habit I have. I'm not proud of it but I don't like ordinary folk to take me for a toff.

She looked at me, head on one side.

'I'll tell you,' she said, 'but only 'cos I know what you's up to, what your gime is. An' I'll split on you if you split on me. Come here and I'll show you.'

And she moved to the corner of the room where the wooden arms of two settles, each backed to their respective walls, enclosed a box-like space, not much more than two foot square. She hoisted herself up, using the arms for leverage, swung her feet in (first letting her oversize shoes slip off and stay on the floor), crossed her arms in front of her thin sparrow's chest, and sank out of view. Meanwhile my heart was thumping and my mouth had gone dry. Did she really know what my game was? Then up came her head again.

'I bin watching you this two, three weeks,' she said. 'You're a naus, ain't you?'

'A naus?'

'Naus Ark. Nark.'

Part III

WAR AGAIN

There is no term for this but class war.

E. P. THOMPSON,
The Making of the English Working Class

12

'Nark?' said I, playing for time, time to recover from the shock. If what I was up to was transparent to a slip of a girl, who else had rumbled me?

'Come on!' She looked up at me with scorn in those greenish eyes. 'Naus. Nark! Informer! Spy. Polis spy.'

'Don't know what you mean.'

'I mean like you take notes on a little pad, when you have a moment to spare. An' ask where people live, an' what their handles are?'

'Handles?'

'Nimes. Then you write it all out in numbers 'stead of proper writing and leave it in a 'ole in a tree atop o' Primrose Hill.'

'Oh shit,' said I.

She put down her planks, came over to the bar, hoisted her tiny bottom on to one of the stools, put her elbows on the counter, and her chin on her hands. Looked up at me all pert, head on one side and grinned.

'Shilling a week,' she said, ' 'an I tell no one.'

I thought of what would happen if she did. They'd tear my

head off for sure. The only doubt was would they do it quick or slow.

'Fine thanks I get for bread and cheese.'

I tried to sound stern but it came out a whimper.

'Ninepence then, and bread and cheese in the mornings. An' you let me go on using my cubbyhole, nights. Like today.' She thought for a moment. 'An' I'll tell you what. I'll do the drop on Primrose Hill for you.'

'Sixpence,' I said. Then, remembering the Duke, 'a tanner. But I'll go on doing the drop meself.'

'Done.'

And she spat on her hand and held it out for me to shake.

We had a bit of a scare from Macpherson. We didn't see him for a day and a night and a day but he came in the second night and, after swearing at her in Gaelic, gave her a slap that floored her, and then tried to pick her up by her hair. But by then she'd put the story round how she wasn't his daughter at all, that back in the room he rented he made her do unspeakable things to him for his pleasure, how he'd got the junior officers of the guard at the Tower to pay a shilling each to watch her do the sword dance naked over their swords which were so sharp they cut her toes, and finally tried to hire her out for the night to a swell in Drury Lane. The consequence was a seaman called Cashman did a berserk, pushed a broken bottle in Macpherson's face, and ran him out of the Three Tuns so he tripped on the icy cobbles, whereupon Cashman and two or three others kicked him in all the softer parts of his body, some of which were well exposed since, like all Highlanders, he was mother-naked under his kilt.

Cashman. No doubt, Mr Cargill, the name is familiar to you, if you've made a proper study of the records of the time. But in case you don't have a picture of him in your head, here is one drawn from memory. He was a smallish dapper sort of a man, very neat the way seamen often are, still wearing his sailcloth trousers though he'd been paid off two years or more and his cutaway donkey jacket over the uniform singlet with pale blue and white hoops. His hair, which was balding a bit in the front, was pulled back into a short tarred pigtail above the collar. In short, he was a regular Jack Tar and, though on the small side, tough as nails, as old boots, as the salted beef and biscuit that had been his diet for a decade and more. He used to boast he was no more than thirteen years old when he was first a top-yardsman and sat at the top of the *Victory's* mizzen during Trafalgar, ready, with other lads not strong enough to handle the guns, to haul in or shake out the t'gallants. Give him a mug of Jamaica rum and he'd tell you how the flags 'England expects' fluttered below him and he saw how the Admiral took the ball in the top of his chest and was carried below in the very moment of triumph.

He himself reckoned he had been hard done by. Coming from an Irish family of fishermen he had been wounded nine times and showed the scars to prove it if a second mug of rum was forthcoming, though the ninth scar, in his groin, he always said was exhibited only to ladies, and then free of charge. He was, he said, owed five years' back pay by the Admiralty, and a sum of one pound a month, which he had made over to his ailing mother, had never been paid.

Well, I had already noted how certain gentlemen of extreme opinions made much of him, talked him up as a popular hero, bought him all the drink he could put away, and the more he took the wilder he became, taking on board (as he would no doubt have put it) the doctrines they put in his mouth as:

Item: Our kings and nobility are descended from a French bastard who landed with an armed banditti and made himself King of England which is, in plain terms, a very paltry rascally original . . .

Item: How come the Duke gets £400,000 to buy or build himself a house, while honest Jack Tar sleeps in a ditch . . .

Item: No reform without revolution . . .

And, of course, he was not alone in all this. Many other workless working men and men who had served before the mast or behind the colours sat or stood round the tables, nursing their small beer and trying to spin it out for as long as they could, listening to the earnest, forceful, but mostly hushed outpourings of the thinkers among them. These puffed at their clays or drank the beer their listeners bought them, leaned across towards each other in the light of the candle, or glanced over their shoulders to see if any stranger might be listening who could be took for one of Stafford's men.

'It's property is the root of it all,' mutters one.

'Aye, that's where the wealth lies,' responds another.

'Take,' says a third, 'all the land and settle it on the people, say I.'

'What you could do, mark me,' comes in the second again, 'is set up a committee in every parish, as would own and manage the land to the benefit of all.'

'Not just the farming land,' the first returns, 'but all the land. The waters, the mines, the big houses, the land the manufactories are on, return all to the people . . .'

And so forth and none did spare a glance for the hairy dwarf who gathered up their empty mugs or brought in from the back a screw of baccy.

Maggie-May had no understanding at all of what this was about. All she knew was what was in it for her: which was a hiding place at night, warm and snug, if cramped; all the food she could eat; a few coppers; and respite from the bagpipes. For the treatment he handed out to Macpherson, Cashman was her saviour, her hero, the star in her heaven, the big brother she'd lost – not I, though 'twas I that fed her and gave her a roof. She'd sit on his knee and reach behind his neck to pull his pigtail, she'd kiss the tip of his nose, and, when she thought I wasn't looking, and MacKillop neither, she'd slurp a noggin of black rum into his ale.

Anyway, it was all coming together, and about the second week of November I was able to put in cipher a message for Mr Stafford whose main gist was a big meeting was planned for that weekend on Spa Fields, that many thousands were expected and that no doubt there'd be a riot at least and a revolution at worst, and I named some names, Cashman's among them. On this occasion a thin, tall figure, dressed mostly in black, with a black umbrella held high above his crushed top hat against the driving rain, so he looked like nothing so much as an undertaker's man at a funeral, was waiting for me. Guy de Bourgeois, no less.

'Too damned wet and chilly to be outdoors more than necessary, eh? Find a snug hostelry, what?'

But instead of heading south towards the gleaming white stucco of Gloucester Terrace on the other side of the park, which would have been a fair step, but would have brought us to one of the many places of some style and comfort behind the terrace, he took me by the elbow and steered me down the hill towards Camden Town. We slithered on the greasy grass and sheep droppings and then had to face the obstacle of a deep ditch where five hundred or so Irish navigators were digging out the new canal. The only way across was on planks not more than three feet wide, loosely bound and nailed together, and even then we had to wait in the rain while a chain of eight men, with sacks on their heads, one corner on each making a pointed peak above their mud-smeared foreheads, came from the other side pushing eight barrows filled with mixed mortar.

'Outta the wayee, yer fockin English bastard,' muttered the leader.

Guy de Bourgeois raised an eyebrow but said nothing.

'Why,' I asked him as we trotted on down the hill, past huge timber gates already in place for Camden Lock where the ditch took a big step down, 'do they use Irishmen for the job?'

'Four reasons,' said Mr de Bourgeois, furling his umbrella (we were now in the doorway of the Marquess of Granby), and ticking them off finger to thumb. 'One, they're desperate with folk starving back home; two, they have no right of settlement to claim relief under the Poor Law as an unemployed Englishman has so long as he remains in his own parish – therefore they feel free to travel; three, desperation gives them strength an English labourer lacks, and four, and most important . . . Shall we go inside?'

He took me to a small table in a corner near the fire, shook his umbrella, took off his hat and shook that, and whistled up the potboy.

'Do you have any mulled claret? No? Then I'll have a dish of tea and so will my friend. Four, they do not have the habit of combination.'

'They combined well enough in the late wars,' I chipped in, for had I not seen the Irish stand together at many a battle through the Peninsula as well as at Waterloo? But he ignored me.

'But they'll never combine in their own interest,' he went on. 'Among themselves they are too democratic, and no combination can work without a leader. So they can never agree on a strike, neither when it should be held, nor what it will demand. And as for collecting and holding a strike fund in preparation, well, they're all thieves and whoever holds it will have bought his passage to Boston soon as he gets his hands on it. Right. What have you got for me?'

He took my paper, which was folded in three and sealed with a blob of wax I'd melted off an old port bottle, and stuffed it in a low capacious inside pocket of his coat. It went in next to at least five other similar sheets of paper – a circumstance that comforted me since it told me I was not alone in my dangerous occupation but caused chagrin, too, to find I was only one among many and therefore perhaps not as highly rated as I had thought.

'But since you're here you might as well tell me your findings.'

He sipped his tea, and looking over the cup gave me a quizzing but whimsical sort of a look. So I told him all I had put together, some of which you've read above, but by no means all, at the end of which he leant back and slapped the table.

'Lord, Master Boylan, I don't know why old Staffers pays

you at all. I've heard it all ten times already and more beside.' Then he leant closer. 'But tell me a bit more about this Cashman fellow. He's a real wild one, is he not?'

There were, as I'm sure you know, Mr Cargill (and may I thank you *warmly* for the mittens), three meetings in Spa Fields in November and December 1816. I know nothing about the third, but I served my masters well I think in the second, and poor recompense I had from them.

The first was held a day or two after my meeting with Mr de Bourgeois, on about the fifteenth of November, and was very well attended though it came to nothing bar a lot of heated speech-making. But the crowd was huge, comprising mainly those made workless and starving by the general shortage of money, thus especially those whose productions were not the necessaries of life but those things that make life worth living, *videlicet* silk-weavers from Spitalfields, clock- and watchmakers, and a fair sprinkling too of laid-off soldiers and sailors, also become a luxury in time of peace.

A Mr Henry Hunt, a noted orator though of honest farming stock, wearing a white top hat for no better reason than to draw attention to himself, was the chief speaker, standing in the window of one of the new houses built overlooking the Fields, chosen because still it rained.

For some reason he took taxes as his theme and ranted on about them to those who would have paid taxes had they first been paid; starvation was their problem, not taxes.

'Is not your loaf taxed,' this Hunt ranted. 'Your beer? Is not everything you eat, drink, wear and even say, taxed?' And so on.

'Give me sight of a loaf,' muttered a poor man near where I stood. He was wearing rags beneath a battered hat stuck with a crow's feather, from the rim of which a steady runnel of water ran down into the collar of the tail coat he'd picked from some dust pile. 'Just give me a loaf and I'll not care if it's taxed.'

Meanwhile Hunt was working himself up into a frenzy. His eyes seemed to distend and protrude, became shot with blood and almost started from their sockets; his voice was bellowing, his face swollen and flushed, his closed fist beat as if it were to pulverise tax collectors everywhere; and his whole manner gave token of a painful energy, struggling for utterance. Well, the poor man was trying to get his voice to carry beyond the first fifty yards or so of the multitude in front of him, else what was the point?

More effective in stirring up hearts and minds, at least of those who had mastered the arts of reading and writing – and there were a good many there who had: it was not all out-of-work labourers but a very fair sprinkling too of shopkeepers, workshop owners, teachers, officers on half-pay and so forth, and even a few of the prosperous sort who may have come out of curiosity or even to take the spring waters and gossip the afternoon away – more effective I say were the penny sheets, hawked about the peripheries of the crowd by those same thinkers who held court in the taproom of the Three Tuns and other ale houses across north London. And the most trenchant of these, hot off the press that very day I believe, Mr William Cobbett's tuppenny trash:

Friends and fellow Countrymen,
Whatever the Pride of rank, or riches or of scholarship
may have induced some men to believe, the real
strength and all the resources of a country, ever have
sprung and ever must spring from the *labour* of its
people . . .

I think I have it about right, Mr Cargill, do I not?

Nevertheless, and despite all this inflammatory stuff and the hunger in many of the stomachs there, the crowd broke up shortly after Mr Hunt ceased his tirade and went home. A premature pall of darkness, coupled moments later with an intensified downpour, may have contributed. The final appeal to all was to return on the second of December by when it was declared the People's Committees would have agreed what

98

steps towards reform, particularly of Parliament, should be laid before King, Lords and Commons.

With most of the crowd dispersed the leaders then did what British revolutionaries always do when faced with the failure of the mob to make more of a revolutionary situation than a day out ... they went to an inn and dined off blackbird pie and saddle of lamb, and drank a few bumpers with appropriate toasts. I know because the inn was our inn and they took over the snug for their meal and I served them myself. There was some considered talk, some a bit strong, and towards the end of the meal some downright wild which reached its highest pitch when one John Castle, a rascally looking oaf, a big man with a dark scar down one cheek linking the corner of an eye with the corner of his twisted mouth, stood and raised his mug of claret and shouted out in his hoarse, rasping voice: 'May the last king be strangled with the guts of the last priest', at which Mr Hunt went somewhat pale, then red again, and shook his head, but bent low over his napkin. He upped and left a few minutes after.

I wrote out my report of these proceedings, but with some heaviness of heart as I correctly supposed at least five or six men in like position to mine would be doing the same, and took it to the Primrose Hill oak tree. And there I found a summons, addressed to me, signed by Guy de Bourgeois Esq., commanding me to attend Mr Stafford at the Home Office the very next day, at eleven o'clock in the morning. But I was warned to take a circuitous route and use the craft, which we call 'tradecraft', I had been trained in to ensure that I was not followed.

I was not, as indeed I now suspected, the only one. There were at least eight of us crowded into Stafford's room in the Home Office. I don't remember all of them. There was an Oliver and an Edwards, of whom more anon, but above all, and I confess I felt a strange tremor of both fear and disgust when he arrived, later than the rest of us, a big man with the heavy build of a navigator or bricklayer, a shock of black hair sticking out over his ears, the width of his shoulders exaggerated by the padding in his jacket (the previous year's fashion) and hands you felt were big enough and strong enough to crush the skull of a smaller mortal between them. And, of course, most distinctive of all, that scar. In short it was none other than Castle, who had been at the forefront of the previous Saturday's event, he who, in our tavern afterwards, had raised his glass to the hanging of monarchs in the guts of priests.

Stafford now harangued us, in his quiet, reasonable but razor-like way, on the banality and feebleness of our reports, all much the same as each other, and none carrying anything that gave him grounds for recommending the arrest of ringleaders for seditious libel or treason.

'Why, look at this,' he said, slapping with his left hand a sheet of paper he held in his right. 'Farmer Hunt's speech verbatim.' And he pushed a pince-nez on the end of his nose. '"Before physical force is applied, it is our duty to petition, to remonstrate, to call aloud for timely reformation . . ." Reformation, gentlemen, please note. Not revolution. Petitions and remonstration, not confusion and bloodshed.' He crumpled up the paper, turned away from us, went to the window and we watched his white fingers churning about at the small of his back like a handful of silver blindworms. 'Gentlemen. These are not hanging matters. And a hanging is what we need. A hanging, gentlemen, is what my Lord Sidmouth has asked me to provide.'

Oliver, or Edwards, muttered something darkly. Stafford turned on him.

'What was that? You can only report what you see and hear? Then, gentlemen, I must ask you to see and hear what I want you to see and hear.'

'What, sir. Make it up?'

'Certainly not. But make it happen. Make it happen, gentlemen. Get in among them, stir them up, urge them on. Not just to shouting. I want more than tavern posturing. I want shops broken into. I want property destroyed. I want blood flowing in

100

the gutters. I want the newspapers the day after to hold up, for the edification of all the propertied classes, the example of the loyalty of His Majesty's troops in the face of a mob, gallantly protecting our right to property. And after that, after the due processes of law properly observed, I want hangings. Now. Let's get down to how this is to be achieved. On second December next, in the same Spa Fields. Right . . . ?'

It was Castle suggested he should bring along a small cart filled with muskets and swords.

'Drink,' I suggested. 'Drink will do the trick. Give me five guineas and I'll give you a hundred ruffians fired up to slit the gizzards of their grandmothers.'

And so on. And so it was.

Mr Cargill, it is not my intention to incriminate myself for a crime which Mr Stafford virtually ordered me to commit, feeling uncertain as I do about the readiness of yourself or your superiors to accept a responsibility incurred by one of their predecessors. I am, however, quite happy to pass on to you a verbal account of the part I took in the events of second December 1816. Perhaps if you would care to call by next time you are in the vicinity of Her Majesty's prison in Pentonville?

13

On this occasion Cargill finds it convenient to take a Hackney patent cab direct from Waterloo station to Pentonville, without first calling at the Home Office. The cabbie takes the route across Blackfriars Bridge, giving Cargill a view of Waterloo Bridge, opened on the second anniversary of the battle thirty-six years ago, which in fact makes it a year older than Cargill himself. Reflections on all this, as the Hackney's wheels run clickety-click but smoothly over the macadamised surface, lead him to consider, not for the first time, just how old Charlie Boylan is. Fifteen at the battle of Waterloo has been suggested, and this chimes with the impression Charlie seems to want to give, but Cargill suspects that this estimate is distorted by Charlie's stature and a desire to appear younger (and therefore more innocent?) than he actually was. Could he in fact be as much as ten years older? That would make the man in Pentonville sixty-three years old.

Certainly, he thinks, as the Hackney crosses Ludgate Hill and passes Newgate prison, almost windowless from outside, made of great blocks of stone left only partly dressed in the rustic fashion, he looks as old as that, even older. But no doubt gaol-fever and its attendant ills are taking their toll and ageing the man prematurely. Almost, he says to himself 'poor man', but really there is nothing much in Charlie's appearance or character to inspire sympathy or pity. On they clop, through Holborn and Finsbury towards Pentonville. At least, and much to the inconvenience of Mr Cargill, Charlie has been lodged in a decent modern prison, instead of that huge stone hulk he has just passed, with its gallows erected outside the Debtor's Door.

Cargill knows all about it. It is, after all, part of his job. Back in the 1780s executions by hanging were moved from Tyburn, with its uncivilised atmosphere of carnival and fun fair, to Newgate, which, on those dreadful occasions, is hung with black in an attempt to stimulate in the crowds, who still turn up in their thousands, sentiments of solemn awe at the majesty of justice carried out according to the law. Yet he has no idea until he has pulled up the spare stool at Charlie's table, and sat himself down opposite the pale and shivering but hairy scarecrow of a dwarf, that it is just such a scene Charlie has in mind and still fears.

'You see, my dear Cargill,' he begins, after yet again hawking and ejecting a slug of green phlegm on to the greasy stone flags, 'the thing of it is, it still could be, a hanging matter.'

'Oh, really?'

'Truthfully, sir.'

A silence, or rather awareness of a man screaming abuse at his gaolers, his lawyers and the world in general, impinges on their ears from maybe five cells away down the gallery. From further away, through the unglazed bars of the tiny window set six feet above the floor, come the distant ghoulish hoots and wails of locomotives shunting freight trucks in the new marshalling yards north of King's Cross.

'Go on then.'

Boylan sighs, leans into the table so his face is less than a yard from Cargill's and Cargill can smell the prison staleness on his breath. Then he puts his hands on the table and laces the fingers.

'Thanks for the mittens, Mr Cargill. Much appreciated.'

Cargill stares for a moment, wondering where the worn black wool ends and Boylan's pelt begins, if the pelt has grown into the interstices of the wool, making a second skin of it, as difficult to flay as the one it has grown over. He shudders, can't help himself. Boylan takes note.

'Cold, innit?'

'Please do go on.'

Charlie Boylan grins, draws in a deep rasping breath, and begins.

'Very well then. Second December 1816. Spa Fields. Islington. The day dawned calm, sunny and frosty. Just as the fifteenth ult. had been a day to depress the spirits and make all stand still for fear of letting the rain spill out of the brims of their hats and down their necks, so the second was a day to feel happy to move about on, spirits lifted by the sparkle on the trees and grass, the cold demanding brisk exercise as swinging the arms and banging them against your sides, stamping of feet and such like.'

'That's enough. I see the picture.'

'I'm making the point it was a day for doing, not standing around.'

'Very well.'

'I can carry on?'

'Please do.'

'Word soon got round, as the crowds began to gather, that I was in funds and spending like a Rothschild with the financial acumen of a Prinny, and the crowd of hangers-on that followed me from hostelry to tavern round the peripheries of the Fields, steadily grew in size.' He is speaking with some relish now, his voice high and rasping, enjoying his own performance, or so it seems to Cargill. 'Soon, at the centre of them and always closest to me and my bottomless purse was seaman Cashman with a crew about him big enough to have manned a ship of the line and Maggie-May on his shoulders. They were well away even before Mr Hunt had begun his customary oration. Indeed they did not stay to hear it.

'Through this crew moved Edwards, Oliver and that giant oaf Castle, urging them on to acts of real treason, inflaming them with promises of anything and everything from unlimited rum until they died, to immortality as the saviours of mankind from oppression and hunger. They handed out the red caps of Liberty and tricolours . . .'

Here Boylan draws breath, wipes the spittle from the corners of his twisted mouth and grins broadly. What a mountebank and player he is, Cargill muses. Now he raises his voice in imitation of the drunken Irish sailor.

'"Oi'm not carrying one of they," bellowed Cashman. "Nine times was oi wounded foighting that rag for King and Country, tis the flag of the allongers and marshongers, no less."'

And here Charlie leans back and gives a short barking snort of a laugh.

'Simple sort of a soul was poor old Cashman,' he says. 'All he ever wanted, 's truth, was the money the Admiralty owed him.'

'"Nay," calls out Edwards, who was the most fly of them, well, bar yours truly perhaps, "'tis not the flag of the French, 'tis the flag of liberty, equality, and the brotherhood of working men."

'"In that case I'll have it," says Cashman, and ties it round his neck, after first handing Maggie-May to me, and then when he has it sitting stylishly to his satisfaction, he takes her back.

'Meanwhile oratory had broken out like the measles all over the Fields, for few could hear Hunt above the din around them so others took the opportunity to sound forth, for the most part urging measures far more extreme than those recommended by the white-hatted farmer. Near us a notorious Jacobin called Watson, Doctor Watson, was sounding off in characteristic fashion. "The Earth was by Nature designed for the support of mankind. The Earth is at all times sufficient to place men above distress. If he has but a spade and a hoe . . ." "Give us then a spade and a hoe," shouted back the crowd, though many there I feared would not know one end of a hoe from the other nor what use to put it to: I mean silk-weavers?

Stockingers? Men who'd served on ships of the line since they were boys? I don't think so. Still, it was enough to get him arrested for High Treason for which he was tried summer of next year, but the case collapsed and others with it when his lawyers showed Sidmouth, through Stafford, had paid John Castle and the rest of us good money to provoke the riot, and we were as responsible as he for what happened next . . .

'Which was this. Old John Castle, who could barely write but cut an imposing figure and had a stirring manner of speech that drowned out Hunt for all but those at the front of the crowd, got on his cart, with a banner in his hands that said "The brave soldiers are our friends" and declared the time had come to take the Tower and the muskets in it, do away with landowners, rob the Bank, and empty the prisons. So saying he leapt down from his cart and he and some as strong as himself began to drag it down Goose Well Road while Watson and another man called Preston hallooed and cheered and waved their tricolours in one hand, and a couple of blown old muskets Stafford had given Castle in the other. And Cashman was just behind, with Maggie-May still on his shoulders, and me trotting at his side and all Cashman's shipmates in tow behind us. Maybe five hundred. No, more. Five hundred seamen, and a pretty vast number of ordinary working folk, women and children among them, many just out for the fun of the thing on a fine day, though a bit bewildered about what was going on and what was expected of them.

'When we got to the Tower, Preston got himself hoisted up on to the outer curtain wall, it's low, you know, so the cannon beyond can fire over it, and called on the soldiers to join him, but, drawn up in line with their officers in front of them they paid no attention until called on to present, aim and . . . but before the last order Preston was down again and scampering back up Tower Hill and into the cart.

'Well, about then the crowd began to break up. Some got as far as Aldgate where they ran into a couple of companies of Life Guards summoned posthaste from the Horse Guards, others headed back towards Spa Fields, then took it into their heads on the way to stop off at the Coldbath prison, but found it now well defended by a hundred or more constables. All this I heard of later, for I was still with that cart which now had no more than the seamen around it, who, sobered up by the march they'd had, were more interested in finding spirits than bringing about the fall of government and the chopping off of royal heads.

'It was about this point, just on midday and all the city clocks chiming oranges and lemons and here comes a chopper, when Castle pulled me on one side, bent down, and said in a hoarse whisper right in my ear: "We ain't earned our money yet. No one's going to hang at this rate and Mr Stafford wants a hanging."

'"Right," said I, "there'll be no hanging matter without some murder and serious mayhem. They've gotta have guns that work."'

And here Boylan slides off his stool and takes a turn round the room, ending with his head cocked up at the tiny barred window above him and his back to Cargill.

'Mr Cargill. I aint proud of what happened next.'

Cargill shifts his buttocks, wishes for a cushion.

'As I understand the records,' he says, 'a gunsmith was broken into in the Minories, the owner refused to unlock the strongroom in which most of his stock was stored, and Cashman shot him with a pistol. What are you ashamed of?'

Without turning, Boylan spreads his arms and palms.

''Twas I. With a pistol I'd carried in a holster under my jacket up under my arm all day. Given me by Mr Guy de Bourgeois. John Castle and Preston was pushing up behind me, and a crowd behind them, just Cashman in front, so no one really knows who looses off the piece. Even Cashman was so drunk he didn't know for sure he hadn't done it himself. Only Maggie-May knew, for she was still on his shoulders and he holding her legs with both hands. But no one paid attention to her and it was me and Castle and Preston gave evidence it was Cashman done it.'

He pauses, sighs, turns away again, ruminating on the final scene the Irish hero graced with his presence.

'He died well, be sure of that. I remember what he said as they pulled him in a cart from Bow Street magistrates, where Stafford presided as clerk, to Newgate, like a common robber. "This is not for cowardice. I am not brought to this for any robbery. If I was at my quarters, I would not be killed in the smoke: I'd be in the fire. I have done nothing against my King and country, but fought for them . . ."

'Then, when the day came, a huge crowd turned up and they had to barricade the scaffold outside the Debtor's Door they come out of in front of Newgate. You never saw so many constables, hundreds sworn in for the occasion. We all stood at the back, me on Castle's shoulders, Maggie-May on Preston's, Oliver and Edwards at our side. Maggie-May understood nothing of it except that the hero of the tragic drama was the same brave seaman had seen off her Highlander a few months back, so she screamed abuse and wept, and shouted again and at the end, when all was over, declared it the best show she'd ever seen, better than the puppets at Hampstead Heath Whitsun Fair.

' 'Course Cashman was drunk, they'd been giving him drink all night, so his courage may well have been of the Dutch variety, but he spoke clear enough. As he came on to the scaffold all fell quiet, even Maggie-May, and he didn't like that at all. "Come on my boys, I'll die like a man; give me three cheers when I trip . . . Hurrah my hearties in the cause! Success! Cheer up!" Two vicars, magpies in black and white, sanctimonious scavengers, tried to raise the tone, but he turned on them: "Don't bother me – it's no use – I want no mercy but from God." So then they settles the Newgate frill round his neck and he opens his mouth for one final shout: "Now, you buggers, give me three cheers when I trip!" and then to the hangman, "Let go the jib-boom!" and down went the trap and choked off his own cheer.

'I told you he was a little man, dinn' I? So he had not the

weight to break his neck and the whole crowd stayed quiet as mice as for two minutes or so he did what they used to call the Tyburn jig, more a hornpipe in his case, then, once he'd stopped jerking about, the crowd began to groan and shout "Murder" and "Shame" and so forth and it was hours before all dispersed, though me and me mates were orf sharpish since there was already talk about we weren't all we seemed.'

Cargill is, and he admits it later to his superior at the Home Office, flabbergasted.

'You shot an innocent man, protecting his property from a dangerous, licentious mob bent on destroying civilisation, in cold blood? And then implicated another man in the murder?'

'That's the truth of it, Mr Cargill, and the nightmare of it plagues me to this day. The horror of his wig flying off, because he was an old man and kept to the wig, and the top of his head after it. A good shot, my hand as steady as a rock.'

Cargill thinks for a moment.

'Let me get this right. Cashman was then arrested for this murder and hanged. But Stafford and Viscount Sidmouth—'

'And Mr Guy de Bourgeois—'

'—must have known of this deception. Must have colluded in the hanging of an innocent man?'

'Worse than that. They incited the murder. That merchant's blood is as surely on their hands as on mine. They paid me well. Out of the Secret Fund.'

'How much?'

'Ten guineas. After I'd made a signed and witnessed deposition of the full truth of the matter, addressed to the judge who tried the case, but never sent to him.'

'But since destroyed.'

'Oh dear me no,' and at this point Charlie Boylan turns and with his usual hideous grin wider than ever, taps the side of his nose, in just the manner, Cargill says later to his superior, of an Israelite, 'dear me no. It lies along with many other depositions in the store of a certain . . . Well, I aint giving you his name or whereabouts, now am I? But he'll see me straight if I pop my clogs in any circumstances other than those of comfort and good care, selling all to the newspapers.'

Cargill twiddles and fiddles with Boylan's pen for a moment and looks thoughtfully down at his restless fingers as he does so.

'Are you trying to tell me, sir,' he asks at last, 'that you are threatening the highest in the land with exposure of evils done by their predecessors in the past?'

'Something of the sort, yes.' And that grin again that Cargill is learning to dislike with a force bordering on disgust and hate comes again.

'It won't wash, you know. It won't wash.'

'Well, we'll see, shan't we? See what you think as the record I'm addressing to you creeps closer to these times we live in. Meantime, speak to the bosses and see if you can't do something for me in the way of a small charcoal burner to take the chill off my quarters and maybe a bite to add to prison fare. I could murder one of Bellamy's pork pies . . .'

Assistant Under-Secretary Cargill sees Charlie properly locked up behind him, and makes his way in a cab back to Whitehall and the Home Office. In his own room, the one where he interviewed George Danby, the Waterloo veteran, only days before, he scribbles a note to his superior who presently sends for him. They discuss Charlie's improprieties for a few minutes before the Permanent Under-Secretary decides the situation does not yet warrant disturbing the Minister.

'So far, Cargill, he has said nothing that can cause us serious embarrassment. Without tangible proofs these tales will remain tittle-tattle, and they took place too long ago to cause any more than a ripple on the smooth flow of government. However,' and here the distinguished civil servant removes the monocle he has been using for his perusal of Cargill's notes, and fixes his gaze on the gigantic nest of timber scaffolding that makes a dead forest along the new embankment, 'however, we must keep him going. Yes, we must keep him going, find out the full extent of the possible harm he might do before we decide what to do with him. Give him his fire. Get him a pork pie. And above all, do what you can to find out where, with whom, he has lodged his depositions.'

He thrusts his hands into the pockets of his trousers and turns. 'What will be next, do you suppose? The Pentrich Rising? St Peter's Fields? Cato Street? Well, we'll see. But keep him writing. Hearsay at third hand no use at all. Get it on paper, committed on paper, eh?'

14

Mr Stafford was wery, wery pleased with me over the Cashman affair but my Lord Sidmouth still did not think we had done enough. London had ceased to be a problem: with trials pending, hangings imminent and soldiers prepared, it seemed, to fire on crowds, things quietened down considerably as the winter deepened. Many of the fomentors, or do I mean fermenters, I haven't had your education, Mr Cargill, fled like old Tom Paine had before them, to America, Willy Cobbett among them, though I have to say Mr Hunt stayed on board but moved north. And it was to the North, well, just north of the Trent, which is north to the likes of you and me, we was presently sent.

But first, my easy readiness with a pistol was what had stimulated their admiration and it seemed they, I mean Sidmouth and Stafford, felt I could become their Specialist in such activities. I withdrew from Islington, went back to my comfortable lodgings in Lambeth which were conveniently situated quite close to Westminster Bridge, though a bit close to the Vauxhall and all the junketings used to go on there before they built the railway slap through it. I was put through a short further course in the tradecraft conducted mostly by Mr de Bourgeois in the basements of the Home Office where I was also tutored by a Captain Quex of the Royal Horse Artillery who had spent much of the previous decade behind French lines in Iberia working for the Duke with the Spanish and Portuguese *guerrilleros*.

Captain Quex (marvel not at the name – it is Norman in origin) was a tall man with a stoop, his hair a premature white – for he cannot have been more than forty years old. You would think from his build and his general physical manner that he was a clumsy, awkward sort of a person, but he moved about his subterranean workshop, which was cluttered with all manner of tools, lathes, chemicals in jars and bubbling retorts, a kiln and even, though it was not always lit and glowing, a small furnace and foundry, with a loping smoothness which at first put me in mind of a large cat such as a puma or cheetah. This was not a satisfactory comparison – later I realised that his loose-limbed gait and seemingly multi-jointed arms and wrists were more akin to those of a large long-legged spider.

This workshop, which was large, possibly as much as twenty yards by twelve, resembled nothing so much as Vulcan's forge, had a high ceiling divided into two vaults of brick, painted white save where fumes had darkened it, smelled of hot metal, acids, the gas that illuminated it and was a source of heat and other noxious fumes. And at the far end from the stairs and double doors that led to it, a tunnel, some twenty yards long, as high as six feet and wide enough to take two men side by side, had been excavated, leading off to the side at right angles to the main body of the hall.

'Ah, Boylan,' the Captain exclaimed, his voice sharp and mandative, on my being introduced into his domain by the same Sam who had been my first guide in the Home Office, 'I gather you are here to be kitted out, kitted out in certain specific ways in order to be able to perform your duties as a government servant licensed to . . . Ah! Just one moment,' and he stooped over a small spirit burner, heating a bluish liquid that was just coming to the boil, and lowered the wick. He never completed the sentence. He did not need to. We both knew the extent and terms of the verbal licence Mr Stafford had just conferred upon me. The blue liquid simmered for a moment and then, as bubbles began to rise through it, it quite quickly became as colourless as water. He dipped a pen into it and wrote three digits on a piece of paper set beside it.

'We'll come back to that when it has dried.' And he moved on to a solid oak work bench. On it there was a very handy gadget, an encrypting device, made up, I suppose, by a master clocksmith, a system of tiny milled cogs which turned to the six figures of whatever the date was on a particular day, say zero six zero two one seven for the sixth of February, eighteen seventeen, and thereby turned other cogs which produced, apparently at random, a six figure number on the other side.

'Now,' Quex continued, 'you take the last two numbers that have appeared, in this case one and two, and they give you the letter "a". One and three, or thirteen, will then be "b" but one and one will be "c", one and four "d" and so forth. However, and mark this most carefully, the letters "e", "t", and "s" are omitted altogether. Can you guess why?'

It took me only a moment's hesitation to come up with an answer.

'Well, sir. No code that does not have a device built into it to counter those who would use the frequency of usage sequence to break it is foolproof. By omitting these letters, among the most common, and yet, given the context in which they appear, readily guessable where they have been left out, you counter that weakness.'

'Good, very good. What else can you say about this device?'

'I must suppose that the likely recipients of any message encrypted by it will have its twin in their possession, which, provided they know the date on which the message was encrypted, will give them the means to decrypt or decipher what otherwise would have appeared to be an enigmatic sequence of numbers. It is an engine which creates an enigma that can only be answered by those in possession of a similar engine.'

'Precisely. Enigmatic. Good. Let us move on.'

Next he handed me a pen, much like the one I am using, but the handle a full eight inches long. A twist at one end revealed a hidden stiletto, round like a needle, and not much thicker.

'It is,' he asserted, 'so thin it will leave a hole in a man's side or neck that an examining surgeon might miss, yet deep enough to stop a heart from beating or fatally puncture the big vein in the neck . . .' He moved on, through his den of vicious machinery.

'And now,' he rasped, his breath somewhat bated in anticipation, 'we come to the finest of all your pieces of kit.'

We had reached the tunnel that branched off at the far end. I peered down it. It was dimly lit by two gas flares set high in the walls. Beneath them stood two life-size dummies, one clothed like a French chasseur, the other in the smock and floppy hat of an English workman. Both were in a sad state of disrepair, their torsos shot to pieces so the straw with which they were filled was bursting out in straggly, untidy handfuls. And the piece of kit? A pistol merely – something of an anti-climax after the exotica that had preceded it. Quex sensed my reaction.

'You are not, I hope, disappointed. This is the improved prototype of a model Spinks and Pottle are about to put into production for the East India Company. It has a standard nine-inch barrel, rifled of course, five seven seven calibre. It is fired by percussion cap, a method still new enough to make percussion caps hard to come by; you will therefore not want to lose the fifty I shall be able to give you. The hammer is controlled by a plain flat bar action lock, simple but utterly reliable. The stock is walnut and pleasantly light in colour. The trigger guard, butt cap and ramrod pipe, with new patent swivel mechanism, are made of brass. It comes with a smart military pistol holster, compact enough to be worn under the arm and beneath a jacket.' He held it out to me. 'Take it.'

I did so, and immediately understood his enthusiasm. It had a balance, a fitness to my hand, an aptness which instantly conferred on me a sense of power.

'Choose one of the targets.'

Since we were no longer at war with the French I chose the figure on my right, the smocked labourer.

'For certainty aim at the centre of the chest. Present. Aim . . .'

But no. I am a good shot anyway and I now felt total confidence in my weapon. I pulled back the hammer. It clicked twice with a satisfying, oiled certainty. The copper button or stud of the percussion cap gleamed in front of my eye.

'Fire.'

The briefest of sparks as the mercuric oxide in the cap fired on being hit by the cup-shaped hammer, a bang sharp and very loud in that echoing space: straw and dust hung for a moment in front of the dummy's head and then cleared. A new black hole was punched into what would have been the right eye-socket of a real man.

'It drops an inch to the left over thirty paces. That's good,' I said, 'very good.'

'Damnit,' cried Quex, 'I told you the chest, man, the chest. Don't take such a chance when in earnest. Choose the bigger target and be sure of it,' and he scuttled, if such a tall man can be said to scuttle, back to the bench where we had started. He picked up the piece of paper he had written on with the colourless fluid and held it to the warmth of the burner. Three spidery, brown characters slowly materialised. He passed me the paper.

I read the numbers.

Zero, zero, three.

'From now on, as far as this department is concerned, that is your name. I have already forgotten the name you had when you came in.'

003.

Who, I wondered, were the two men who had, prior to myself, been licensed to kill?

15

The secret number, passed to Sam's successor, also a Sam, who takes it down to the basement with a formal request signed and stamped by Cargill, releases a trawling netful of documents from the archives below. The bent old man with his trolley who rules the place like a Library Ghost trundles them to a hatch set in the wall by the spiral staircase and loads three open stiff leather boxes on to the shelves of a dumbwaiter. Sam II pats the old man on the shoulder, signs a chit for him, a form of receipt, and climbs to the third floor. There he opens the hatch, hauls on a rope that runs against the wall of what looks like, and may well once have been, a chimney, and brings the dumbwaiter up. He unloads the boxes from it, and with the smell of ancient paper, ink and leather in his nostrils, and something sulphurous too, carries the three boxes down the corridor to Assistant Under-Secretary Cargill's office.

Cargill is looking out of the high window down into Whitehall, one side of which is now being demolished. The widened thoroughfare will link the new Palace of Westminster with Trafalgar Square. The Admiralty want to call it Nelson Street, the Horse Guards have in mind Wellington Parade, the

Home Office will arbitrate and it will end up unchanged as Whitehall.

None of which bothers him. What is exercising his mind is the strange behaviour of Mrs Cargill the night before. Although his own breath was tainted with brandy when he joined her in their large faux mahogany bed from Heal's he felt he could detect the odour of gin upon her. Worse still, when he pushed his way into her with a view to pleasuring himself, as was his custom on Wednesday nights, he found her, well, sort of wet. Moreover, she locked her ankles in the small of his back and refused to let him go, even when he had finished. Not even the whores he uses during her monthlies behave like this and frankly he was deeply disgusted, indeed still is. Yet he cannot help feeling a sort of pleasant warmth in his loins, a stiffening of his member, at the memory of it. Is she suffering from erotomania, a condition treated in a paper from the Department of Mental Health he was asked to read in the line of duty a month ago?

He acknowledges Sam's arrival and waves to the table behind him indicating that the boxes should be left there, turning to them once Sam has gone with some relief. The boxes are all labelled, simply, 003, followed by dates from and to. He selects the first box, January 1817 to December 1820, and the folder bound in parchment paper marked April 1st to June 30th 1817. Inside there are five reports each of several small pages of strong but thin paper, close to the quality of that used for banknotes, and covered with a thin brown spidery writing. The paper rustles a little as he smooths it down. He peers at it through squinting eyes, moves it six inches further away and grits his teeth. Soon, he knows, he will need spectacles. Is this the penalty he must pay for overindulgence in marital intercourse?

April 10th, Año Dom 1817, Chatsworth House
Proceeding according to Mr Stafford's instructions I left Westminster on the 5th inst. using the stage to proceed

to Bakewell, in the county of Derbyshire, where I was met at midday on the 8th inst. by a Mr Norton who took me to Chatsworth House in a pony and trap.

Gracious, thinks Cargill. Three days to get from London to a village halfway between Derby and Manchester. Three hours now, or not much more. How things have changed in thirty-five years! What a vastly different world it is now! Has ever life changed so quickly? Will it ever do so again?

Mr Norton is a secretary to William Cavendish, Duke of Devonshire. He has arranged that I should stay in his spare room in his house in Chatsworth village. This is a small settlement occupied exclusively by servants and workmen on the estate where all are excessively deferential to the Cavendish family, for their livelihoods depend on them and they have seen so many of their relations driven away by enclosures and so forth all live in fear that deprived of employment they will be the next and do nothing to upset the Duke.

'Excessively!' remarks Cargill to himself. What could Boylan possibly have meant? One cannot be excessively deferential to people like the Cavendishes.

The next day I was given the opportunity to present to his grace the letter of introduction and so forth that my Lord Sidmouth had been gracious enough to supply me with and was gratified to hear his grace instruct Mr Norton that I was to be given every assistance in my work that I might require. It will now therefore be my chief concern to assume the role of journeyman engraver and insinuate myself into the councils of the local revolutionaries.

I remain etc your most humble and obdt. servant . . . 003.

119

Cargill handles the paper carefully, takes it to the window, rubs it between thumb and forefinger. With the forefront of his mind on what he is doing, and the deeper recesses still troubled by his wife's extraordinary behaviour, he is able to ignore the collapse of a wall across the way and the ensuing flurry of dust and powdered snow from the caved-in roof, even the screams of a couple of workmen caught in a shower of tiles and bricks fall on deaf ears. He is in no doubt it was written in solution of copper sulphate and the writing brought to light by heat so it appeared to have been penned in brown copper-coloured ink. He places it carefully back into the folder and slips out the next.

April 21st, Eastwood, near Nottingham

Having made my preparations I walked the thirteen miles to Eastwood on the twelfth April arriving at the Sun Inn shortly before sunset. There I bespoke a room at the back of the main building overlooking the yard and stabling (receipt attached, item one), washed my hands and face, changed my jacket and boots and went down to the main public room where I ordered a cut off the fine leg of mutton that was being turned on a dog-spit (receipt attached, item two). Shortly after I had begun my repast seven men entered and, having ordered pints of Burton bitter beer, the beer of choice, preferred over the landlord's home brew by those with a farthing extra to spare, they sat at a table near the fire and began to speak revolution, in the most bloodcurdling terms. Among them I recognised the figure of my colleague William Oliver, and he me, acknowledged by the agreed sign of each of us, in as natural a way as possible, viz. by picking our noses.

Presently, having finished my tranche of mutton, I pulled my clay from my pocket, left my table and joined them with the pretext of begging or buying a small plug of tobacco since I was, I asserted, freshly out

of that commodity. Oliver himself obliged and, while I
rubbed down the baccy and filled the bowl of my clay,
he introduced the assembled company. They included
the following. Jeremiah Brandreth, Isaac Ludlam,
William Turner, Thomas Bacon, all from Nottingham
or its environs, and Joseph Mitchell who had
accompanied Oliver from London. Bacon, a middle-
aged man with a red face and a squat turned-up nose, it
was who took a straw from the floor, lit it at the fire
and passed it to me so I might set my pipe going. It
later transpired he is long-reputed a dyed in the wool
Jack who works as a cast iron dresser at the Buttery
iron works. He was accompanied by his son, Bob, him,
who was so like him in looks it could have been him
twenty years ago.

'It's a poor thing,' I said, 'that honest Englishmen are
forced to lead lives as miserable as that dog's,' and I
gestured to the Jack Russell, imprisoned in his
treadwheel above the fire from where his poor
scrambling paws, by a system of toothed cogs, turned the
spit from which my mutton had been sliced.

'So it is indeed,' grunted Jerry Brandreth. 'A Jamaicy
negro slave's be no worse; at least he know where his
next meal be coming from.'

'I could not,' I went on, 'help hearing some of your
conversation and forming an estimate of its general
tenor. And I should like to say it chimes most
harmoniously with my own views and those of many in
the city I was in but a week ago.'

'And where may that be?' asked one of them . . . I
recall it was Isaac Ludlam, a sharp, small man with red
hair like a fox.

'Bristol,' said I.

'You don't speak like a West Country man.' A
suspicious kind of a fox, then.

'I am no country's man,' I replied, 'nor any man's

121

either. I travel about selling my trade where I can and hope to find a living hereabouts in Derby or Nottingham, for as long as I choose to stay.'

'What trade is that then?' barked Brandreth. He was a big man with black hair, black moustache and beard, and beetling black eyebrows to match. His complexion though was not swarthy, but rubicund rather. He looked like a farrier or a smith, though I already knew from the file your worship gave me to study that he had been a stockinger, and five year back had been a follower of General Ludd, escaping the executions and transportations through lack of hard evidence against him. Another thing I must say about him. He was noted for the three heavy woollens he liked to wear beneath his coat, which he wore turn and turn about, week by week, each knitted in outrageous patterns and brightly coloured yarn.*

'Engraver,' said I.

'You make pictures, that can be printed?'

'Of course.'

'Wa-hay, we can find a use for you, then.'

'That is what I hoped. I can embellish handbills for you, fill in spaces on ballad sheets, or even broad-sheets. Look, I'll show you.' And I went back to my table and pulled from under it my carpetbag, that had in it engraver's tools, burins, scrapers and so forth, and half a dozen untouched copper plates, octavo and quarto, and a folio of prints, all supplied by Captain Quex. They included hangings of noted Jacobins, poor Cashman among them, cartoons depicting

---

* The eminent commentator and broadcaster Gyles Brandreth has been known to claim that his ancestor Jeremiah was the last Englishman to be publicly beheaded for treason. Not so. Arthur Thistlewood (see below) was hanged and beheaded nearly three years later. J. R.

landlords and mill-owners trampling on the faces of working men, and so forth, all done with a crude sort of vigour that pleased my new acquaintances no end as they passed them around. They served their purpose, which was to be my passports into the confidence of traitors.

One man there had so far said little, but sat on a settle below the jutting stone frame of the fireplace and had contrived to keep his face in shadow.

'I see you have there a likeness of Johnny Cashman,' he now murmured, and I recalled this was Joseph Mitchell, a man older than the others, with a face lined by age and maybe suffering too, and with a fringe of white hair round his head like a tonsured monk. 'It aint a bad one.'

He did not speak in the Nottingham way at all, but like a Londoner.

'You have good reason for saying so?' I asked.

'I knew him a little. And I was at his execution.'

'I knew him too. I also was there.'

'Just a month ago.'

'Not quite a full month, by my reckoning.'

'The crowd was immense.'

'It was.'

'And deeply hostile to authority.'

'Yes. Deeply so.'

Mitchell looked round the others with satisfaction on his face. I, however, was puzzled. These were the lines, rehearsed and learned, I expected from Oliver, but he leant back in his chair, took a pull of his Burton bitter and wiped a mouth which could not quite conceal a smug smile.

The younger Bacon now chipped in.

'Are they ready to rise in London?' he asked, with great conspiratorial earnestness. 'Without them we can do nothing.'

123

'Oh, they are ready,' I said and took a long look at the bowl of my clay which was now just about through. Then a memory tugged at my mind like a puppy on a trouser cuff.

'And in Bristol, too,' I added.

'I was indeed wondering,' Mitchell now remarked, 'how it is you come from Bristol but were in London less than a moon ago.'

'Just like I said: I travels around a good deal.'

Had I said that? I thought I had. Mitchell came back at me.

'Somehow,' he said, 'I'd got the idea you'd been in Bristol some time, earning your living at the engraver's trade . . .' and he fixed me with his watery eye and I noted how the fist he made on the table between us tightened a little and relaxed.

Not long after I went into the yard for a piss and Will Oliver, whose real name was Richards, followed me.

'What's with this Mitchell then?' I asked, out of the side of my mouth. Shoulder to shoulder, or rather my shoulder to his elbow, and the piss hissing in the midden, we could not be eavesdropped upon.

'He's a very canny bugger,' said Oliver, 'and an old hand at the game.'

'Our game?'

'Not at all. He's a professional Jacques for twenty years and more, and how he's escaped hanging is a mystery, but I guess mainly by taking care of his connections. The others know him, or know of him, and if he gives the sayso they'll believe it.'

'So how did you get to him, being he's so careful?'

'He trusts Charlie Pendrill, and Charlie got me the intro.' And turning to me he shook his peg and put it away.

'Did Charlie know what he was doing?'

'Oh yes. Mr de Bourgeois has Charlie by the goolies,

you see, has turned up evidence he was in Colonel Despard's plot to kill the King. It may be thirteen year back, but it's still a hanging matter. But to the Jacobins, he still rings true, true as minted gold.'

But I'm not happy about it, Mr Stafford, not happy at all. I think this Mitchell has his suspicions of me, and if I'm to do the business the way you want me to, I'd like him off the scene. That's plainly said, and plainly meant.

Ever your humble and obdt. servant 003.

Cargill lays the three sheets he has just read carefully on the table and goes back to his window. Then he takes a pace or two to the fire and looks up at the young Queen and her Consort . . . nicely engraved, and aquatinted, but not by Boylan. Marital troubles temporarily forgotten, his mind is clearer than it has been all morning. It is dawning on him just to what extent this Boylan is chameleon-like. He'd read what the man had written about Waterloo and then the Miss Tarrant St Giles scandal and all that farrago, not to mention the poor Belgian wench he'd rogered on the battlefield. He'd met the man and found him a wheedling, cringing, creepy sort of a cove. And now, these rather lucid reports written, what, some thirty-five years ago by a man who displayed quite another sort of character altogether. Or so it seems to him.

Had these really been penned by the hairy, corrupt, whingeing dwarf now lodged in Pentonville? And he recalls, that that is precisely what he has been commissioned to find out. So far he is no wiser, to be frank is making no sort of a fist of it at all. He goes back to the file and pulls out the next sheaf of old, yellowed stained paper. Stained? Could be beer or blood, no saying after all this time.

May 10th Año Dom. 1817 at Chatsworth
I have my commission now to perform as best I might to catch Brandreth in a trap similar to that Cashman

was taken in, so it be my intention now to keep low, but close as I might to Brandreth, leaving the main stirring of revolt to Bill Oliver. He was down in Nottingham at the back end of last week and arranged to meet old man Mitchell at the Trip to Jerusalem in the castle walls where Mitchell was taken by two Runners sent for him and tipped off by Oliver and is like to be taken from Nott. gaol to Cold Bath Fields which is good news for me. He'd raised suspicion against me by asking me to engrave a picture of a female Liberty wearing the tricolour for which of course I do not yet have the skill.

There's still doubts among the stockingers and such hereabouts that London really is ready to rise, and they will not come together here until they believe it . . .

I have put it about that I am going on to Birmingham for a fortnight in case suspicion has attached itself to me following the taking of Mitchell, but in fact I am hiding up as before with Mr Norton.

Your obedient servant
003

June the First, AD **1817, back at the Sun Inn, Eastwood**
I went to Jerry Brandreth's between six and seven this evening. We left his house and met Turner and walked up Sandy Lane. Turner said I should have been here on Monday night. He stated there was a London delegate who reported there was about 70,000 in London ready to act with us, that they had arms and would take the Tower; I supposed this delegate was Bill Oliver, and yes they said, that was so, and I added my bit saying they are very ripe too in Birmingham and that twenty thousand there would rise on the same day and that all was fixed for June 9th. I asked where was Oliver and they said he'd gone on into Yorkshire to spread the word of a general uprising. Such is their conviction, Mr Stafford, and such

their fervour that all this will happen, I almost believe it myself . . . In any event, rise they will, and the place is set for Pentridge, a village a few miles north-west of Eastwood, and the date Monday the ninth, before first light. I am confident I shall find opportunity to do my duty.

June 15th, Año Dom. 1817 Chatsworth

Mr Stafford, I am satisfied you are already cognisant of the events that took place here all but a week ago, but am persuaded that an account from one of the chief witnesses of the events, and indeed protagonists, will be of interest.

We met at the Sun Inn on the afternoon of Sunday the eighth of June last, that is Brandreth, Turner, Ludlam and your obedient, and after a solid repast of hot raised mutton pie provided by the landlord, whose sympathies with our enterprise reached as far as feeding us, if no further, set out the ten miles to Wingfield Park, a recently enclosed common, close to Pentrich. Dusk fell and no one came save some young lads who were out poaching rabbits and, seeing us, fell in out of curiosity. Brandreth sent these and others of our company out to the hamlets thereabout but mainly to Alfreton and Swanwick, these being the largest, and by midnight there were fifty of us, some with pikes and a couple of guns, but mostly billhooks or no more than the clothes they stood up in. Brandreth declared it was enough, for were we not merely a small company marching to join the thousands assembling at the castle gates in Nottingham?

Off we marched through the night, picking up more at Pentrich itself, Ripley and Codnor, on the way and calling at houses as we passed them. All the time I was looking for the opportunity to present itself at which I might do the business. It was not long in coming and fell out at a small country house of some slight distinction,

127

the owner being a Justice of the Peace, a Mr Lancelot Rolleston, who first bid his servant, one Jonathan Glew, to cover his departure with a fowling piece, then took horse with the intention of riding to Nottingham. Brandreth and two others tried to intercept him whereat this Glew raised his piece. Brandreth had a musket which he attempted to fire, but it was raining a little and the powder in his pan, already dampened, merely flashed. I took the opportunity and a second later scored with my Spinks and Pottle pistol which proved the reliability of its percussion cap and the efficacy of mercuric oxide in producing a spark when firmly struck, for the ball took the ostler in the mouth – he drowned in his own blood some six minutes after. In the dark and confusion, the only light being a horn lamp held behind us, it was not difficult to persuade all, and even Brandreth himself, that the spark had taken in his musket, and after a fractional delay had fired off the ball that killed Glew. Since in the confusion and darkness I was able to drop the musket in a well there was no one to say whether it had fired or not.

By now we were two hundred strong and shortly after daybreak came back into Eastwood and to the Sun where the landlord had left a couple of barrels in the yard, shouting down to us that we might avail ourselves of the contents, but asking us not to attempt to enter his premises which he had barricaded. Indeed we found all the houses and so forth boarded up, and the residents either escaped into the surrounding copses, or keeping very low.

It was raining heavily by now, and many had reached that tired stage of drunkenness where all effort carries with it three times the cost it normally does, and the thought of a feather bed is heaven indeed. Many expressed a desire to get home, but Brandreth sent me round by the outlying lanes to come at them from the front with my cloak pulled round me.

128

'Give us three huzzahs then,' I shouted, 'I am come from the city where all is going our way, the town hall burning, the constables hanged from the castle walls and the cavalry on our side . . .'

This cheered them, and we pushed on through the rain. Brandreth tried to get us to sing a piece of doggerel he, or another like him, had composed for the occasion.

> Every man his skill must try
> He must turn out and not deny
> No bloody soldier must he dread
> He must turn out and fight for bread
> The time is come you plainly see
> The government opposed must be . . .

And a little later, become cognisant that in the wet dawn he was losing more men than he was gaining, he gathered all round at a crossroads and stood on the hummock by the signpost to get their spirits back.

'Nottingham will be given up before we get there,' he cried, 'and we'll go on from Nottingham to London, take the Tower and the Mint, men from the North will come like a cloud and sweep all before them . . .' and when someone shouted back he'd no intention of leaving wife and kids to go to London, Brandreth, with some desperation, promised him roast beef, ale and rum in Nottingham and even a pleasure trip on the Trent.

Thus as far as Giltbrook where, turning a corner, we found a troop of the 15th Hussars drawn up and waiting for us, sent to halt us, following the news Mr Rolleston JP had taken to the authorities in the city. They came at us at a steady trot with sabres drawn and that was that. Brandreth caught my arm and said he was off to Bulwell where his wife's sister would look after him, and meanwhile it was a case of *sauve qui peut*.

Mr Stafford, it was your obedient servant who passed

on this intelligence to the magistracy as a result of which Brandreth was taken and charged with sedition, treason and the murder of Jonathan Glew, and I claim the fifty pound reward . . .

Your obdt. etc

003

Again Cargill puts up the paper and sits musing for a while in front of his fire. He is, for all his failings, a man of imagination, goes to the theatre to see Shakespeare, often musicked into the like of opera, reads the novelists and so forth, though favours those of the last century, especially Mr Fielding, over such moderns as the Bells, who some say are women, and are read by Mrs Cargill with unhealthy enthusiasm, and D'Israeli, a young Jew who had just achieved cabinet rank in Lord Derby's administration. At all events he feels he can see that rag, tag and bobtail of out-of-work textile workers stumbling, drunk, through a grey wet dawn, the rain dripping off the leaves and down their necks, the cuckoo a half-mile away changing its tune to cu-cuck-oo, the ring of their iron-tipped shoes on the occasional stones.

Many of them would already be apprehensive of the outcome of what they were doing since a murder in which they were by association implicated had been committed, so the shock, the panic blow to the diaphragm, when they turned a corner and found the road blocked by tall moustachioed troopers on big horses, would have been all the greater. Their harness and accoutrements jangling, the word of command, the curved sabres drawn and catching the dawn light, and the command given: 'Trot on . . .'

He looks round his room, crosses to the wall opposite the fire. It is entirely taken up with a large bookcase, glass-fronted and locked, filled with reports bound in yellowish brown leather. He fiddles a key chain out of his trouser pocket, finds the right small key with a brass clover-leaf end and pulls open the door. It creaks a little. His finger runs horizontally along the spines of several large tomes in one corner until he finds the dates 'Jan. 1816 to Dec. 1827' under the title 'Lists of Executions, Vol. VIII'. He takes the volume from its shelf and places it on the table by the window, reflecting as he does so that not many yards away, and only just out of sight, is the very spot on which the regicides erected their scaffolding for the murder of King Charles I just over two hundred years ago. The official prose is plain and to the point but its very bluntness opens up the scene for the Assistant Under-Secretary.

> November the seventh, 1817. Brandreth, Ludlam and Turner. Already known as the Pentrich Plotters. The penalty for treason, hanging, drawing, decapitation and quartering, mercifully commuted to hanging and decapitation. Cavalry present. A large crowd. The men hanged for a half-hour then beheaded, the executioners masked and their identities kept secret. Brandreth's head exposed to the crowd which looked for a moment likely to riot. Fourteen others transported to Australia.

Cargill is in no doubt about it all. Brandreth and the two others who had been in the forefront of the march were executed not for treason but for murder, and this was the reason why the common people had not made martyrs of them. Boylan, if it was he, had done his job well.

Musing further on the whole business, Cargill cannot leave it alone. Having found one reference to the affair and replaced the tome in which he found it, his eyes scan the shelves looking for more. The 1821 Census. Would that have a record of how things had turned out for any of the participants Boylan's dispatches to Stafford had named? The County of Nottinghamshire. Pentrich. 'Ref: Morleston and Litchurch Hundred – Pentrich Parish. The entire parish of Pentrich contains 2143 inhabitants. The Population has decreased one-third in the Township of Pentrich since 1811, which is said to be owing to the insurrection which took place there in 1817, in consequence of which the Duke of Devonshire's agents destroyed many houses.'

131

16

Cargill replaces the volume and returns to the papers brought up from the vault. And with some excitement. For if Pentrich had been a small affair, indeed pathetic and somewhat mean-minded in the way it bamboozled a couple of hundred men and women into believing they were part of a national uprising, what Boylan claimed next to have played a very significant part in had turned out to be a milestone in Sidmouth's campaign to crush or at any rate stifle mass dissent. But he is in for a disappointment, runs into a cul-de-sac. These papers are no longer written in a brown ink in Boylan's spidery hand, but in long sequences of numbers. That damned enigmatic machine, he realises, lies behind them. And without the twin of the machine Boylan used to encrypt his report, and not even knowing the date they were written on, so even having the machine would have been no use, there is no way he is going to be able to decrypt them.

It will mean another visit to Pentonville. His gorge rises at the thought. The cold dampness, the prison odours of mould, rancid fat, sour milk and something even worse which he cannot help recognising, the smell of fresh semen. It all adds up to an aura he brings back with him so his neighbours on the Clapham train pull away from him, or open the window and let in gusts of sulphurous coal smoke to smother it. And home at last, his wife makes him change and bathe and bundles his clothes into the boiler in the basement. Well, cellar really. No. He'll send a message, a request that Boylan should get back to his pen and paper.

Late in the afternoon the answer returns.

Sorry squire, but we could be talking up a hanging matter again. Come and hear me tell it like it was. Not many alive now can do that for you; you'll be one of very few who know the real story. And why not bring a bottle or two of porter or something stronger, for it's a long tale, and I'll be dry in the mouth before it's properly done. Your Obd. 003.

So here he is, three hours later, sitting on his stool, watching the little hairy man attempting to cope with a bottle of porter. Charlie untwists the tiny knot and eases the cradle of wire it secures up over the cork, then places the exposed half-inch of cork in the side of his mouth, and pulls on it.

'Fuck,' he says, and passes the teak brown bottle across the deal table to Cargill. 'You do it. Old gnashers all cracked up. Scurvy and whatnot on those buggering islands in the Pacific. All of twenty years ago. Ruined them.'

Cargill, wondering what islands Charlie is referring to, lifts a buttock from the stool, pulls a large handkerchief out of the tail pocket of his coat, and gives the bottleneck a fastidious wipe before making a clamp out of his right forefinger and curling it round the cork. No luck. It won't shift. And he'll be damned if he'll put it in his mouth and use his teeth, even though he's wiped it. He curses himself for buying an inferior brand rather than Sir Arthur Guinness's brew whose bottles have glazed ceramic tops and wire clips which submit to a slight pressure from both thumbs.

133

'Get the screw in,' suggests Charlie. 'He'll do it.'

George, the Screw, is duly called for, and being a big burly man, clearly accustomed to opening bottles of cheap porter, achieves what is wanted with no difficulty at all. However, the bottle has by now been so shaken that it spurts out a fountain of yellowish foam, losing about a quarter of a quart bottle, and spraying Cargill's shoulder and his hat which is on the floor beside him, thus further enhancing his aura. George, the Screw, then offers the bottle to Cargill, who waves it away with the handkerchief he is now using to mop his soused garments. Screw puts bottle on the table, ignoring the pewter cup Charlie holds out to him, and with much swinging and rattling of his keys lets himself out, locking up behind him. Charlie carefully fills his half-pint pewter mug, empties it down his throat, and refills. Then he leans back with his thumbs in the armholes of a moleskin waistcoat several sizes too big for him, clears his throat, and once more launches his accustomed slug of phlegm so it lands within inches of Cargill's foot, and grins.

'First I knew of it,' he says, 'I was called by Mr de Bourgeois to the usual rooms in the old Home Office and reported at the time appointed to Mr Stafford's room, or the one he used, which, as I think I've already told you, was linked by an inner door to the one where Lord Sidmouth entertained those of his colleagues with whom he wished to talk in a quiet way, without secretaries or amanuenses, unrecorded, off the record, if you take my meaning.'

He takes another, shorter pull at his porter and wipes his mouth on his sleeve, momentarily revealing the dog-like pelt that begins at his wrist. In spite of the porter he is speaking lucidly and with an accent and tone that might, under other circumstances, have almost passed him off as a gentleman, certainly as a man of some education. Again Cargill wonders at his interlocutor's chameleon-like qualities and recalls that still he knows nothing of the man's, or dwarf's, origins.

'Little cabal sitting in their nice chairs with red leather backs at a table with a veneer you could comb your hair in, and portraits of the Pitts, the Admirable Nelson and Prinny himself, done by Lawrence, no less, looking down at them and drinking tea from Meissen or Sèvres or some such . . .'

'Cabal?'

'Prime Minister Lord Liverpool, Home Secretary Lord Sidmouth and Master-General of the Ordnance his grace the Duke of Wellington.'

'Well, I'm blessed,' murmurs Cargill, and then again, 'well, I'm blessed,' because a thought has occurred to him. He is fairly sure he knows which room Boylan is remembering, and if he is right the portraits are now of Liverpool, Sidmouth and Wellington. 'Sorry, go on. And you were privy to what these great men were talking about?'

'Great men, my arse. The great men are the grandees, the magnates: the Grosvenors, the Cavendishes, the Seymours, the Cecils, the Sackvilles and now the Rothschilds too. The politicians are their tools, their puppets. Addington was a doctor's son, Robert Jenkinson the grandson of a countryman, and no one knows who Wellington's ancestors were because they were Irish, not bog Irish I grant you, but pretty well shrouded in mystery since, but for an adoption, his name would have been Colley not Wesley, and Wesley not Wellesley, had not the family wanted to avoid confusion with the founders of Methodism. And for what reason his father was made an earl, damnit, no one seems to know.'

Boylan's voice had assumed the accents of an educated Irishman, a drawl superimposed on a brogue, and again Cargill marvelled at his protean qualities.

'You seem well informed about these personages.'

'Well, one way and another I've been given time to study and reflect, study and reflect. It's not all been bustle and go, y'know?'

A pause while the Irish gent took another pull at his tankard and then topped it up from the bottle whose contents were now less than a bare half-pint.

135

'And you overheard their conversation?'

'On this occasion, and one or two others, yes.'

'How? Surely the inner door was closed?'

'Ay, well, it were like this. Old Stafford went off for a piss' – gone was the Irish gent and back the wheedling cockney spy – 'an' left me there on my own. I could 'ear their voices and the clink of that classy china, so after a moment I gave the door a gentle rap', and to illustrate the sound he rapped the deal table, 'and let myself through. "Shall I remove the doings, me lords?" I asks. "Not just yet," replies Sidmouth, "nearly finished." So I takes up a position by the door with my hands by my side and my head up and with like no expression at all on my face and thus I disappear . . .'

'Disappear?'

'I becomes a flunkey. No one sees a flunkey. Bear in mind I was a young lad in those days and on account of me height taken to be younger than I was, and dressed smartly too in white breeches and a neat cutaway black coat, an' I listens to them. They was discussing the Six Acts.'

'Hang on a moment. When was this?'

'Summer, 1819. July, I'd say.'

'Ah!' cries Cargill, a crow of triumph. 'You're a charlatan after all. The Six Acts weren't passed until November, as a consequence of . . .'

'Hang on, squire. Passed maybe. But discussed, and longed for and begged for for many, many months before. Now, harkee, this is how the talk went, for part of my training was to recall verbatim what I heard and most of it stays locked up in here,' and this time it is his forehead he taps.

'The Dook was speaking and took it up again. He was sitting with one knee over the other in them new-fashioned dark trousers beneath the high-necked red jacket of a Field Marshal, for he was off to some military function before dinner, with his Garter star on his chest and the ribbon over his shoulder. Quite a dandy was the Dook, got away with it on account of his nose always gave him a dignity a fop might lack. Anyway, he picked up a piece of paper and I recognised the hand of Joseph Nadin, the Deputy Constable of Manchester, whose reports often reached the desk of John Stafford.

'The Dook frowned, tapped it: "It's said here the rabble have been drilling."

'"Precisely, Arthur," said Sidmouth, narrowing his already weasel-like eyes and passing a hand over his dome of a forehead. "That's why we asked you to drop by."

'"From a military point of view, Harry, it's of no consequence – at least for as long as they are doing it with staves and even billhooks. Without muskets, it's of no consequence, and where are they going to get them? But the intention, the mood it speaks of, is another thing. You know why we drill so much in the army?"'

'"It's occurred to me to wonder." Sidmouth stretched his narrow mouth into an obsequious grin. "And I'm sure you're going to tell me. To instil discipline, I imagine."

'"Much more than that, Harry. Drilling makes one man, one article, a part of a much larger whole, not even a part, but an addition, a constituent, makes it impossible for him to act save as a part of the whole. A rabble that has done its drill, knows the Dundas Rules and Regulations for the Movements of His Majesty's Infantry, is no longer a rabble but an animal of a very different colour. The unfortunate thing is that there are several thousand men on our streets who have practised them in Portugal, Spain, the Low Countries and America, most of whom now lack useful employment. If there are a few good sergeants among them they'll drill the rabble so they'll stand in front of a regiment of redcoats, take a volley and then go in, even with only billhooks. They might even learn to form squares against cavalry." His eyes went dreamy, he looked past Liverpool and at the grey sky above the roofs opposite the yard. Perhaps he was thinking of the squares along the crest of Mont St Jean four years earlier. Then he looked back at them, Sidmouth and Liverpool, and there was maybe a twinkle in his eye. "And that, Harry, could be quite an embarrassment. It's my view we need an Act to forbid drilling."

'At this Robert Jenkinson, Lord Liverpool, a sunny-faced man with a rubicund complexion, which would have looked good on the more prosperous, educated sort of a farmer, poured himself another cup of best China.

'"Arthur," he said, "we want more than one Act. Harry here reckons six will do the trick."

'"Six, by God. You'll never get six through the Commons. What are they?"

'"Three for the press to strengthen the seditious libel laws and tax newspapers out of the reach of working people, one against drilling and another allowing us to search any house where we think arms might be hidden, and a sixth against meetings of more than fifty. Henry wants to suspend habeas corpus again, but there are too many old buffers in the Commons who'll make a fuss over that one."

'"Quite right. And as for the rest . . . Can't be done. Not without we give the better sort in the country such a fright they forget all the claptrap about the Englishman's freedom to do this or that despite what their betters tell 'em."

'"Well, Arthur, that's precisely what we aim to do," the genial Jenkinson chimed in again. "Nadin and others, inform-ers and so forth Harry and his man Stafford have working for them, know Hunt and others are planning a big parliamentary reform meeting . . ."

'"I'm no lawyer, Robert, but a meeting for parliamentary reform is not a crime . . . We ran into that problem after the Spa Fields business, that and your oaf Castle letting it out Stafford paid him . . . Whole damn lot got off except that sailor who shot a gunsmith."

'Here, Mr Cargill, you may be sure I found it not easy to sup-press a self-gratified little grin, but suppress it I did, in true flunkey style. Meanwhile Jenkinson, Lord Liverpool, continued to plough his farmer's furrow.

'"You're right, Arthur, but the idea has caught on and must

be stamped on, and we can do that by making any meeting seem to be not just for reform but revolution. The weavers are out of work because of the recession and a second bad harvest on the way, so they'll turn up, and the Spenceans too with all their land reform claptrap, and giving it all back to the common people; in short there'll be a huge crowd and enough of the Jacobin persuasion to justify treating it as seditious, maybe reading the Act and so forth. Harry has a plan, it looks good to me, but we want your opinion of it and then your advice about troops and so forth . . ."

'"This meeting," asked the Dook, "how big is it likely to be?"'

'"Very big indeed," grunted Sidmouth, and wiped his thin mouth with a linen napkin before snapping off half a cat's tongue biscuit between his squirrel teeth. "Fifty thousand, Nadin reckons, might not be too high an estimate. Many hands out of work, you see, holiday month, many villages and the smaller towns having fairs and so forth anyway . . ."

'"Is anyone going to oblige me by telling me where?"'

'"Manchester."'

'Follows a long silence, then the Duke uncrosses and recrosses his legs, sits up a touch straighter and taps off his points on the palm of his left hand, one by one.

'"The main thing, gentlemen, is to have your aims, what you want to achieve, perfectly clear in your heads. Many a campaign, many an action have I seen go awry because the commanding officer was not sure what he wanted to get out of it, or, worse still, changed his mind halfway through. Take Beresford at Albuera . . . Well, anyway. Now, from what you've said, and I agree most wholeheartedly, what you most fear is reform of Parliament, doing away the rotten boroughs, widening the franchise and so forth. If we have manufacturers and bankers voting, then manufacturers and bankers are whom they'll vote for. So far then as the working men and the hands are allied with the middling sort of people in wanting reform, so far we're in danger. But what the working men want, the scally-wags among them, that is, the scum that floats to the top, is not reform, but revolution, the full doings. Now they'll never get it. Not in this country. So what we have to do is—"

'But at this point, Mr Cargill, old Stafford returned, spotted what I was up to and hauled me into his office by my ear. Mind you, he had a laugh at it too, saying it showed how much I'd learnt of my trade that I could be standing in a room with the three greatest schemers in the country and they not notice me. Then he sat me down opposite him and his desk so the window's behind him and was about to give me my commission when the door part opened and that great nose comes halfway round it, and those piercing eyes.

'"Charles. Charlie. Did you ever get that sixpence I promised you?"

'"No, your grace," said I.

'"By thunder, you're in with a gang of sharp characters, aint you? Mr Stafford, my respects. Give the lad his tanner, there's a good fellow." Then he looked at me again. "Never forget a face, Charles. I don't and I don't suppose you do either," and he was off, and we could hear that laugh again that rattled the windows as, like the ten thousand men he was, he marched off down the corridor.

'Stafford never gave me the sixpence but he did give me my commission.'

'Which was?'

'To go to Manchester. Mr Cargill, if you'll pardon me for saying so, may I suggest you call George back and get him to open the second bottle? Yes. Manchester.'

The honours done, Charlie's throat again saved from a drought an Egyptian fellaheen or Hindoo might have found difficult to cope with, the hairy dwarf took up his tale again.

17

Have you ever been to Manchester? Well, the last time I took a look was when I got off the Boston packet at Liverpool some four years ago, and it was pretty horrible then, but at least there were some good municipal buildings going up among the mills, the roads were properly cobbled, the railway terminus busy and there were signs of very reasonable prosperity, though the hands still looked wan, thin and miserable, especially the children, and the smell of coke-fired furnaces was carried on the soot that was everywhere. But what an improvement over thirty odd years ago! There was nothing fancy about it then, believe me.

No railway then, of course. My, but haven't things changed? The stage again, and it took three? four nights? I forget where the last stage was, up in the hills somewhere, pleasant country; we stopped for a change of horses and a bit of lunch at a country town, all grey stone and steep hills I recall, and a spa . . . Buxton, that's it, little boys selling jugs of the water for a farthing, then up another rise or two and then down the other side, and those great rolling hills with mist scarfed over their tops to the right and on the other side a big rolling plain of forest, orchards and fields stretched beneath us, but a couple of villages deserted with their roofs fallen in, and a wild pig or two nosing through the churned-up gardens for old roots.

But the great thing of this panorama was that at a distance of twenty miles there was a black pall of smoke lying dense like a blanket, not rising for there was no wind and the day was fine, though hot and sultry with a lilac coloured sky. As we got nearer and lower we could see the forest of brick trees that sprouted this sulphurous fumy cloud instead of foliage, and as we came in under it it was like moving into an unnatural dusk, a gloomy hellish place where it seemed the sun never shone properly but was only ever visible as an orange disc the size of an orange held at arm's length . . .

I was waited for, of course, Mr Stafford saw to that, and taken up Deansgate to the Prince Regent's Arms, a favourite resort of Joe Nadin. The man who met me was Edwards, one of Mr Stafford's lot – you recall I'd met him already – but just then known as Roberts, thought to be a Spitalfields silk-weaver and Spencean, thought to have come up from London to help the local Spenceans organise the big meeting, then put down for ten days later.

After he'd seen my bag stowed in a tiny attic room with a dormer I was to share with him at the back of the inn he took me out into the town to meet the other Spenceans who had arrived, first telling me to take my engraving kit with me, which I did, it being packed up in its carpetbag as before, separate from the rest. We went back down Deansgate and across a corner of St Peter's Fields which was where the Meeting was to be, and found that there was a fair on, on the green, a country fair.

There we were, surrounded by red brick painted black by the soot like the painted face of a savage, the big mills on two sides, many floors high and long like they were huge barracks or prisons and the interminable serpents of smoke trailing themselves upwards for ever and ever, and in the middle a

Lammas-tide fair with stalls selling cheeses and honey and barley cakes and corn dolls. There were shepherds down from the hills, each with four or five ewes too old to lamb but would sell off to make mutton pies, and gypsies selling ribbons, white heather, lavender, clothes pegs carved at the top with comic heads and other fairings too, just as if Arkwright and Cartwright and William Horrocks from Stockport had never invented their infernal machines and the hands to run them had never been driven from their villages by the enclosures to man them . . .

'You sound like a political economist of a radical persuasion,' Cargill comments dryly.

'Exactly so. Mr Stafford often complimented me on the way I had it off so pat no Spencean could fault me. Mind you, it's more difficult now with the sort of talk you get in the Red Lion, Windmill Street, with these German types; a rum lot they are, especially the one with the big beard, but that's all for the very end of my story . . . Yes, Mr Cargill, I knew my stuff, I'd done my homework . . .'

Anyway. We walked through this fair at which, I have to say, very little was being sold and the only real activity was a group of out-of-work or absconding hands, men and women, having a bit of a dance to a fiddle, fife and drum, but they were wearing the heavy clogs hands wear to protect their feet from machinery and hot coals and it was more of a clickety-clacking tapping-dance, if you take my meaning, than the old country-style.

We made our way south a quarter-mile or so into a warren of new housing, terraced cabins in brick, with a chapel here and there, rising like a man of war above a fishing fleet, and it was in a tiny hall at the back of one of these, Unitarian as I recall, that I met or was introduced by Edwards, or Roberts, to a committee of Spenceans. They were already discussing ways of turning the march and meeting from a demonstration of support for annual parliaments and one man one vote into something with a bit of go in it, such as hanging the aristocracy and thieving their land off them.

Who was there? The Watsons, doctor and son, Arthur Thistlewood, Thomas Preston, John Hopper and others. On this occasion my reputation had gone ahead of me and they knew me from the Pentrich affair as an engraver and by now I truly did have the skills though in a roughish sort of way.

'Roughish is fine,' said Thistlewood, a decent sort of a fellow and well spoken, though with a marked Lincolnshire accent; short he was, not short like me but a sturdy compact sort of a chap, about forty or a bit more, close-shaven hair, widely-set eyes beneath brows like two triangles, good broad chin. Strong hands, very dry. He'd done a bit of farming, done a bit of soldiering, knew his arse from his elbow, if you follow me. Educated too. And soft spoken though he was, he was more for bloody revolution than any of the others, no matter how they ranted and raved. He really did want to see Prinny's head on a spike.

He went on to me: 'Citizen Boylan,' for he used the form of address modish among would-be Jacobins, 'the originals you'll be working from will be pretty rough to be sure – these aren't landscapes by young Turner or Haydon's historicals to be reproduced for the minor gentry, you know! The classiest we have are old Billy Blake's, but they're a bit weird, and old hat too, and I doubt we'll use them,' and he spilled out a portfolio of sheets showing the likes of Cashman and Brandreth on the gallows, or the executioner holding up Brandreth's head, gamekeepers and soldiers driving country folk in smocks and straw hats off the commons, and even the Duke with his nose done bigger than ever, and Sidmouth looking more weaselly than a weasel, and Prinny as gross as the biggest pig you ever saw with a weaver stuck on his fork and a napkin like a Union flag round his neck ... you know the sort of thing. All done crude and exaggerated, many of them engraved already, but of course we didn't have the plates so I had to copy them on to mine. And he explained to me how these were to go on posters, bills and throwaways with text yet to be chosen and, I daresay, written beneath them.

'It would be best,' I said, 'if I did the work here or any road not back in my room where the light isn't so good, and I might be recognised in the town from the work I did at Spa Fields and Pentrich for the cause and spied on, for be you sure, sir, I mean brother, John Castle may not show his face, but there are other spies everywhere and I daresay thicker on the ground than ever before as news of the meeting and its size spreads all over.'

All this I said, of course, so's I'd be among them and hear their innermost counsels.

'Well thought of,' cried Thistlewood. 'Pull that table there under the window so he can see, and let's have one of you cleaning the soot off it . . .'

So within minutes I was at it, but not so's I couldn't hear every word was said and every plan they laid which was as well, because they used Roberts, or Edwards, as a runner or messenger boy, even sending him to get some pigs' feet and ale for their suppers, on account he was lean and long-legged, though short and ferret-like, and got around the town and even the countryside as quick as if he had a horse to ride.

I was at it every day for a week and more, scratching and gouging away at my plates and was only ever out of that small dusty hall to take them down to a secret press they had back of a tool-maker's shop who used to do repairs for the mill-owners' machines, two streets or rather alleys away. And bit by bit it got clearer there was trouble among them, trouble between the reformers and the revolutionaries, just as the Duke had said. And one day, less than a week to go, who should come by but Orator Hunt himself and he had a long confabulation with Thistlewood, like they were old friends who agreed to differ, but the upshot was Arthur agreed this time not to spoil Hunt's meeting with urgings for a mass rising and the cutting off of heads, and the redistribution of land, which Hunt agreed was what he wanted too in the long run, but step by step starting with reform. Anyway, as I say, this Thistlewood agrees to back off this time and says he'll clear off to London, not muddy Hunt's waters and all.

The thing of it was, the whole business had been organised by the Manchester Patriotic Union Society, all honest men who wanted no more than fair dos for the workers, and Hunt and Thistledown thought they'd call it off if they thought revolution would be talked up and maybe even tried.

Well, every evening Roberts, or rather Edwards, and I would take ourselves back to the Prinny's Arms, knowing we were followed, suspected of being spies because it was Joe Nadin's pub of choice, but it being so obvious and us making no attempt to disguise the fact, it was thought being Londoners we knew no better. We went in the back way, the service entrance where the vittles were delivered and straw and such like for the horses of any gents might be staying there, and up a twist of narrow creaky steps to our room. What the Spenceans didn't know was there were attic passages took us round two sides to the top of another flight of wider stairs down to the first-floor room where Nadin and his Mancunian cronies met of an evening to sort out what they'd do about the Big Meeting in such a way as would please Sidmouth and his Whitehall cronies.

This Joseph Nadin was a character fit for those times and his occupation. By 1819 he was fifty-five or thereabouts, a big man, big head, dark complexion so you'd say there was some gypsy not so far back or even a Hindoo or A-rab further back than that. He had a big nose, beaked, but not boney like the Duke's, a lowering brow, and an angry suspicious look to his dark eyes. It was a coarse face as matched his fingernails and his manners.

You'll know his history, Mr Cargill, from your files ... No? Well, as a young man he worked as a cotton-spinner but gave that up maybe thanks to Mr Arkwright's spinning-jenny and became a thief-catcher instead, scoring a couple of quid for every thief successfully prosecuted. Course he didn't look for thieves, just for people whose circumstances would convince the Justices they were thieves. He also got a Tyburn ticket for each which he could sell for ten pounds. A Tyburn ticket? It exempted you from public service like juryman, or maintenance of public building, that sort of thing, as a reward for sending a felon to gaol.

From thief-catching he progressed to protection, especially of brothels and the like. Soon, in part by reputation as a scourge of criminals and in part by bribery and blackmail, he got to be Deputy Constable of Manchester and secured himself for ever in the minds of the local dignitaries, mill-owners and the like, by arresting forty weavers at a seditious meeting. King of Manchester, the radicals and reformers called him, and not only them, but the minor gentry, mill-owners and so forth too. He was not a nice man, not at all.

He and his cohorts and equals and sometimes superiors met every night in that first-floor front room overlooking the main entrance and ate beef and parsnips off a fine polished oak board with silver candelabra and drank a couple of bottles of claret each, smoked their pipes or cigars brought in to Liverpool on the sugar boats from Jamaica but smuggled there from Cuba. Rolled on the thighs of negro girls, they said.

Well, I'd brought my Spinks and Pottle with me and was wondering who I'd have the honour of using it on, Thistlewood perhaps or even Orator Hunt, and who'd end up on the gallows for the murder I'd been licensed to do. Towards the end of the week I got from the gist of it all that Arthur Thistlewood was in the frame which gave me a moment or two of bother, for, albeit he was all for the most bloodthirsty sort of revolution and not just parliamentary reform at all, in himself he was a decent sort of a cove. Anyway, or any road as they say up there, he took off, back to London, for the reasons I've given you and bit by bit as the week wore out and there was only three days left, I came to understand that licensed killing was not the plot this time at all. Not at all. Ha! Well not by yours truly, any road.

And when we told Joe Nadin that Thistlewood was gone he damn near had an apoplexy on us there and then, he was so angry.

'Fuck that,' he cries, 'fuck, fuck, fuck.' You'll pardon the language Mr Cargill, in the cause of hearing a truthful, verbatim account. 'With Thistlewood gone we'll never get that cunt Willy Hulton up to the mark.'

Well, already I knew who Mr Hulton was. He was Chief of the Justices in Manchester, the Chairman, but a young 'un, in that position on account he was a proper gent and also had an Oxford degree in law. Which was fine up to a point, except he knew what the law was, and if it weren't broken then my Lord Sidmouth's clear intentions, as arrived at in consultation with the Duke, would not be executed at all, and the likes of Joe Nadin would not get the rewards they had been promised.

So, once he was over his anger, this Nadin, who had a cunning head on his shoulders for all he was an oaf, came to me and . . . Well, you'll see how it turned out.

' . . . the second bottle's empty, Mr Cargill. And forgive me for mentioning it, but I have to ask myself, why has my good friend neglected to bring with him the pork pie as requested? You know, Mr Cargill, this is the third time in my life I have been placed in a position where the edibles available have been virtually inedible or more or less not there at all. You cannot imagine, Mr Cargill, what cravings present themselves under such circumstances, how the mind dwells on what it lacks, invents feasts out of all proportion to what is wise or in good taste.'

And here Charlie leans across the tiny table and puts his face right up against the Assistant Under-Secretary's nose . . .

'Mr Cargill. I . . . want . . . a large . . . pork pie. With a thick outer crust that might almost break your teeth, a doughy dumpling-like lining to that crust, the rich brown jelly, and the meat succulent, not without fat but not too fatty, lightly spiced with fine white pepper and salt and with a subtle hint of sage. A Bellamy pork pie, Mr Cargill. I'll see you with one tomorrow perhaps, with more porter and maybe a pint of Hollander as well. Then . . . then I'll tell you the full story of the battle of St Peter's Fields.'

18

Or will I? thinks Charlie Boylan as he rolls himself once more into his cocoon and waits in the darkness for the fetid warmth to build up. Slowly, as is the case on every night, the prison asserts its presence more surely in the dark. The smells, the noise. The ringing rattle of keys, the echoing heavily booted footsteps, the endlessly repeated monotone of the very old man three cells away who cries again and again and again the same wretched mantra, in a not quite perfectly pitched minor doh, re, mi, fa, so, the words: 'the jury was fixed, the jury was fixed, the jury was fixed . . .' And then the noises that really make the prison a prison because they come from outside its high spiked walls: the clip-clop of a trotting horse, and the squeal of a wheel, the raucous but distant chanting of a gang of drunks thrown out of one pub and looking for another, the whistle and clang of shunted rolling-stock, the ee-yip of an owl, and, towards dawn, the rustling pitter-patter of a thousand tiny hooves, the occasional yap of a collie and the plaintive baa of a lamb separated from its dam as the shepherds drive them down the Caledonian Road to Smithfield. Lambs to the slaughter. Was

St Peter's Field like that? A bit. But there was more to it than that.

It started the night before. Towards dusk Charlie and George Edwards, known as Roberts, their hands smudged and their fingernails caked with ink, left the radical engineer's workshed with two satchels each filled with pamphlets and handouts, a thousand divided into five different lots, still smelling of turpentine soap, linseed oil and lamp-black, and humped them back to Deansgate. As soon as they were clear of the narrow alleys that separated the rows and rows of workers' terraces they became aware of strange presences in the gathering gloom, beneath the never shifting shroud above them. There'd been no wind for three days and even out in the country it was sultry Lammas-tide weather, weather for flies and stickiness, for rumbling thunder up in the hills and flashes of sheet lightning along the horizon to the west, weather when the coke fumes in the town flattened the oxygen-depleted air into the streets so they stank of drains, sweat, grease, stale beer, sewage and the dyes used in the mills. Weather when men and women shifted from catatonic moods of sullen numbness to sudden passions of which anger and lust were the most pronounced.

Strange presences? Soldiers. Soldiers marching in that easy ambling motion that had taken them relentlessly across the *mesetas* of Spain and through the sierras too, soldiers never in more than a company at a time moving into prepared billets about the town centre and settling quickly and silently into the darkness so no one could say just how many there were, what sort of a threat they presented. But one thing was sure. None of them was local. A battalion had marched, so it was said, by byroads and country lanes from Liverpool and were Irish; others had slipped over the hills during the day from the Borders, Geordies and even a company of kilted, bonneted Scots. If they had bands they did not play. If they had colours they remained cased. And out on the outskirts, in the fields, but no more than a fifteen-minute ride away, it was said four squadrons of Hussars, the 15th, just like the ones who did the business at Pentrich and could be trusted, were bivouacked.

But these were presences, rumoured, guessed at, exaggerated or diminished according to your temperament. What were obvious were the normal forces of law and order: four hundred special constables in their flattened hats and armed with nothing more menacing than their bludgeons and boots, and a full turnout of the local mounted militia, the Manchester and Salford Yeomanry. They were evident all right.

Charlie and Roberts, consigned to the public rooms by Nadin for the time being, told to report back later, found a couple of score of them fighting to get to the counter, swilling strong ale and claret, stuffing their mouths with the landlady's pasties filled with cheese, onion and bacon, or Lancashire hasty haggises. They were a dreadful crew – volunteers, of course, raised for the sole purpose of keeping those who labour under the thumb of those who don't. They had to provide their own horses and uniforms and while most county yeomanries used the standard light cavalry sabres and pistols, a few swells among this lot prided themselves on being different by arming themselves, illegally, with axes. These had hafts as long as your arm and blades like those of an executioner's.

Their uniforms consisted of bucket-shaped shakoes, wider at the top than at the rim, with a plume in the front which was edged with gold, long blue coats with red collars, white leather bandoliers worn over the left shoulder, white breeches tailored tight to accentuate buttocks, and padded privates, boots to above the knee. And those with axes had a further wrinkle to this ensemble: they wore cotton sleeves, tight at the wrist and elbow over their coat sleeves, in the style of butchers and penpushers. These, they boasted, were to protect their uniforms from the blood they would be certain to shed.

The majority were tenant farmers of some standing or small landowners or their sons, though some came from mill-owning families who prided themselves on keeping up connections with the landed gentry. But among them too were a dancing-master, a butcher and a cheesemonger. Their common sports, apart from guzzling and boozing, were hunting and shooting, cock-fighting, gambling on bare-knuckle bruisers and whoring. Almost all were porkers for fatness, and none had a civil word for any sort but their own sort. They were foul-mouthed in speech save in the presence of ladies they knew, with whom they became even more red-faced than before and quite dumb. Until, that is, they married them, when they took to raping and beating them.

Charlie and Roberts soon gave up on getting to the counter or even catching the attention of the many serving maids called in especially. They found a corner in the empty inglenook, smoked their clays, and waited, listening to the raucous boasting and bluster around them.

'Well, lads, what'll we do tomorrow?'

'Chop the buggers down my brave boys, chop 'em down.'

'Aye, that's right. For when all's said, it's our fucking beef and puddin' they want to take from us.'

'An' another thing. Think on this. The more we kill the less poor rates we'll have to pay.'

'That's it. Be brave, lads, show your spunk and loyalty, King and Church say I—'

'Aye, that's it. God save the King, poor mad bugger, and Prinny, God bless him too.'

It wasn't long before Roberts got tired of waiting to get some liquid or food inside him and was making for the door when a flunkey came halfway down the stairs, blew a whistle at them through his fingers and signalled them to follow him back up to Nadin's room.

The King of Manchester was sat at the head of the table in a big carved oak chair with arms, a knife in one hand and a tankard of claret in the other. All round him sat or sprawled his bully boys, a captain of Hussars, and the Chief Constable who was no chief to his deputy, but a lawyer with an office in Salford and a big house out in the hills.

'Right, lads. Yer be Stafford's men, baint you?'

The big man was half-cut and Charlie had to restrain himself from telling him that he knew damned well they were.

'Yer job tomorrer is simple enough but mark it well and be sure you unnerston.'

The two of them nodded. They were standing to the side of him, their hats in their hands over their stomachs.

'All through the morning, while the crowd comes in, you hand out them pamphlets and papers, but first you leaves samples of them here, say ten of each, for us to send to London. Especially the ones that is blasphemous and seditious. I like the one of Prinny rogering Britannia from behind so gold guineas come out of her mouth, that's witty that is, says a lot . . . You know what ladies say when they come? They say they're spending themselves, and so does Britannia when the likes of Prinny fucks her.'

He sliced a lump of Wensleydale off the cheese in front of him.

'Then about one o'clock you, Edwards, slips away, for I don't want you seen, and you go to Mr Buxton's house in Mount Street, the back of it looks over the Fields, and that's where we'll all be. But you, Charlie, you go round the back of the hustings to the mill I've told you of, and you meets the men you've put there, and you waits for the sight of a big white kerchief waved from Mr Buxton's house, then . . . well, you know what then. Am I right?'

Charlie nodded, but with a distinct sinking feeling in his stomach, for the long and the short of it was the ten guineas Nadin had given him were still in his bag on the other side of the inn yard, and he hadn't actually met any men at all to do what Mr Nadin wanted; indeed, the fact of the matter was that he was in two minds he might take the ten guineas down to the docks at Liverpool. Ten was enough not just for a passage to Boston, but a passage in style, dinner at the captain's table, that sort of thing. Meanwhile, drunk as he was and half-forgetting what he was about, Nadin blundered on with a belch and a fart to introduce what he still had to say.

153

'And you time it so you'll leave the hustings by one o'clock when that fucking clown Hunt is due to appear and that's when the men I've put in will shout sedition and treason for all they're worth. There'll be some of my lads around you, they'll join in. Then if you go to your posts like the good obedient lads you are and do what we decided, all will be well. Reet, be off wi' yer. No. Wait.'

He took a last pull at the claret.

'It's gorra be timed just right. Go off early, half-cock and there'll be trouble after. There's gorra be witnesses, real witnesses ready to swear they heard real sedition, real treason called for from the platform itself or bloody close to it. But there's gorra be confusion, noise, muddle. Let that ol' cunt Hunt get into his stride, about one man one vote and parlyments every year, and people'll forget there was sedition and treason preached and it'll be clear that when it happens it's staged, a put-on. Gorra get it reet. One of yer stays in Buxton's house, where we'll all be met, and one goes, like I said, over to the mill . . .'

Then suddenly he leaned forward, so his chin almost touched the table, flung out his hand so the tankard flew out of it and clattered to the floor, and, 'Fuck up,' he bellowed, then dropped his voice to a hoarse whisper. 'Fuck up, especially you, Charlie, and I'll have you hunted down like a rat, even if you gets to America, and you'll die so slow, with your guts round your neck and your balls in your mouth, you'll wish you'd never been born, you'll wish you never met Joe Nadin.'

And his cheek hit the board and he was gone. With barely a nod at the three or four other worthies there, who were as well out of it as he was, Charlie and Edwards slipped away.

Shit, thought Charlie, can the old devil with his talk of America, read minds as well?

'So where you going to get these men from?' Edwards–Roberts asked, with a sneer, as he followed him down the warped and twisting passages and up the steps towards their room.

'Why, I have 'em already,' Charlie replied, holding his candle above his head, glad his fellow spy and *agent provocateur* could not see his face. 'Indeed, now I think of it, I'll go and seek them out, make sure they've got what's needed and know where to go.'

'Oh yeah? Well you be back by daylight or I'll tell Joe Nadin you're gone, and he'll have you in irons long before you get to the Liverpool dock, and then he'll do what he said. With your innards and your testiculars.'

But Charlie was already clattering down the backstairs and out into the dark streets. Edwards hesitated for a moment then stumbled down after him.

'Hey, wait up,' he shouted. 'I'm coming too.'

Charlie set off in an easterly direction, taking a corner off the Fields where Edwards caught up with him and took his arm. Together they went round the church and into a warren of older streets. Although it was now well past midnight there were still a couple of small ale houses on street corners open, light streaming from their doors and shouts and singing of a sort rising and falling, like waves, on the terraced cottages opposite. From one end of the alley it was 'And it's no, nay, never, No nay never no more, Will I play the wild rover, No, never, no more . . .' and from the other end 'The pipes, the pipes are calling, From glen to glen and down the mountainside', then all came together with one apparently spiritually communicated consent, 'Though lovely and fair like the bright rose of summer, Sure 'twas not her beauty alone that won me. Oh no 'twas the truth in her eyes ever dawning, That made me love Mary, the Rose of Tralee'.

But while most of the singers were struggling to recall the first line of the next verse, competition of a more robust nature broke out: 'I don't want a bayonet up my bum-hole, I don't want my cobblers minced with ball, For if I 'ave to lose 'em, Then let it be with Susan, Or Meg or Peg, or any whore at all . . .' and this last sent a shiver up Charlie's spine and a very mixed feeling of fear and a sort of joy like a dagger in his heart.

'It can't be,' he said to himself, but aloud because he was so moved, 'it really cannot be. I won't believe it.'

'Believe what,' Edwards asked, tightening his grip on Charlie's arm.

And as the last bellowed ditty climaxed two figures appeared in the doorway of the inn across the way from them, one tall and lean but tough, the other smaller and stocky, the first more drunk than his companion and leaning on him with his arm round his shoulder. Charlie knew them. He didn't have to come any closer to know what the number was on the breast badges that joined their diagonal white belts over their red coats: 88. The Connaught Rangers.

And the tall one lifted his head, and the light fell on the curls of his red-gold hair and spilled across a face more lined and worn than Charlie remembered, but still tanned like red cordovan leather, and then he looked back down on the straw-coloured almost white hair of his mate.

'Fock me, Kev, but I'm a deal dronker than I tought I was.'

'How's that then, Patrick?'

'Look up dere. Across t' way. And tell me dat isn't dat hairy little ront Joey. Joey Bozzam.'

'Who the fuck is Joey Bozzam?' Edwards–Roberts asked an hour later as they made their way back to the Prinny's Arms. All had been arranged, just as Joe Nadin wanted it, and the bag was lighter by only six guineas. As Corporal Kevin Nolan had said, that's two each and two for the sarge who'll cover for us at roll call.

'Joey Bozzam?' asked Charlie. 'Never heard of him. In point of fact his real name was Bosham. Joseph Bosham.'

And that was all he had to say on the subject, then, at any rate.

'Is that thunder I can hear? A spot of rain on my wrist?'

156

19

'That was very nice, squire, just the ticket, but if you don't mind I'll leave the second half until tomorrow. But we'll wrap it back up most carefully. Mice, you know.' He taps the side of his nose again and then pulls the crinkly, crackly paper, printed with the three-feathered badge of the Prince of Wales, Prinny himself, By Appointment Suppliers to, and 'Bellamy' in the newly fashionable gothic lettering, around the remaining half of the raised pork pie Cargill has brought him. 'Now, if you don't mind, the stopper out of that Hollands and I'll have a good nip to wash it all down. Water? A splash. Not more than half and half. Your health sir, your very good health.'

He leans back, so much as a man can when sitting on a backless three-legged stool, sips his Bols and grins.

'That's good. Very good. A man does miss little comforts in a place like this. Tell me, it seems not quite so cold now, as if we might have entered an unseasonal warm spell?'

'That is so. Most of the snow has melted and for the moment we are blessed with a gentle southerly breeze and rather more sun than we had before.' Cargill is relieved his investment in a bottle of quality gin and a large pork pie is turning out so well, for he doubts the Treasury will reimburse him.

'Just such a change of weather, though in a contrary direction, heralded in the morning of the sixteenth of August 1819, a Monday as I recall. There was a thunderstorm late that night that lasted an hour or so, nothing like that which preceded Waterloo, you understand, but enough to clear the atmosphere and give us a sight of the blue sky. A breeze, too, from the west if memory serves, and strong enough to push the flags and bunting about and give everything a jolly atmosphere, a holiday feeling, you know? Yes, I'll have a drop more before I get properly started. Are you sure you won't? I understand. A clear head if you're to write it all up this evening.

'First thing, not long after first light, we could hear the hollow echoing banging as carpenters and chippies erected the hustings on the south side of the Fields, backing up to the big new mill. Not always a pleasant sound for the bangs and sawing that go with the erection of a scaffold at a place of execution are very like. George and I, George? Roberts or rather Edwards, was George, had a breakfast of small beer and bacon butties at Mr Nadin's expense, then, with our satchels of pamphlets and throwaways slung over our backs, sauntered down Deansgate into Alport Street, took a left and wandered out into the middle of the grass. Already it was a brave sight, much like one of the old country fairs, indeed more so than the sorry business I'd seen at Lammas-tide. There were stalls going up round the edges of the green, selling comestibles for the most part and drink too, holiday fare; a lot of it, like new apples dipped in treacle, candies, sausages in butties, small pies, flummery and so forth, and a couple of butts of frumenty well laced with rum.

'These last attracted one class of customer particularly – members of the Manchester and Salford Yeomanry, whose horses and so forth were corralled in St Peter's churchyard next to Mr Buxton's house, made frequent trips, indeed they procured buckets and churns to take the stuff back to their companions . . .' He rambles on, and his eyes fix on the wall above Cargill's head and lose focus as he plays the scene again across the phantom retinae of his mind . . .

At first there were just small groups of locals, people from the housing near by, mill-hands and out-of-work loom weavers for the most part with their wives and kids, some with bowling hoops and tops to whip and some with skipping ropes, most in their holiday best, those that hadn't pawned them. And wherever they could be put there were flags, mostly the Union flag but a few tricolours, too, and banners stretched from pole to pole with slogans and exhortations on them, such as 'Liberty or Death', 'Corn Laws Repealed' and 'Votes for All'.

By midday the big battalions were arriving from the outlying towns and districts, each contingent or regiment sometimes several thousand strong. Often the hands themselves marched, in good order, in files four deep or six, smartening up their gait as they drew nearer, encouraged and often sworn at by the many ex-soldiers who were there, heads up, arms swinging, mostly in step. Some carried staves shouldered like muskets, but for show only, no hostile intent, and many followed bands, often military ones from disbanded regiments. They played the tunes they'd played from Torres Vedras to Waterloo: 'God Save the King', 'Rule, Britannia!' and 'See, the Conquering Hero Comes'. In nearly all cases the columns were accompanied by the wives and children of the men, scampering alongside them, these too in their holiday or Sunday best. Some of the women formed their own columns and a couple of hundred from Rochdale swung by looking particularly grand with happy smiles and occasionally introducing dancing figures into their marching when the music prompted. Another group from Oldham, a club of female reformers, marched behind a white silken banner inscribed 'Annual Parliaments', 'Universal Suffrage' and 'Vote by Ballot'.

Other contingents had made efforts to appear uniform and tidy, as all the men wore black waistcoats over white shirts or all the women had wide-brimmed straw bonnets tied down with bandannas of muslin and knotted beneath their chins. The aim was not to look like uniformed soldiers, though some of the press made out this was the intention, but to show they were decent folk, only anxious to do a good day's work for a fair wage, and not a rabble of malcontents.

The sun grew hotter and the sky remained clear; it was as perfect a day for an outing as you could wish for. Marshals engaged by the Patriotic Union Society shepherded the groups as they arrived to appointed places, but it soon became apparent that far more were coming than had been expected, and it became a matter of some concern to get the people to close up and move forward so later arrivals could be accommodated on the green, in the Fields, rather than in the alleyways around. Yet all was done with cheery goodwill, and little in the way of disputes. Apart from the staves, which were no more than four by twos cut to five-foot lengths and not the quarterstaffs they were accused of, no weapons were visible.

And through it all Charlie and Edwards and maybe a score more of Nadin's men moved, handing out sheets and throwaways and muttering treason and sedition at any who looked likely to approve. Which was not many; indeed most took one look at their papers and crumpled or tore them with looks of irritation and even disgust on their faces. One woman, head and shoulders above Charlie, grasped him by his stock and lapels and stooped to put her face into his.

'Be off with yer, you scamp. We'm not here for revolution but work at a fair wage,' she growled, and turning him round pushed the throwaway he'd offered her down the neck of his coat.

None of this caused the agents concern: that their papers should be found littering the place in the aftermath would be enough.

The clock on St Peter's square tower struck the half hour, half twelve, and Edwards sought out Charlie, touched his elbow.

'I'm off now to Mr Buxton's,' and he gestured over his shoulder at the big house that stood in front of the church, that is,

160

seen from where they were standing ten yards or so in front of the hustings. 'Watch out for the handkerchief.' And he grinned and pulled out the corner of a big napkin he had pushed into his trouser pocket.

Charlie reached up to slap his shoulder. 'I'll check out the lads,' he said, and he turned away, pushing through the throng where it was thickest, ditching his satchel and what sheets were left of his literature to ease his passage.

It was when he was working round behind the hustings that he saw him, a tall lean figure, shoulders slightly stooped, wearing black beneath a hat that would not have disgraced an undertaker, but lank hair resting on his shoulders.

'Mr Bourgeois,' Charlie called, raising his voice above the general hubbub. 'Hi there, Mr Bourgeois!'

He considered it a bit silly to honour the man's name with its frenchified prefix 'de'.

He felt no surprise to see the man; after all, this was his 'control', and presumably the control of the other men, agents and spies from Mr Stafford's secret battalion, who were now scattered through the vast crowd. But he was a touch mortified when the figure, retreating and keeping his back to him, ignored him and slipped away, as neat and almost as quick as a shuttle through a confusion of threads. Less slick in their movements were the three heavy, thickset, red-faced bully boys who appeared to be following him, clutching knobbed bludgeons in ham-sized fists. Were they in pursuit to do him some mischief? Or were they his minders in a crowd and place which could be very hostile to Mr de Bourgeois if knowledge of his occupation got around?

Charlie didn't hang about to see. Already on the platform itself there were gathered some notables of the Patriotic Union, a band of fiddlers and a fat madman with a waistcoat cut from a Union flag who capered about pretending to be John Bull. At that point this harmless fool was perhaps the most significant symptom of riot or disorder that could have been seen among a gathering that had already reached sixty thousand and was still growing.

161

Charlie rounded the side of the new mill that the hustings backed on to, crossed the track that circled the open ground, climbed a fence, dodged through some small outbuildings and got into the street on the other side. The ends were corded off by the marshals who endeavoured to persuade the people to go on to the Fields at the other end, facing the hustings, so suddenly all was quiet, save for the distant rumbling of the crowd – like surf heard from a distance.

'And I know what I'm talking about,' says Charlie, suddenly coming out of his spoken reverie and fixing Cargill with his sharp eye before taking a swig at his gin and water. 'For did I not listen to surf without a break for three years upon the Galapagos?'

He got in by the main door without difficulty for the mill was owned by one of Nadin's cronies and he had had it left unlocked. After a quick look round the deserted halls he climbed the wide wooden stairs, dusty with cotton waste and coke dust, to the first floor. Here the machines, the power looms, stood in serried ranks like a regiment of armoured monsters, tethered by their looping driving belts back to the steam-powered machinery that drove them from the end of the building where the boilers and furnaces were sited. A place where on a working day wheels and shuttles rolled and flashed with a raucous deafening racket, but were now silent and shrouded in a dim, heavy light save where sunbeams penetrated at a steep angle from the street side through the high arched windows.

'Paddy? Patrick? Kev?' Charlie called, but not too loud. Nevertheless his voice echoed up into the high spaces above, crissed and crossed by the broad driving belts. A sparrow chirped and fluttered among them.

No other answer. Had there been a misunderstanding? Were they on the second floor, the floor above? Charlie scouted along the north-facing wall, passing embrasured window after window until he came to the end, the east end, the last window, the one nearest the house, Mr Buxton's house. At two hundred yards he could make out the magistrates assembling, on the first floor too, just about on a level with him. And there, leaning in the corner made by the window frame and the alcoved wall, he found not one or two Irish redcoats, not Patrick and Kevin, but what looked like a flintlock with a long barrel. Instantly he recognised it for what it was – a Baker rifle.

He knew about Baker rifles. They were accurate to two hundred yards and could kill at twice that.

A note was attached.

dear Joey
This is the best we can do for ye. Tis loded.
Yor freinds.

'I don't know why they persisted in calling me Joey,' Charlie says, head on one side, a question in his voice as if wondering whether Cargill will challenge him on the matter. He coughs and spits to cover the unease he feels.

20

So. Charlie was to do the business himself. He didn't like it. He was terrified. He stood back from the window, hefted the rifle, studied it; it felt familiar enough, he had handled them before, but not often. He knew all he had to do was pull back the hammer, clickety-click, put the butt to his shoulder, take aim and pull the trigger. Simple. But more likely to work out if done by an experienced sophomore than by a relative tyro. The Spinks and Pottle was more his sort of thing. There was also the problem of getting away to consider. If his intervention in the proceedings was noted, and why should it not be since upwards of seventy thousand people were, by now, facing his window, how was he to extricate himself?

He soon realised his anxiety was unfounded. Already a serious commotion was taking place below. A couple of hundred, at least, special constables had been marched round Mr Buxton's house and were pushing their way into the crowd. What they were up to was not immediately apparent, but gradually their purpose became clearer. They were endeavouring to form two lines to make a narrow corridor between the hustings and the house, and even as they did so a mighty cheer rose from the whole crowd, a huge cheer from eighty thousand throats, such as would strike terror in the heart of any man who had not heard such a sound before. And very few had. If any. Perhaps we would have to go back to Roman times and the vile games that took place in the Colosseum to hear such a noise. And the cause of the cheer? The arrival on the platform of Richard Carlile, John Knight, Joseph Jonson, Mary Fildes and last, last because he was the most important, instantly recognised by his white top hat, Henry 'Orator' Hunt, carrying a staff with a liberty bonnet on it, red knitted wool, with a blue, white and red cockade. Behind him, and filling the spaces at the back were the gentlemen of the press, from *The Times*, the *Leeds Mercury*, the *Liverpool Mercury* and the *Manchester Observer*.

'So all through the riot, you remained in the upstairs hall of the mill?' Cargill asks.

'It was no riot, not until the constables and the soldiers made a riot out of it,' says Charlie, eyes, in spite of the gin, suddenly keen again. 'And I doubt they would have done that had I not done my duty.'

'Technically it was a riot.' Cargill, with a bureaucrat's pedantry, was sharp in return. 'The Riot Act was read, so, it was a riot. It's the reading of the Act makes a riot, not the behaviour of the people.'

Charlie slowly, elaborately, unwraps his pork pie again, cuts another slice, nicely judged to leave a good third of the original still intact, and silently holds out his mug for more gin and water. With a sigh, Cargill obliges.

Charlie finishes with a gulp of liquid and his thumbs return again to the armholes of his stained waistcoat.

'If you're wondering if I knows at all what went on in the upper room of Mr Buxton's house, the answer is yes. George was there and he told me it all in very particular detail.'

It was a largish room in a house built some fifty years earlier, possibly as a rectory, when the Fields still had the appearance of a large village green outside a church. Originally it had been a withdrawing room in the evenings, a place where tea was served, the fortepiano played, and, in a general way, the manners of the upper classes aped by their superiors, the new bourgeoisie, who should have known better. Mr Buxton, himself a magistrate, kept it on as a *pied-à-terre* in the suddenly enlarged town, from which he conducted his business as a cotton factor, though he and his family resided for the most part in the countryside, a couple of miles away in Rusholme.

By midday the tall sash windows had been thrown up in part to allow in a cooling draught but mainly so the magistrates, of whom there were a dozen or so, including Mr Buxton himself, could the better observe what was happening below.

William Hulton, a young man but, as we have seen, educated in the law, was both nervous and anxious to act in as proper a way as possible. At half past eleven, or thereabouts, persuaded by his fellow magistrates, some of whom were close to Nadin and had been schooled by him, that no good could come of such a huge gathering and that it should be dispersed before it got any bigger – lives and property were clearly at risk and this is one of the parameters that makes a riot a riot – he formally made the proclamation that constitutes what is known as the Reading of the Riot Act. This meant that he was now constitutionally obliged to disperse the crowd if they would not disperse of their own accord, and was enjoined to use all necessary force to do so.

But there was a problem: how to inform the vast gathering that the Act had been read? Nadin said that the only way that could properly be done was from the hustings themselves.

Hulton was standing in the middle of the three windows. He turned, picked out the boroughreeve from the group immediately behind him, caught his elbow and pulled him to his side.

'Edward,' he said, having first sketched out the fix they were in, 'you'll have to take your men, form a corridor or passage between here and the hustings we can walk down, without being jostled or worse, so I can get on the platform and inform the crowd that the Act has been read.'

Edward Clayton, a thin man, by trade an undertaker to the moneyed classes, and boroughreeve because he enjoyed the dignity the title gave him, chewed his thumb knuckle for a moment.

'I'll need every man I've got to do that,' he said. 'The full four hundred.'

'Nevertheless it must be done.'

'I'd rather form them up in two files along this side and have them clear the Fields. You can walk behind them, and announce the Act has been read as we go.'

'And if the line breaks?' Nadin intruded and made a threat of it. 'What then? My constables are stout men, but they are not the thin red line that saw off Boney's hordes at Waterloo.'

Actually some of them were, but no one was prepared to point this out.

'All right,' said Clayton. 'But if they don't disperse, what then? My men will be committed to holding that passage – they won't be able to assist in moving the crowd.'

The answer was so obvious no one chose to give it. But Major Thomas Trafford, 'Old Trafford' as he was usually known, buckled on his belt and sabre that were lying on a chair at the back, smacked on his blue, feathered shako and cleared his throat.

'I'll tell the lads to saddle up,' he said, saluted, and went.

'Who was this Trafford then?' asks Cargill.

'Officer commanding the Manchester and Salford Yeomanry.'

'Of course. Silly of me. I forgot his name.'

'Not one they're likely to forget in Manchester.'

They watched with growing amazement as the four hundred constables marched out. Instead of their having to fight or even push their way through, the crowd parted before them like

167

the Red Sea. Oh, no doubt there was a little jostling, but more joshing than physical resistance. Remember, I was in a position to see this for myself. Many of the constables were known. There were jibes but mostly humorous, and no doubt a high hat here or there was knocked off but, all in all, the crowd let them do just what they purposed to do – it let them form a corridor, nearly two hundred yards long from the back gate of the house to the steps at the front of the platform. And before long the constables were offered drink, some of it strong, and vittles, 'For,' as one wag put it, 'it would be shame on us if we, as have all brought us snap with us, don't share it with you, who hasn't.'

Up in the big room the stillness of the crowd, its good humour and almost perfect behaviour, produced consternation, for it was proving precisely what Liverpool, Sidmouth and the Duke most feared. At the superficial level it was becoming clear that an announcement that this was a riot would be greeted with laughter since it was clearly a meeting and offered no threat to life, limb or property. But more deeply it spoke of something far more serious. A vicar, a man of the cloth anyway, standing near George muttered to himself as much as to anyone in particular: 'A people thus united, will never be defeated.'

And his neighbour, a ship-owner, commented: 'With this sort of organisation, on this sort of scale, they'll become ungovernable.'

'Except by themselves, except by themselves.'

The ship-owner was flummoxed by the enormity of this. All he could do was walk away, muttering obscenities about Methodism and its evil influence, Church and King were the pillars on which good government rested, not the consent of the people which was an irrelevance, and so forth.

And thus they remained for some ten minutes or more, riven with indecision, while below me the platform party busied themselves in the ways such people do, viz., who is to speak first? Do we need a Chair to introduce the speakers? Who is to tackle which particular theme so we don't repeat ourselves too much, all stuff no doubt rehearsed already that morning, but needing to be carved in stone before they began. And the crowd continued to cheer and sing.

Meanwhile, in the upper room they seemed to have forgot that the purpose of the corridor of constables was to allow Hulton et cetera to announce the Act was read so all could hear, and the talk took another direction.

'Well,' said Nadin, 'the Riot Act is read, those fellows are in contravention of the law. Your worship must do something. In fact, you had better arrest the ringleaders.'

'The ringleaders? Who are the ringleaders?' asked Hulton, suddenly petulant.

'Why, those on the platform. Not just the speakers but the wankers in the Patriotic Committee, or whatever they call themselves.'

'We need warrants then. Properly drawn up. The accused named and so forth.'

'I have them here.'

Nadin thrust out a hand, sort of half behind him, and one of his cronies smacked a sheaf of papers into it.

'All they need is your worship's signature. Jack. Give his worship a pen and hold the inkpot for him.'

Hulton at last did his duty. Wm Hulton, he wrote at the bottom of each sheet.

'Right then,' he said at last. 'I reckon with the help of the Specials, drawn up as they are, the police should be able to execute the warrants. Send them in.'

A hiss of indrawn breath from Joe Nadin and he shook his head.

'Never,' he said, 'with or without my specials, nor with ten times the number, nor with all the special constables in England.'

'You seem to mean that it cannot be executed without military force?'

'It cannot.'

A long pause, then poor William Hulton, caught between a rock and a hard place, if, Mr Cargill, you'll excuse a very overused and misunderstood expression, heaved a deep sigh.

'So be it,' he said. 'You shall have the military force. Major Trafford . . . Where the devil is he?'

'Already down in the churchyard.'

'That's devilish forward of him. Call him back. I need to give him very specific instructions as to how it is to be done.'

And that was the moment Joe Nadin gave the nod to George, and George pulled out his napkin and gave it a great wave before burying his face in it in a fit of simulated sneezing, and I saw the white of it in the right-hand window.

This is it, I thought, nothing for it now but to do my duty. I smashed in a window pane with the butt of the Baker, reversed it, took careful aim at the top light in the middle window above Mr Hulton's head and loosed off the one ball I had.

Mr Cargill, you know I'm a good shot.

With shards of glass falling about his head Mr Hulton, doubled up, yelled out his order. Or his curse. 'Get out there. Get the bloody bastards. Clear the Fields and arrest Hunt and all his damned desperadoes with him . . .' And so forth.

Almost at once, with or without this final confirmation that Church and King, and grandees and magnates and landowners and mill-owners and professional classes and merchants and traders of England all expected him to do his duty, Major Trafford drew his sabre and bellowed: 'Right, lads, now's your chance to show we are the masters . . .'

At first they performed as troopers should, forming a long line two deep, sabres drawn but held relatively smartly, in an upright position so the sun flashed from the blades and made a grand sight of them. The very back of the crowd, turning at the sound of hooves and jingle of harness, thought they were part of the show, the occasion, for were they not all stout, some very stout, Mancunians? So they gave them a cheer. Then Trafford rammed spurs to his horse's flanks, got the lumbering beast into a trot, and urged it among them. Someone behind him had the wit to blow a bugle, the high held note signifying a charge, and soon the entire Manchester and Salford Yeomanry, a hundred and fifty of them, waving their

170

sabres above their heads, dashed into the thick of it and began cutting the people. And remember some of them had not sabres, but axes.

'Down with 'em, chop 'em down, my brave boys,' shouted Trafford, puffing and blowing through his fat, inflamed cheeks, while others, recognising known troublemakers, or hands they had a personal grudge against, went for them particularly, so the line quickly fell apart.

They had been drinking frumenty for two hours and most were drunk and their horses were quite unused to crowds of this sort.

Their sabres were plied to hew a way through naked upheld hands, and defenceless heads; and then chopped limbs, and wound-gaping skulls were seen; women, white-vested maids and tender youths were indiscriminately sabred or trampled. Among the first to go were a dark-haired mother and her child, a three-year-old, and she holding up an arm in front of the brat to save him.

They cut, they wounded, they sliced and they slashed, and occasionally they killed, but in no way were they achieving what they were there for. Isolated in ones or small groups of five or six they caused eddies and spaces and whirlpools in the crowd, but they themselves were in front of the main exits from the Fields, which were either side of St Peter's. The others were between Mr Buxton's house and the mill Charlie was in, and here the crowd was thickest and least willing to go, for it was also nearest the hustings.

Mr Hulton watched it all for ten minutes or so, as the Yeomanry got more and more split up and in one or two cases even a trooper was pulled off his horse and disappeared beneath the sea of bodies and feet around him. But at last he sent for Lieutenant Colonel L'Estrange, commander of the regular military, scribbled a note and handed it to him. Clear the Field and arrest the platform party, signed Wm Hulton.

'Good God, sir,' added the magistrate, 'don't you see they are attacking the Yeomanry? Disperse them!'

171

Four squadrons, six hundred troopers, of the 15th Hussars, breast-plated and wearing the high plumed helmets of gleaming brass designed by Prinny himself, well mounted on proper chargers, not hunters and farmers' nags, in perfect order, trotted in from the other side of the church and headed straight for the hustings.

This was a more serious business altogether. The people were now in a state of utter rout and confusion. The panic was heightened by the rattle of some artillery, two six-pounder guns, crossing the square, shrieks were heard in all directions and as the crowd dispersed the effects of the conflict became visible. Within ten minutes the Field was an open and almost deserted place. The hustings remained with a few flag staves erect and a torn and gashed banner or two drooping. While over the whole Field were strewn caps, bonnets, shawls and shoes, trampled, torn and bloody. Several mounds of human beings remained where they had fallen, crushed down and smothered. Some of these were still groaning – others with staring eyes were gasping for breath and others would never breathe more. All was silent save those low sounds . . .

Charlie pauses, wipes his mouth.

'How many were killed, Mr Cargill?' he asks.

'Eleven.'

Charlie offers a high scoffing laugh.

'That was the number of dead found on the Field,' Cargill asserts stoutly. 'And four hundred wounded.'

Again the laugh. 'Mr Cargill, you knows as well as I do, official figures always lie. How many were carried away by grieving families? How many died later, five minutes later in an alley, three weeks later of gangrene? And how many did the troopers pursue down the alleys and out into the countryside, murdering as they went? I was at Waterloo, Mr Cargill. And before that . . . well, never mind. But I can tell you this. Most men who die of a battle, die slowly and later.'

A pause while both ruminate on this observation, and the

madman down the corridor continues his monotonous assertion that the jury was fixed. Then Cargill looks up.

'And you, Charlie? What happened to you?'

Me? Yours truly? I watched, transfixed for a time with horror at what my single shot had brought about, and yet I felt a sort of exaltation, a sort of god-like power, arising from what I had done. But I was mistaken as I was about to find out. Let me tell you.

Some five or six of the crowd, perhaps reckoning some of the Yeomanry or the Hussars themselves had fixed on them personally, broke into the mill from below, reckoning no doubt the horses would not follow them in and up the stairs. Hearing their approach I moved to the second flight which was made of iron with pierced steps and up I went, as quietly as I could, ducking beneath the belt drives as I went.

I found myself in a second machine room, but the looms this time smaller, more narrow, perhaps designed for narrower widths of finer cotton with a patterned weave. To tell you the truth I wasn't that interested. And there at the end of this long room I found one of the nastiest sights, and I've seen a few, I've ever come across.

Two bodies very slowly turned in the draught from an open window, hung by the necks from a beam above them. Their hands were tied, and both had had their throats cut before they were hanged. I knew them, and not by their red coats and their brass badges, but because they were familiar to me from long ago when they had been my mates . . . Patrick Coffey and Kevin Nolan, no less.

I froze, almost in a catatonic trance, for I do not know how long, but I heard the fugitives below eventually making their way down the first flight of wooden stairs. Then I moved towards those old mates of mine, and my foot kicked an object on the floor. A leather wallet, one of those that fold over like a book, the leather soft and worn. I picked it up. A footstep behind me.

173

'Mine, I think, Charlie. Give it to me. There's a good chap.'

Guy de Bourgeois, of course . . .

'Why "of course"?' Cargill interjects with what sounds like genuine bewilderment.

'Do you not see?'

'I cannot say I do.'

'Could Patrick and Kev be trusted not to blab about their part in the business? Of course not. They had to go. Two Irish soldiers, sent by the authorities to be a picket in the mill, found by a group of rioters who murdered them and used one of their pieces in an attempt to assassinate the Chief Magistrate, that's how the bodies could be explained if necessary. You see, Mr Cargill, what I then perceived was how I was not the god in the machine, but a mere cog, a minor part in a system such as drove those looms about me, not even a tool but a minor moving part, easily replaced and counting for nothing.'

'And this de Bourgeois?'

'He took his wallet, which he had dropped or had fallen out of his pocket, there must have been a struggle even though he had his bully boys about him, he took his wallet and went. And shortly after, I followed him. Back to London.'

'There was no mention of soldiers murdered or a shot fired in the reports and inquiries that followed.'

'Was there not, Mr Cargill? Was there not? Well, no doubt there was enough evidence to justify the reading of the Act and the arrest of Hunt and the others, without falling back on an episode that would have blown Mr de Bourgeois's and my own cover, had it come to court. The rule I learnt over the years in my occupation was that more was always planned than in the event was brought to bear, such was Mr Stafford's and Lord Sidmouth's desire to make every possibility of failure, safe.'

21

Minutes of the Cabinet Committees . . .

There are twenty-five folio volumes each of five hundred pages closely written in a tiny copperplate hand that varies minutely, but enough to show that several scribes were employed at different times all of whom strove to conform to standards regulating the layout of each entry as well as the style of calligraphy. Each is bound in cinnamon- (shit-?) coloured leather with the title stamped on the spine in tiny Roman capitals with dates, infilled with gold leaf.

Minutes of the National Safety Committee . . .
Minutes of the Committee Regulating Permanent Defence Requirements and Consequent Requisitions.
Minutes of the Committee Regulating Appointment and Recruitment.
Minutes of the Committee Responding to Secret Societies dedicated to Insurrection and Overthrow of the Crown . . .

That might do, Cargill thinks, and thumps the huge leather-bound volume on to the big table. A tiny puff of dust, musty with the smell of old leather. The binding creaks as he opens it. The pages are dry and brittle but this has not always been so – there are damp marks, grey and blotchy, spreading from the bottom outer corner, but diminishing towards the middle of the volume and finally disappearing. With a dull feeling of boredom, that is growing to the physical presence of a headache, Cargill slips his thumb under the last page which bears the mark and lets the pages flicker down towards the first where the stain is largest. It puts him in mind of a gadget, a toy, Emily, to whom he was then engaged, was much fascinated with eighteen months earlier in the Great Exhibition. There the release of sheets was achieved by mechanical means but the effect is the same. On that occasion, through the optical illusion, a sailor danced a hornpipe. This time the stain simply grows and grows.

But it isn't much use to him. Each entry records the name of the Secret Society, lists its members, and its specific aims, the committee's response to them and their considerations concerning further action.

Back to the three huge piles on the floor beside his chair, and the awareness that the weariness is increasing. A volume thinner than the others catches his attention and, because of its thinness, appeals; curiosity proves to be an antidote to ennui, and he heaves to one side the three volumes that are on top of it. A thought crosses his mind, prompted perhaps by recollection of the wonders housed in that vast glasshouse: it would be wonderful if someone could invent an engine that could search through huge masses of words, picking out and listing one particular word or item, listing where it occurred, a bit like a Concordance of the Bible, but . . . an engine, not a book, a search engine.

Minutes of an Ad-Hoc Committee. That's all. But the dates are from 1819 to 1820. Inside, the title page is more specific. In letters decorated with curls and arabesques showing a penmanship less dull than that he has so far perused, he reads these words: *An Informal Sub-committee to the Cabinet with the brief to*

*consider in the frankest and fullest way possible all possible steps
necessary to maintain the integrity of the State.* Then, in smaller
letters: *The understanding is that these minutes will be used for reference only and only with the permission of the highest authority. It
is understood that speculative and original thought may lead to statements that could be construed as prejudicial and contrary to strict
understanding of law and custom: freedom to resort to such projec-
tions and considerations without in any way impugning those who
offer them is considered a prerequisite for arriving at radical solutions
to radical problems.*

Cargill turns the creaking pages at random.

*Minutes of a meeting held at the Home Office on the fifteenth day of
March, in the year of Our Lord eighteen nineteen. Present: The
Prime Minister, the Secretary of State for Home Affairs, the Master-
General of Ordnance.*

The very three who had met not long before the Riot in St
Peter's Field, who had ignored Charlie's presence, taking him
for a flunkey. That, in fact, must have been a meeting, rather
than a tea party, of this Ad-Hoc Committee. Interest floods
back, headache recedes again, though a desire for a searching
engine remains. Cargill turns back to the beginning, page after
page, skimming them as he goes, his eyes hunting for a word, a
name that will show he is on the right track. Thistlewood, yes,
it occurs often. Also Watson, Carlile, Davidson, Brunt, and
then Lord Harrowby. He is on the right track. And then at last,
yes, Boylan, Charles. He flips back to the date when what
already looks like a sequence of meetings dedicated to the same
subject begins ...

*The Twenty-Third day of September, Y of G Eighteen-Nineteen.
The meeting convened in Room 101 in the Home Office at eleven
o'clock in the morning.
Present: The Prime Minister, the Secretary of State for Home
Affairs, the Master-General of Ordnance.*

Agendum: Consideration of the events following those that occurred on 16 August in St Peter's Fields, Manchester.

His Grace the Master-General of Ordnance requested that the meeting should not refer to the events in St Peter's Fields as 'Peterloo'. Their Lordships concurred with his request . . .

'Peterloo! They're calling it Peterloo. Damned newspapers! It raises a stupid muddle on a small scale to the level of what was, I am the first to admit it, something of a muddle, but on a very large scale indeed with very important consequences.' His grace swung a booted foot across the knee of his other leg. 'Can we not think of something else to call it?'

'Difficult,' the Home Secretary replied. 'You see, the other term is "massacre", specifically the Manchester Massacre, which you may find even more offensive.'

'Indeed I shall. How can the deaths of less than a dozen out of eighty thousand be correctly styled a massacre? But I tell you what, Sidmouth. They'll impeach you for it. Mark my words. Ha!' And the big laugh racketed around the room.

'Arthur might be right, Henry,' Lord Liverpool interjected. 'And after what happened the other day, you won't be able to claim that your intention was to deter further riots on a similar scale. But the more important thing about it is that it shows that your plan to drive a wedge between the parliamentary reformers and the revolutionaries is looking a little – how shall I put this without prompting you to a resignation I will not accept – is looking a little sick.'

'You mean, Prime Minister, because three hundred thousand turned out here in London to welcome Hunt and the reformers' return from the North? And it was all organised by the revolutionaries, by the Watsons and that fool Thistlewood? You think that betokens an alliance? I tell you what it really betokens, it betokens something that has always been the case, and always will be. That any movement for change will always be spearheaded by those with the greatest tendency towards militancy.

They will be the organisers, at meetings and riots the most vocal and violent, and once the vast majority sees they have served their purpose to the general cause and from that point can only serve to bring it into disrepute with the vast body of middling, middle-of-the-road Englishmen, they will be thrown out, discarded. Wat Tyler was the first, then came the Levellers and the Diggers during the Civil War, the Baptists and all their crew in the 1680s, the Jacobins thirty years ago, and the Luddites the day before yesterday. I'm talking of England, not the Continent you understand . . . Your average Englishman, be he never so liberal, dislikes militants.'

'You're talking damned good sense, Henry, if I may say so, so don't get in a huff about it,' his grace interjected. 'Robert likes to tease, don't you, Liverpool? And I was joking when I talked of impeachment.'

'Thank you, Arthur. You're very kind. Thank you.' Somewhat mollified, Sidmouth continued his apologia. 'Anyway. The other thing about them is they can never agree among themselves and always tear themselves apart. Already Stafford, who has men at their meetings as you would expect, reports that the Watsons are at loggerheads with Thistlewood.'

'Over what?'

'Thistlewood believed the huge turnout would develop into an insurrection. It didn't. So he's talking up assassination—'

'The devil he is!'

'Whereas Watson says the only way revolution will come is when twenty thousand march on the Tower, the Bank or Parliament, instead of just listening to ranters like Hunt. You know, storm the Bastille, that sort of thing.'

'And Hunt himself. What's he up to?'

'Apparently he's in a state of confusion. Shock. Peterloo . . . sorry, St Peter's Field, quite overwhelmed him. On one side he takes it as a matter for celebration almost, with himself as the chief figure of honour. He is immensely flattered by the fact so many turned up, flattered even that we thought it worth a few lives to put a stop to it. On the other hand, he's frightened,

179

frightened of revolution and revolutionary talk. He's on bail on charges of sedition and he doesn't want to be identified with the revolutionaries when it comes to trial. As a leader he has two failings. One. He enjoys being the leader, the hero, but fears to make decisions because, two, he is terrified that he might hang.'

'So what do you want us to do right now?'

'Well, Arthur, not a lot. We need the Six Acts but I'm not going to ask Robert to call back Parliament before its due date in November. With Peter . . .'s Fields still uppermost in what pass for many people's minds, there'll be opposition. Sir Francis Burdett and the other radicals will have their say in the Commons as well as in the press and keep things spinning longer than need be. No. What I want you to do, so long as Liverpool agrees, is simply keep troops on hand loyal enough to do their duty in case we need them, but in barracks, and sensibly distributed, and meanwhile we sit it out, at least until Parliament reassembles, but knowing we can call on you if necessary—'

'You know very well that lies outside the scope of my duties as Master-General of Ordnance. HRH Freddie is still Commander-in-Chief . . .'

'Old York? He'll march them up and he'll march them down and he'll damn well march 'em where you tell him to. Right, next. Sidmouth? Any particular point you'd like to raise before we adjourn?'

'The success of our endeavours, Prime Minister, depends entirely on intelligence, knowing what the beggars are up to. Arthur will agree with me—'

'Certainly. Kicked the French out of Portugal and Spain because I always knew what was happening on the other side of the hill. Broke their ciphers, read everything they were saying to each other, that's how I caught Marmont at Salamanca. Damn near lost the Waterloo campaign because I didn't know Boney was going for us first. We thought he was going for the Austrians in the south until the day before the first battles . . . I say, I'm not boring you, am I?'

180

'Not at all, Arthur. But wandering a touch further from the point at issue than . . . never mind. Where were we? Yes. So you'll both agree with me that our intelligence gathering should be properly funded.'

'Of course, dear fellow. Of course.'

'Understood,' Liverpool chipped in. 'As soon as Parliament's back we'll vote an increase to the Secret Fund—'

'No. I need it now. It's not just a question of paying our . . . informers, and we have nearly two hundred now, it's a matter too of bribes, of buying our way in . . .'

'Don't worry, Sidmouth. I'll get Chancellor Eldon to sign a chit *ante diem*. Just give us a number and we'll double it. Now. Who's for a second cuppa? Arthur, will you do the honours? Home Secretary, I take it you are after all continuing with your overall strategy of driving a wedge between the reformers and the revolutionaries? I'd be obliged if you'd tell me what your next step will be in that direction.'

'First, Prime Minister, I've had contradictory reports from the North. Strikes, riots, marches, some say they are for revolution, others assert parliamentary reform is the main object, the cure-all for their ills. Stafford is sending his best men up there to get the measure of what is really going on. Here in London, I aim to exploit the divisions between the Watsons and that oaf Thistlewood—'

'Sounds fine, Home Secretary. Thank you, Arthur. Tell me, you and your brother are old India hands, what do you think of this story that some botanist fellow has found wild tea plants growing in Assam? If that comes to something it'll do us a world of good, get the Chinks off our backs, what?'

The meeting closed with some animadversions on the possibilities of tea production in the north-eastern highlands of India, which were not germane to the workings of the committee.

Marvelling that a commodity now so universally preferred for flavour strength and cheapness had been unknown a mere thirty years earlier, namely Indian tea, Cargill closes the volume, having first marked the place with a slip of paper, a corner of a bill he finds in his coat pocket. Then he sits back and muses for a moment on what he has read, chewing the end of his pen as he does so. Which of these enterprises was Charlie involved in: the disturbances in the North or the arrest and prosecution of Arthur Thistlewood?

The answer, of course, is both. Or so he will claim. And at the back of Cargill's mind the question nags, prompted by that slip of paper, a monthly account requesting prompt payment of fairly trifling sums; the total came to seven shillings and six-pence, presented with thanks for your valued custom. Why is his wife resorting to the local Apothecary, Pharmacist and Chemist residing at twenty-one Clapham Common Road South, Clapham Village, at least twice a week to buy items that appear to be cheap but are not identified? But before the significance of this can be examined further, he is interrupted by the arrival of a package brought by special messenger from Pentonville prison.

He breaks the sealing wax on the knots that bind it, undoes the string, for Cargill is careful about such things, and folds back the waxed paper wrapping. Fifty sheets of quarto, each covered with Charlie's spidery writing, lie in the nest he has exposed. Here is good news then – Boylan has taken up his pen and at least for a few days Cargill will not have to go and listen to him and then laboriously write up what he has heard. It is not just a matter of the time consumed, it is the fact that he has now developed such an aversion to the place that even the thought of Pentonville produces feelings of nausea.

22

In late September of 1819, Mr de Bourgeois, he of the saturnine appearance and manner, came to my lodgings in Lambeth. This was a time when I could claim to be living in a style that befitted, or nearly so, my antecedents. I was tolerably well off. Mr Stafford paid me a regular stipend to which were added emolumentary one-offs for each mission satisfactorily accomplished. These payments I supplemented by giving lessons in Spanish and French to the upwardly aspiring youth, both male and female, of the neighbourhood. All sought to get into commerce or banking and some facility with these languages was deemed a useful prerequisite. Consequently I was able to rent, and furnish according to my personal taste, the two first-floor rooms in a new terrace house just south of Lambeth Palace and close to the Vauxhall Gardens. All of course now demolished, apart from that squat brick palace, to make way for the Waterloo, Clapham and Woking railway line.

My landlady, a stout personage of Irish extraction whose husband was foreman to the speculative builder who had put up the street on land leased, I believe, from the Duke of

Westminster, or possibly the see of Canterbury, ushered my caller up the stairs.

He paused on the threshold, looked down at me and then over my head.

'Doin' well, aint you, Boylan?'

I took his high dented hat and his long black coat and slung them over the back of a chair. As I did so Mr Bourgeois took himself off to the fireplace and, lifting his threadbare tails, warmed his bum over the glowing coals.

'Not badly, Mr Bourgeois,' I concurred. 'And what can I do for you?'

'Nothing for me unless you can persuade your good lady to bring up a dish of bohea. But I have a commission for you from Mr Stafford.'

This was no surprise. A shock, however, was on the way.

'You are to go up north. Birmingham, Sheffield, Manchester, Newcastle, in your usual guise as a radical engraver, and mingle with hoi polloi in the ways in which you are so adept.'

'With any particular purpose in view?' I asked, mindful of Licence 003.

'Not as yet. But there is very considerable unrest in the wake of Peterloo, and our masters are in a state of some anxiety regarding the direction it is taking. Reform or revolution appears to be the question. You are, as I say, to mingle, and then send Mr Stafford reports as to the mood and tenor of the general populace, which way its disaffection tends and so forth. Are you with me?'

'I think so.'

'I doubt it.' He did not exactly sneer but came near it. 'The fact of the matter is, and I'll be direct with you because we know you to be an intelligent fellow, we are already advised that reform is the word. For every Jacobin or Spencean there are a hundred reformers. But that is not the picture our masters wish to present to Parliament when it reassembles in six weeks' time. It is important that evidence should be available such as will ensure the passing in the Commons of certain Acts

184

designed to postpone the threat of reform in the name of suppressing or preventing revolution. Now are you with me?'

Well of course I was. Liverpool's government, and no doubt many to follow over the centuries, used and will use occasional terroristical events to promulgate laws that are repressive in a general way. But now came the rub.

'I'll pack my bag and engraver's gear immediately,' I cried, 'and get myself aboard the mail coach for . . . where did you say? . . . Birmingham, right away.'

'Well no, Boylan, actually . . . not. To give credibility and verisimilitude to your, um, cover as a humble perambulatory artisan or journeyman, you'll walk.'

'Walk! To Newcastle?'

'Via Birmingham, Sheffield and so forth. There we are then. If you're sure no pot of tea can be got for me, I'll be on my way.' And he shrugged himself back into his coat and I handed him his hat.

'Ta-ta, Boylan. Be good.'

Ta-ta? I understand that the term, signifying 'goodbye', is now common among children and the more playful of adults, but it was the first time I had heard it.

I did not, Mr Cargill, make the mistake of trying to buck Stafford's instructions. Spymasters who know their job, and Mr Stafford certainly knew his, employ spies to spy on the spies – indeed I had already done this sort of work for him, and on one occasion had used my Spinks and Pottle to eradicate or rub out a poor fellow, a tinker, who really was a tinker, and not a gentleman pretending to be a tinker, in short a doubling back sort of a cove, whose chiefest allegiance was not to his pocket, which Mr Stafford kept reasonably full, but to his mates in the trade.

Picture me then on a blustery day toiling up over Hampstead Heath, pausing only to glance over the shoulder of a dauber who was endeavouring to capture the fleeting shapes of the clouds above the city below, his brush alternately swirling and

stabbing at his easeled canvas in something approaching
dementia, for of course the clouds shifted and changed more
quickly than he could possibly keep up with them.

'The task you have undertaken,' I murmured, 'would seem to
be Sisyphean,' as he flung aside a spoiled canvas and dragged
another out of the capacious bag that lay at his feet.

'Fuck off,' he replied, but not unamicably.

'That cloud,' I continued, 'is almost in the shape of a camel.'
He painted on.

'Yet now it looks like a weasel.'

'Or a whale?' he suggested.

'Very like a whale,' I replied.

'You know your Hamlet,' he said.

'Oh am I?' quipped I.

At which he laughed and added: 'Ay, as sure as I am Johnny
Constable.'

Which was well put since I never saw a man less like a constable in my life. Though, of course, he may well have been a
police spy.

I toiled on – remember, I was lugging my bag of engraving
tricks as well as a change of clothing, and a few other odds and
ends – past Lord Mansfield's country retreat at Ken Wood,
stopping for a cheese Sandwich and a pint of small at the
Spaniards Inn. Then it was downhill into Hertfordshire,
through market gardens, deserted villages, and common land
enclosed and given over to wheat and pasturage. And at about
three o'clock, just as I was despairing of reaching St Alban's, my
goal for that first night, a most wonderful thing happened.

I was descending a gentle slope and cursing to myself none
too gently for a mail coach had just thundered by, its postilion
tooting on his squealing horn to get me out of their way, its iron-
shod wheels slicing a muddy puddle and splattering my trousers,
when I heard a quite different noise approaching, also from
behind. Wheels, yes, but turning at a civilised rate. Hooves,
but those of a pair of shaggy ponies, blinkered and moving at a
leisurely trot, and music too, but not the peremptory squeal of

brass but the merry trilling of a flute. There was singing too: 'Oh don't deceive me, Oh never leave me, How could you use a poor maiden so', or some such maudlin ditty of maidenhood betrayed.

Behind the ponies a trap, a trap indeed for it contained, I was going to say a bevy, but how many do you need to make a bevy? of girls, though probably not maids, five in all, such as might trap any unwary male. At first glance I had an impression of muslin high-waisted, big bonnets, and posies of flowers, but this was wishful illusion. They were dressed in scraps and rags – oh yes, there were muslins and chiffons there, and mutton-chop sleeves, but such as had been pulled from waste bins or bartered for at market stalls, and real rags as of sacking and jute and so forth as well. Posies yes, but of such flowers as grow by the wayside rather than in the glasshouses of the rich. Nevertheless, they made a cheering sight as they passed me, waving and chaffing at my stature and so forth, which I'm used to, and I was already smiling as the tailgate drew level and went by.

And there she was. Perched on the back, her legs bare almost to the knee, her reddish-blonde hair blowing about her face, her fingers idly twining together a daisy chain, wearing a scarlet shawl over a royal blue dress far too big for her and still with a scrap or two of lace at the neck and the cuffs. 'Twas she recognised me rather than the other way about.

'Cha-arlie,' she hollered.

And . . . 'Magg-ie,' I shouted in reply, and stumbling I ran to catch up, slung my bag in beside her, and clambered aboard.

23

Even then, she could not have been more than twelve, thirteen at the most, but looked sixteen, an imposture she in part maintained by wearing the flame-coloured shawl low slung across her shoulders so it concealed the lack or small size of her bosom. And of course her eyes and mouth flirted as ever in the manner of a society miss (girls were far more forward in those days, Mr Cargill), and what her complexion lacked in fineness of texture was more than compensated for by the constellations of freckles, kisses of the sun, scattered across her cheeks. She budged up for me, my buckled shoes nudged her ankles above the pair of swinging fodder buckets that hung below us, she bussed my cheek and put her hand upon my thigh, above my knee, as if we were as close as any Darby and Joan.

Behind us the bevy chattered and carolled: 'Maggie's got a beau! Where did you find him Maggie, in a freak show or a circus? What's his name Maggie-May, Tom Thumb?' and so forth until she told them to stow it, it was no fault of mine I was hairy and small of stature, and I'd done her a great good turn three years back, getting her away from the monstrous Macpherson, so it was right and fair to do me a good turn now.

Then when a sort of silence prevailed apart from the clip-clop of the ponies' hooves and the rumble of the trap's wheels, she turned to me.

'So, Charlie, where are you going then?'

'North,' said I, 'and you?'

She frowned. 'Nottingham,' she said, 'for the Goose Fair. Is Nottingham north?'

'On the way,' said I.

'Then we'll take you there.'

This was a great boon, and were I shadowed or looked for by one of my colleagues, one of Stafford's crew, I felt it would not be held against me. Bumming a lift in a trap would not blow my cover, the way a paid-for window seat in the mail coach might have done.

Presently I asked Maggie-May what was the purpose of this trip to Nottingham, she and her companions were making. Not, I presumed, to buy geese.

'Why, to make money, of course.'

'But how?'

'By buzzing, dipping and finger-smithing. By angling and hooking. And if we have a bad day of that we'll do a bit of tail-trading, scrudging or rumping in the evening but waiting till all the johns are pissed so we never, never do the full charvering.'

By which I understood her to mean various forms of thieving and prostitution, though in the latter case cheating their customers of the complete works.

Her four companions were, severally, Kate, a tall thin brown-haired lass who spoke as if she were gentry and held the reins of the ponies and a long-lashed whip to the manner born; Jude or Judith, a girl with dark tresses, high cheekbones and a curved nose which suggested, as did her name, Hebrew origins; Tiger Lily, who had an oriental cast to her features; and Tess, a blonde of white gold with a skin like peaches and cream. The trap was really more a small cart than a trap and quite capacious, with an assortment of carpetbags and the like, and a couple of bolster-shaped bundles wrapped in coarse hessian

189

bound with a collaboration of string and leather straps. As soon as we reached the next appreciable rise it was all out bar Kate and we walked, occasionally helping the ponies, a chestnut and a pure white grey, whose grandiose names were Copenhagen and Marengo, by pushing.

Meanwhile, Jude, resting her chin on my shoulder, added to what Maggie had said.

'At fairs we also do tableaux such as Titania and her court and the death of Cleopatra. That sort of thing. We have a tent—'

'Well, more a sort of booth,' Maggie interrupted . . .

We reached St Alban's at nightfall and found lodging in an inn in the market place overlooking the Eleanor Cross. The girls shared two rooms above the stables and I slept in the trap, an arrangement that pleased them since they lived in terror it would be stolen with Copenhagen and Marengo, and one or two of them usually spent a chilly and fearful night in it. But first I watched them exercise their various talents and skills on the other travellers. Their proceedings really were most unfair for their winsome charms and flirtatious ways left boys and men alike exceedingly vulnerable and by the end of the evening, when we all retired to one of the two rooms they had taken, there were two purses, three handkerchiefs and a gold watch, all of which they reckoned would fetch a round ten guineas at the pop shop in Stony Stratford, for it was their practice never to sell booty in the town where it was taken.

And so we proceeded, following in reverse the melancholy trail of King Edward's mortal queen, only leaving the route at Grantham where Tess nearly had us all locked up. Having been caught angling in a grocer's shop by the sharp-nosed daughter of the proprietor, a severe man, a Wesleyan lay preacher, she attempted to seduce the father by wheedling her fingers into his breeches while laying her head upon his chest and sobbing for forgiveness. Had not the needle-eyed daughter been present I think she might have got away with it.

*

But long before Grantham, probably on the way out of Dunstable as I recall it, I asked them where they had got the ponies and the cart from, guessing that, whatever else, they were not paid for. But here I was in part wrong. It seemed that Kate Bramshaw really was gentry, and the ward of a Squire Easton, her maternal uncle, her father having been killed at Waterloo and her mother of wasting away in consequence, who had a substantial holding in Kent not far from Sissinghurst. Kate's fortune, which she could not enter into until she was twenty-one, was very considerable, being land that marched with her uncle's and fifty thousand pounds in the Consolidated Funds and such like, all of which would pass to the Eastons if she died before achieving her majority.

I was not then surprised to learn that the Eastons, father and son, mured her up in the top room of a towered folly overlooking a lake with bulrushes and weeping willows, and surrounded by elms, where they left her to starve to death, for such is the stuff of so many novels it must occasionally happen in real life too.

Now the top boughs of these elm trees provided the foundations of a rookery of some twenty nests or more. Imagine then Kate's joy, when on the third day of her incarceration she was roused by the hideous cackling of the crows to look out of her window and saw, a bare six feet from her, the face of Maggie, with Jude behind her, peering back. As hungry, almost, as Kate, they had climbed the elm nearest to the tower with the aim of robbing the rooks of their eggs.

Squire Easton had left the key to the chamber, the cell, on a hook just inside the ground-level door. Within twenty minutes the three girls had rescued Copenhagen and Marengo, at that time going under the names of Nuts and May, who were also close to being starved to death as being of no use on a farm, and harnessed them to the pony cart that was in a shed next to the stable. Within an hour they were trundling up the London pike towards Tunbridge Wells. It was Kate's purpose now to

191

remain on the move for the six and a half years that still separated her from her inheritance.

After a month or so on the road they joined a circus where they met up with Tess and Tiger Lily. Tess's father managed a small troupe of bareback riders and knew horses. He was pleased to take on the ponies and used them in a performance in which two dwarfs re-enacted a burlesque of the battle of Waterloo, hence the new names given to their steeds. Tiger Lily's father, however, was a Chinese, and used to perform magic tricks in the guise of an oriental wizard, tricks that involved the use of fire and gunpowder, such as fire-eating, juggling with flaming torches and so forth. He was also a drunk, and contrived to blow up a keg of gunpowder during a tented performance at the Whit Fair on Hampstead Heath. He died in the blaze, as did several of the audience, the magistrates moved in and arrested all but the children, who decamped . . . with the trap and ponies . . .

At this point Cargill breaks off, after leafing forwards through the seven or eight pages which took the equipage the rest of the way to Nottingham interspersed with tangential accounts of sundry adventures enjoyed by the infamous five in the past. Why has Charlie put in all this stuff? Is it to delay revelations that shamed him? A desire to make a full life story out of his account, rather than simply sticking to what is germane to Cargill's inquiry? Or, horrid thought this, is it in code??? Whatever, right now he can't be bothered with it.

And so to Nottingham, which we reached on the last day of September, the day before the Goose Fair officially opened, the road through Radcliffe and along the bank of the Trent already full, and indeed blocked, so we were reduced to the pace of a goose. Mr Cargill, can you imagine the scene? A thousand white backs separated into squadrons numbered in tens and hundreds, a thousand long necks with beady eyes and yellow darting beaks, a hissing noise magnified to the volume of, yes, yet again, the thunder of surf on a rocky shore, the slap,

slap, slap of all those webbed feet, the yapping and snarling of dogs, much like sheepdogs or collies, the shouting and cussing of owners trying to keep their flocks separate, and, just about worst of all, worse than the bedlam and the frustrating tardiness of our progress, the slimy brown and dark green excrement underfoot, rendering footholds precarious and through which one slithered and waltzed much as if one was wading in half-frozen slush. And the smell! And this was only one corps or division of the army that was descending on the town by all the roads to the east and north that led out of the fens of Lincolnshire.

Fortunately this host was quartered a short distance from the town centre in parkland and fields where pens had been set up for the purpose. We pushed on through streets and alleys still crammed but with people now, and all heading towards the market square which is, by repute, the largest in the land, shaped like a wineskin or alchemist's retort with a long slanting neck. It was already packed with stallholders and crowds of holiday-makers, for these were not only people who had come to buy or sell geese, but working people, farm labourers, hewers of coal, weavers, spinners, boot-makers and lace-makers and so forth, who had walked in from upwards of twenty miles around, to spend a few pennies at the biggest fair in that country, get drunk, and even pick up a wife or husband.

Yes indeed, for one of the first stalls we passed was like a hustings on which men were selling their wives and daughters by auction as freely as blackamoor slaves were sold in Kingston market, more freely, since in this case most of the women were happy to go along with the commerce in order to escape men who would do anything to buy drink and keep out of work.

Do I really want to read all this? thinks Cargill again, and skips through another half-page or so to . . .

There was even a shadow puppet show which caught a good throng of radical-looking types since it was showing *The*

Lamentable Slaying of Harold, The Last English King, and the Horrid Imposition of the Norman Yoke under which all true-born Englishmen have laboured and starved . . . When I get the chance, I thought, I'll be back here and follow the likelier personages to whatever snug or bar they plot and gossip in.

Perhaps the biggest attraction of all was not in the square at all, though its waggons, two huge closed-in box-like affairs, *pantechnicons* is the new word for them, each pulled by a team of four shire horses, were parked outside the Corn Exchange and added much to the general congestion. The lettering on the sides read *Madame Tussaud's Waxworks, Meet the famous face to face, patronised by Royalty and the Greatest in the Land, See the guillotine fall on Robespierre and Marat mudredered* (sic) *in his Bath; the Death of Nelson, and the Iron Duke victorious at Waterloo.* A crew of men in blue coats with gold buttons were unloading the figures, wrapped in cotton shrouds, always holding them upright, one to one, so they looked as if they were dancing up the steps with ghosts. In a sense they were.

'We'd better set up our booth directly,' Tess, who was walking next to the trap and holding on to its side, fluted, for her voice resembled her instrument, as loud as she could above the general bedlam that surrounded us, 'while we can still find a space for it.'

'No,' cried Jude, who was sitting in the back and running a heavy comb through her long black tresses, an occupation she indulged in often since it allowed her to arch her back and thrust up a bosom of which she was vain, for it already gave promise of becoming a formidable embonpoint, 'let's find a room and stabling first.'

I doubted this would be possible with so many strangers jostling around us, but was soon proved wrong since, along with boasting the largest market square, Nottingham also provided space for more inns and ale houses than I have ever seen anywhere else. We tried fifteen before finding accommodation that suited us, which may seem a lot, but it left, I understood later, a hundred and thirty-five we had not tried. Every alley corner on the square had its boozer, and there were at least five or six in every side street and most offered a room or two and a small yard, if not actual stabling. We ended up at the top end of the square where it narrows into Angel Row on the one side and Long Row on the other. Long Row was a sight to see, for these were rich merchants' houses and places of business and had climbed storey by storey to scrape the sky at seven floors high. The overhangs came out over the street and were supported on brick pillars that made a pleasant arcade.

Our inn, the Bell, was on a corner of Angel Row, and one of the oldest, largest, and I daresay most expensive, but I had already discovered that Kate had not left behind in Sissinghurst the tastes of the gentry, and always chose a place for us to stay that was comfortable and boasted a respectable clientele. As she said: she had four girls in her charge, all about twelve to fourteen years old, and she owed it to them to give them safe lodging. She could make herself seem twenty, and when, on occasion, she put on her grandest airs, innkeepers and the like jumped to do her bidding, this despite the fact that the other four were dressed in cast-offs and even rags. An added advantage was that, were they pursued, accused of filching, dipping or whatever, their persecutors usually conceded their error when faced with the best hostelry in town.

All in all and never mind the fair-time crowds, I was beginning to realise that Nottingham is a grand place, especially in contrast to the raw new squalor of Manchester.

24

We left Copenhagen and Marengo lodged in a stable next to a big shire horse, a grey, whose owner, a farmer all the way from Newark, was already boozing himself stupid on Burton ale. Once the girls had established themselves in one large room on the second floor of the Bell, but at the back, overlooking the L-shaped yard, we manhandled the trap back into the crowd. We tried to find a pitch in the square itself but this soon proved impossible, and so, on the advice of a helpful porter, we retraced our steps back past the Bell, up Bar Gate and at the top, just where it became the Derby Road, found another smaller square not yet full where there was room for us.

Here the girls arranged a tiny stage out of the trap, enclosed in a hessian tent on poles and with ropes, leaving a space where twenty could stand at a time and view the tableaux they mounted. Next, a score of onlookers were admitted, at one penny a person and a halfpenny for children in arms, to be faced with a screen painted with flowers and birds. When all were in, the screen was removed to reveal Titania with her fairies about her, and they sang a lullaby, and she went to sleep. Back came the screen and behind it Kate, who was Titania, rerobed herself

196

and browned up her face to a rich copper colour, changed her silver crown for a gold one, and so forth, then the screen opened again. This time we had Cleopatra with her three maids about her, fastening the asps to her breastbone above the hem of the imitation cloth of gold wrap she had put round her. Then some lines from the Bard of the We-shall-not-look-upon-her-like-again nature, and Good night sweet husband, before she died.

Again the screen and this time the grand finale ... Kate had now deepened her hue yet further, and was as black as a blackamoor, and even more gorgeously dressed in gold crusted with coloured glass and bits of broken mirror and all sorts, and this time she was The Arrival of the Queen of Sheba, enhanced by Tess playing the music of the late Mr Handel on her flute while the others beat tam-tams and shook tam-bourines in time.

Then it was a ten-minute break while the first onlookers were chased out and the next lot ushered in. This time Kate began with Sheba, cleaned up through Cleopatra, to be silvery white again for Titania. And thus, through the afternoon and into evening and night, when lamps and candles added a deeper mystery to the Tableaux Vivantes, she continued from silver to copper to black to copper to silver to copper to black to copper to silver, and we all made our slighter changes in concert with her.

We? Yes I. At first my role was to take the money and usher one lot in and push the other lot out, but then Jude, I think, recalled Titania loved an ass, and what did they do but cast me in the role. Why not Copenhagen? I cried. But they would not be deflected from their course, for Maggie herself with Tiger Lily had been off to the Shambles behind the square and pro-cured the ears of a slaughtered bullock which they attached to my head. Then they made me strip off to my undergarment and oil my hairy pelt, and lo, I was an ass. Held and fondled by Kate you'd think I'd revel in the role, but she was a scrawny, boney thing and I wished she'd give Jude or Maggie the part.

And, what do you know, but in spite of this rough disguise, I was recognised, but not yet pricked out. It was under the lamps for the first time that I saw him, though I must have taken his penny as he came in, a young lad with a cloth hat and a red kerchief round his neck above a moleskin waistcoat, very fair hair, plump red cheeks and a button nose. He stared at me as if trying to put a name to the monster he saw, and I stared back, trying hard as I might to place where I'd known him before.

Come about half past seven and the night well in, the crowds began to thin, at least of women and kids who made up much of our audience, for women are always on the lookout for a touch of beauty and mystery in their lives and also love to have their infants instructed in the finer things of life, and Kate declared 'twas time to pack up.

We resumed our everyday clothes, packed all into the cart and pushed it back down Bar Gate to Angel Row and the Bell. But as we did so I could see down Beast Hill and across Market Square to Exchange and how there was still a crowd, of men mostly now, in front of the shadow theatre, still playing *Harold, The Last English King*. As soon as all was stowed I took my leave of the ladies and myself off to the show, catching the last performance, the very end, when, in shadow play, Harold took the arrow in his eye, and William the Bastard put on the crown, and that was the end of Merrie England, for as Tom Paine said, from then we have been ruled by naught but a band of *banditti*.

Not my opinion, Mr Cargill, but that of the simple country folk who moved off in a group, with me among them, to the George and Dragon in Long Row.

Well, I had picked the right place, for the rooms were crowded, mainly with working men, and the tapster's lads were kept busy passing out pint mugs of Burton ale and the kitchen too with platters of Collier's Pie, a flat flaky pastry filled with a layer of cheese and a layer of diced bacon. Well, I paid up my pennies, kept back from what I'd taken at our show, for I thought all in all I had earned them and knew Kate in her generosity would not grudge them, took my platter of pie and mug of ale to a corner under the stairs, and from this inconspicuous (I thought) cranny watched and listened.

Well, Mr Cargill, what I heard was rank sedition, treason and blasphemy, especially from those whose blackened faces and the preponderance of creaking heavy leather in their garments signified those of the coal-quarrying trade. I say quarrying because at that time no pits had been sunk in the area. But others there were, who from their talk I took to be cotton-spinners, weavers, croppers and stocking-knitters put out of work by the machines which, as had been the case in Manchester, were easily managed at far less cost by women and children. As the evening wore on they broke into song, maudlin chants for the most part though some with a touch of defiance in them such as:

> Chant no more your old rhymes about Robin Hood
> His feats I but little admire.
> I will sing the achievements of General Ludd,
> Now the hero of Nottinghamshire . . .

Apart from this there was not much in the way of exhortation to frame-breaking and destruction of other machinery, but plenty about the Manchester Massacre, praise for Orator Hunt and terrible proposals for what should be done to my Lords Liverpool and Sidmouth and even the erstwhile hero of the hour, his grace the Duke. But my feeling was that this was pub talk, and these men would stay quiet on ten shillings a week, even though it was their wives who were earning it. Perhaps, because it was their wives . . . In short, and as I have said before, a clear case of when this pub closes the revolution starts.

Then looking through the lamplight and the smoke I saw him again, the red-faced, snub-nosed, yellow-haired lout who had peered at me so close in my guise as the ass loved by the Queen of the Night and this time a name came to me, Bacon. Thomas? No, he had been in his forties. But Bob, his son? That was it. And for the first time it came properly home to me that where I was, that is Nottingham City, though this was the first time I had been inside the city walls, was but a couple of leagues from Pentrich and Eastwood. Bacon. One of Brandreth's lot. How had he escaped hanging or transportation? I knew not, and at that moment cared less. He was looking at me, and talking out of the side of his mouth to his neighbour, a giant in collier's leathers, and he knew I was looking at him.

I was in a quandary. What to do? Hail fellow well met? How have you been these three years? Or slink away on the qt while I had the chance? I began to wish I had Spinks and Pottle about me, but he was in my bag at the Bell, along with my engraver's kit.

Well, Mr Cargill, you know I have never been one to take bulls by the horns; my size is against heroics of that sort, whereas my physique does make it an easy matter to slip between men's thighs in a crowd and so disappear.

'Your pardon, sir, I'd be most obliged, sir,' and I was almost at the door when a hand, black and brown and the size of the end of the largest branch off the largest oak in Sherwood Forest, clamped on my collar and hoisted me right up so I banged my head on the ceiling.

'So, what have we here, me lads, but the snivelling hairy little runt who led us into the path of the Hussars three years back!' he bellowed in a voice that rumbled and grated like a load of coal tipped off the back of a collier's cart. I can't do the dialect, Mr Cargill, so you'll have to take that as read, but believe me it was as thick as the goose-shit on the streets outside.

'Ay,' cried another, 'and there are those as say it was he killed young Johnny Glew up at Squire Rolleston's house and not Jeremiah Brandreth at all. Watch out, Arnold, he don't have that little stinger of a pistol about him right now.'

'He'll not hurt me,' thundered Arnold, the collier, and bumped my head on the ceiling again. Then he dropped me, just like that, so my legs gave under me, and I was on the floor in the straw and beer spillings, half-eaten pies and dog-shit, for there were a couple of lurchers leashed in to a table near by. And then he kicked me with his heavy metal-bound clog, and a few others, those who could get near enough to do so, including Bob Bacon, and one of them got hold of the hair on the back of my head, which was long and wiry, and pushed my face into a dog-turd one of the lurchers had thoughtfully provided. Then he picked me up by the collar and the tails of my coat and chucked me out into the square.

I rolled a yard or so down the hill and came to rest at the feet of a pair of passing constables.

One looked at the other and said: 'Trouble in the George then, ol' Bill?'

'Ay,' answered ol' Bill. 'Best keep clear of it.'

And they continued on their way, slowly striding up the hill, swinging their sticks behind them.

It took me a moment or two to be sure the pains I was suffering from were not the torments of hell, but the results of the kicking I had received. I got myself to my knees and hands, was about to try standing when the door of the George and Dragon opened again, throwing light across the slimy cobbles, and I heard voices of the men that filled the gap.

'You let him go, Arnie? You let the fucker go? The man who killed Johnny Glew and brought about the hanging of Jeremiah and Ludlam? They cut their heads off you know. We should do the same. There's cleavers as'll do round the corner in the Shambles. Aye, and a meat hook we could hang him on . . .' And so forth, not just the one man speaking but three or four, severally and in turn.

They'd find me, I knew it. I had to run for it. Downhill across the Square to Angel Row and the Bell. Could I do it? I'd bloody have to. Fear overrode the pain. I got up, but bent double, my back wouldn't straighten, and scampered and slithered away. They saw me, of course, but I thought I'd get across ahead of them with the twenty-yard start I had. But one of them at least seemed to know where I was headed for, Bob Bacon I reckon, since he'd seen me in the show with the girls, and scooted across the neck of the square to head me off. I swerved. My hunters likewise; Arnie went into a skid in the goose-shit and two others went arse over elbow over him. Steps loomed up in front of me and I realised I was on my hands and knees again, but somehow I scrambled up them and tumbled through a door still open and unlocked. I rolled over and over and straight into a big basket, the sort women going to market carry cabbages in, knocked it flying and smacked into the wooden frame structure that stood behind it.

'Twas not cabbages rolled out, tumbling and bouncing towards the door, but severed heads. The first in after me kicked one, then saw it by the lamp that still burned in the doorway, screamed, turned and took the full weight of his mate coming in behind him, smack, face to face and both fell outwards.

I was sitting with my back to the big timber-framed engine, and some vibration in everything going on set it off, and wheeeeh, clunk, down came the blade and took two inches off my hair, which I wore long, the hair on my head, I mean; it was the blade of Madame Guillotine did it.

I scuttled away, half bent double, half on my hands and knees, through a crowd of ghosts, sheeted figures, standing about the place, lit by the moon showing through a high row of arched windows, making for a low dais at the far end, and stumbled on its step. Clutching at the sheet of the figure in pride of place in the centre of the raised area, I came to rest a little beyond it, with the sheet wrapped round me. I looked up at the noblest face in Christendom, the high forehead beneath the fore and aft cocked hat, the piercing eyes, the lean face, the nose like the ram on the front of a quinquereme, his grace, done to the very life, the Duke of Wellington. I swooned.

I came to in the cold light of a grey morning, just twenty minutes before nine o'clock and the scheduled opening of Madame Tussaud's Waxworks Show. My shoulder was being roughly shaken by a constable, ol' Bill no less, who had done nothing to save me the night before. But it was the lantern-shaped, melancholic, ashen face of Mr de Bourgeois that looked down into mine.

'You're blown, Boylan,' he rasped. 'Fucking blown. You've come to Nottingham once too awfen.'

Like Robin Hood in the old ballad, I thought, and fell back into my swoon.

202

25

Minutes of an Ad-Hoc Committee.

Minutes of a meeting held at the Home Office on the tenth day of December, the Year of Grace, eighteen nineteen. Present: The Prime Minister, the Secretary of State for Home Affairs, the Master-General of Ordnance.

The Master-General of Ordnance spoke first, commenting on the apparent seriousness of events in the North during the previous six weeks.

'A near run thing, eh, Sidmouth? What? I'd say so. I quite thought we were in serious trouble a month ago.'

'So did I, Arthur, so did I.' It was Liverpool who got this in. Sidmouth remained silent, a pleased, almost smug little smile stretching his thin lips as he poked his way through the pile of loose papers he had in front of him.

'It was the arming that worried me. The taking up of arms. Pistols and pikes,' Liverpool continued.

'Pshaw! Nothing a whiff of grapeshot wouldn't have seen

off,' declared his grace, the Master-General of Ordnance, unwittingly echoing the technique for crowd control another Great Man had resorted to some twenty-five years earlier. 'But the numbers were impressive. Especially in Newcastle. A hundred thousand?'

'Rubbish,' murmured Sidmouth. 'Fifty at the most.'

'And they kept so cool, the newspapers said,' the Prime Minister continued. 'All in order, and disciplined, no drunkenness, no looting. If there'd been a Bastille, there would have been no stopping them.'

'There was, is, a castle. Used in part as the county gaol.'

'Whiff of grapeshot,' repeated his grace. The other two said nothing but kept their thoughts to themselves. After the reaction to Peterloo they knew the use of artillery against the mob really would have brought the house down about their ears, especially a mob that was behaving itself. Damnit, this wasn't Frogland.

'The fact of the matter is,' Sidmouth at last asserted, 'for the vast majority the bearing of such arms as they had were for defensive purposes. That's what they said, and most of our fellows who were there believed them. Pikes to keep at arm's length any more mounted Yeomanry the magistracy might have chosen to employ. And then there was the Armed Association of the Newcastle Church and King Party. With that lot of grocers and farmers strutting about with muskets on their shoulders, the working classes judged a pistol or two not to be out of order, and I can hardly blame them for that. When all's said and done it turned out as I said it would. Nine out of ten were radical reformers. The revolutionists may have organised, but the rank and file were reformers, not bent on revolution at all.'

'You're very sure of this.'

'I am, Arthur. Very sure. Stafford's people did a very thorough job. We had literally hundreds of reports and they all agreed as to the general mood. Horror, indignation on the surface over St Peter's Field; underlying fear, which is what I wanted, that we really would use the army if need be, and a fundamental belief in the English way of doing things, bit by bit, step by step, with reform of Parliament as the first step. Look, look at this. A report from Y. Amusing but typical. Y had got himself employed as agent and salesman to a smith, Naaman Carter, up in Manchester, who was making pike-heads that could be carried in the pocket and fitted when needed on to a stave. Here he is calling on Carter and his wife . . .' Sidmouth pulled on his half-frame spectacles, looked over them, cleared his throat. 'I won't attempt the northern dialect . . .

'"I found him and his wife fighting – I told him it was foolish to fight on the Sabbath-day, they had better adjourn it till Monday, when they might fight it out. The wife said, I shall not be beaten by you, I will have you put into the New Bayley for making Pikes – She said this, just as he was pushing and kicking her out of the door . . ." and so on, and so on. Mind you, one of Carter's customers is reported as saying, when he bought one of these blades, "This'll do the business for the Prince and every bugger of them" . . .' Sidmouth looked over his specs. 'I confess, gentlemen, that as far as Prinny is concerned a similar desire has crossed my mind once or twice.'

'Most amusing, I'm sure, Sidmouth.' His grace sounded a touch stuffy. He was noted for the exaggerated respect he had for the concept of royalty however corporeally manifested. Then the grin returned. 'Anything from that young rogue Boylan or Bosham or whatever name he's going under at the moment? His dispatches are usually amusing.'

'Very little. He was sent north by way of the Birmingham pike. However, he chose to ignore his control's instructions and went through Nottingham instead, where he was of course recognised, and his role in the Pentrich affair recalled. I am afraid he was given a quite severe kicking and beating.'

'But he recovered? I'm sure he did, for if ever a rogue was born to hang . . . Damnme. I do believe I once promised him a sixpence which I doubt he ever got. Never mind. Go on, Henry, what's next?'

'Well, Arthur, I think we're over the worst. For the time being anyway. Winter is settling in nicely and so long as the price of bread stays within the reach of a hardworking and thrifty man he'll not go out of doors north of the Trent except to work. With the Mob indoors it's the time of year when the revolutionists are left to fend for themselves, and they're at loggerheads with each other. The one I'm after is that fool Arthur Thistlewood—'

'Didn't he make a monkey out of you, a couple of years back? After the Spa Fields affair? As I remember it he bought tickets to America for himself and his family, and then when you dropped the case against him after that fool Castle had owned up to being one of yours, tried to sue you for the cost and called you out when you wouldn't cough up—'

'Really, Prime Minister, you can't imagine—'

'No indeed, Sidmouth, imagination is a faculty the fairies left off their list at my birth . . . But it argues a sense of mischief in the fellow, which some might find amusing. So?'

'My Lord, Thistlewood favours the use of assassination as a means towards revolution.'

'Does he, by Jove?' Liverpool remained cool, though interested.

'Then he's a fool!' the Duke exclaimed. 'We all know what a pistol ball can achieve. We'd still have poor Perceval on our hands instead of your lordship, if Perceval hadn't been shot and I suppose that is something to be grateful for. However, this Thistlewood would have to go through the entire peerage, their male offspring, the professional classes and the landed gentry before assassination achieved anything. None of us is so indispensable that we cannot be replaced by another.'

'Oh thank you, Arthur. I see you are determined to keep me in my place. Nevertheless,' the Prime Minister went on, 'forgive me if I do take the threat personally.'

'Me too,' added his Secretary of State for Home Affairs. 'And not because of what this clown did in the past but because I have no desire to take a bullet in my head from him. He has got it in for me, you know?'

'Infamy?' remarked the Duke, who, since Waterloo, had been a touch hard of hearing. 'What's infamy got to do with it?'

Sidmouth sighed, raised his voice. 'Anyway. Stafford and I intend to take him at his word and ensnare him in a trap of his own making. And he'll hang. And most people, and I mean most, including the reformers, will judge he gets his deserts. There is another angle to consider as well. A plot to assassinate the entire cabinet is what we are looking at and such a plot exposed will concentrate wonderfully the minds of the Commons when they meet to debate the Six Acts.'

'You're a cunning bastard, aint you, Sidmouth? I've always thought so.'

'Your grace is kind enough to say so. My only aims are to preserve the peace and give satisfaction.'

26

Mr de Bourgeois took me back to Lambeth in a cart and for ten days I was confined to St Thomas's hospital believed to have a lung punctured by a broken rib and a kidney ruptured by a kick. But either the diagnoses were wrong, the injuries more slight than supposed, or my constitution stronger than my frame would suggest for I soon felt able to discharge myself from the company of the old, dying and nearly dead and have myself brought back to my former lodgings.

For a time it seemed these might now prove to be beyond my means for Mr de Bourgeois, possibly acting on the instructions of Mr Stafford, but equally possibly pocketing what was due to me himself, announced that I would receive no bonus above my usual meagre stipend for my recent adventures since, by going to Nottingham instead of heading north through Birmingham and Manchester, I had disobeyed instructions. I argued that my incognito was as compromised in the latter town as much as in Nottingham, through the part I had played at Peterloo, but in vain. Consequently I was ripe for the picking when the next commission came along, though it looked likely to prove as dangerous and exposed as any I had yet undertaken.

First, Mr Cargill, I must insist that in the newspaper reports and the trial that followed the affair I am about to describe, the role I played is much diminished, much of what I did being ascribed to George Edwards, this being in part because of the fellow's overweening desire to make a place for himself in the history books but also so that I might maintain my already somewhat tattered cover.

You will recall that I was already known to Arthur Thistlewood from my engraving work done in Manchester in the run up to Peterloo; that said Thistlewood had left Manchester days before that event out of respect for Orator Hunt's desire to keep bloody revolution off the agenda, so when I turned up at his lodgings with my engraving kit, he not only remembered me but had no reason to question the part I had played in the events that followed his departure.

He had a couple of rooms in a house in Stanhope Street, just by Clare Market, not far from where the Cumberland and Chester Terraces on the east side of Regent's Park now stand, the land just then as I recall being cleared for their erection. Because of the building that was undertaken in the area, the canal as well as the terraces, and the clearing of the St Giles Rookeries to the south, it was a run-down area filled with Irish navigators, the prostitutes and hucksters that leeched off them, and those who had come home one evening to find a hole in the ground where their dwelling had been.

Though a gentleman by birth, albeit of farming country stock, Thistlewood lived in abject squalor. It was said he was an adventurer who had lost his fortune gaming, but this was not so: he made an unwise loan to a friend of almost all of what capital he had, and declared himself well rid of it, the ownership of capital being against his principles. In this he seemed to me to be standing in the path of an oncoming train with more stupidity and obstinacy than any follower of Ned Ludd.

The outer room, though scarcely more than twelve feet by twelve, was a meeting place for like-minded artisans, radicals,

Spenceans, deists and Jacobins; indeed, the inner circle contrived to be all these things at once, and the parlour was often crowded. The only furniture was four or five three-legged stools, and a printing press with its fonts in their racks stacked up alongside it. The curtains were sacking, white with the flour they had contained, but rendered useless for that purpose by the knives of those who had plundered it the winter before when the price of bread was even higher. There was a tiny fireplace on which Susan Thistlewood, a thin severe sort of a woman and a Jacobin as radical in her own right as her spouse, endeavoured to keep a kettle going from which she topped up a cracked teapot every ten minutes or so, though I never saw anyone actually add tea leaves to what were already in it.

The inner room was their bedroom and contained a large bed with a horsehair mattress piled with rags and rugs. It was often the case that a handful of small children lay asleep in it which I took at first to be the litter the Thistlewoods had spawned, but later learnt were street children come in for the warmth and shelter.

Thistlewood welcomed me into this noisome den with expostulations of delight.

'This is most opportune, my dear Charles, we have a hundred texts and bills and pamphlets need the embellishments you can provide . . .' and he ushered me across the threshold into the crowded room, filled with tobacco smoke, the smell of printer's ink and that of the Great Unwashed. 'You must meet my friends and colleagues, citizens all . . .' and he reeled off such names as Brunt, Adams, Harrison, Davidson, Ings and . . . Roberts . . . 'whom I think you know? Was he not in your company at Manchester? I think so.'

Well there he was, the little ferret, and I shook his hand, for, like me, he was no better than a fucking Judas.

Indeed in the *conversazione* that followed he was more forward than any of them in promulgating schemes for the assassination in one fell swoop of all the main instruments of tyranny.

210

'Blow up the House of Commons,' he cried, when all were sitting on the stools in a circle and those who had none were standing behind them. Yours truly, meanwhile, was in a corner gouging away with my burin on my plate, doing a copy of Fogg's cartoon of the Manchester Massacre, the one with the Yeomanry charging in, all fat and red-cheeked, slashing at a woman and her child, except I was adding word-balloons of a vitriolic obscenity Fogg himself had not thought of. 'Blow them to smithereens . . .' Edwards concluded.

But Thistlewood would have none of that – there were good people in the Commons, people like Burdett – nor would he countenance barrels of gunpowder in the cellars of the Spanish Embassy during a fiesta to which the government had been invited, which was the next suggestion of Edwards, since ladies would be present.

'There was women enough at St Peter's Field,' James Ings offered.

'But would you then have us tarred with the same brush as our enemies?' riposted Thistlewood, albeit gently, Sweet Jesus that he was.

All of which presented a problem which Lord Sidmouth, Mr Stafford, Edwards and I set about resolving. We met in the room next to Room 101 in the Home Office about a week after my induction into Thistlewood's circle.

My lord stroked his chin and said: 'So this quixotic fool will murder the cabinet, but the cabinet only; there must be no contiguous casualties. That will not be easy to arrange, at least not unless we find a way of allowing him to think he can blow up the cabinet room in number ten.'

'My Lord,' said I, 'how about if you were all invited to a private dinner party?'

'A social event,' said he, 'without women? Wives, or if it is to be, um, informal, mistresses? Unlikely. The cabinet does not dine together and alone, even as the guests of one another.'

'Does Thistlewood know that?' Mr Stafford asked. 'I doubt he is aware of such niceties as regulate polite society.'

'Or perhaps, my Lord,' said I, 'it could be it was put about that the cabinet, wishing to discuss informally a pressing topic without the presence of minute-takers, might dine in the house of one of its members. May I make so bold as to offer a suggestion as to which?'

'Go on.'

'There is among Thistlewood's coterie a malcontent called William Davidson, a black man, who pushes a pen for Lord Harrowby—'

'I know of the man,' Stafford interjected. 'He is the bastard son of the Jamaican Attorney General. I have a file on him. His father sent him to England or rather Scotland where he got some education studying law in Glasgow. Latterly he was a sailor, then a Wesleyan preacher, a position he lost after he attempted the seduction of one of the younger girls in his flock. Well, to be blunt we paid her to seduce him for he was combining revolution with sermons of brotherly love. Naturally, being negroid, it was easy to persuade the elders of his congregation that the boot was, so to speak, on the other foot, and that his savage instincts had got the better of him. Finally after these and other vicissitudes, Harrowby, out of consideration of his friendship with his father, gave him work as a clerk. He's been on the fringes of the reformers for some time but has since moved towards the revolutionists and is a member of the Spenceans.'

Lord Sidmouth chewed the cud over this for a moment.

'My Lord Harrowby, President of the Council, has recently acquired the lease on a house in Grosvenor Square with, so he has told us, a most excellently well-appointed dining room. But he is notorious for being slow in returning the hospitality he owes every one of us. I'll put it to him.'

Mr Stafford and I looked at each other. We both thought it proper that it should be he rather than I who made the point.

212

'My Lord, forgive me, but the success of the exercise depends on you, and the rest of the cabinet, *not* being present.'

'Ah yes. Yes, of course.'

Two matters now had to be put in hand. First, Thistlewood must be convinced that the cabinet, with no woman present, were to meet on a particular evening for dinner and private discussion at Lord Harrowby's. The second was that a place near by should be found for the assassins to gather where, armed and ready, they might be apprehended without endangering the lives of innocent bystanders, let alone the cabinet. Mr Stafford undertook the first. He approached Lord Harrowby, who was thereby advised of what was going on, and invitations to the entire cabinet were duly sent. However, Harrowby himself now took fright: 'Supposing,' he said, 'the conspirators overpower their would-be apprehenders, or even that just one or two escape and determine to do the best they can without their accomplices. I shall be alone in m'house, and in they'll burst and I'll be done for. In short, Mr Stafford, I think for that night I'll take the opportunity of visiting m'mother in Twickers.' By which he meant Twickenham, then a still fashionable resort for those who valued serenity and landscapes restfully disposed about the river.

I meanwhile sought out a place for the assassins to meet. This was not easy. The vicinity of Grosvenor Square was even more select then than it is now. There were no pothouses, or not such as would accept a meeting of an obviously impoverished and rough-looking group of Spenceans in its upper room, armed to the teeth. Even the several mews were tidy, well kept and occupied by trusted ostlers and coachmen to the nobility who lived in the large houses. In the end I settled on a hayloft in Cato Street, a mews nearly a mile and a half north-west of Grosvenor Square. The place recommended itself for several reasons. It was in a cul-de-sac and therefore could be easily contained, surrounded by a *cordon sanitaire* of constables or foot soldiers; the building itself was dilapidated and unoccupied;

and the quarter it was in, part of Tyburnia, was owned by Lord Harrowby himself.

The next thing was to persuade Thistlewood and the rest that this was a suitable place to meet, the problem being the distance.

'Would it,' asked Arthur, 'be possible for five or so of us to march the distance, with whatever arms we can muster, through the streets of London, without exciting the interest of the Bow Street constables? Especially bearing in mind that they are always thick on the ground in the Mayfair area on account of the wealth and importance of the residents.'

However, I was able to persuade him that the Cato Street hayloft could not be bettered, the final temptation being the very word Cato itself. Arthur prided himself on his classical education, received at the hands of dominies at Horncastle Grammar School, and recalled with a little prompting from me that Cato was a notable republican, associated with the assassins of Julius Caesar, though not present at the actual event.

'Five! With pistols? That will not serve the purpose at all,' cried my Lord Sidmouth when I rehearsed this conversation to him. 'The whole point is to present this plot to the better sort as a real threat to lives and property throughout the kingdom. Only that way will we get the Six Acts through, only that way will we have the excuses, nay reasons, we need to lock up or transport a hundred like-minded fellows and draw a line beneath these constant riots, meetings and the distribution of seditious and blasphemous libels. Come, Stafford, what do you think?'

'My Lord is right as usual. But I think if Boylan was to go among the taverns south of the river and maybe as far east as Dartford, he might be able, with the judicious outlay of a crown here and a half sovereign there, recruit a company of losels and loblolly men . . .'

'What about weapons?' I asked.

'Well,' answered Sidmouth, 'I think I might persuade his

grace to lend us a few old Tower muskets left over from the wars, and maybe some grenades too. Pikes and cutlasses you should be able to pick up in pawnshops and the like.'

In the event recruiting was not a problem. The fact of it was that word had got about in the London underworld that something was afoot, and something more than twelve inches, as the wags put it, and several lunatics, malcontents, and even two or three more spies who had not been part of Stafford's and Sidmouth's plot but wished to earn themselves their employers' approval, volunteered themselves. Indeed, the day before the event, when the dinner had been noticed in the *New Times* by arrangement with Stafford, notice which was taken as proof positive that the rumours were true, Arthur Thistlewood was turning would-be murderers away.

The weaponry was another matter and in the end, with time running out, it was all piled into a covered cart and sent round to the Thistlewood establishment with an anonymous note: *These might be of use in your magnificent enterprise, a Well-Wisher.* Having inspected the load, Arthur declared himself pleased and the lot was immediately moved on to Cato Street without further ado and stored in the hayloft. All that is save the sword of a captain of foot, gilded in the hilt and engraved with a legend that said it had served its master well at Waterloo, presumably later pawned by a half-pay officer or his penurious widow. This, Thistlewood himself took a strong fancy to. He was an accomplished swordsman, knew the art of fencing like a gentleman, which, in a way, he was. However, the blade was dull and the point broken an eighth of an inch from its tip. I took it to a cutler whose shop was a mile off in St Martin's, and he put an edge and point on it sharp as a demon barber's razor.

One last chore remained to be done. Edwards and I slipped round to the Cato Street hayloft and there emptied the gunpowder out of the grenades and replaced it with a mixture of fine sand and coal dust.

It was about midday, a cold February day, the day of the

attempt itself, Wednesday the twenty-third in the year 1820 by Christian reckoning and round about thirty-one in the minds of revolutionaries, when the blow fell. Most of us were gathered in that upper room partaking of a lenten stew of onion shreds and some potato whose flavour suggested that, in the distant past, there had been some presence of mutton bones long since departed; the blow being the sudden arrival of Davidson, himself in a stew and out of breath, having run all the way through Mary-le-Bone from Grosvenor Square.

'Friends,' and then catching a warning eye from Susan Thistlewood, he added, in his deep velvety voice, the voice of a Jamaican negro, 'Citizens, Lord Harrowby is gone. Departed. This half-hour gone to Twickenham to visit his mother. He has taken his body servant and luggage and told major-domo Hanks not to expect his return until Monday. It cannot be but that the dinner is cancelled.'

Amid exclamations of rage and disappointment, some exaggerated to cover a certain relief, from most of the dozen or so of us there present, I took it upon myself to cry: 'You must be mistaken. There must be some mistake . . . let me look into the matter.'

Davidson caught my elbow.

'It is not my custom to lie to my friends,' he boomed.

He was a big man, more negro than white, with tight curly black hair trimmed short, eyes that flashed lightning bolts from their dark fathomless depths, and a grip in his huge black hands as tight as a tiger's jaws. He wore a dark blue coat with a high collar and a white stock, bleached and starched, wound to his chin.

'Of course not,' I managed to stutter. 'But let us be sure you have not mistook the situation or misheard what was said.'

'Let him go,' cried Arthur. 'What harm can be done?'

So Davidson set me on the floor again and off I went, cutting across Mary-le-Bone Road and into the alleys behind Oxford Street. It was perishing cold, a fog was descending, and the ice that had formed the night before was scarcely melting at all. I gave a horse dropping the size of a tennis ball a kick and hurt my toe, so frozen hard it was.

A pothouse door opened and exhaled a vapour that carried on it not only the fragrance of hops and malt, but also those rich odours that speak of beef and oysters, rich gravy and a crust you could break your teeth on. I thought to myself, I have twenty minutes to get to Grosvenor Square, ten minutes to spend there and twenty minutes to get back. I can have a pie and a beer and maybe a tot of gin, and smoke a pipe too before it will be time to return.

Hardly had I sat down to this rich repast when who should appear in front of me but that ferret Edwards.

'Budge along, Charlie,' he rasped for, like many of us that winter, he had the illness of the throat doctors now name laryngitis, which all lived in terror might turn into the scarlet fever, 'I knewed you'd be here and you're damnably lucky I could put myself forward as the one to see you were truly on your way.'

'How should this be,' I cried, and the mouthful of meat and a chewy oyster I had between my teeth turned to ordure in my mouth.

'Yon Davidson, the Blackie, took against you, said he'd always had suspicions of you.'

'By God,' I swore, 'I promise you I'll see him hang . . .' then looked anxiously around, 'but won't they send another to check on you?'

'Nay, they trust me, be sure of it. I've been too forward in their counsels for it to be otherwise.'

Well, to cut it short, Mr Cargill, we went back in due time and together protested that butler Hanks had admitted himself mistaken, Lord Harrowby had gone across the Park only to visit his whore on the further side, where the better class of that sort conduct their trade, and would be back by four o'clock in time to entertain his fellow ministers.

27

Dusk was falling and the fog forming even thicker so the brand new gaslights in Oxford Street glowed like haloed oranges whose light hardly reached the paving below them. The big new shops round the Circus were already putting up their shutters and the last dozen or so of the more fashionable shoppers summoning their coaches or Hackneys, their horses steaming, the hooves of their nags slipping and banging on the ice. Thistlewood, or rather his wife, who was of a more practical frame of mind, split us up into five groups of three and four apiece, and gave to each a different route, some through Mary-le-Bone, some by Cavendish Square and Wigmore Street, another straight down Oxford Street and up the Edgware Road, and another to go south down Tottenham Court Road through Soho Square, across Regent Street to Hanover Square, past old Handel's house, back to Oxford Street and up Mary-le-Bone lane. She had it timed that we would all meet at Cato Street at just about five o'clock, where we would make our final arrangements, arm ourselves, and set off back to Grosvenor Square, aiming to be there at about half past six when, it was supposed, the cabinet would be dipping their spoons into their turtle and sherry soup.

As we left she embraced her husband warmly and murmured

to him the words that were to hang him, for it was I, not Edwards, heard them.

'Be mindful, love, if all goes wrong we are to meet at my sister's house.'

Now I already knew, for I had been on an errand there for her, that her sister lived at number eight, White Street, over near Moorfield Pavement. It's long since been pulled down and a new thoroughfare built called, and pray mark the irony, Liverpool Street, after the very man these people sought to undo. Anyway, off we all trooped in our several battalions, and arrived at Cato Street at the appointed hour.

Now Stafford's plan was all should be apprehended almost as soon as we were there, but, as usual, when the military are involved, there was a cock-up and most of us were armed and listening to Thistlewood's Periclean exhortation by the time the constables burst in on us.

First he drew his captain's sword and gave it such a flourish that those of us who stood near by, and were mindful of how sharp it was, ducked or shrank back.

'Friends and citizens,' he began, in a low solemn voice for this was no great crowd he had to address in a big space like Spa Fields or Hyde Park, but a mere couple of dozen gathered beneath a hurricane lamp whose rays did not penetrate to the further corners of a cobwebby hayloft, 'today we take on us the mantle of Brutus and Cassius, Marat and Robespierre, William Tell, the Levellers and the Diggers and even of such men as Washington and Jefferson. All, indeed, who have stood up against the oppression and tyranny of, um, tyrants, kings and nobles, the tyranny above all of those who by stealing the land from those who work it steal the fruits of their labour and live in idle and purposeless luxury. What we do this evening, bloody and dangerous though it be, will mark the dawn of a new era, when all shall benefit to the full from the land they work, or the land their manufactories are built on. The mill-worker, the quarryman, the miner, will stand beside the farmer and the day labourer in the fields, in the unity of the harvest sickle and the industrious hammer, to push back the plunder of the ages . . .'

Sensing he was losing his thread and we might be somewhat delayed while he sought it out, Ings now interrupted with a shout: 'Come brothers, now is the time. Let's go forth and win his rights for every citizen and citizeness in this land which labours beneath the Norman Yoke,' and 'Glory, glory Hallelujah,' boomed Davidson in his rich black voice, adding a diapason to the strident oboe of his mate . . . 'the Lord of Hosts is on our side'.

I wax lyrical, do I not, Mr Cargill? Diapasons and oboes, forsooth! Arthur Thistlewood, though, frowned somewhat, being as he was a deistical if not downright atheistical sort of a fellow.

'Enough of that,' he cried. 'Now let us just remember the practicalities of what we have decided. I shall ring his lordship's bell, and declare that I have a package for Lord Liverpool, most urgent dispatches just come from the Continent . . .'

'Would it not be better to say Lord Castlereagh, he being the man for foreign affairs . . .' chimed in one Gilchrist by name, a dapper chap, a cobbler, I believe.

'Gilchrist, you're a fucking oaf,' said Ings. 'Yon Castlereagh will already be there. At Lord Harrowby's.'

'Damnme. So he will,' cried Gilchrist.

'It hardly matters,' replied Thistlewood somewhat tetchily, 'so long as all rush in with me once the door is opened, rush in and bind the servants, killing those that resist, occupy all passages in the house while I and Ings, Wilson, Bradburn, Cooper, Tidd, Boylan and Davidson go to the dining room and kill all there as mercifully as we can.'

'Might not be so easy as that,' said Gilchrist again, who was becoming something of a nuisance, 'with the long-nosed bugger that beat the French among them.'

All might then have fallen into dispute, wrangling anyway, except at that moment Mr Richard Smithers of the Bow Street Patrol threw open the wooden door at the far end of the loft. He had a pistol in each hand. One he loosed off into the

220

roofing and produced a shower of old plaster, lathes and a slate, the other he levelled at Thistlewood's broad brow.

'Stand where you are,' he cried, 'or I blow off your head. I am an officer of the peace and you must lay down your arms.'

In point of fact not many of us were armed at that moment for cutlasses, bayonets and pistols were laid out for us on a carpenter's table at the top of the stairs and it was understood that we would each take what suited our abilities and preferences as we passed on our way out.

Nevertheless, this was, I have to admit it, courageous on his part, for, as I shall make clear, he was momentarily, on account of the layout of the place, virtually a man alone.

There were two ways into this hayloft, you see. One up a flight of ordinary stairs to a landing on which the patrol might have assembled, but this had been covered on Thistlewood's orders by one of our number left below. Edwards had volunteered himself for the post and all would have gone well if he had got it, but Thistlewood appointed another. Not wanting there to be any general alarm during which the murderers would have opportunity to see to their weapons, Mr George Ruthven, the constable in charge of the arresting detail, therefore took the second route which was by an outside ladder to an opening haylofts generally have exposed to the outer world, but it being a ladder his men could arrive only singly before or behind him. Consequently, Smithers, who had preceded him, was for the moment alone.

This perhaps emboldened our Arthur, though by now you will have realised he was a man, who was, whatever else you could lay against him, imbued with a reckless disregard for his own skin, or indeed for those of others. At all events, just as Ruthven emerged from behind Smithers he lunged at the latter with his second-hand sword, which went into the poor man's chest on the right-hand side, as smoothly as a hot skewer into butter, but quite to the side, glancing between his ribs but well away from heart or liver.

Men can survive such a blow.

Seeing this I put the confusion that followed to good use. I pulled down and extinguished the one lamp and plunged all into darkness. In the mayhem that ensued Thistlewood, and some fourteen or so with him, managed to escape down the stairs, eschewed the door and made their exit through a ground-floor window. I, meanwhile, was able to complete the work he'd started by giving Smithers his certain quietus with the poniard Captain Q had given me so many months before. It pierced his heart, I'm sure of it, but with so fine a point, scarcely more than a needle, it was never noticed by the surgeon who examined the body later.

They should of course have been caught in the yard outside by a company of Guards who were supposed to have surrounded the place and sealed off the cul-de-sac. However, they were led by Captain Adolphus Fitzclarence, a bastard son of William, then Duke of Clarence, later William IV, who had contrived, in the way to which Guards Officers are prone, to lose his way.

Thistlewood and a dozen more thus made their escape, and where did they go? Why, to number eight, White Street, Moorfields. Where, the following morning, he was apprehended by a constable Lavender, in bed, with his stockings and breeches on. In his pockets, ball, cartridges and flints, and the black sash he had worn at Cato Street.

Thistlewood, Davidson, Ings, Tidd and Brunt were found guilty of high treason and Thistlewood of the murder too that I had perpetrated on his behalf and which convinced all, not just the jurors, but many up and down the land, that he was nothing more than a ruffian brute and no gentleman at all, and fit to be hanged. Others were transported and a couple of Stafford's men got off for turning King's evidence. Not I, nor Edwards: to maintain our cover we were presumed to have escaped.

And yes, Mr Cargill, I attended their execution on the first of May 1820. And it damned near caused my own demise.

It was a lovely day, warm and balmy and sunny, one of the first like it after a hard winter. Cherry blossom in the parks and the first swifts mewling down Fleet Street and over the scaffold in front of Newgate, draped as it was, as I have already mentioned, in black to give solemnity to the occasion. Not that it needed it. An immense crowd had turned out and stood in utter silence as the men were paraded on the scaffold. There was none of the jeering and cheering as you got when a highwayman or common murderer was swung.

Thistlewood tried a last speech, of course; he was in his way as fond of his own voice as Orator Hunt was of his. It went something like this as I recall.

'My genius is so great just now. I don't think there is any man alive has so great a genius as mine at the moment . . .'

By 'genius' he meant attendant spirit, allotted, according to his deistical beliefs, to every person at his birth to preside over his destiny in life.

'If it is the will of the Author of the World that I should perish in the cause of freedom – his will, and not mine be done . . .' you'll note again, Mr Cargill, the messianic touch, 'it is a triumph for me . . .' and he threw his arms about so some said he was insane, and the executioners had a hard time of it binding them.

Ings then burst into song with 'Death or Liberty', and Thistlewood, somewhat unfairly I thought since he had had his own vociferous display, reprimanded him.

'Quiet, Ings,' he called. 'We can die without all this noise.'

They all, apart from Davidson the negro, whose brief had ill-advisedly pleaded that he could not have a fair trial on account of prejudice in the jury against men of colour, turned away from the ordinary. Davidson, though, who considered himself a man of the cloth, did say a short prayer with him.

This being done, the chief of the executioners gave the signal and all dropped together, and a deep sigh or groan spread across the vast crowd like a dark blanket before an almost perfect silence returned. However, as the death throes continued there were sporadic shouts from here and there, demanding mercy for their suffering and so forth.

Tidd went first, being a big man. Thistlewood struggled slightly for a few minutes, but each effort was more faint than that which preceded, and the body soon turned round slowly, as

223

if the hand of death gave it a nudge. Ings struggled the most – being small and light, he danced a long and wretched jig, kicking and twisting, his hands straining at the bonds to reach for the halter. Davidson they had to pull on, that is pull hard on his legs, and after three or four heaves he became motionless. Brunt suffered terribly and the executioners had to haul and heave, two or three at once to shorten his agonies.

Then, when all were dead meat, came the butchery. No quartering, just decapitation, and that, Mr Cargill, was when emotion got the better of me. For when the executioner who cut off Thistlewood's head (and let me say I never saw a worser crew of bunglers than this lot were) hoisted it up for all to see, he let it slip from his hand and . . .

'Butterfingers!' I cried, and raised a titter or two from some of those that heard me.

And thus it was that I drew attention to my presence, which on account of my stature might well have gone unnoticed but for my indiscretion, for now many looked in my direction, and among them a group of working men come all the way from Nottingham for the event and, perched on the shoulders of two of them, Maggie-May and Tiger Lily, her oriental friend.

'Charl-eee!' called Maggie.

'Is eet Char-ree Boyran, then,' cried Tiger Lily.

'Why if it baint that rascal Charlie Boylan, the Pentrich traitor,' cried the oaf who carried her. The louts put down the girls and began to push through the crowd to get at me and surely would have done for me this time had they got through.

However, one advantage my diminutive size bestows on me, one I believe I have already remarked on, is the ability to slip through a crowd with ease.

De Bourgeois heard of it. Stafford was told. And a few weeks later I was ordered abroad to be out of harm's way, for, as Mr de Bourgeois put it, 'It's not your courage or your good sense we doubt, Charlie, but who knows what indiscretionary talk a man might fall into in the presence of those who can't wait to pull his head off.'

Part IV

THE DROWNING

My spirit's bark is driven,
Far from the shore, far from the trembling throng
Whose sails were never to the tempest given;
The massy earth and spherèd skies are riven!
I am borne darkly, fearfully afar . . .

PERCY BYSSHE SHELLEY, *Adonais*

28

And that is the last of Charlie's fifty close-written pages. Cargill stacks them neatly, slips them into a Treasury folder and ties the red ribbon. He sighs. Back to Pentonville, for what he suspects, from all that he has gleaned already, will turn out to be the outset of what Charlie will claim as his most notorious exploit. No. Notorious is the wrong word, since almost no one knows about it. Nefarious? Execrable? Odious?

The Minutes of an Ad-Hoc Committee set the scene and will, he suspects, give some of the background . . .

However, as he reaches for the spice-coloured hide of the not so weighty volume, a clock chimes; flicking up the Sheffield plate lid he checks his own watch, and slips it back into his watch pocket. Five o'clock. A not unreasonable time to go home. All along the corridors of the ministerial palaces that are springing up to tower above the alleys and warrens of old Whitehall many of his colleagues, especially those whose certainty that they are always right, conferred on them by an education at Rugby School or Westminster and even Cambridge and Oxford, are already shrugging on their top-coats. Hackney carriages queue to take them to Kensington and Belgravia. Coming from a somewhat humbler background, Cargill feels that to justify what seems to him (though not to most of *them*) a more than adequate stipend it is necessary to stay late and work hard. He is also keenly conscious that without the benefits of an armigerous name and the patronage of a titled if distant relation, diligence, perseverance and even wit, if not actual cleverness, are the only ropes capable of hoisting him above the status of a mere pen-pusher. He looks forward to the day, only three years off did he but know it, when entry to the Civil Service will be by examination and merit, and meanwhile he seeks promotion by staying late. Nevertheless, it is too late for a trip out to Pentonville and a fresh chapter of Charlie's life, there is nothing left for him to do in the office, and he resolves to be off, a full hour earlier than usual.

At least Mrs Cargill, Emily, will be pleasantly surprised to see him.

He crosses Westminster Bridge, with several hundred others, all of whom seem like ghosts looming up through the thickening fog which lies low over the river, he did not know death had undone so many, and turns left with most of them towards the Terminus, partially covered by high glass roofs which catch the ruby refulgence of a late February sunset softened by the smoke and steam. He brushes aside the blandishments of the ladies who idle along York Road beneath the Portland stone that supports the raised courts of the station like the massive walls of a fortress or prison.

'Need a friend for the night, guvnor?'

'I've two daughters at home, both virgins, waiting for just such a gen'l'man as you are, sir.'

'Have a quick one, sir, I've a place just round the corner.'

With that hour in hand he's almost tempted but falls instead for a bunch of snowdrops thrust under his nose by a child who has made a snood out of a tatter of tartan rug, and whose nose drips over scabbed lips. But she has blue eyes as well as blue fingers.

'Gawd bless you, sir, oh Gawd indeed bless you,' for he has given her a silver thrummer instead of the penny she expected.

Warmed by his own charity, and still clutching the tiny bunch of pearl and emerald, he hurries up the steps and through the Arch. Some thirty-five minutes later but still at least an hour earlier than usual he uses his latchkey to let himself into number eight, Waterloo Villas. At the top of the house Deirdre hears him, puts aside the book she is reading, hurriedly pins up her hair, reties her apron, and asks herself what the divil is going on, isn't it a full hour before the auld fool is due back and a good half hour before the mistress is expected? And she runs down the two flights of stairs to welcome him, take his hat, his coat, his case, his umbrella, and . . .

'Put these in some water for me, Deirdre, and perhaps leave them on the piano where Mrs Cargill will see them.'

Jasus if it isn't snowdrops the auld fool's brought in.

Then . . .

'And tell Mrs Cargill I'm back.'

'Ah, to be sure, sir, the mistress is out.'

'Out? As late as this?'

'Yes, indeed, sir.'

'Where? Where's she gone at this time of night?'

'I'm sure I wouldn't be knowing that, sir. But she did say she had something to collect from the chemist down in the village. Some medicament, I shouldn't wonder.'

'That'll do, Deirdre. No. Er, perhaps a pot of tea?'

'The India or the China?'

'The India, Deirdre.'

And she bobs him a curtsey, a habit he cannot approve since she is tall and thin, big-boned with red elbows, and it looks silly. He can hardly ask her to bow though, can he?

He fidgets about for a couple of minutes, goes to the window and peers across at the common. The trees, chestnuts he thinks they are, are black where the gaslights pick them out, and merge into the blackness beyond. They look like giant insects marching out of nothingness. He shudders, turns away, then back again to draw the heavy velveret curtains across the bay window and wonders at the morbidity of his imagination. Is he

229

sickening? Perhaps. He has spent too long in the spiritual company of Charlie Boylan, his imagination has been infected. He sits in his armchair in front of the fireplace which is giving off more sulphurous smoke than heat, and unfurls *The Times*. No comfort there. Cholera reported in Alexandria. A doctor recalls the outbreak of three years earlier when fourteen thousand died in London alone. How long before it visits London again? A year, the doctor predicts. He shifts uneasily against the brown moquette and scratches his crotch. And of course at that moment Deirdre returns.

Why the blazes couldn't she knock? Because she is carrying a tray. Standing above him she pours the tea, just, she believes, as he likes it, but in fact adding too much milk.

Where is Emily? Where the devil is she? She should be here to pour his tea.

He fumbles with the newspaper, trying to get it to refurl on its pearwood stick, knocks the occasional table, which is round, on a single pedestal above a three-toed claw, grabs at it as it tips away from him, and of course the lot falls in his lap. It scalds. He leaps to his feet and bellows. Deirdre rushes back in, rushes back out, rushes back in, this time with a cloth; he hears the latchkey click in the tiny hall, and here is Emily standing in the doorway, watching as Deirdre, on her knees in front of him, rubs away at his trousers.

She says not a word but walks, no glides, through to the back room, opens the small escritoire which is her own, unlocks the sloping lid, places the small package she is carrying, wrapped in blue paper and sealed, in one of the pigeonholes, raises the lid, relocks it, puts her small reticule on top of the escritoire and unpins her hat.

'Got home early, did we?' she says. 'How nice!'

Fortuitously his accident has conferred on her a transient superiority she enjoys and it shows in her solicitous smile, which contains just a tiny zest of mockery, as she takes his trousers from him.

'I'll hand them straight over to Deirdre,' she says, as they both head upstairs to their bedroom. 'They won't be dry by morning so tomorrow you'll have to wear your second pair.'

The perversity of language conceals the truth. In fact the trousers in question are not the second pair, but the second best. They are actually the first or at any rate prior pair.

'They're too tight in the waist,' Cargill remarks petulantly.

'You'll have to breathe in then when you do them up. You are not going to leave on your, erm, underthing are you?'

She means his long johns. Heavy wool, a sort of creamy off white, except where the tea has soaked through the trousers and stained them a rusty brown colour.

'No, I suppose not. Would you mind?'

He expects her to withdraw to the landing, but she merely turns to the window, which, since it is on the first floor and overlooks the common, she has left undraped. There is a reflection, blurred by the slight waves in the glass, but distinguishable. She catches the briefest glimpse of his buttocks as he lifts his voluminous shirt tail, the first time she has seen them. Not, she decides, a pretty sight.

She gathers up the garment he has shed.

'There then, I'll leave you in peace. I'll take these to Deirdre.'

Peace is not on the cards. Cargill, as he struggles with buttons of mother-of-pearl and bone, is tormented by a confusion of emotions, all unworthy. He has been humiliated, made a fool of, in front of . . . women. There is no way in which he can turn the blame on them. Even the unstable table, ten years old, dating from the Regency, was left him by his grandmother. His thighs still smart with eye-watering intensity, but no one has suggested an application of yellow petroleum jelly to keep the air away from the inflamed skin and soothe it. Above all, he is aware that Mrs Cargill, Emily, used the fracas to lock up a package she did not want him to see, a package she had brought into the sitting room, unconcealed because she had not expected him to be there. What could it be? Something bought at the chemist, Deirdre had suggested. What might she buy at a chemist that she did not want him to see? Cargill has no idea: but assumes it must be something that relates to her femininity or femaleness, something to do with her sex, or even just sex, plain and simple.

Nothing fattens the maggots of paranoia so readily as ignorance, and ignorant about sex is what Cargill so blazingly is.

Emily, too, but at least she is trying to do something about it.

'Have you finished the book I lent you?' she asks Deirdre as she hands over the tea-soiled garments.

'Nearly, ma'am. I would've if the ... master had not come home early. Do you want it back?'

'No, Deirdre. It would be better if you kept it for me in your room. Under the mattress of your bed. I'll ask you for it if I need to refer to it again.'

'Very well, ma'am.'

The book in question is *Everywoman's Book, Or What is Love?* by Robert Carlile, in a pirated edition. It advocates trial marriage, contraception (prescribing the use of a sponge in the vagina as practised by the French aristocracy, the sheath and *coitus interruptus*), and recognises that infidelity in women is no less reprehensible than it is in men. Indeed, not that reprehensible at all.

If Cargill discovers it his paranoia will become insupportable both for himself and his wife.

29

Minutes of an . . .

> '"As I lay asleep in Italy
> There came a voice from over the Sea
> And with great power it forth led me
> To walk in the visions of Poesy.
>
> I met Murder on the way –
> He had a mask like Castlereagh –
> Very smooth he looked, yet grim;
> Seven blood-hounds followed him:
>
> All were fat; and well they might
> Be in admirable plight . . ."

'This is pretty wretched doggerel, isn't it?

> '". . . For one by one, and two by two,
> He tossed them human hearts to chew
> Which from his wide cloak he drew."

'Oh I say, Sidmouth, this is a bit much, isn't it? Has Robert seen this?'

'I take it you mean Londonderry, Castlereagh as this chap persists in calling him?'

'Yes, damnit, I do.'

'No, Arthur, he hasn't.'

'Well, he'd better not. He's in a bad way as it is, horribly overworked. He'd be mortified.'

'I should think that is part of this scribbler's purpose, is it not?' Liverpool drawled. 'Go on Arthur, read us a bit more.'

> '"Next came Fraud, and he had on,
> Like Eldon, an ermined gown;
> His big tears, for he wept well,
> Turned to mill-stones as they fell.
>
> And the little children, who
> Round his feet played to and fro,
> Thinking every tear a gem,
> Had their brains knocked out by them."

'No, hang on a moment, Henry's next . . .

> '"Clothed with the Bible, as with light,
> And the shadows of the night,
> Like Sidmouth, next, Hypocrisy
> On a crocodile rode by."

'Got your number all right, don't you think, Henry?'

'Damnit, Arthur, that aint fair. Anyway, why a crocodile?'

'The tears, Henry. Crocodile tears. And the propensity the monster of the Nile has for snapping up unconsidered trifles. Like small children.'

'Are we in it, Arthur? Has he anything to say about us?' The Prime Minister was eager.

The Duke scanned with the practised eye of a gentleman

who has been besieged with paper for most of his working life, even on as well as off the battlefield, turning the sheets one by one. Ninety-one stanzas . . .

'No, Robert, nothing. I'm afraid we do not rate in this gentleman's catalogue of villains, not by name at any rate. It's an honour I can live without. But there's some stirring stuff. Harkee!

> '"Men of England, heirs of Glory,
> Heroes of unwritten story,
> Nurslings of one mighty Mother,
> Hopes of her, and one another;
>
> Rise like Lions after slumber
> In unvanquishable number,
> Shake your chains to earth like dew
> Which in sleep had fallen on you –
> Ye are many – they are few."

'Hang on a moment,' the Hero of Waterloo turned on through some four or five pages. 'Yes, I thought so. Our doggerelist thought highly of that last stanza and repeats it at the end of the whole vile production. Well, Henry, what have we here? Who is this man?'

Sidmouth looked coy, was not yet ready to give a direct answer. A wave of his hand took in the pile of files and papers that sat like the plinth of a monument on the end of the table.

'We've kept an eye on this young gentleman,' he said, 'for some eight years, ever since he wrote a pamphlet disputing the existence of the Deity, for which he was expelled from Oxford.'

'Quite right,' the Duke interpolated. 'I've said it often and no doubt I'll say it again: educated men without religion are but clever devils.'

'Yes, Arthur. Anyway, during the years since he has produced a steady outpouring of verse, not all of it doggerel like this, and some prose pamphlets and effusions too, advocating,

235

if you can penetrate his somewhat turgid manner, Liberty, violent overthrow of government and religion, incest, the end of marriage . . . and so on and so forth. One of his favourite targets is what he, along with Cobbett, calls paper coin and the national debt which he sees as a clever plot whereby the government pays out vast sums in interest to all the patriotic gentlemen who bought bonds during the late wars, interest now paid for by the taxes we raise, taxes which he insists fall most grievously on the poor.'

'Not the view of my bailiff or my banker.'

'Probably not, Arthur. There is worse stuff, particularly in an extended pamphlet called "A Philosophical View of Reform".'

Sidmouth's fingers, white like the fingers in the underneath of a crab, whispered through the papers.

'Let me give you some examples. He talks of the "dilemma of submitting to a despotism which is notoriously gathering like an avalanche year by year, or taking the risk of something which it must be confessed bears the aspect of revolution". Now the expression there is a touch weasely, but properly interpreted it can lead only to outright advocacy of revolution. He talks about how a system of capitalist accumulation makes factory hands work sixteen hours a day where they only worked eight, how children are turned into lifeless and bloodless machines at an age when otherwise they would play before the cottage doors of their parents.'

'Or run about breaking their neighbours' windows,' Liverpool intervened. 'At least child employment keeps them off the streets.'

'Quite so, Prime Minister. He advocates universal adult suffrage—'

'What, women too?'

'It would seem so. I haven't read all this myself, of course, but I've had it marked up and a digest prepared. The end and aim appears to be this: "the equal and full development of the capacities of all living beings".'

'What the devil does he mean by that?'

236

'Arthur, I don't know. Here we go again: "Labour and skill and the immediate wages of labour and skill is a property of the most sacred and indisputable right and the foundation of all property—"'

'That's Cobbettese if I'm not much mistaken.'

'Possibly. None the less reprehensible. What becomes increasingly clear is that this man is arguing himself into a position where he advocates a mass movement and, if all else fails, revolution. "The last resort of resistance is undoubtedly insurrection. The right of insurrection is derived from the employment of armed force to counteract the will of the nation . . ." that, I take it, is a reference to the Manchester Massac— the events of sixteenth August last. Ah. More poetry . . .'

The Home Secretary laid his hand upon his breast and read, with mock heroics . . .

> '"Men of England. Wherefore plough
> For the Lords who lay you low?
> Wherefore weave with toil and care
> The rich robes your tyrants wear
> The seed you sow another reaps
> The wealth you find another keeps
> The robe you weave another wears . . ."

'Oh, and so on. And here is what he thinks of our royalty . . .

> '"An old, mad, blind, despised and dying king,
> Princes, the dregs of their dull race, who flow
> Through public scorn – mud from a muddy spring . . ."

'Well. There you are, gentlemen. In the last case sentiments we might share but have the manners to keep to ourselves.'

'And this fellow remains at large, not locked up?'

'That's the problem, Arthur. At the moment he resides in Italy with a ménage or harem of at least three women, all of whom have borne his brats . . . His legal wife, not one of his concubines, is Mary Godwin, illegitimate daughter of that old fool the philosopher and *his* concubine, Mary Wollstonecraft, who aped Thomas Paine with her *Vindication of the Rights of Woman*.'

'Dear me. You don't say. We're not talking about Lord Byron, are we? No? These modern men of genius are sad fellows, don't you think? Why have we not heard of this one before?'

'Through the happy good sense of the booksellers and publishers he has called on to print his stuff, very little of what he has written has been spread about at all. Editions of a hundred copies have sold ten, other work has not been printed at all. It has been my judgement that to bring him to trial would give him a notoriety that might induce less wary printers to make more of him and present him with a readership he does not at the moment enjoy.'

'So why are you asking us to consider him now?'

'This latest . . . effusion we have before us, merits, I think, a closer consideration. You may call it doggerel, Arthur, but I believe even you found a strength, a muscle in the stanzas you read to us. It is clearly intended to have a wide appeal, it is a conscious and intentional call to riot, rebellion and revolution, and was inspired, if that's the word I want, by Peter . . . by the events in Manchester last year. It is quite clearly a seditious libel—'

'And you can't reach the fellow because he resides in Italy.'

'That certainly makes his arrest and trial a matter of some difficulty.'

'So what do we do?'

'Apply a gag. At the moment that is not a problem. The man in question—'

'Whom you have still not identified.'

'—sent this, and all the other stuff I've read, all of a similar tenor if lacking the same immediate appeal, to Leigh Hunt, the editor of the *Examiner*, who is a friend of his of some years' standing. Now Hunt will not publish—'

'Why not?'

'Because the Six Acts hang over him like a sword of whats-isname. Because if he does he'll go to prison for five years and pay a fine of, oh, what, five thousand pounds? Because he has six children and is damn near a pauper already. No, it was from Hunt's house that we, er borrowed, this most recent stuff, and at the time Stafford's men, John Castle, Charlie Boylan and a couple of roughs they had in tow, pointed out to Hunt the consequences of ill-advised publication. However, when our man discovers Hunt won't publish, I've no doubt he'll try elsewhere.'

'So what are you proposing?'

'Arthur, I'm loth to be too specific. I know you harbour feelings of justice and proper dealings in your breast which do you nothing but credit. However, our man has wild habits, wild recreations, and I cannot help feeling he might meet with an unfortunate accident. He rides like a cavalry officer, he shoots though only at inanimate targets, he sails small boats in dangerous waters. He keeps raffish company, including Lord Byron—'

'Damnme. He's clearly a scoundrel to enjoy that sort of company, but what you have said implies too that he might be a gentleman.'

'Precisely, Arthur.'

'Oh come on, Henry. The man's name, damnit.'

'Arthur, he is related, I have to admit it, to a family with whom you are on intimate terms.' This said with the twisted half-smile of someone who has a card up his sleeve, but has doubts about the reception its revelation might provoke.

'Damnme, Sidmouth, you don't mean the Arbuthnots?'

'No, Arthur. The Shelleys. Our man is Percy Bysshe Shelley, presumed heir to a baronetcy, his father is Timothy Shelley, Member of Parliament for Lewes, son of Sir Bysshe Shelley and a connection of Sir John Shelley.'

A long silence.

His grace the Master-General of Ordnance drummed fingers on the inlaid marquetry bosom of Galatea in her triumph, then snapped open his watch (gold, of course, not Sheffield plate) and looked around.

'I must leave you,' he rumbled. 'I have an appointment with His Majesty to discuss the coronation and the problem of the Queen who threatens to be there. What is it the cockneys say: Tee-hee?'

'Ta-ta, Arthur. Ta-ta.'

The Prime Minister and the Home Secretary waited a moment or two as the martial boots and spurs rang down the corridor. Then . . .

'Did you see that?' chortled Liverpool. 'His grace was *not* amused. Proof positive I'd say that the gossip that says he's been humping Lady Frances Shelley carries a grain of truth, eh Sidmouth?'

'I'd say so, Liverpool. I'd say so.'

'Anyway this Shelley feller. It wouldn't surprise me if he fell off his horse, you know, or got on the wrong side of a condottiere or whatever. We'll leave it to you, Sidmouth. I'm sure you'll be able to arrange something.'

30

Cargill closes the Minutes of the Ad-hoc and sits and thinks for a moment. Reading them has been the least unpleasant experience of what is turning out to be one of the least pleasant days in Cargill's life. With his second-best, first-bought trousers constricting the digestion of the breakfast Deirdre has cooked for him (oatmeal porridge, devilled kidneys) and a certain soreness on the fronts of his thighs, he descends the wide stairs from the room where he has been working, goes out into Whitehall and, on finding the stand where the Hackneys usually line up for custom empty, flags a cab. And another and a third and a fourth. Must he resort to an omnibus? Lord knows what time of day it'll be before he reaches Pentonville if he does.

The answer to that is an hour and a half later, about midday, having nearly frozen to death on the top of the 'bus, the interior seats all being taken, and put up with the deafening shouts of the driver as they halt at each stop ('Tra'aggar Square, Cherrin' Craws, The Ald'itch, *The* Alditch, alight 'ere for Wa'erloo Bridj and the styeshun acrawss the rib-ber, *if* you please . . .'). He is thus in no mood to hear the news that awaits him in the guard-room, as relayed by the duty officer, a white-whiskered cove, in his sixties, late of the Guards and wearing the Waterloo medal pinned to his long coat.

'Mr Boylan? Mr Charles Boylan? Sorry, sir, he aint 'ee-ah!'

And, in response to Cargill's repeated enquiry . . .

'Flown the coop, he 'as, sir, flown the coop and in a word . . . *gawn*. No sir, not escaped, but released according to due and proper exercise of his rights under 'Abeas Corpus, the Magna Carta and the Bill o' Rights. Not on police bail but in his own recog-nye-zances. A Mr Guppy from the firm of Kenge and Carboy got his case heard by the local Justice who found no warrant existed either in fizzical form as might be a piece of legal paper properly drawn, nor in moral form neither, for holding the gen'leman incarcerated any longer agin his will. No sir, no forwarding haddress was left.'

Nothing for it then but to return to Whitehall. This time a 'bus takes him to King's Cross, where, after queueing for ten minutes, Cargill is able to commandeer a hansom cab.

There is worse to come. Back at the Home Office he does what he can to check the records, sends a messenger across to Scotland Yard, and establishes that after Boylan's arrest the Home Office was informed, and the police were given a written instruction to put him in Pentonville. This the police had done without the formality of going first to a magistrate. Since the instruction was signed by a Permanent Secretary at the Home Office itself, the superintendent who had Boylan in a cell in the basement of Scotland Yard was afraid it would seem an impertinence to ask for further authorisation.

Having filled in what was left of the day with routine tasks and left a memo for the Permanent Under-Secretary, Cargill duly arrives home at the usual time. Even as he lets himself in and divests himself of his hat and topcoat in the narrow hall he becomes aware of an odour that is as disagreeable as it is familiar. Pungent, acid, stale, alcoholic and slightly urinary, it is not just the odour of gaol, it is the smell of Charlie.

'What the blazes, Boylan?' cries Cargill as he bursts through the door, then, as he comes properly in and sees his wife sitting

242

on the further side of the fireplace, 'I'm sorry, dear, I did not realise you were here too. However, I must ask you now to leave us.'

'Oh, should I? Mr Boylan has been entertaining me with so many interesting accounts of his extraordinary life, I would prefer to stay.'

'Please go.'

But she won't budge.

Cargill ignores her and spins on Boylan, who is sitting in *his* chair, Cargill's chair, the black leather buttoned one, with his head well below the antimacassar (as recently recommended in *The Ladies' Journal* to prevent stains from the macassar oil some men, not Cargill, smear in their hair), and his toes swinging above the faux turkey hearth rug.

'Answer me, Boylan, what the devil are you doing here?'

Charlie looks up at him with a gleam of glee, even a sort of triumph in his eye.

'Waiting for you, dear boy, taking tea, and conversing with your very charming wife.' For the occasion he has adopted the manner and accents, albeit stagy, of the upper middle classes. 'She tells me her family come from Newport, in Monmouthshire, where they have a tannery that does well supplying the iron-masters with heavy leather. That she came to London as a governess—'

'Boylan, I know my wife's antecedents and history without your help. Please answer my question. What the devil—?'

But Emily Cargill has risen from her high-backed chair.

'Thomas, that is the third oath you have resorted to since you came in. I shall leave now, not because you have told me to but because you seem to have lost all sense of what is polite in front of a lady. I hope to return when you are in a better temper.'

She sweeps out and the crinoline of her underskirts hisses across the Axminster.

She's back in a moment, before Cargill can take her place facing the interloper.

243

'And you need not think you can throw Mr Boylan out into the street. He has made it quite clear that his present circumstances, that is with no lodging or money, are the result of your negligence in not following the proper legal steps when you arranged for his incarceration. Therefore, I have told Mr Boylan he may remain with us, using the spare room next to Deirdre's, at least until such time as he can afford lodging of his own.'

This is the longest speech Cargill has ever had from his wife's lips. What's more she closes the door with some force when she leaves and he can hear her footsteps on the stair and the floorboards creak as she storms into the rear first-floor room which is intended one day to be a nursery and where now she keeps her pianoforte. Presently the strains of Chopin's *Revolutionary Etude*, albeit somewhat hesitantly played, filter through the house.

Meanwhile, Cargill takes up his position in front of the fire and looks down on his unrepentant and unbidden guest.

'So, sir. Explain yourself.'

'Nothing to explain, squire.' Charlie's tone and accent revert to those of a wheedling trickster. 'On learning he was holding me in prison without proper recourse to the law, the Guvnor slung me out. Where else could I go?'

'A lodging-house?'

'Without readies? I borrowed a shilling from old George, the screw at Pentonville, took a bus to Waterloo and the train to Clapham. That, with a pasty and two pennyworth of gin, took care of the bob.'

Cargill takes a turn about the room. He needs advice. He looks at his watch. The Permanent Under-Secretary will have left the Home Office at least an hour since. He recalls that Boylan claims to have deposited an account of his life, such as might compromise the Great and the Good, both living and dead, at a secret address and that it will be published if he disappears. And that the Permanent Under-Secretary instructed him, Cargill, to find it. And he's done nothing about that, having no idea at all of how to approach the problem. He contemplates going to the nearest magistrate and swearing out a warrant (was that the right term, the right procedure?) and have Boylan charged with the one crime that could not be disputed: that he entered the lobbies of the newly built House of Commons, armed with a loaded pistol. But as it is now a month since the offence was committed, and he has to hand no evidence or witnesses, he cannot see this working out.

'Where were you living when you were, er, taken in?'

'None of your business, squire,' said with the same wheedling grin, splitting the stubbled cheek, revealing the blackened teeth. 'But it won't be available to me, I can assure you of that.'

With frustration and ill-temper mounting like steam in a patent pressure cooker, Cargill takes three more turns about the room before coming to a halt again over *his* chair.

'You really cannot expect me to let you stay. You are, after all, a self-confessed murderer—'

'Oh hang on, Mr Cargill.'

'You have confessed several murders to me—'

'And there will be more, I promise you. But, between you, me and the doorpost, Mr Cargill,' and here Charlie casts a sly eye round the entire room, 'given the right circumstances, say an undertaking from your superiors to pay me the pension I'm due, I could be persuaded to withdraw every one of those confessions and much else too, much else. In return for a pension I might even tell the truth.'

And he taps the side of his nose.

Cargill feels a wave of dizziness. What is going on? *What* is going on? He looks down at Charlie who looks back up at him with the sort of trusting smile on his face that you might imagine could appear in the eyes of an old and faithful dog.

Cargill sighs, pushes a hand over his heated forehead. If he throws Charlie out, what then? If he gives him money for a night's food and lodging? He'll lose him. He'll never find out where those blasted papers are or even if they exist.

'All right then. You can stay. For one night . . .'

'Spoken like the true gen'lman I know you to be.'

'But first Deirdre will draw you hot water for a bath, and take your clothes and put them in the boiler.'

'Deirdre the lady of the house . . . ?'

'Deirdre is the maid of all work.'

And he pulls the tasselled bell sash that hangs by the side of the mantelpiece.

'He will dine with us.'

'He will do no such thing. He'll have supper with Deirdre.'

'Thomas. Mr Boylan is the first guest we have had in our house. I will not have him dine with the servant.'

'Charlie Boylan, Emily, is a . . . um . . . well, not to put too fine a point on it, by his own admission, a murderer.'

'That I cannot believe. He would not have been allowed to walk out of that dreadful prison, if that were the case. He is a gentleman. Moreover, he has every right to style himself a viscount—'

'A WHAT?'

'He told me his grandfather supported the Young Pretender in the 'forty-five rebellion, and escaped to Rome with the Prince. In recognition of his services and the sacrifices he had made he was raised to the nobility with the title of—'

'Oh this is too much!'

'Mrs Cargill, that was quite delicious. Allow me to compliment you on the table you keep. The crème brûlée was quite the equal of any I have had in France or Spain.'

Boylan leans back, dabs his lips with his napkin, sips claret from crystal, the first time it has been deployed as tableware. He is wearing Cargill's carnation-patterned silk dressing gown, with the sleeves rolled up so they look like the cuffs on the coat of a dandy from the previous century.

'Oh, Mr Boylan, or should I say my Lord? You are far too kind to say so. But I must confess I hardly noticed whether or not the comestibles were *au fait* so entertained was I by your accounts of the battles of Salamanca and Vitoria.'

246

'Ah, perhaps tomorrow then you will allow me to tell you of my exploits at the battle of Waterloo.'

Oh no you don't, Cargill says to himself, recalling the first of Charlie's reminiscences he read.

'Well . . . ! That is something to look forward to. Meanwhile, I'll take my leave, I have a little sewing to do. I'm sure my husband would like to share a glass or two of port wine with you.'

'We haven't any.'

'Madeira then. I know there is Madeira for we bought a bottle so your aunt could have a glass when she called. And a cigar too. I believe the cigars Mr Cargill buys are quite the best. They are his little extravagance, you know, aren't they, dear?'

Make no mistake. On the page our Emily seems simperingly polite: but there is steel in her voice, a note her husband is beginning to find occurs more frequently than he can readily accept, but so far has not found the courage to censor.

'Since I'm stuck with you, at least until tomorrow, you might just as well continue your story. It broke off at the execution of Thistlewood and his co-conspirators. You were, to use the terminology you employ, *blown*.'

Cargill is dissembling. What he feels, but cannot quite admit to himself, is a reluctance to go upstairs and rejoin his wife. He rather hopes she'll be asleep when he does, and to that end is prepared to give Boylan an hour or so.

'You went abroad, I believe,' he continues, 'with a commission as I understand it, to assassinate the poet Percy Bysshe Shelley.'

'My, Mr Cargill, you have been doing your homework. Or rather one supposes you have been at it "overtime", as the trades unionists call it, in the archives of the Home Office.' Charlie draws on his cigar, expels an attenuated plume of smoke through pursed lips, which Cargill notices for the first time are thickish and wet, and watches how it is sucked under the breast of the fireplace. 'Yes, I did indeed go abroad, but not initially to Italy. Initially, the commission to kill Shelley was not handed to me but to incompetent bunglers. Stafford and Bourgeois decided it were best I should lie completely low for a year or so and I went to Pau, in the south-west corner of France, a delightful town on an escarpment overlooking the Gave d'Ossau, with the high Pyrenees to one side and the coast, including the fashionable resort of Biarritz, some leagues away on the other. The verdant plains of Béarn roll between, providing every necessary and delight man, or woman, can wish for—'

'Stow it, Boylan. The reason you went to Pau was not because it had been recommended to you as a picturesque and commodious place—'

'No, indeed not. You are your usual perceptive self. I believe I mentioned at dinner that I was present at the battles of Salamanca and Vitoria—'

'At some length, Boylan.'

'Dear me. I do hope I was not tedious. Your delightful wife seemed, well, I do not think I exaggerate, enthralled. Whatever. The fact is I was an ensign in the 88th, the Connaught Rangers, and also personal servant to Captain Branwater—'

'I have heard some of this story before, Boylan, and I have checked the army lists. No Charles Boylan was an ensign in the 88th.'

'No, indeed not. But you see, at that time I went under the name of Joseph Charles Edward Bosham, Viscount Bosham, in the county of Sussex. Which, indeed, is what I am.'

'This is cod, Boylan. I don't believe it.'

An angry flush now suffuses the little man's cheeks, which, divested of their usual grubby stubble by Cargill's own razor, and already rouged with the effects of claret, Madeira, and a good coal fire, now glow like twin plums.

'Watch it, Cargill. I've called chaps out for less. And you already know I have a steady hand when it comes to pistoling.'

'Oh, for heaven's sake, get on with your story.'

Boylan giggles at the small pretence he has just made of gentlemanly concern for the manners of others.

'Another drop perhaps . . . ?' he adds.

Silently Cargill refills his uninvited guest's glass with the thick dark topaz wine, the decanter clinking musically on its rim. It is at least the smaller, port-sized glasses they are now using.

'Where was I?'

'You mentioned a Captain Branwater.'

'Yes, indeed. Like many of his brother officers who had fought for several years across the dried up *mesetas* of Spain and through its icy passes, he found the rich champaigns of Béarn particularly inviting. Which was the point about them I was trying to make. On returning from the war in America he sold up his estates in Ireland and transported himself, his horses and his new wife to Pau, where he bought an apartment on what was soon to be called the boulevard des Pyréneés. I already knew the place, for in 1814, after the battle of Toulouse, I returned there and took a place as usher in a girls' school where I taught English and Spanish—'

'You were released from the regiment?'

'In a manner of speaking.'

'You deserted.'

Boylan shrugs. 'I had no wish to fight against the Americans in the swamps of Louisiana. This is not relevant. To return to where I left off and to cut a long story short, following the execution of Thistlewood *et aliorum* I returned to Pau in the summer of 1820, discovered the marriage of Captain Branwater had been blessed with two children, who had happily survived and were now of an age when they might embark on the elementary stages of Mathematicks, a little Latin, and so forth, and I was employed to that end. Incidentally, this occupation filled no more than three or four hours a day and I amused myself for the rest of the time in writing up a history of my life. The rough first draft I left in Pau, but the second fair copy I made is with my other papers, which, as you know, constitute my insurance for a contented old age. My cigar appears to be finished, and bless me if my glass is not empty again too.'

With a sigh he makes no attempt to conceal, Cargill sees to his collocutor's needs.

'Thank you, kind sir, thank you kindly. The spring of 1822 brought two events which were to intrude upon this happy state of affairs and bring it to an end. The first was an unfortunate misunderstanding with Captain Branwater over a missing purse, the second was a letter from Mr de Bourgeois inviting me to meet him in Marseilles . . .'

Charlie warms happily to his tale. Indeed, he is feeling more than usually secure for there is yet another aspect to his release which we have not explored and which of course he does not divulge to Cargill. He has not told the whole truth about his departure from Pentonville. Mr Guppy had arrived in person with the Order for Release and they left together. On leaving Pentonville with the said Mr Guppy, a young man of prepossessing appearance, well-groomed hair and clothes, and a keen disposition to please, they went to Charlie's most recent lodgings. There he put into Mr Guppy's hands a substantial bundle of papers.

'Take these, sir, and this sovereign, and hide them. Hide them well, where no one will read them.'

Mr Guppy declared he knew just the place. An old mad drunk had a house near St Paul's. There he let out rooms but in his own room he kept piles and piles of old legal papers, briefs, submissions, letters, anything. Some he came across and kept, others were put in his care. But the whole point was, this alcoholic madman was an illiterate, a non-reader. He tried and tried to master the art, his overriding ambition, apart from the next bottle of gin, was to be able to read the vast heap of paper he had in his charge. But he never would.

With this happy arrangement at the back of his mind, as well as all the other aspects of his changed good fortune, Charlie spread himself, and began.

31

Thirty years ago, Marseilles lay burning in the sun, one hot day in June. There was no wind to make a ripple on the foul water within the harbour, or on the beautiful sea without. Boylan, Bosham, however you choose to think of me,* walked to the end of the southern mole, as near to the Fort St Nicholas as the *poilus* who guarded it would allow, and turned back to survey the city, one arm thrown up to shade his eyes against the glare from the staring white houses, staring white walls, staring white streets of the old town. Then he turned towards the distant line of the Italian coast, just visible through light clouds of mist, slowly rising from the evaporation of the sea . . .

'Boylan, your geography is at fault.'
  'It is?'
'Marseilles faces west, towards the delta of the Rhône.'

* I imagine no editor or reviewer who has read John le Carré's *A Perfect Spy* will wish to query the apparent confusion of third and first person narrative in this chapter. J. R.

'Well, I'm not the first, um, author to get that wrong. May I go on?'

'Do. But do not expect me to attach any credibility to what you say.'

Distantly the midday bells rang across the scum and flotsam of the harbour, some chiming the hour, others measuring out the Hail Marys of the angelus. A fisherman who had been straightening nets set out to dry some fifty yards back down the mole removed his sailor's cap and bowed his head, clasping the cap with both knobbled hands in front of his chest. He ignored the tall, thin dark shadow of a man who passed him, and the thin dark shadow of a man ignored him.

'Boylan. We make a connection at last,' Guy de Bourgeois remarked, coming to a halt five paces short of his quarry. 'You've been a deuced difficult chap to find these last three months or so.'

He looked about him with some irritation. Gulls swooped by, pursuing one of their number who carried a fish-head in its beak. Whether by accident or out of cunning it was not easy to say, it let a morsel drop, in the spirit of Atalanta staving off pursuit with her golden apples, and those gulls that were harrying it wheeled away, diving and squabbling to the surface where it landed. A more raucous screech sliced the hot air through several hundred yards and a plume of black smoke curled into the sky. The new paddle-driven steam-powered tug was towing a four-masted brigantine through the roads towards the open sea.

'And what sort of a place is this, to set for our meeting?' de Bourgeois concluded.

'One where a sudden knifing would be seen, a single pistol shot heard. And a long run back to the quays before you'd feel safe.'

'If you know a reason why you might be the victim of an assassination plot, you should keep it to yourself. For we know nothing of it.'

'We? Stafford, Sidmouth?

'Stafford, yes. Sidmouth bowed out six months ago. We have a young man now, Sir Robert Peel, but things go on much as before. Indeed he's a law and order man, talks of a metropolitan police force on the French model, but nothing will come of it. Our whigs and radicals will see to that. Look, it's deuced hot out here. Can't we walk back to the town, find a place we can have a drink? I promise you I have no designs upon your person. What do you say?'

The lean black shadow hurried on, and Boylan had perforce to quicken his pace almost to a run to catch up with him.

'Really you know, Charlie, you have nothing to fear from me. I come with a commission. You still have your special licence and we require you to use it.'

'Why me? There must be others in England.'

'Because the target is in these parts. Well, not far away.'

Bourgeois, with a nod of his head in the right direction, contrived to indicate the purple line below the cloud on the eastern horizon. Well, actually, no. Not, Mr Cargill, if you are right about the alignment of the port of Marseilles, but at any rate it was towards the east that he nodded.*

'And you are the nearest. And the best. I assume you can take a boat from here to Leghorn?'

'Livorno? Yes, there's a packet once a week. Takes twenty-four hours if the wind's right. Or there's a daily sail to Genoa and one could take a coaster on from there, I would think.'

The traffic at the port end of the mole now thickened around us making further conversation difficult. There were mooring hawsers to step over, lobster pots to walk round, and as we came on to the quays the full bustle, noise and confusion of a busy port, a forest of masts, a Babel of tongues, the trundling of barrels, the crash and crunch of huge crates dumped on the granite flags or swung dizzily through the air

* An intention to plagiarise the opening paragraphs of Dickens's *Little Dorrit* got me into this mess. J. R.

into the maw-like holds of the waiting traders. Bourgeois threaded a way through it all, as if confident he knew where he was going, found an alleyway through a stack of baled Egyptian cotton, and suddenly all was dark and cooler, though the noise still echoed down the medieval canyon they had entered.

Boylan skidded on a discarded sardine and clutched his elbow.

'This might be a good place for a sudden stiletto thrust,' he murmured.

'Oh, do be quiet. I promise you I have no such intention in mind.'

The alleyway opened into a tiny square with a small church and opposite it a smaller tavern with benches attached to its slimy walls and a sad looking orange tree in a tub by the beaded doorway.

'This will do.' Bourgeois sat, pulling his coat-tails over his thighs, in much the manner of a raven or vulture adjusting its cumbersome feathers, then, to the urchin who had appeared like a genie through the rattling beads, holding a tin tray, '*Une bouteille de vin rouge, deux verres et une carafe d'eau froide, s'il vous plaît.*'

'Things are different since Sidmouth moved on,' he continued, as if there had been no break in the conversation. 'We are now, how can I put this? less *official* than we were. Sir Robert is a man of probity . . . not that Sidmouth was not, I would not suggest that, but Sir Robert prefers not to know about everything that goes on, keeps his finger, as it were, out of the pie. Almost he expects us to *guess* what is required of us. There is sense in this. If something gets out or goes publicly wrong he can offer the Commons and the press what he calls a plausible denial of complicity—'

'And as a result the artisans, the mechanicians of his designs, can swing for them?'

'No, no, indeed not. They inhabit now a world that is even more shady than it was, and when pressed can merge into the shadows and be forgotten.'

'But not unrewarded.'

'No, indeed not,' the raven repeated. 'The secret fund remains in place, is annually renewed, and most years increased. Ah. Our wine.'

It was not, Mr Cargill, as good a wine as the one you provided this evening. Sour, yet with a hint of liquorice. I drank it much watered down. But the business of drawing the cork, pouring, topping up from the terracotta jug of water was enough to signal a change of subject to something more gritty, more germane.

'Three persons who have in the past caused our masters some irritation have, or are, coming together in the vicinity of Leghorn with a plan which the powers that be view with some concern. Two of them have been exiles in Italy for a couple of years or more and beyond our reach and have both written and published, one with more success than the other, numerous poems, pamphlets, essays and such like inciting the common people to revolution and enlisting through specious arguments the support of educated people who should know better. The third, only recently arrived after a peculiarly long and hazardous voyage via Biscay and Gibraltar, is an editor and publisher of such stuff. And the point is all three are come together with the aim in mind of printing and publishing a new periodical to be called *The Liberal*. The notoriety of both writers and the very considerable popularity of one of them will ensure a wide readership and possibly considerable influence. In short and to put the matter plainly, this must not happen. It must be stopped.'

My curiosity was aroused, as no doubt is yours, as to who these people were.

'Lord Byron, Percy Bysshe Shelley and Leigh Hunt,' was the reply. Ah. I see you start and look up with what appears to be a wild surmise.

Cargill, who, what with the fire, the wine, the food and the relentless monotone of his interlocutor's voice, not to mention

255

the trials and tribulations of a difficult day, has been dozing, but these names have indeed brought him back to wakefulness.

'But I thought . . . I, er, read . . . there is a file, minutes of a committee—'

'That says what, Mr Cargill?'

'Oh, nothing. Just that it was dated spring 1820, not 1822.'

'And it suggested negative action against all or some of these men?'

'Something of the sort. But it's not for me to say. Forget what I have said.'

Boylan ignores this last instruction.

'I recall, I think, what you are talking about,' he touches the side of his sly nose. 'About that time, and shortly before I removed to Pau, I did call on Mr Hunt in Hampstead and, well, not to put too fine a point on it, put the frighteners on him with regard to printing Mr Shelley's work. At the time that was probably enough but, having put himself beyond the reach of the law by removing to Italy, well, the situation was altered.'

He takes up his tale again.

The commission Bourgeois had thus at last got round to issuing to Boylan was simple: *The Liberal* must be stopped.

'By what means?' asked Boylan, brushing aside a troop of flies that had homed in on the seated pair.

'Any means,' Bourgeois's tone was dry. 'But it would be . . . nice if there was the appearance of an accident.'

'The chinks?'

'Fifty per person removed, and all reasonable expenses.'

'Guineas. In gold. None of your paper coin. And a return to my regular stipend. With back payments for two years.'

'Bless me, Boylan, you want the earth.'

'Look. I'm here. I'm your man for this sort of business. How long will it take to find another and get him to Leghorn? More than the time it'll take to get this new paper out, *The Liberal* you call it? Take it or leave it.'

'I'll see what I can do. But you are driving a hard bargain.'

'Take it or leave it.'

'Oh very well.'

'Twenty down. Now. To cover my initial layout.'

'No. Payment on results.'

'Mr Bourgeois, do I look as if I could find the chinks for a passage to Livorno?'

I duly used the first of my twenty guineas to purchase a passage from Marseilles to Genoa, arriving there about the thirteenth of the month. I found the city an altogether more attractive prospect than Marseilles, being subject to the cleansing influence of the cool winds that blow off the Ligurian Alps, and generally better kept. There were fewer foreigners, almost none of those of dusky hue from North Africa who make the French port both filthier and more dangerous, and generally speaking I find the Italians, those of the north of the peninsula anyway, more ordered, cleaner and more efficient than the French: no doubt this is in large measure the result of the imperial Austrian presence.

I spent a day or two making enquiries and found that Hunt and his large family, now much weakened by a long and tedious voyage, the children squabbling and peevish, Mrs Hunt feverish and weak, had just arrived, perhaps on the same day as I.

They planned to sail as directly as they could, at least as soon as they were in part recovered from the privations they had suffered, to Leghorn, from where, I assumed, they would complete their epic odyssey by coach over the last ten miles to Byron's place at Pisa. It was not difficult to unravel all this – they had an English servant with them, who was happy to tell me all I needed to know in return for a bottle of grappa and a dish of squid rings fried in batter. He had none of the local currency about him, indeed none at all, having not been paid since they left England at the New Year, such were the hand-to-mouth straits through which the Hunts managed their domestic economy.

But this was not all. From a different source, um, namely

through the offices of a serving girl in the hostel where they were staying, I was able to peruse some of the correspondence Mr Hunt left lying about the room they had taken, and from this learned that the Shelley household was not at Leghorn or Pisa but had established itself at a tiny resort close to La Spezia, halfway between Genoa and Leghorn, called San Terenzo, close to the rather larger but still small fishing port of Lerici. I decided to investigate this first, feeling it would be easier to observe this smaller household and possibly insert myself into it, than the much larger establishment Lord Byron maintained at Pisa. Consequently it was a small coasting felucca that I took, trading down the coast, from Genoa to La Spezia . . .

Boylan's voice meanders on, rising and falling, sometimes rumbling, more often squalling and trilling. Cargill, bemused by the tiresome day he has had, the fumes of his cigar and the third glass of Madeira on top of a large meal and a bottle of claret, sinks into a semi-somnolent state in which the events Boylan narrates assume the painted reality of a dream.

To an eye peering across a gunwale hardly more than eighteen inches above its surface, the wide sea seemed violet in hue and dusted like a grape with yeast. Only if you stood up, and, so steady was the vessel, one hardly needed to clutch the stays that supported the masts to keep one's balance, one could see across that scarcely ruffled sheet that now, with added height, took on a sapphire hue, to a chain of bays, coves and tiny sandy beaches. Beyond them the piled-up foothills of the Apennines, rugged with outbreaks of rock between the pines, oaks and cypresses, climbed to the sheltering sky, an inverted bowl that burned, staining the white radiance of eternity with lapis blue, and heated the air that lay like a miasma between, depriving it of those constituents that make breathing a lightsome pleasure rather than a chore.

The two heavy lateen sails hung like the wrinkled dugs of a fat old woman, trimmed with the rat-tails of their reef-points, scarcely swelling and only then at their boomless hems. You could not say the water lapped against the clinkered planks; a kitten makes more noise. The only sounds were the muted snore of a peasant woman hung with green and pearly ropes of freshly plaited pungent garlic, and the very occasional swish of the steering oar as the helmsman made the tiny adjustments needed to reap the fullest benefit he could from the slightest shift of a breeze that lacked the strength of a baby's sigh . . . but was strong enough to spread the strong sharp odour across Charlie's nostrils and into the wake of the felucca. She was overfreighted with barrels of salt and sugar, both off-loaded from a Spanish merchantman in Genoa, and bound for La Spezia, and had three passengers beside Boylan and the garlic-wreathed woman. One, a Dominican friar with a big black-rimmed wideawake hat, who muttered at his beads for almost the whole trip, had, as they cast off from the Genoan quay, berated the master of the three-man crew for overloading the slight craft.

'Squalls,' he said, 'are sudden on these coasts and can come out of a blue sky.'

He was not reassured when the answer came that if this happened they'd throw some barrels overboard, and this was the reason no doubt why he resorted to his feverish pleas to the Virgin that she should pray for him now and at the hour of his death.

Presently they rounded the craggy headland that marks the entrance to the Gulf of La Spezia, and began the snail-like process of beating up against a virtually non-existent breeze: this, the last league or so, would take them to their destination. And as they made their listless progress, they heard, coming from behind their heavily drooping sails, a distant magical music, which, albeit almost inaudible, carried with it all the allure of the songs the Sirens sang.

Boylan, alone of those on the felucca, understood the words, for they were in English.

259

We meet not as we parted,
  We feel more than all may see:
My bosom is heavy-hearted,
  And thine full of doubt for me:
  One moment has bound the free.

That moment is gone for ever,
  Like lightning that flashed and died –
Like a snow-flake upon the river –
  Like a sunbeam upon the tide,
  Which the dark shadows hide.

That moment from time was singled
  As the first of a life of pain:
The cup of its joy was mingled
  – Delusion too sweet though vain!
  Too sweet to be mine again.

The voice, a sweet soprano, towards the lower end of the register, almost a mezzo, not strong but nevertheless certain and confident, died over a suspended cadence, a broken chord from the guitar that had trippingly supported it, then, a man's voice took its place . . .

'Is that it, Shelley?'

'That's it, Edward. That's as far as it so far goes.'

And at that moment their craft came in view, passing behind the felucca, coming out as it were from the stagelike curtains of its tired sails, only twenty paces or so behind them, gliding on the sheeny silk with the purposeful thrust of a swan with wings upstarting, half unfurled.

'Ahoy, there,' continued the same voice, then, to his companions: 'Are they awake or do they dream? The crew of this painted ship upon a painted ocean?'

He meant us, for their passing had spilled what little wind there was from our sails which now hung like sacks from a line. Their boat, however, surged on – in spite of the near calm the water veritably rustled beneath its prow in a glassy bow-wave. Although not more than twenty-four feet long, she had two mainmasts, was rigged like a schooner though with topsails, and had two or three jibs on each pole as well. She moved like a gliding swallow and seemingly as fast when there was more than a puff of wind, and her lines put you in mind of the same bird. She had only one visible flaw – a large patch on her forward mainsail where a large piece had been cut out and replaced. Visible? There were other flaws, not so evident.

32

I, the garlic wreathed lady and some of our cargo were put down at La Spezia two hours later – it took that long to beat up the narrow gulf against what airs there were. Almost immediately our felucca stood out again into the bay, with mountain cheeses in place of what had been dropped, but still with our bead-telling priest aboard. He, bound for Leghorn, yclept Livorno by the natives, was now in a state of terror for a huge pile of cloud-capped palaces, surmounted by an ominous anvil, had risen on the far horizon and he and all aboard the felucca feared a storm, which was why she put to sea so hastily, hoping to make a further reach down the coast, and thereby escape the squall that blackened the horizon beneath the cloud. With the light airs behind her she was soon a mere triangle or shark's tooth of white which I watched diminish as certain condottieri, customs officers and police gathered around me, smoking cheroots, and even in the case of the most senior officer present, drinking coffee from a tiny cup held beneath his chin by forefinger and thumb. They subjected me to intense and irritating bureaucratic investigation for a tedious six hours or so stretched well beyond nightfall.

As the sea got up for the last hour of daylight, with the wind knocking against the doors and shutters, and the rain gusting in from under the dense black cloud, I was held in quarantine in a tiny cell behind the town hall. What this quarantine was meant to achieve I never discovered, but disbursement of two more gold guineas foreclosed it in time for me to make a late supper. Converting the Spanish I already had into Spitalian allowed me to communicate with ease with the natives, and following a not undisturbed sleep on a flea-filled palliasse in the taverna I set out the next morning to cover the five or six miles to Lerici by road and mule track.

Descending through pines, cypress and scrub oak I could see it was not much of a place: a huddle of cottages about a church and a square, a quay faced with rough-hewn stone, a mole and a beach with a half-dozen or so fishing boats pulled up on it and nets set out to dry. I made enquiries, principally of an Italianate Beauty who looked like a Raffaello Virgin apart from her moustache. She was putting out washing on a line while the bambino on her back peered over her shoulder and prattled instructions in bambino-italiano. From her I understood that the mad English lived a mile or so back up the coast, possibly beyond the next headland, on which a small brown castle brooded like a cockchafer, though their boats were here in Lerici having been brought in the night before to be safer from the storm.

I took a look at them, tied up as they were to the quay. One was the boat like a swallow I had seen before; the other, larger, twice the size, a three-master, American rigged, with a brass cannon in its forecastle, was called the *Bolivar*, a name which meant nothing to me at the time, though when I learnt the man in question was a South American revolutionary I understood why Byron should have named his boat for him.

Mad? The English? They stay up all night, my Raffaellesque lady continued. They swim in the sea with no clothes on. They sail their boat in all weathers and at a speed that leaves the dolphins behind – like a witch on a broomstick. They kiss and maybe fuck each others' wives. She didn't exactly say 'fuck' but linked her forefingers in a most expressive gesture. They never eat meat though Lent was over three months ago. Such was the gossip in Lerici.

I retraced my steps for a half-mile, back up the hillside, and then took a left down a steep track, dusty and grooved, occasionally laddered with the roots of the pines and oaks that shaded much of it, until I came back on to the beach, a continuation of the one at Lerici, with its castled headlands. A dozen cottages, certainly no more, stood back from the sea clustered round a tiny church with a cupola like a baby's bonnet. Two hundred yards further on was a much larger edifice, which was aptly named, considering the size of its neighbours, Casa Magni.

From the back, which is how I approached it, it was a plain wall faced with honey-coloured stucco, pierced on the upper two floors with tiny shuttered windows, not more than three or four of them, and shaded by timbered eaves beneath the usual tiles set over and under in the style that has been current since Caesar came and saw and conquered.

There was no rear entry that I could see, so leaving the squalid and closed-up cabins to my right and stooping beneath the branches of a large and fruit laden fig tree which looked like nothing so much as a giant, green candelabra I made my way round the side. A flight of six blue and green, arrow-tailed, long-beaked bee-eaters swirled up from its branches and made off into the pinewoods I had left, and a hoopoe on the edge where coarse grass merged with coarse sand gave up raising and lowering its crest, uttered an annoyed hoo-hoo and with its rowing, roller-coaster flight followed them.

I paused for a moment and, with my back to the hamlet and the castle, took in the scene. My gaze followed the shallow arc of the bay right round for a mile or more back to Lerici itself, and, somewhat to my chagrin, I realised a walk along the shore would have brought me far more quickly and easily to where I was than my scramble over the hill. Perhaps my Spitalian

264

had not been as efficient a mode of communication as I had supposed.

My eyes winced at the glitter of sunlight on a surface that was for the most part deepest sapphire but modulated to emerald just beyond the reach of a tiny jetty. Above this and the beach itself rocks had been piled into a short sea wall some eight feet high with, cut into it as it were, a portico of five or seven arches, I forget exactly how many, the middle one wider than the others. Square shuttered windows above them looked out over the bay and a projecting roof like an awning set against the main body of the building rose to a top storey behind. This façade was finished off with a crumbling balustrade which attempted to give a sort of second-rate nobility to what was, in effect, a boat house. The largest room, as I was about to discover, lay behind the arches, and was, when it all served its original purpose, where the boats were kept.

Standing on the corner of the portico, and hidden, should I wish to be, by the squared-off end pillar that supported it, I became aware that I was witness to a commotion or crisis. The lady I had seen in the boat the day before, she who sang and played the guitar, dressed now in muslin *déshabillé* and with her luxuriant and dark hair tumbling about her shoulders, paced to and fro in the portico, twisting a tiny lacy handkerchief between her fingers. Her eyes, shaded by her palm, were fixed on the bay, and particularly distant Lerici, and she muttered, sighed and gasped to herself, giving evidence of the greatest agitation. Then, when she turned in my direction, I caught, just as I ducked out of her sight, a glimpse of the front of her robe and saw that it was splashed with . . . blood!

It was now that, above the swish and drag of the waves, my ear caught the distressing sound of a woman crying out, sighing, and moaning in pain, and the voice of another who alternately gasped and wept, neither set of sounds emanating from the one in front of me. I must not give the wrong impression. None of these expostulations was loud or even dramatic – I sensed there was an effort of control behind them and that they were forced from between clenched lips by the exigencies of the situation. In short, they confirmed what I already knew: that these people were British. Had they been Italian I make no doubt the air would have been rent with screams, prayers and imprecations.

They were interrupted by two circumstances. First, a ringing clatter as of something large and metal, a huge saucepan perhaps or cauldron being dropped on a stone or tiled floor, then a screech as it was pulled along. This was followed by a sudden and most un-British wailing, as suddenly reduced to a whimper, signalling the arrival of a second actor on the stage-like portico. This was a small child, not above three years old, dressed in the fashion of the time in a long gown, also bloodied, and with a mop of long hair too, so I could not be sure whether it was a boy or girl. It clutched a twig of liquorice on which it chewed for a moment before giving vent to another prolonged Waaaaaaah! Then it caught the visible woman's hand and stared up at her.

'Mama will be dead by din-dins,' it said.

The woman lowered the hand that shaded her eye and with a clenched fist made a brief gesture that seemed to express hope, then she bent her knees to bring her head to its level and took the child's free hand.

'I don't think so, Flo,' she said, flinging out her other hand towards Lerici. 'For here comes your father, and I'm sure he'll have the doctor with him.'

The eyes of the girl, as I now took her to be, and my own, followed the direction of her arm and we could see the sails, all up and fully stretched though the distance to be covered was small, of the swallow-like boat which surged through the swell as if hunted by Neptune's tritons.

'He's on his way,' she now called out, directing her voice to the room beyond the pillars. 'They'll be here directly.'

'The doctor?' came the reply.

'Not that I can see.'

'Oh, my God! Who is with him then?'

'Just the three of them. Eddie, Trelawny and Bysshe.'

266

She turned back from the interior and, holding little Flo's hand, waved her handkerchief at the approaching boat, still with her back to me. Presently she was joined by another child, a little older than the first, a girl also, I think, about whose shoulder she placed her arm and hand in an intimate gesture offering comfort. This intimacy led me to believe she was the mother. This second child placed her thumb in her mouth, the first continued to chew on her twig of liquorice and thus they stood and waited until the boat slid up to and past a buoy, a small barrel, that bobbed ten yards or so beyond the tiny quay.

Sails rattled down. One young man in front dropped hempen fenders over the side, in the stern a big, dark, bearded man with a mane of black curly hair put the helm up and brought her round as the third leapt nimbly across the decreasing gap between gunwale and pier.

This was the slightest of the three. He had a high brow beneath a mop of dark hair, a long straight nose, sensuous but shapely lips which could take on a sulky look, a slightly recessive but well-sculpted chin. His figure was lissome, fit, not thin but by no means fat, tanned as I could see for his white shirt was open, his breeches unbuttoned below his knee, his long brown feet bare. His hands were strong, the fingers long and thin. But as I was to discover later it was his eyes that held you. Large and dark, they rarely smiled though the rest of his face might break up into manic merriment. His eyes, however, remained always solemn but burned with a dark intensity that questioned you and the universe they inhabited.

This was Shelley – the man I had been sent to kill.

I was caught. My squared pillar would not conceal me from both the quay and the rest of the portico. He had a sight of me, paused in his stride and those eyes burned me up for a second, then he surged on up the steps, and into the room behind. I heard his voice ringing out, instantly in command.

'Mary, what the divil . . . ? Come, you should not have left your bed—'

'She was, she said, too hot—'

267

'Never mind that now. No, Claire, I do not have the doctor with me, but yes we have a boat-load of ice, one big block. Now come on, let's stir about, waste no more time. Claire . . .' then voice raised, 'Jane, help Mary into the bath if you would . . .'

The lady on the portico relinquished the children and hurried in after him. The man I later understood to be her common-law husband, Edward Williams, completed the mooring of the vessel, and he and Trelawny, the giant dark-bearded Cornishman, began to try to lift a huge block of greenish ice out of the space between the masts.

Shelley came back out, saw their difficulty, swung round and fixed on me.

'Here. You. Whoever you are, lend a hand.'

I did as I was told. With Shelley one usually did.

By the time we had the block, which was six feet by three by three and most awkward to handle since it was already slimed with melt, he had returned with a sledgehammer and a long-handled axe. Williams found a two-handled cane basket of some capacity, Trelawny and Shelley set about breaking up the ice and I with hands that fast became frost-bitten endeavoured to fill the basket while Williams used a shovel. He then rushed it indoors, returning within seconds for the next load. This was done four times before voices within declared they had enough.

We downed tools and trooped into the large shadowy room that lay behind the pillars, I standing somewhat behind the others.

The ceiling was high and divided into three or four vaults, the walls hung with nets, rigging, sails, boathooks, oars and the like as befits a boat house though this was not true of the rest of the furnishings. These were an elegant glass-fronted bookcase, wicker- and cane-bottomed chairs, a humdrum table with turned legs, woven floor mats, children's toys including a hobbyhorse, tops, a hoop, beach buckets and spades, a chaise longue, bloodied, and a hip bath. Sand drifted across the cracked stone flags. A naked woman half-sat, half-lay in the hip bath, head back and corpse grey, one hand thrown, like Marat's in the painting, along the edge. Her raised knees rose from the pile of broken ice she sat in, which, where it lay above her lower stomach, was already rouged with the blood that melted it. Shelley knelt beside her, held the hand that dropped over the rim. Presently she opened her eyes and a wan smile drifted like a sunbeam across a devastated landscape.

'Thank you, Bysshe,' she murmured, and returned the pressure of his grip. 'I think I'll be all right now.'

At this the woman called Claire caught a sob in her throat and turned away. Trelawny slapped his hand against his thigh and cried: 'I'll see the sails are properly stowed, coming Williams?' and Mary's child Flo looked across the bath at me, and said: 'Who's that?'

Shelley rose.

'Yes, indeed. Who do we have to thank for some timely help? An imp, it seems, but not I think from hell, but summoned perhaps by the wild fantasies the present state of affairs has produced in our minds. Speak, Spirit! If thou art not damned.'

Well, I could not. Unprepared I could find nothing to say.

'Is he dumb? Deaf too perhaps? *Un uomo sordo! Un sordo-muto?*'

A deaf-mute? It was a role I was happy to adopt and I did so for as long as I could maintain it convincingly, for the next week or so.

33

Let me pre-empt any possible confusion you may labour under and quickly recapitulate the members of this *crew*. Starting as it were at the bottom of the ladder there was Charles Vivian, whom you have not yet met, a likeable lad of eighteen or so who acted as ship's boy aboard the *Don Juan*, for that was the name of their speedy boat. More of that in a moment. He had been left in Lerici, since there was not reckoned to be room for him with the block of ice, but he arrived shortly, having run along the beach behind them. Then the children. The eldest was a girl, the daughter of the guitar lady, who was Jane, known as Williams, she who had stood out in the portico watching for the arrival of the *Don Juan*; then came Percy Florence, or Flo, the son of Shelley and his wife Mary, whom I had, on account of the fashions that did not distinguish the sexes in one so young and whose nickname Flo had further confused me, presumed to be a girl. Born in Florence he was named for that city, a foolish conceit which I imagine will not be adopted by many. Finally there was a baby, the offspring of Jane and Edward Williams, whose name or sex I never established with any certainty as it was variously apostrophised as

Boojum, Mustardseed, Beelzebub or Bub. So much for the younger members of the party. Now for the adults; I will not say for those who had reached an age of discretion, for none of them had.

There was the aforementioned Jane, a tall and beautiful lady of some presence and stature who sang and played the guitar with equal accomplishment. Her lover was Edward, or Eddie Williams, a very British sort of person, very, how shall I put it, *physical*. He was always on the go: sailing, swimming, working on the boat, shooting, riding, indulging in pranks and other mischief, with a jolly laugh and a quip for everybody. He was shy only of his inamorata whom he clearly worshipped, though she treated him often as a joke. However, he was muscled, fit and young and no doubt gave her a good time in bed.

Trelawny, the oldest there, also Edward but always referred to by his family name, was an adventurer, a traveller, a doer, and, on the qt I discovered, a bully. Big, dark, bearded, he looked and behaved like a Cornish wrecker, though had pretensions the others accepted to be a gentleman. More too of him anon.

He had a companion, a Captain Roberts whom I hardly saw at all for he had lodgings in Lerici, there being no room for him in the Casa not-so-Magni. He it was who had designed and built the *Don Juan* in Genoa, had come with Trelawny on the *Bolivar* and, after Trelawny had taken the *Bolivar* back to Livorno, remained in Lerici to continue to improve the rigging, ballast and so forth on the *Don Juan*.

Then there was Claire Clairmont, the daughter, by a previous liaison, of Godwin's second wife, and so a sort of sister, though no blood relation, to Mary. She had heretofore been the concubine of Lord Byron, one of many, whose child by him, Allegra, had recently died while in the care of nuns to whom my lord had given her in charge. Claire was a flirtatious piece much of the time, often at loggerheads with her stepsister, jealous of Jane, prone to fits of melancholy but jolly enough when her bereavement was off her mind. Named Jane at birth, she called herself Claire as a result of a whimsy and for no better reason.

271

Finally, the Shelleys themselves. Mary was already famed as the creator of Frankenstein and his Monster, not out of Promethean fire but more the result of a *bet*. She was at present struggling to complete her second and third novels, but struggle it was, plagued as she was by constant travels and removals, financial crises, the deaths of all her infant children bar Flo, the miscarriage I had just attended, and the neglect of a husband who idealised and probably seduced any of their female acquaintances who came within his reach, often requiring her to maintain *ménages à trois* or even *quatre*. No wonder she was, in the brief time I was acquainted with her, melancholïc, withdrawn and prone to illusions.

And finally her husband. What can I say? Atheist, revolutionary, libertine, he yet exerted a power in which attraction and repulsion were precisely balanced, so one was part driven away by loathing of vice and extreme self-love while held by passion, sincerity and the sense that he was in touch with elemental forces beyond the ken of ordinary folk. I have heard comparison made between him and the Devil as portrayed in Milton's *Paradise Lost*. A cursory glance, no more, of that work, is all I have been able to give, my life as you know has been too full of other concerns to find time to do it justice, but I daresay there is a correlation to be made between our Percy and the Light Bearer who was also the Prince of Darkness. He, at any rate, thought so. Mark this, taken from a lengthy manuscript I came across during my sojourn at the Casa Magni.

Milton's Devil as a moral being is as far superior to his God as one who perseveres in some purpose which he has conceived to be excellent in spite of adversity and torture, is to one who in the cold security of undoubted triumph inflicts the most horrible revenge on his enemy . . .

Or put it another way, Milton's Devil is a failed revolutionary, while his God is a Liverpool, Wellington or Sidmouth or a Trinity made up of all three.

The same document ends thus:

It is impossible to read the compositions of the most celebrated writers of the present day without being startled with the electric life which burns within their words. They measure the circumference and sound the depths of human nature with a comprehensive and all penetrating spirit, and they are themselves perhaps the most sincerely astonished at its manifestations, for it is less their spirit than the spirit of the age. Poets are the hierophants of an unapprehended inspiration, the mirrors of the gigantic shadows which futurity casts upon the present, the words which express what they understand not, the trumpets which sing to battle and feel not what they inspire: the influence which is moved not, but moves. Poets are the unacknowledged legislators of the World.

Well, Mr Cargill, that may have been true in Shelley's brief lifetime but let us be grateful that poets have since returned to their proper business of writing about the beauties of an idealised nature and an idealised past, when they are not dwelling on the mysteries of their own navels.

Having made a mark both as a helper in the ice-block episode and as a deaf-mute, I continued to hang around in as discreet a way as I could manage through the rest of the day and indeed the week or so that followed. That day itself saw the belated arrival of a doctor who said Shelley had done well with his ice which had staunched his wife's bleeding, and who pronounced her out of any immediate danger. Claire and Jane now set out a simple repast of olives, bread, goat cheeses and watered wine which all pronounced excellent, their apparent fancy being to pretend they lived the simple life of the local peasants. Since, from the smells that were wafted across the short sandy space that separated the Casa Magni from San Terenzo I was able to surmise these were dining off broiled

273

tuna, lobster and sardines, I felt that this was yet another illusion these people cultivated among themselves.

Shelley then saw his wife back to her couch on the upper floor, where Claire read to her until she slept; meanwhile, Jane nursed her youngest within the portico, while the men, satisfied that what was essentially a female crisis was over, took their whizz of a boat back to Lerici where they and the aforementioned Roberts continued to make improvements. Under his direction they now set about rerigging her, a task that took several days interspersed with several trial relaunchings and rebeachings.

During this time I learnt that the boat had been recently built in Genoa under the direction of Roberts and Trelawny, Lord Byron paying the costs as they arose which Shelley had promised to reimburse, and they had had her in Lerici for a month. Byron, out of what motive no one knew – it might have been sheer egoism or to make the point that he was still owed for her, or possibly just as a cruel joke – had christened her *Don Juan* after the hero of the scurrilous lampoon he was then writing. This had been bad enough but what was worse for Shelley was that Byron had caused this name to be painted indelibly across the fore mainsail. For a week Shelley and his friends had scrubbed at these offensive words, eventually giving up hope of removing them and requiring a Lerici sail-maker to replace the width of canvas on which they had been inscribed. Such is the vanity of men who, though friends in every other way, considered themselves rivals on Mount Parnassus. Privately Shelley renamed her, to himself, *Ariel*, after the tricksy sprite in Shakespeare's play, a name he kept to himself though I heard him use it when he uttered it in my presence believing me still to be *il sordomuto*.

The intention that lay behind the rerigging was to make her yet faster not only by increasing the span of canvas she could spread but by altering her balance in such a way that she would require less ballast of pig-iron nuggets to keep her stable, thus lowering her waterline by a good three inches. This required the nicest calculations, much theorising and scribbling, and many sea-borne trials. They achieved their object, but, said Trelawny, possibly at the expense of safety. Shelley rejected this consideration as mere calculus; what he wanted was speed.

Speed and an early death. Why do I say this? On more than one occasion he required me to walk down the beach to Lerici and post his letters. These, following the requirement of my profession, I duly opened, first having borrowed his seal so I could restore them to a state that would not excite their recipients' suspicions. One of them, which I posted about a week after I had arrived, was to Trelawny who had departed, being captain of the *Bolivar* which Lord Byron required him to take to Leghorn. This letter included a request for 'Prussic Acid, or essential oil of bitter almonds because it would be a comfort to me to hold in my possession that golden key to the chamber of perpetual rest'.

I had intercourse only once more with Trelawny, at the very end of this episode, when, having learnt that I had acted as Shelley's postboy, he accused me of opening his letters, indeed of being a spy for the Austrian or even British police. This he was able to do since in the course of his interrogation he extracted an expletive from me by kicking me savagely from behind, thus blowing my pretence at being a deaf-mute which I had kept up for so long. It is for this reason that I was able to make the categoric assertion that he was a bully.

Before that, however, things went on very well without him. I continued to haunt the Casa Magni without ever becoming an accepted part of the household. They understood me to be a sort of village idiot from San Terenzo or even Lerici itself once the people of San Terenzo had denied knowledge of me. Or perhaps I was the whelp of a whore travelling with the armies in the late wars, dropped in the neighbourhood and surviving by begging, thieving and the exercise of my wits on the peripheries of human habitations. I made myself useful when occasion arose, made sure I was in their vicinity or near the parts of the house where they cooked when food was being prepared, slept in outhouses or in the woods behind the house where I also hid what was left of de Bourgeois's gold. If they expressed irritation or even fear at my presence, I kept away for a day or two or performed some signal service, and before long they accepted me the way one does a feral tom, petting me when I let them, offering me scraps, even playing with me, but never admitting me fully to the hearth.

This suited me. Considering the commission I had been given I had no readiness to learn to like them.

The weather became hotter and hotter and they did not know how to handle it. Being British they threw open all the shutters and doors, allowed sunlight to fall through casements and heat the rooms further, in short did everything against local custom. Their neighbours in the villages sealed their houses during daylight, only opening them long after nightfall when the temperature did drop a little, and living and playing by night rather than by day. They even tended their plots and sorted their catch by lamplight. But the Casa Magni sweltered. The stones of its floors and walls continued to give off heat through the night and the air inside was often warmer than on the headland where almost always it moved a little. Sunburn and heat rashes made the children miserable and they whined and mewed through the day when they should have slept, and cried and squabbled at night when their elders endeavoured to make them sleep.

A sort of madness fell on the place, the heat a fog, a miasma of unreality. They saw visions. Dark passions shifted below glassy surfaces like sharks. The bay became infested with jelly-fish, purple Portuguese men o' war that drifted beneath the surface like bloated apparitions; sheet lightning filled the western sky at night, an impotent display of fireworks that brought neither thunder nor rain nor even a sudden gust of wind. The moon grew to fullness and, big-bellied, made a day of night.

Mary drifted through the upper rooms, hardly ever coming down again, and never out, weeping when on her own, or when she thought she was on her own, or sighing 'he cometh not'.

And when he did come she perversely pretended to be reading or even writing and soon he left her on her own, taking the stairs as quietly as he had mounted them.

The men on the other hand affected a jolly boyishness for as much of the day as they had energy for, first fixing up the boat then sailing her. They made a great fuss about the work they were doing: they exclaimed at the satisfaction they got from planing wood, driving in nails, shinning up the masts to fix the new rigging. How there was pleasure to be had from physical labour and such like nonsense. To myself I took leave to doubt they would have taken so much pleasure from it had they been doing the same work for someone else, for pay, for hire.

Jane was mostly with them, her laughter and her song chiming like crystal droplets in a breeze across the glaucous water, trailing her white hand in the wave, or strumming the very beautiful guitar, inlaid with flowers like a posy or wreath around the sound-hole, which Shelley had given her so she could accompany herself singing the love songs he wrote for her. Occasionally Williams sulked if she ignored him too much, but for the most part she and Shelley were always able to mock him into better humour. Claire drifted between Mary and the men, not entirely welcome with either, or busied herself with the children, though this caused her pain at times as memories of her own child came back.

Often, while Roberts, Williams and Vivian, the ship's boy, worked on the boat, Shelley would write or read, leaning against the mast if they left him undisturbed, or in an upper room of the house if they did not. I caught glimpses of what he scrawled. It was strange stuff.

34

'The chariot rolled, a captive multitude
Was driven; – all those who had grown old in power
Or misery, – all who had their age subdued

By action or by suffering, and whose hour
Was drained to its last sand in weal or woe
So that the trunk survived both fruit and flower; –

All but the sacred few who could not tame
Their spirits to their conquerors – but as soon
As they had touched the world with living flame

Fled back like eagles to their native noon
Or those who put aside the diadem
Of earthly thrones or gems . . .

'Bugger it, Sordomuto, I'm stuck for a rhyme for noon and soon.'
It was of course on the tip of my tongue to suggest June and
Moon, but I managed to restrain myself and continued to push a
little heap of sand and seawrack round the floor with my witch's
broom, real broom, cut from the hillside and tied to a pole.

278

Shelley sighed, dipped his pen, and across the bottom of the page began a quick sketch of the *Don Juan*, or *Ariel*, but that quickly dissatisfied or bored him too. Aware I had glanced round his elbow he turned brusquely and fixed me with those burning dark eyes that seemed to skewer me to the rough-cast wall behind me like a butterfly in Mr Darwin's collection. Well, more a bug really. A cockroach. And like a King's Counsel, or rather Queen's, he began a catechism in exactly that dry and offensive tone prosecutors use in court.

'What, *mio sordomuto*, would you say is the greatest evil that can befall a man . . . ?'

Again an answer was on my lips almost before I could suppress it into a crow-like cry. The ingratitude of princes was what I was about to say. Well, their spymasters anyway.

'I'll tell you, Sordomuto, since you choke on your answer. Boredom, Sordomuto. *L'ennui, la noia*. The dull sweat secreted on the forehead by that monster accidie. I'm bored. Pardon the expression but I am fucking bored. And bored with fucking. My dear wife has kept me from her bed since she knew she was yet again with child, and now she has miscarried will keep me at arm's length a few months more, while monsters fill her brain and do unspeakable things to her in the moonlight of these hot nights. Claire I've had, and Jane I'll have. But it bores me. All that bores me. Especially in this heat. Skin cleaves to skin instead of slipping like silk across it. Sweat mingles with semen. It's a messy business. Mind, between men it need not be so messy . . . Athenian love, maybe that's what I crave. I'm not alone. Poor Eddie hungers for me, and Trelawny too sees himself as a modern Alcibiades.'

As this monologue proceeded he paced the room round me like a caged cheetah and at times I felt like the festering leg of mutton zoo-keepers throw to such beasts. Almost all the time his eyes remained on mine, mine flinched away, but when I looked up again, his would dart in like a fisherman's spear and transfix them again.

'Eddie wants me. Eton, you see. Like me he did time. Old

279

habits die hard. And then the Navy. As a very young lad. Well . . . Doctor Keate and the birch. Buggery. Mr Midshipman Easy. Very easy. That's why he countenances my flirtation with Jane. He hopes, maybe, for a threesome as a prelude to just the two of us. Meanwhile, vicariously he enjoys what he imagines she and I do together. It's the heat you know. The long nights, when no one sleeps until dawn, the roar of the cicadas, the murmur of the waves, the moon embroidering a skein of golden threads across the mantle of the sea. Oh GOD . . .!' And his fist banged the table so the inkpot would have toppled had I not snuck out a hand and caught it just in time, 'I'm beginning to sound like that cockney bastard. Weep not for Adonais . . .

'Where was I? Through these nights unspeakable things begin to seem possible. Orgies. We dream of a wonderful shared fuck where we all come together, tearing our souls through the gates of life, and some nights we get near it. Trelawny leads us on with tales of dusky maidens out on this or that paradisiacal island, and how they offer themselves to the sailors, and even Mary argues most coolly and rationally for what she calls free love. Almost we are all ready to fuck each other. And we never do. Do you know why? Because we're British. We've lost the habit. Oh no doubt scenes of debauchery such as plague in phantasy my waking nights occur in bordellos off St James's or on the south side of the Park, but that's not what I am talking about. What all of us want to do is dash into the moonlit sea, scatter the green streaks of lightning that slip along the crests of its waves, dance a while, then hurl ourselves on to the sands and there take hands, curtsey and . . . what? You know what. I know what. And we never do, and never will . . .

'And if we did do you know, Sordomuto, what would spoil it? I'll tell you. Sure as the sun rose today one of the brats would wake and begin to squall, and set the others off, and it would be back to soiled napkins, and gripe water, and toast for Flo to chew his latest tooth on.'

I of course managed to keep up the pretence that I was as deaf as a stone and continued to chase imaginary particles of dust

around the room with my broom. Room and broom? It seems I rhyme more easily than the gentleman I was with. He gave up on June and Moon, but murmured as his pen scratched away:
'Let me see. All but the sacred few . . .

> "Were there, of Athens or Jerusalem,
> Were neither mid the mighty captives seen
> Nor mid the ribald crowd that followed them,
>
> Nor those who went before fierce and obscene,
> The wild dance maddens in the van, and those
> Who lead it – fleet as shadows on the green,
>
> Outspeed the chariot, and without repose
> Mix with each other in tempestuous measure
> To savage music, wilder as it grows,
>
> They tortured by their agonising pleasure,
> Convulsed and on the rapid whirlwinds spun . . ."

'Sordomuto, you still here? Devil take it, bugger off now, there's a good chap.'

Which, by then, I was ready to do. I don't know about you, Mr Cargill, but I find this sort of stuff vaporous, self-regarding, emotionally cheap, and so, in no very long run, boring. But hardly seditious, hardly likely to bring the Mob into the streets or bring about the storming of the Tower.

So much cannot be said for a very different piece of writing I came across a day or so later. It was during that hottest, most languorous part of the day, between perhaps three and four o'clock in the afternoon. Hardly a breath of air stirred on land and the wavelets in the bay seemed to heave themselves up the sand with a sigh followed by a groan as if it were all too much and scarcely worth the effort. The *Don Juan*, or *Ariel*, was halfway to the horizon skimming deeper waters under full sail with Williams and Vivian as crew, Shelley at the helm and Jane as bait for the zephyrs that longed to cool her cheeks and no doubt other parts as well. You see I too have a poetical sensitivity when I choose to turn it on. Mary continued to languish upstairs.

And I? Having lent a hand with the launching of the boat and watched her sails slowly fill and belly out, and heard the tinkle of that guitar fade and mingle with the murmur of the waves, I turned back into the big lower room, the boat house, and flung myself on to the cane or wicker chaise longue. In the rafters above me spiders fixed their nets like aerial fishermen. A swallow swooped in and out. I began to hanker for a cigarillo and I thought I knew where I might find one. I have spoken of the glazed bookcase that stood at the back of the room. In fact it was more a cabinet than a bookcase though combined the functions of both. It was in the Sheraton style, standing almost six feet high, the top half glass-fronted with a simple but elegant tracery of wood in interlocked pointed arches, above a lidded desk, the lid barrel-shaped. Beneath the desk four drawers and it was from the top one of these that I felt sure I had seen Trelawny take a thin cheroot a day or so earlier, just as the sun had touched the horizon in front of us and the sky suddenly flashed with gold and green.

I was right. And there was a saltpetred wick too, mounted between a flint and milled wheel, and before long there I was, standing in front of the bookcase, cheroot in my mouth, lifted from between the cedar leaves of its box, and puffing to my heart's content, with my hands behind my back, perusing the volumes and so forth in front of me, like a gent in his library or personal den.

The top shelf was taken up with poets – Milton, Shakespeare and so forth and anyway was almost beyond my reach; the second politics and philosophy – Plato, Locke, Voltaire, Rousseau, Tom Paine, Godwin, Erasmus Darwin and Mary Shelley's mother Wollstonecraft; but the lowest was a repository for a stack of papers, many yellowing and tatty looking, most bound with ribbon, a few printed, most handwritten. A first glance showed me these were a collection of my host's unpublished work, not poetry as far as I delved, but pamphlets and such like. Again I recalled the duties due to Mr Stafford and the Home Office and I took a closer look, but deterred by the spidery italic of the penmanship and the frequent corrections I went for one of the few printed ones.

An Address to the People on The Death of the Princess Charlotte by Percy Bysshe Shelley: that caught my attention for I recalled that the date of that event was exactly the day before the execution of Brandreth *et aliorum* in November 1817. The Princess Charlotte (I doubt you will remember this, Mr Cargill) was the only child of the Prince Regent, later George IV and his, um, controversial wife Caroline, later Queen, though notoriously never crowned, she who was excluded from the coronation by locked doors though the London Mob were behind her. But that's all by the way.

Well, I settled down on the chaise longue with my smoke, and began my perusal of the said document. It began harmlessly enough, though somewhat lugubriously and with a downright plagiarism from Wordsworth:

THE Princess Charlotte is dead. She no longer moves, nor thinks, nor feels. She is as inanimate as the clay with which she is about to mingle. It is a dreadful thing to know that she is a putrid corpse, who but a few days since was full of life and hope: a woman young, innocent, and beautiful, snatched from the bosom of domestic peace and leaving that single vacancy which none can die and leave not . . . but then he went on to count this death as of no more importance than the deaths of countless women, all women who die young, and especially those who die in poverty or childbirth.

Next he praised the habit that makes a nation mourn when some great thinker or benefactor dies (the unspoken, so far, assumption that the defunct princess need not be numbered as such) which was not unreasonable until one took in the examples he gave: Milton, Rousseau and Voltaire! Finally, in this section he wished that we might mourn national calamities such as the rule of foreign or domestic tyrants (did he have in mind the House of Hanover?), the abuse of public faith and concluded: *When the French Republic was extinguished, the world ought to have mourned.*

And then quite suddenly he shifted his ground and I confess I felt the ground give way beneath my feet.

The news of the death of the Princess Charlotte, and of the execution of Brandreth, Ludlam and Turner, arrived nearly at the same time . . . and he describes in the most harrowing terms, and as if he himself had been a spectator at the event, the executions I had witnessed and indeed been the main begetter of as if they were a greater calamity than the death of the Princess, rather than a cause for popular rejoicing, dwelling on the fears and suffering of the men and their families, and the horror of the vast crowd of onlookers.

He then loses the plot a little with a dense page or so arguing that the ills that have fallen on the poorer sort in our time are the result of the taxes raised to pay the interest on the loans the government raised to pursue the late wars to their triumphant conclusion, arguing that these fall on the poor who did not make the loans and are paid to the rich who did. However he cunningly returns to it: *So soon as it was plainly seen that the demands of the people for a free representation must be conceded if some intimidation and prejudice were not conjured up, a conspiracy of the most horrible atrocity was laid in train . . . thus much is known, that so soon as the whole nation lifted up its voice for parliamentary reform, spies were sent forth. These were selected from the most worthless and infamous of mankind* (the most worthless and infamous of mankind? Moi?) *and dispersed among the multitude of famished and illiterate labourers. It was their business if they found no discontent to create it . . . It was their business to produce upon the public all impression that if any attempt to attain national freedom, or to diminish the burthens of debt and taxation were successful, the starving multitude would rush in, and confound all orders and distinctions, and institutions and laws, in common ruin. The inference with which they were to arm the ministers was, that despotic power ought to be eternal. To produce this*

salutary impression they betrayed some innocent and unsuspecting
rustics into a crime whose penalty is a hideous death. All was pre-
pared, and the eighteen dragoons assembled in readiness no doubt,
conducted their astonished victims to that dungeon which they left
only to be mangled by the executioner's hand . . .

Eighteen? It seemed more than that at the time. But by now I
was breathing in short gasps and my heart was hammering. How
did this man know all this so well? In such detail? Had he, like me,
stood in that room in the Home Office and listened to Liverpool
and Sidmouth formulate their policies, send forth their battalions
of spies under the command of Mr Stafford? Had he been a fly
upon the wall? They say the devil is the Lord of Flies.

But one thing he got wrong, though Brandreth got it wrong
too. *On the word of a dying man, Brandreth tells us that OLIVER*
brought him to this, that but for OLIVER, he would not have been
there. And *Turner exclaimed loudly and distinctly, while the execu-*
tioner was putting the rope round his neck THIS IS ALL OLIVER
AND THE GOVERNMENT.

In conclusion he returns to the Defunct Princess and praises
her as a woman who might one day have made a good Queen
(much as her glorious niece has done) but then seems to say
that Liberty too died at the same time and this was the greater
loss. But to tell the truth, I skipped these last paragraphs with
eyes blinded by cigar smoke and chagrin that yet again that bastard Oliver, like Edwards, had stolen the fame and fortune that
was due to me, and the recompense too that I am now, through
these depositions you have read and heard, Mr Cargill, endeavouring to claim as my rightful due, being now advanced in years,
and deserving of the sort of pension that might support a worthy
servant of the state with dignity into the sere and yellow.

However, I still have much to recount, not least how I rid
the nation of this pestilent knave whose house I was in, and
whose wife was even now looking down at me with some surprise and not a little disapprobation.

As far as I knew, she had not left her bed upstairs since her
miscarriage.

35

'Ah! Sordomuto. I detected the odour of the weed, it gets everywhere, and I detest it.'

She plucked the last inch from my nerveless fingers, and floating in a nightgown or daydress, I really would not know which, though it all but concealed her bare feet, went out through the central archway on to the rocks below with its tiny jetty whence she committed it to the waves. Then she bent her knees, rather gracefully I thought, one raised, the other parallel to the stones, in the pose of Venus Anadyomene, but too thin, indeed very thin. And still very pale with dark circles around her eyes.

She dipped her fingertips in the water and rubbed them together until she was satisfied all trace of the tobacco smell was gone, before completing the pose by placing her right elbow on her left knee and staring out across the indigo ocean to the distant pattern of superimposed triangles that marked the position of the *Don Juan*. She was then beating north towards La Spezia, a mile or so offshore. Mrs Shelley sighed, but whether out of distress at her situation or appreciation at the transitory delights of the scene, it was difficult to be sure.

Back in the shade, almost the darkness, of the big room, but silhouetted against the blazing light of sea and sky, she stood over me for a moment, looked down at me, and a sort of quizzical smile, not altogether friendly, lifted the corners of her small but pretty lips. Had not her form and the passing expressions on her face always mirrored the intensity of her emotions and the subtlety of her thought, had she been able to relax into easy acceptance of her beautiful body and the appeal of her almost elfin face, she would have been a most attractive object, a worthy prize for any man of breeding. But always there was that restlessness, that curiosity, that inner activity that betrayed a spirit more akin to that of a philosopher or a dominie than an odalisque.

She took her husband's 'Address to the People' from my hand and glanced at it.

'Twenty copies they ran off,' she murmured, 'and then they took fright. Can't blame them. Bysshe always went too far, said too much, thought himself charmed, invulnerable, they wouldn't dare put him in the dock as a common felon, he was a gentleman, heir to a baronetcy. He was . . . Shelley! In fact his problem is: he doesn't care.' Her voice suddenly caught as some deep emotion welled up, 'He simply does not care. What happens to us, to him.'

She dropped the sheets on the cottage table, not a match for the Sheraton, seemed to recover, looked back at me and a small, pearly tooth gently chewed her lower lip for a moment. 'This quarterly, *The Liberal*, Leigh and George Gordon are getting out with him, that must cause the nabobs some concern. Printers, publisher, a notable author or two, all out of reach here in Italy . . . if he writes stuff like this for it . . . they'll want to stop him.'

She drifted, floated back into the archway, with her back straight in front of me, one hand set on her hip, and her voice, clear like a bell, came back to me.

'Sordomuto, are you really deaf? Is your muteness assumed? After all, it appears you can read.'

287

She turned.

'A spy perhaps? An assassin even?'

She returned, stood at the foot of the chaise longue, and looked down at me, head on one side, quizzical.

'All in all, Signor Sordomuto, you're not only an enigma, you're a bit of a monster, aren't you? I'm something of an expert in monstrosity, you know? When my Frankenstein put together his creation it seemed right, poetically just, to make the monster large, and gifted with enormous strength, but was I right? After all, he was prototypal and I think my Frankenstein possibly did too well at his first attempt. Perhaps he should have produced a dwarf, covered with a pelt of hair, misshapen—'

I squawked. I couldn't help it.

'Ah!' Her voice was suddenly sharp, a rapier thrust. 'You heard that, did you not? Come Signor, or should I say Mister, I think it is time you were more frank with us.'

I could have answered in the tongue we shared. I could have run for it. Instead I kept my head. I made frantic gestures with my hands signifying a desire for writing materials. She understood instantly and produced a pencil and a notebook from the drawer where I had found the box of cigarillos, and put them on the table with a flourish and decisive bang. I swung myself off the chaise longue, went to the table, took up the pencil, and hesitating for a moment only, began to write:

My father was English but lived in Spain. My mother was Italian. I consider myself to be English . . . so far two-thirds the truth, a higher proportion than you will find in most communication between men . . . *I lost my hearing almost but not quite entirely and the power of speech completely on the field of Waterloo. I am not misshaped. Only small.*

I resisted the temptation to embroider further. This was a lily that needed no painting. Bald and unconvincing it may have been but I felt there was no immediate need for corroborative detail to aid verisimilitude. Let her ask, if that was what she wanted. She took the pencil from me.

You have a name? Or have you forgot it?

Joseph, I wrote. *Joey or Pepe will do.*

She took a long, slow look at me, tapped the pencil against her teeth, then turned back to the arch, walked out on to the jetty.

'They're on their way back, Joey,' she said. 'We'll see what Bysshe and Eddie think.'

But before the menfolk could arrive further intercourse between us, of a private nature at any rate, was foreclosed by the sound of prattling children. Flo and Jane's elder child came scampering in, followed shortly by Claire who was carrying the younger Williams in the crook of her arm. The big room echoed with their idle chatter about the starfish they had found, the crabs they had chased, and the treasure, in the shape of tiny marble pebbles, washed round by the centuries and ground by the sand to pearl-like smoothness, they had collected.

Using the commotion that followed I slipped away into the shadows, and back up the hillside into the woods where I had my nest or den in a hollow lined with pine needles and dried lavender. It was also a vantage point from which I could look out over the bay and presently I saw the *Don Juan* skimming homewards on the last breeze of evening. Hearing shouts, calls, and detecting a note of excitement in what was going on, I slipped back down the hillside just as the lad Vivian was mooring the boat to the small buoy that bobbed in the opalescent swell, a few yards away from the jetty. He hauled in the tiny canvas coracle that was attached to it and, making two trips of it, he, Williams, Jane and Shelley were ferried on to the jetty where Mary, Claire and the children welcomed them.

I used their preoccupation with each other to climb into the fig tree on the corner of the house and hid among its generous leaves, which were enough to hide more than my privates. There I sat out the next several hours, suffering cramps and later an urgent desire to relieve myself, before I found an opportunity to descend.

Meanwhile, Shelley was full of news.

'She sails no more,' he cried. 'She flies instead like a bird, like a swift, no, a tern. Mary, you really must come out with us tomorrow, it's an experience that has no equal. I have never, never felt so elevated as when sailing her.'

But she demurred, frowned, looked peeved. Ignoring this he rushed on.

'We stopped off at Lerici. There were letters, and why the *postino* could not have brought them along I do not know, from Hunt at last. The dear fellow is at Genoa, he's had a most terrible time of it, family poorly, short of money as always, but determined to push on and meet up with us at Livorno or Pisa where Byron, he has written too, is waiting.'

Well, of course I could have told him the Hunts were at Genoa, had been there a week, but had had no occasion to do so.

'You will be anxious to join them there then.' I could see how she twisted her scrap of lace in her fingers, could hear the anxiety in her voice.

'Of course, my love. But listen, our vessel is so fast, I am sure we can forestall him, be at Genoa before he leaves. He talks of staying until the end of the week, to recover from their frightful voyage; Marianne was really quite ill it seems. We'll sail at very first light in the morning, we'll be there by midday. You've no idea how fast she is, with new topmast rigging, three spinnakers—'

'Bysshe, NO!'

I swear she stamped her foot.

'I beg you not to go,' she went on, moderating her voice to a plea rather than a command. 'I am not well. Flo is not well. He vomited again this morning. You will not leave me ...' she looked round at the other two women '... us – alone for what may be days.'

'My love, not days I promise you. We will be back the day after. I keep telling you how nimble she is—'

'But what's the point? Fast she may be but you cannot think to bring Hunt, Marianne and all their children back with you. And their baggage. No doubt he has a library of books with him. No. It's out of the question.'

She turned away, back into the house, for all I know back up the stairs to her lonely bed, leaving the Atheist nonplussed and as indecisive as Hamlet, kicking at the ground.

'She's right,' Williams murmured.

'What'll we do then?'

'Hunt will take a packet down the coast to Livorno and the diligence to Pisa,' Claire Clairmont now intervened. 'That will be best for him and his family. Once he's established at Pisa with Byron he'll send for you. Really, Bysshe, that will be best.'

Another pause. Then . . .

'Oh damn and devil take it. You cannot believe how happy his letter made me, how desperate I am to see the dear fellow. Hang it. Hang it all!'

Pushing a leaf aside I saw how he leapt down the piled-up rocks and set off, kicking at a sandcastle left by the children, heading towards the headland and the tiny ruin at the north end of the bay. Jane, choosing her footholds more carefully and holding her gown almost as high as her knees, followed and presently caught up with him. She took his hand, he bent his ear towards her, and she gave a little skip of . . . pleasure, delight? At all events she alleviated the temper he had got himself into. Not so her child, the younger one, who gave a wail at seeing his mother leave so shortly after she had arrived.

'Charlie!' Williams called, hoisting the brat into the crook of his arm. I nearly fell out of my tree with surprise. 'Get the poor thing a beaker of water, he's dying of thirst, there's a good chap.'

But of course he meant Charles Vivian.

Such was the fright I'd had, and such the continued comings and goings on the jetty and within the shade of the portico, I remained where I was. Night fell with that flash of greenish

291

light I have already described but brought no respite from the heat which continued to lie like a blanket on the sea, the woods, the Casa Magni. The sea, reflecting a bowl of stars, glowed with an unearthly light edged by glassy ripples beneath darting phosphorescent flashes. A silvery shoal of flying fish, each curved like a barbed hook, skimmed the surface a hundred yards out and fireflies glowed and died, pinpoints among the purple boughs. An owl yipped high up on the wooded hillside, and one hoped the vespers of a song thrush might prove to be a nightingale.

You get the picture.

Still Shelley and Jane remained abroad. No one seemed to know where, and if they cared they did not say so. Presently the last turquoise light faded from the horizon leaving a wall of charcoal-coloured haze above it. Emerald Hesperus punched a hole in the veil so big you felt you could stick your finger through it. Out in the bay, a solitary fisherman rowed his tiny skiff close to the rocks. He had a lamp cunningly designed to throw a beam into the water, and a trident that would not have disgraced Neptune himself with which presently he speared a quite substantial octopus, lured by the light.

Moonrise was an hour off and I knew this was the darkest the night would get until she set, so I slithered down my fig tree's trunk, smooth and grey, much like the leg of a pachyderm, and made my way as silently as I might back to my den in the woods. But, my goodness, I was hungry.

36

The next morning, the twenty-third of June I believe, or it might have been the twenty-fourth, found me only shortly after sunrise scouting round the back of the house where there was a pit into which the fisherman's daughter, who came in for them most days to spend an hour clearing up, threw their rubbish. For people who concerned themselves with the privations of the poor, they were wasteful – whole loaves could end up there, goat cheeses a touch mouldy on one side but wholesome on the other, a melon gone soft. Unfortunately, there was nothing more substantial since they kept a vegetarian table. Shelley's view was that 'avoiding meat does not mean self-mortification. It is both for you and for the natural environment you belong to. You will be rewarded for this.' I also heard him ascribe longevity to the practice. Much good it did him. And 'natural environment'? What sort of a thing is that?

Mrs Shelley herself sometimes also took the air at this time and had recently resumed the habit, it now being a clear week since her misfortune, for it was cool enough for her to be out. I felt that if I could have ten minutes with her (hers being a generous soul for all the outward severity of her manner) I might have been able to allay whatever suspicions she may have raised in the minds of the company regarding my status as spy, assassin or merely *mutilé de la guerre*, as the French have it. But, this particular morning, she remained in her bed until the forenoon was fairly advanced.

Having satisfied my morning hunger tolerably well off a couple of almond-flavoured sponges which put me in mind of the *magdalenas* the man I used to call my father broke his fast with, and a coddled egg that had been no more than cracked, I slipped down to the seashore. I was just about to climb up on to the piled rocks of the jetty, heading for my fig tree, when a cloud of tobacco smoke preceded a figure coming out on to the portico and I heard Williams's voice quite loud and clear.

'Personally, Bysshe, if I were you, and if the little runt appears again, I'd fetch your crop and give him a damn good hiding before sending him on his way.'

I have been called 'little runt' often enough to suppose that when I hear the words they refer to me, and for the rest of the day I proceeded with a somewhat exaggerated caution, hiding in a small outhouse, in a tiny cave, and eventually, when the coast was clear, up my fig tree. The problem was, having learnt that things were likely to move in the next few days, that the three conspirators would, whatever Mary Shelley's anxieties on the subject, meet up and put in train the production of *The Liberal*, I knew the time had come for action. After all, I was on a hundred and fifty guineas, nay more, if I could achieve the assassination of all three, whereas if I failed and the sheet came out, I'd get nothing. So I made sure that I was able to piece together, albeit piecemeal, what was happening.

Shelley, having agreed not to attempt to meet the Hunts at Genoa, was all for sailing the very next day in the opposite direction to Leghorn whence he would proceed to Pisa where Lord Byron had his substantial establishment housed in a palazzo. Hunt would be there before him, or very soon after. This Mary opposed. She was still not well enough to support herself and their child on her own, no, not even with the help of Jane and Claire, who, in any case, had Jane's children to look after as well.

The discussion, I nearly said argument or even row, but these people cultivated a measured discourse in which voices were never raised, and cool politeness was maintained, even when they were severely at odds with each other, waxed and waned throughout the morning, coming to no certain conclusion. Eventually, with some impatience Shelley declared he would take the *Don Juan* out for a spin, perhaps as far as the headland at the northern end of the bay, furthest from San Terenzo and Lerici. Mary yet again refused to accompany them and all split up with barely concealed signs of irritation if not actual antagonism.

I realised that this excursion, planned to take them not out into the bay but close to the land, might provide me with the opportunity that had not yet presented itself. I hurried back to my foxhole, retrieved from it a small but powerful spyglass Captain Quex had recently given me, one which, by means of a prism, allowed superior magnification without unwieldy length, and my old friend Spinks and Pottle. I then scrambled through the wood and arrived on the headland, actually in the ruins of the fort which, judging by the smell and the goat droppings, had served the local goatherds, young lads for the most part, as a pen during the heat of the day. From this vantage point I had a clear view of the *Don Juan*, already arrived, sails down, and anchored in a tiny natural harbour, about twenty paces beyond pistol shot, in clear crystal water.

Out of pistol range but sound carries well over water and I could clearly hear the song the lovely Jane sang.

> 'The keen stars were twinkling,
> And the fair moon was rising among them,
> The guitar was tinkling
> But the notes were not sweet till you sung them
> Again.'

Odd, I thought, no rhyme for *Again* – unless of course it was *Jane* and she had left it out to spare her so-to-speak husband's feelings. She continued.

> 'As the moon's soft splendour
> O'er the faint cold starlight of Heaven
>   Is thrown,
>   So your voice most tender
> To the strings without soul had then given
>   Its own.
>
>   The stars will awaken,
> Though the moon sleep a full hour later,
>   To-night;
>   No leaf will be shaken
> Whilst the dews of your melody scatter
>   Delight.
>
>   Though the sound overpowers,
> Sing again, with your dear voice revealing
>   A tone
>   Of some world far from ours,
> Where music and moonlight and feeling
>   Are one.

'Oh Bysshe, it's so lovely!'

'I say, old chap,' chimed in the more official of her lovers, 'did you really dash that off this morning? Just like that?'

I imagine Shelley merely assumed a modest look, for I did not hear his answer.

Of course what I suppose she understood, and perhaps Eddie Williams did not, was that in the third verse there was promise of another tryst in the evening to come – when the moon would rise an hour later.

Jane now laid aside her guitar and said, with a wistful voice: 'Oh how I wish we could explore that castle, storm it from the sea as the Corsairs of old must have done. Do you suppose there is treasure there, perhaps a skeleton lying across a chest of doubloons? I'm sure there must be.'

The saucy minx, she well knew what she was up to.

'Not a problem,' Williams asserted. 'It's scarcely ten paces before we will be able to wade.'

'Oh come on, Eddie, you know very well I can't swim,' Shelley chimed in. 'And you're not a lot better. Remember what happened on that canal between Livorno and Pisa, back in April. You damn near killed me.'

'But surely we can get the boat in closer. Even beach her.' Jane was not to be put off.

'I don't think we should beach her. Not a breath of air closer in.'

'But we could, what do you sailors call it, Eddie, you know, pull up the anchor, throw it forward and then haul ourselves up to it.'

'Warp.'

'Eh?'

'Warping. That's what it's called.'

'Oh, I do beg your pardon. I thought you, um, burped. Those eggs. At breakfast. They were a bit nesty.'

Seemed all right to me. The one I had, anyway.

Warping is what they did; it took them twenty minutes to cover five yards but they did it. With Jane leading, they waded ashore over pebbles and sand, exclaiming about the fish that darted from them, and warning each other about sea urchins. Jane was wearing muslin, which floated up round her armpits when she first lowered herself into the glassy water and moulded itself like a second and transparent skin to her breasts, which were buxom and fruitily nippled, and then her rounded belly and her thighs, as she made it to the shallows. The men, I am sorry to say, were even less modest, stripping to the buff and leaving their shirts and frayed linen trousers behind.

I primed and cocked Spinks and Pottle but with little hope

of success. To get a fatal shot in on the Poet, and yet evade capture by Williams, seemed, well, a long shot.

'Ooof!' cried Jane. 'I hate this, it's all clingy . . .' and she hauled her gown over her head, leaving herself as naked as they. Eve and two Adams. I wondered which would have her.

I didn't have to wait long to find out. Presently Shelley, leaning over her, was pouring fine sand from his cupped hand into the gap between her breasts and no doubt muttering things about the sands of time running out, *carpe diem* and so forth, while Williams sat up, knees pulled in, and lobbed small stones at invisible targets in the water. It's been said that if all the men in Britain were placed at ten-yard intervals right round the coast, within two minutes all would be throwing stones into the sea.

After a time the caresses the supine pair were sharing became more intimate, indeed seemed to be approaching a significant moment as it were, and Williams hauled himself to his feet and looked down at them.

'God, Shelley,' he said, and his voice was quite hoarse, 'I never saw anything so beautiful.'

Nevertheless a sense of decorum, or possibly brute jealousy, drove him to turn his back on them and the sea, and he began to clamber up the rocks, away from the beach, and straight for my hiding place in the one small turret that still retained, amidst the bay trees and scrub oaks, its original form among the tumbled stones. I backed away from the doorway or embrasure I had been using as my lookout, and pressed myself at the back of the tower into a deep patch of shadow where the stones had collapsed and a tangle of briars, brambles and a prickly sort of myrtle had grown up, around and over them. It was no use. He came straight into the embrasure, placed his legs apart and began to piss.

Maybe it was dust disturbed, perhaps it was the smell of his urine. Anyway, I sneezed.

I could have shot him.

I don't know why I did not. It would of course have been a

foolish thing to do since almost inevitably it would have led to my arrest, but I doubt I worked that out on the spur of the moment. Instead I ran, ran straight into the brambles and briars which lacerated my shins; I twisted my ankle, stumbled and, since I had my pistol in one hand and my spyglass in the other, fell heavily and gave myself a bloody nose. And as I scrambled to my feet again, a quite substantial piece of rock, the size of a cricket ball, caught me a glancing blow on the top of my head which instantly ran with blood the way scalp wounds do. The fucking bastard was throwing stones at me as well as abuse!

I got away. After all, I was shod while my pursuer was Adam-naked. I spent the rest of the day up on the hillside, licking my wounds and only venturing back to my fig tree at nightfall.

It was not all loss. I had, during the whole episode, been presented with one morsel of information that was all I needed to make fulfilment of my mission a possibility. I knew that Shelley could not swim.

37

Wake up, Mr Cargill. We're nearly done. With the Shelleys anyway. Mind if I help myself to another glass of Madeira? And for you? No. Perhaps best not. Now then, where was I?

That night was the strangest of all, the night the heat really got to them. And it was the twenty-fourth, the Eve of St John. St John the Baptist's Eve.

First they all came out into the portico after they had finished supper at about six or seven o'clock I suppose, not long before sunset. This was a custom, a routine, a sort of discussion circle at which one of them, usually Shelley, would introduce a theme or make a possibly contentious remark, and invite their comments. The men, including Charles Vivian, carried out wicker chairs and arranged them in a semicircle for the use of the ladies, Mary Shelley taking the middle one. The table was brought out and sitting at it with an Argand lamp to assist her, she began to sew. The men disposed themselves in a sort of defensive outer circle around them, standing with arms in a sad knot or sitting on the top step. Williams chucked his cigarillo whose smoke Mary Shelley had been ostentatiously batting away with her lily-like hand whenever it came near her. Shelley cleared his throat and opened the proceedings.

'I wish,' he said, 'I knew how it would feel to be free!'

'Oh come on, Bysshe. Few people on earth could claim to be more free than you.'

Including, I thought, ten paces away in my fig tree, being free with other men's women.

'If you believe that, Williams, I cannot suppose you have a very considered idea of what constitutes freedom.'

'You have. And you're going to tell us.'

'No. That was not my motive in bringing up the subject. I wondered, aloud, how it would *feel* to be free.'

'From which,' Mary paused in her sewing, needle poised in the lamplight, 'we must assume that you do not consider yourself to be free.'

'You are the freest person I know,' cried Williams again.

Shelley directed his attention to Claire whose face I could see most clearly, in delightful chiaroscuro thrown by the lamp.

'Would you, Claire, say that of me?'

She pulled back a little, as if aware that her face and expression were exposed, and that what she had to say would be easier said from shade.

'Why yes, I believe I would. The first great enemy of freedom, as you yourself have often taught us, is poverty. You are not rich, but you have a sufficiency, at least now you do. It was not always so. More important perhaps, you have freed yourself, and others, through your own intellectual efforts, from the tyranny of superstition, and hypocritical morality. Yes, Bysshe, by and large I should rate you the most free of men. And not least because you never wear a stock but always go about with your shirt open.'

She laughed, and looked around hoping that others might share her merriment. None did.

'I think we are agreed,' said Mary, biting off a thread and proceeding to rethread her needle, squinting into the circular and self-reflecting glow of the Argand patent wick, 'you are the freest of men. So now you will tell us why you are not. Or why you are so unfree that you can wish you knew how it felt to be free. And pray do not chafe because I have asked you not to sail to Livorno tomorrow – you have always equated freedom with love and if you love me you will stay here a few more days yet.'

This said with great placidity and as uncontentiously as may be. The text beneath the surface was clear: *I am not making a fuss about this, but I do want to forestall any attempt on your part to turn a discussion of freedom into an argument that favours your sailing tomorrow.*

His gambit refused, Shelley withdrew to higher ground. He also stood up and paced about a bit, once or twice coming close enough to my screen of leaves as to make me think he must see me so I tightened my grip on Spink and Pottle while bracing my foot in the crotch of bough and trunk where I was stood.

'As long,' he began, 'as there is one man or woman enslaved on a sugar plantation, a manufacturer in a workshop toiling for fifteen hours a day for a shilling, a navigator digging out a tunnel that might fall on his head to keep his children back in Ireland in bread, a sailor hauling in canvas on the mainyard of a merchantman in a storm, as long as people work themselves to an early grave, die of diseases inflicted on them by the labour they are forced to do, as long as any of these dreadful things continue to occur while I continue to enjoy the wretched annuity their labours have bought for me, then I cannot count what that annuity has bought me freedom. For with it I have bought the slavery of others and their slavery is my slavery, and I am as unfree as they.'

'That has a rational ring to it, but examine it closely and you find the logic is poetical rather than rational,' Williams remarked.

'I hope, Williams,' said Mary, without lifting her eye from her sewing ring, 'you do not count the logic of the counting house superior to that of the Poet.' She looked up, at her husband's back, for he was now watching the last glow of the sunset fade in front of him. 'And I hope you, Shelley, do not have it in

302

mind to renounce the trifling income you have in exchange for what should have been your inheritance on the death of your father. At least not until I have finished *Valperga*.'

He shrugged dismissively.

Jane, who had not yet contributed, now began, measuring her words carefully.

'Is it not the case,' she murmured, 'that each of us is made to contribute in our own particular ways to the common good of all? That some have gifts of muscle, and strength and can hew, and carry water, and plough and dig and so forth, for the bene-fit of all, while others have gifts of soul and mind, intelligence and the power to make and create, and would not the best and freest society be the one where each did what he was best at for the good of all? Is it not freedom to be able to do what one is best at?'

'But which depends on which?' Shelley rushed in. 'Which should reap the greater reward? Does any deserve more from the common coffer than the other? I'll tell you. If there is to be any difference then the greater share of the blessings human society can bestow upon its members should be bestowed on those whose contribution is most vital, on whom all else depends, on those without whom we are no more than beasts of the field, the mountain or the jungle.'

'Surely it is our intellectual powers, more present in some than others, that raises us above brute creation, and it is there-fore right that those most intellectually, indeed spiritually gifted, should be given most. If only because it is in freedom from physical toil that intellectual and spiritual labour can take place, and what we know as civilisation be thus advanced.'

Williams again, the male Williams.

Shelley took a turn along the whole length of the portico and back again, humming and hawing to himself as he did so, then he swung at them, his face lit by Delphic ecstasy . . . and the lamp.

'Where does civilisation start?' he cried, and thrust an accusatory even minatory finger at Williams, then let it track round the circle from face to face. 'I'll tell you. The dawn of civilisation was that very day, that one day, when one man having produced enough food for himself, went on and produced more—'

'One *man* . . . ?' Ever mindful of the literary legacy of the mother she had never known, Mary's tone was cutting. Shelley took the point.

'One man and his wife. His woman.' Still Mary bridled, no doubt at the use of the possessive, but this time kept mum. Shelley, oblivious, went on. 'The day they produced enough for themselves and their children by midday, but laboured on to sunset, that was the dawn of civilisation, for on that day they liberated another, others, who may have spent the time thus gained making up a poem, telling a story, modelling the clay from the riverside.'

'It doesn't,' remarked Claire, anxious perhaps to regain some credibility as a thinker after her somewhat inane remark anent Shelley's open-necked shirts, 'have quite the dramatic, grand ring of Promethean fire about it, does it? Nevertheless,' she went on at some speed, the words spilling out of her mouth before another could interrupt, 'I see your point. By producing a surplus, he, she, they set the world free.'

'But they themselves were bound, chained.'

'How so, Jane?'

'Because the ones who took their surplus did not in fact paint pictures or make sculptures, they invented swords, whips and chains, took the land from the food-growers and allowed them to keep only what they needed to keep themselves alive and working.'

'In other words, they took over, they took control of the means of production.'

At last Charles Vivian had found the temerity to make a contribution. He created thereby a silence. Shelley broke it.

'Yes. I suppose you could put it like that. Or, put it another way. They stole from the producers of food the time they had earned by producing more than they themselves needed. They

304

stole from the tillers and reapers the freedom they had won for all to share.'

'And you will not feel properly free until you have given it back to them.'

'That's right. The first duty of any society is to make sure that those who produce more food than they need for the benefit of all should be rewarded as highly as their judges, law-givers, poets, and, if they are still needed, priests and philosophers too.'

At which moment the local producers of surplus food made their presence felt. There was an almighty bang, an explosion, a flash of white light that instantly turned into orange and red flame and limned against the night sky to the north the Gothick outline of the little fort which had been my lookout post until that oaf Williams started hurling rocks at me.

'Good God,' he now cried, 'what the hell was that?'

But he was barely heard for that initial explosion was followed on the other side by a similar explosion a mile and more away in the castle on the southern tip of the bay above Lerici. Then came the pealing of both church bells, San Terenzo's and Lerici's, and a fusillade of shots, explosions and the ignition of ten or twenty bonfires along the beach between the villages.

Instantly I recalled my childhood, spent in a village near Salamanca in Spain, and the Fires of St John, the festivities that marked the shortest night of the year, exactly six months from Christmas Eve whichever way you approach it, the day on which the Baptist begins to decrease and the Christ child quickens in the womb. The day on which the food-producers earnestly hope to break the drought of summer with gunfire and powder charges so the grain will swell and the olives and grapes plump up. The day, the night rather, when firecrackers are tied to the horns of a bull which is set free to charge up and down the alleys of each village. The night, so my father told me, wise before his time, when Jupiter Feretrius struck the oak, made the mistletoe glow like a Golden Bough, and a new King of the Wood took the place of his precursor through ritual combat and sacrifice before offering himself in service and marriage for a year to . . .

And here, prompt upon her cue as ever, and an hour later than the night before, shining like Athene's shield through the black silhouettes of oak trees on the crags behind us, she came, the Queen of Heaven, the true wife of the sky-god. For she too loves the solitude of the woods and the lonely hills, and sailing overhead on clear nights in the likeness of the silver moon looks down with pleasure on her own fair image reflected on the calm, the burnished surface of the bay of Lerici. Except, of course, she's Artemis, not Athene.

Such extravagant expenditure of black powder cannot be maintained for long without the resources of a Mapoleum or Willingdone and soon what seemed like a calm, after the initial bombardment of our ears, fell over the scene. This was, however, a matter of contrast rather than fact – the bonfires continued to burn and round them we could see how the villagers, pranked out in masks and costumes one would normally have associated with February Carnival than the shortest hottest night of the year, mopped and mowed in wild, and if pressed I must admit it, obscene dances. I would spare your sensibilities, Mr Cargill, so will merely add that they involved the use of large erect pizzles strapped to the men's crotches.

Mrs Shelley declared the whole business had given her a headache and that she would prefer to go back to bed. Claire Clairmont helped her up the stairs. Shelley said he had work to do and, picking up the Argand lamp, followed her. Presently I saw how it illumined the end room and I could see the shadow of his head thrown upon the further wall. Williams used flint and wheel to light a cheroot, the glow briefly illuminating his face. He sat down on one of the vacated wicker chairs to smoke it. Vivian declared himself tired and withdrew to the attic space they allowed him at the back of the house. I came down out of my fig tree and, keeping to the rocks and their shadows, approached the nearest of the bonfires. As I think I have mentioned before, Mr Cargill, I am by nature as curious as a cat and in a spirit of enquiry I conceived a desire to see how these country revels would turn out.

I have not mentioned Jane, have I? Jane Williams. Well, she was there before me, an alabaster pillar in the moonlight, standing back from the crowd and looking every now and then over her shoulder, as if to say he comes, he cometh not. For her he came all right, his unbuttoned white shirt also catching the moonlight, his hand first clutching at hers and then circling her waist.

After a time the fires burned down a little, the dances became less frenzied, but a new sport took their place. The younger men now launched themselves at the fires, leaping across them, but angling their leaps so none at first went clear across the middle where the orange flames still leapt high beneath an upward rush of spiralling sparks. Those who made the jump were mocked by those who did not for not risking the centre of the fire which burnt round a cave of almost white-hot embers, like a volcano.

Shelley disengaged his hand and, barefoot, took a run at it. He passed right through the flames but fell short, kicking into and skidding amongst a suburb of charred timbers that exploded into sparks as he landed in them. A fisherman grabbed his out-flung arm and hauled him clear, rushing him straight across the sand and shingle and into the sea, where he leaped and hopped about as if he were doing the Tyburn jig, while Jane waved, and cried, and hallooed from where the wavelets brushed her feet. The assembled peasants and fishermen, and their womenfolk, all broke off their sport to join her and applaud the mad English Milord. Then he took her hand again and led her away from the fire, walking through the water which sometimes reached as high as their knees, until the flames no longer threw their shadows in front of them and they had only the moon to guide them. Presently, somewhere beyond the Casa Magni, they left the sea and went up into a cove or maybe the woods, and no doubt did what they had met up to do.

38

It seemed a good opportunity to go up to the study where Shelley wrote and see what he was up to. The main room, the boat house as it were, was in darkness in so far as the moon and the flashes of Fool's Lightning which had begun to illumine the banks of cloud that lay below her on the western horizon allowed of any real darkness at all. There was no sign that any of the four remaining grown-ups, nor their children, were anywhere but in their rooms, and I slipped in like a shadow. The Argand still burned and threw a line of light into the passageway. I eased the plank door open, careful of the squeak I knew it could make if handled brusquely. I turned the key deftly, locking myself in. It was some days since I had paid the room a previous visit and I glanced round quickly to see what was different from before.

It was much the same. A table, round and made of dark wood, a desk on which the lamp stood, piles of loose papers and notebooks roughly bound with string or ribbon, a pewter mug filled with trimmed quills and pencils, a penknife, a stick of sealing wax with a wick, a couple of ink pots, the travelling sort with milled screwtops made of brass, three or four books left open, one of them turned over, binding uppermost, *Paradise Lost, Books I to VI*, another in Greek. I don't have a lot of Greek but I was able to spell out Aeschylus from among the other heathen letters in the title. The third was *Lamia, Isabella, The Eve of St Agnes and Other Poems* by John Keats.

I sat down at the desk, turned up the circular wick and looked around. Two large open bookcases against the longer wall, pictures on the shorter: a print of the Venus Anadyomene and another of Fogg's cartoon of Peterloo, the one I had copied for Thistlewood in which an overfed, beefy yeoman raises a sword or axe in front of the Union flag and is about to bring it down on the woman who kneels in front of his horse, holding her baby, but looking up at the brute with defiant pride. I confess I shuddered a little – it brought back memories which on the whole I prefer not to recall. Under it a scrap torn from a notebook was inscribed with one verse:

> Then she lay down in the street,
> Right before the horses' feet,
> Expecting with a patient eye,
> Murder, Fraud, and Anarchy.

Shelley's truckle bed, unmade, and which he used or had been pretending to use since Mary's miscarriage, was pushed away under one of the bookcases.

I pulled one of the books out from under the lamp, and read from the open page which came near the end:

No greater evidence is afforded of the wide extended and radical mistakes of civilised man than this fact: those arts which are essential to his very being are held in contempt; employments are lucrative in an inverse ratio to their usefulness: the jeweller, the toyman, the actor gains fame and wealth by the exercise of his useless and ridiculous art, whilst the cultivator of the earth, he without whom society must cease to subsist, struggles through contempt and penury, and perishes by that famine which but for his unceasing exertions would annihilate the rest of mankind.

So, perhaps it was reading this stuff that had prompted his discourse that evening on the production of surplus food. I turned to the title page. *Queen Mab, a Philosophical Poem with Notes.* It was one of the latter that I had been reading. *Printed by P. B. Shelley, 23 Chapel Street, Grosvenor Square, 1813.* Did this mean it was his own work? Printed nine years ago? I glanced through some more – I shan't bore you with what I read, Mr Cargill, but be sure I could soon very readily understand why this boy, this youth, this man had been kept under the tightest surveillance by my masters. He was, make no mistake about it, a bloody revolutionist and for once I savoured the moral nature of my trade.

Next I glanced at two sheets of paper written over densely and much corrected, and a third which seemed to be a fairish copy of the others. I scanned it briefly, found nothing seditious but a rather obscure lament that a certain She had left him at that moment in the night when the Moon begins her downhill journey to the West, that She had tamed all passions, which, however, were now returning to plague him in her absence. It ended strikingly enough with a description of the time before dawn when the fishing boats leave . . . scattered o'er the twinkling bay,

> And the fisher with his lamp
> And spear about the low rocks damp
> Crept and struck the fish which came
> To worship the delusive flame . . .

At this point I heard a footstep on the boards of the passage, the latch on the door lifted, but the lock held, just as I held my breath.

'Shelley? Bysshe? Are you there?' A hushed whisper, but recognisable. 'I know you are for your lamp is lit and the shadow of your head is cast upon the wall. See, I've been outside to see. Let me in, Bysshe.'

Claire. Claire Clairmont. She went on.

'Mary's asleep, I promise you. I read to her until she slept.'

A longer pause, then with harder tone but still quiet.

'You have Jane in there, don't you? I know it. Never mind. I don't blame you. I'm sad company, amn't I, since my darling died?'

And the footstep diminished down the floorboards. But was she really gone? Or did she hang about not wanting to return to her lonely room?

What she actually did was go out on to the portico where she met Shelley returning along the beach, hand in hand with Jane. I heard their voices, raised in doubt and consternation. As quickly as I could and without standing, indeed with as little movement as possible, I reached up to the lamp which stood on the table between me and the window, and turned down the wick until the flame was extinguished, but not before my shadow had been observed.

Silence. Then Shelley's voice.

'The Magus Zoroaster, my dead child, met his own image walking in the garden.'

And Jane: 'What do you mean?'

'He means,' murmured Claire, who could affect a feyish manner when she wanted to, 'that to see your own double is a sign of death approaching.'

The night was not over. I hid in a closet in the passage and heard much of what occurred. Although the carry-on down at the beach continued until dawn the household had, as far as I could tell, drifted off to bed, their own beds I supposed, two or three hours earlier, and by three o'clock or so I had decided I could probably take my congee and return to my den in the woods. Unfortunately I mistook my way in the darkness, for the moon had now set and what pre-dawn light there was was coming from the other side of the house. Thus I blundered into Mary Shelley's room without realising it, she having, I suppose, left her door open because of the heat.

At this moment I heard a hoarse scream from down the

passage and then a terrible bang. Shelley, half-awake, in part noctambulising, had come along from his study, where he had had what he called a vision but you or I would call a dream or at most a nightmare, and walked into the door of my closet which I had left open, banging his face on it in the dark. He then swung into his wife's room, with blood streaming down his face from his nose, and, in spite of the darkness, saw my figure leaning over his wife's body. At this moment she woke up, sat up, and I, desperate with the apprehension that I was about to be discovered, grasped her shoulders and pushed her back into the pillows.

She, however, retained some presence of mind and more strength than I would have expected in someone who had been so ill so recently. She pushed me aside, sidestepped her husband, and got across the passage and into the Williamses' room. Soon, too soon, all were back in the master bedroom, with a candle or two, I was under the bed, and they were piecing together what they thought had happened.

Shelley claimed a couple of visions, though you or I, Mr Cargill, as I have said, would call them dreams or at the worst nightmares.

In violent tones, with many gestures (he was sitting on the bed and it rocked and the springs rang above my head as he continued), he described them.

'You, my dear Edward, with Jane behind you, rushed into my room and bent over me. You were both naked but your bodies were streaming with blood as if you had been lacerated by a . . . by a lion, no, a griffin, a sphinx or perhaps by harpies, yes by harpies. You screamed at me, both of you shaking me with corpse-cold hands, that I was to get up for the sea was flooding the house and it was all coming down.'

Get up he did, and thought, as a good husband should, of his wife first.

'I ran to Mary's room, but on the way encountered a fiendish giant, armed cap à pie, who lifted his visor and revealed the laughing scornful visage of my father, my own father, but with

312

grave worms coming from his nostrils and the corners of his mouth. He smashed me with his mailed fist. However I pushed on past him, and on entering this room encountered the worst visitation of all – the figure of myself, strangling my own beloved wife . . .'

And here his voice broke and the springs jangled and dipped towards me, as he no doubt folded the poor woman in a distraught embrace.

He concluded this hair-starting tale by telling her how earlier in the evening he had seen the figure of himself from the terrace, and this time Jane and Claire lent credibility to his story.

The discussion continued until dawn. I was much bothered by the fluff and feathers beneath the bed, and the smell of the chamber pot, but managed to choke back a desire both to sneeze and vomit. The upshot of it, of the discussion I mean, was that Mary finally extracted a promise from them to give her a full week to complete her recovery, and indeed get over the setback the events of the night had brought on. It was fixed that they would sail to Livorno on the first of July.

'After all,' she said, 'we have heard no more from the Hunts and we know they expect to make their way to Pisa via Livorno, and they'll not move from Genoa until they have recovered some of their health and spirits. Now, if you don't mind, this room is grown stuffy, and the sun is about to rise which will make it more so. I would like fresh air, on the terrace, and a cup of tea or warm milk.'

And, to my grateful relief, they all made the move. Except they didn't. Shelley remained stretched out on the bed, in the attitude of the poet Chatterton after he had overdosed himself on laudanum and other medicaments taken to cure a chronic cold. Presently, however, he rolled off the bed, knelt beside it, and, reaching for the chamber pot, took hold of my clammy hand. Of course he screamed again when he saw me, but, give him all credit, not with fear but rage. Fear? Why not? He genuinely, I am sure of it, atheist though he was, thought I was a demon.

'You Goddamned Imp. You little runt of a Devil. Get the fuck back to Pandemonium where you belong.' Uttering similar imprecations he chased me out, between the pillars, past the ladies sitting at their table waiting for Vivian to come up with their tea, and up into the woods where he finally caught me, not far from my den, and plucking a switch which had sprung up from a fallen oak the way they do, gave me as sound a whipping as I've ever had.

Believe me, Mr Cargill, I made sure he paid for it, and the whole damned crew. After all I knew where he and his tricky little boat would be in a week's time, and I knew he couldn't swim.

Not a lot more to be said, is there?

I made my way, mostly on foot, to Livorno or Leghorn, fifty miles to the south, arriving there towards the end of the month, and took a room above a tavern that overlooked the quay. Tied up to it, dwarfing the feluccas and other coasters and fishing boats, was Byron's three-master, the *Bolivar*. On the first of July the *Don Juan* came out of the sunset like a bird and moored alongside. Using my spyglass I was able to ascertain Shelley, Roberts, Williams and Vivian were on board, none of the women. Officials, like carrion crows in black uniforms, immediately flocked around and forbad them from leaving the boat until their superior, now off duty, had examined their papers to be sure they had come from a neighbouring port. If they had not, then they were liable to be quarantined. Meantime no intercourse was permitted with any on shore. The crew of the *Bolivar* threw them some cushions to spend the night on and all was settled by the time darkness had properly fallen.

Next morning Byron and the Hunts turned up on the quay. The reunion was frantic. Shelley embraced everyone in sight, Byron beamed with glee face to face and sneered behind their backs, Leigh Hunt shook everybody's hand again and again, and Mrs Hunt, still looking poorly, endeavoured to keep her brood in order or at least from pushing each other into the

314

harbour. His lordship sorted out the quarantine situation and they and Shelley departed in carriages and on horseback for Byron's place at Pisa, ten miles or so inland. However, Trelawny, Roberts, Williams and Vivian remained behind on board the *Bolivar*, having first moved the *Don Juan* down the quay to a proper berth. I was not bothered by this. As long as the *Don Juan* remained at Livorno, and the women at Lerici, I knew Shelley would be back. And there was no point in going to Pisa. Byron's establishment was large, and much increased by the huge Hunt family, six children I had counted, and there was no chance I should be able to dispose of all three of my quarries at once. Not without resorting to a mine or petard. In any case I had resolved to make Shelley my first priority.

The question was . . . how? Walking up to him with Spinks and Pottle and blowing his head off was clearly not an option. But on the night of the seventh of July the local priesthood took a hand. For a month, the clouds that the dying sun briefly transformed into a blazing Valhalla remained piled on the horizon, and the electric storms that flashed along their foundations remained sterile. The figs and peaches dried on their boughs, the wheat shrivelled before it swelled, the pastures dried up and the cattle developed huge cavities in their sides and their ribs stood out like *cordilleras*. There was no milk. On that night solemn processions were formed, banners, images, crucifixes, censers and huge candles on gilt sticks were brought out of the churches and in front of the assembled populace the local monsignors and so forth called upon their rain god to do his stuff.

He took his time, but sent messengers of his intent ahead. Gulls flew inland. Sharp gusts of cold air blew down from the Ligurian Alps or even further north, and bumped into lumps of hot air rolling in from Corsica and Sardinia. Real thunder at last prowled round the horizon and in the mountains lightning flickered like cracks in stucco.

Already, through the careful distribution of a couple of guineas in the post office, I had been able to obtain brief possession of a handful of letters, two of which were addressed to the Casa Magni in San Terenzo. They indicated that Shelley planned to return within a day or two. The one to Jane Williams ended thus: 'I fear you are solitary and melancholy at Villa Magni. How soon those hours passed in which we have lived together so intimately so happily.' I may not have it exact, but that was the gist.

On the night of the seventh, in the company of a rogue of a sailor who seemed assured that he knew what he was doing, I boarded the *Don Juan*. Together we lifted six of the nuggets of pig-iron out of the small gunny sacks they were tied up in, and dropped them overboard, replacing them with wood shavings. Then we cut off the reef-points from one side of each of the two mainsails which had only been loosely furled. Satisfied with what we had achieved, I took the old pirate to a tavern on the quay, filled him with grappa, hit him on the head with Spinks and Pottle's butt, weighed his feet with two more of the pig-iron nuggets and tipped him into the harbour. Well, actually, no. I tell a lie. Knocking large men on the head and drowning them isn't my style, is it, Mr Cargill? Let's just say he drank so much grappa at my expense he had, by morning, forgot all of the previous night's events.

At about midday on the eighth, Shelley returned to the *Bolivar* and immediately preparations were put in hand for both boats to make sail and leave the harbour. Again I had to deploy some gold and arranged for the *Bolivar*'s departure to be delayed. Her papers were found not to be in order. Shelley, having promised both his wife and certainly one if not both of his mistresses that he would be back at Lerici by nightfall, the wind blowing strongly from the south, insisted on sailing without the company of the bigger ship. He took Williams and Vivian with him, leaving Roberts and Trelawny to follow when they could.

The *Don Juan* crossed the harbour bar just after two o'clock in the afternoon, under full sail.

The catastrophe came sooner than I could have hoped. I watched it through my spyglass from the upstairs window of my

316

lodging house. Low clouds were rushing in from the west but above them towered, heaped high upon each other, great bolsters of thundercloud capped with the flat anvil shape that invariably predicts a squall. Beneath it stretched a black haze of curtaining, driven rain. Out of it came two feluccas, their single big triangular sails reefed down to almost nothing, streaking for the safety of the harbour they had just left.

A third felucca stayed close to the *Don Juan* until she was swept over by a giant wave. The master of the felucca later described how, using a speaking trumpet, he had urged the English to reef, to take in sail, even to abandon ship and come aboard his craft, and how they had ignored him though one of the *Don Juan*'s crew had striven to reduce her spread of canvas but was hampered by another and how they could not even tie in reefs because there were no reef-points; how she had come beam on to the wind and the surf and her leeward gunwale had tipped into the sea as if she were ungovernable, would not respond to their efforts to bring her round and let her run before the storm. Then she disappeared in the murk.

You know the rest, Mr Cargill. The whole world knows. The bodies were washed ashore ten days later, much damaged by the sea and the fish that had fed off them. Williams had in his pocket the copy of *Queen Mab* he had been studying, Shelley the last collection of poems Keats had published, the one that had been on his table. A romantic fantasy has grown up around their cremation on the beach near Viareggio, organised by Trelawny and in the presence of Hunt and Byron. A pagan send-off for that most pagan of poets. The fact is, Mr Cargill, it was done to satisfy yet again the rules of quarantine. The body could not be taken from the beach for fear of infection. Ashes were allowed.

There. That's it.

Cargill stirs in his big armchair, and briefly farts. Charlie Boylan stands, stretches, goes out and up the narrow stairs to the privy and pees. A grey cold light suffuses the house on

317

Clapham Common except where the heavy drapes still keep it at bay. It carries that low icy glow, like the touch of death, that comes with a new fall of snow. He returns to find Deirdre, the tall, spectre-thin, Irish woman, leaving after pulling back the curtains.

'This room smells like a brothel or a shebeen,' she says, and continues, 'it's ten past eight. Mr Cargill has usually left by now, but I'll bring him a cup of tay to send him on his way, and a slice of toast.'

Cargill pulls himself together remarkably quickly, as if he wants, Charlie surmises, to be out of the house before his wife appears. He complains the tea has a bitter taste.

'Sure and hasn't it been stewing on the hob this last half-hour? Put some more sugar in it.'

He does. And he drinks it.

Charlie begins a lengthy peroration the gist of which is that he never got his fifty guineas for sending Shelley to a watery death, since, according to Mr Bourgeois, none of the contemporary accounts made any mention of the presence of an imp-like character in the neighbourhood of the Casa Magni. It was one of his main grudges, his chiefest complaint.

'Thirty years ago, Mr Cargill. Think of it. Fifty guineas in the seven per cents for thirty years, compound interest . . .'

But Cargill pays no attention. Suffering from stomach cramps and already late for work, he bustles about, finds his papers, some money, his muffler, his coat and his tall hat. The front door bangs behind him.

His wife, in a long dressing gown and with her hair all anyhow, the flush of a better night's sleep than she has had for a long time still on her, joins Charlie in the front room.

'Still here, Mr Boylan?' she asks, somewhat archly. 'I'm sure Mr Cargill will want you to remain for as long as is necessary. Do ask Deirdre for anything you might require . . .'

Part V

MURDER

Murder most foul – as in the best it is.

WILLIAM SHAKESPEARE, *Hamlet*

39

'Ah. Cargill.' The Permanent Under-Secretary takes his monocle from his eye, gives it a polish on the handkerchief he pulls from his trouser pocket, replaces both. It all amounts to the displacement activity he often resorts to, almost unconsciously, whenever a possible rebuke to a junior colleague is on the horizon. 'Deuced embarrassing this business with that chap Boylan.'

'Bosham.'

'Bless you!'

'No, I mean his name now seems—'

'Can't blame you. Not your fault. But hardly that of the police either . . . I say. Are you all right?'

'Yes, fine. Sir. Touch of, um tummy trouble. It's wearing off.'

'Glass of water?'

'No thank you.'

'You're sure? Quite so. Where was I?' He looks out of the window. The last of the scaffolding has been taken down. The stone gleams, a pale, rosy, honey colour. Gilding flashes in a passing sunbeam. But even though only a year has passed since the part of the Palace of Westminster he can see from his window was finished there are already streaks of black beneath ledges and ornamentation where the rain gathers or runs off. 'Yes. Deuced embarrassing. So where's he gone to ground? Do we know?'

The embarrassment the Permanent Under-Secretary feels is nothing compared with what is now afflicting Cargill.

'We do know, sir. For the moment, though not under restraint, he does seem to have a fixed abode where we can, er, find him when needed.'

'Can we be sure of that?'

'As long as he remains without funds I think he'll stay put. Especially if he continues to believe he can, er, raise the wind from . . . us. I mean he will, under these circumstances, remain where he knows we can find him.'

'So. Nothing immediately on the horizon to keep us awake at night.'

Considering Charlie has already cost him most of a night's sleep Cargill's assent is half-hearted.

'What's the latest exploit he lays claim to then?' the PUS continues.

'The assassination of the revolutionary poet Shelley. Back in twenty-two.'

'Fiddlesticks.'

'He produced a lot of circumstantial evidence.'

'Of course he did. The whole business has been very well aired in public print by all the survivors who were there. It's like all these other murders he lays claim to. I don't believe he did any of them. He's just trying to blackmail us into paying him off.'

Cargill shrugs. He's feeling none too good, spasms and pain in his abdomen. A feeling that he might have to excuse himself quite suddenly. Meanwhile the PUS takes a turn back to the big window. Goodness, Lord Aberdeen and that young Gladstone already on their way down Whitehall? He looks at the clock on his mantelpiece – Cargill was dashed late in his office this morning. Is the poor chap really all right? He clears his capacious throat.

'Have you got anywhere tracking down these papers the old rogue says he has hidden away?'

Cargill's fevered blood runs cold for a moment. In truth, once again, he's forgotten all about the cache Boylan claims to have as his insurance, having pushed it to the back of his mind as an empty ruse invented to give muscle to the old reprobate's claims.

'Er, no, not actually. I've had a couple of men looking into it,' he lies, 'but they've made no progress with it yet.'

'Because, and this is why I called you in, something, um, requiring attention, and careful handling, has cropped up.'

What can Cargill usefully say? Nothing. He says nothing. The PUS goes on:

'And your chap Boylan seems to have been involved.'

'Ah.'

'The Duke . . .'

Although there are a few dukes around, a dozen or more Cargill guesses, and even though the old man has been dead these five months, one instinctively knows to whom his superior has referred.

'He left a lot of papers. That was to be expected. Of course, there is little that need worry us in any of them that relates to anything in which he himself was directly involved. Occasionally he could be acerbic, very acerbic, but almost never without justification. In everything else his every act was above reproach. An amazing man. Amazing. However . . .'

He clears his throat again, looks round his big room. Is Cargill really a person to whom one would entrust the sort of information he is about to lay before him? But that is not the point, is it? For, whatever else, Cargill is the route to Boylan, and Boylan could turn out to be very much the point.

'However. He was also the Chief Executor of the Will of His Majesty King George the Fourth. And that is a very different kettle of . . . fish. More a tin of worms, if you'll pardon the expression. There's a mountain of stuff, the personal stuff you understand, and much of it unsavoury, and I'm afraid to say your chap Boylan's name does crop up a couple of times. Now, what I am getting round to is this. All the papers that relate to the scandal that all this is concerned with, were destroyed. And the gentleman most concerned in it all, um, disappeared. But. The point is, he may have made copies, more than one set of copies, of the relevant papers, and Boylan, just conceivably, might have them in his cache . . .

'So,' and having come to the nub, and reasserted to himself the decision he has already made regarding Cargill's discretion, he at last sits down in his big chair behind his desk, leans back and looks across the sea of Aubusson at his Assistant Under-Secretary. The monocle winks like a heliograph in the sort of imperial adventure story that is already achieving huge popularity in the bookshops. Yet he still cannot help playing with a gold-mounted steel-nibbed pen that lies across the top of his cordovan blotter. As supplied to Her Majesty by Joseph Gillott, 37 Gracechurch Street, London and The Works, Graham Street, Birmingham. The nib that is, not the blotter. 'So. I'd like you to have a word with him about the whole matter. As the Duke himself would have recognised – we need to know what lies on the other side of the hill. All right. Report back to me, personally and verbally. Nothing in writing until we know, um, where we are.'

He looks up at Cargill, eye contact. Signal: we're in this together. Trust me. Poor chap does appear pale and has a sheen of sweat on his forehead.

'I'd see a sawbones if I were you. Not been anywhere near the docks have you? The MOHs are on the lookout for cholera, y'know.'

Cargill gets a grip. Is it his malaise, whatever it is, his lack of sleep? Is it really the case that the PUS has actually given him no hint at all as to what he is talking about? Frightened and confused though he is, he goes for it.

'I'm sorry, but I really have no idea, sir, just what it is you suppose Boylan was mixed up in. That could have been mentioned in the late King's . . .' (is that right? After all William IV has come and gone since then, though hardly noticed) 'in King George's papers.'

'Are you implying I have not made myself clear?'

Emboldened by indigestion, if that is what it is, which is a powerful psychological irritant, Cargill shows a readiness to be blunt that he would normally have suppressed.

'Frankly, yes sir.'

'Just mention Cumberland, Sophia and Garth to him, and see what happens.' He pauses. Again the heliograph winks in code. 'You see what I mean? Our very dear young Queen would be most distressed if that particular nest of adders went public. Worse than that. It could aid a revival of the republican senti-ments that last year's shindig did so much to allay.'

He means the Great Exhibition, although now, February 1853, it would have been more accurate to say the year before last. Cargill gathers up his papers and holding them to his chest with one hand, and his stomach with the other, puts his hand on the porcelain doorknob. PUS, back behind his desk, clears his throat.

'Cargill. This really is very important, you know. We really do need to know what Boylan has got. Our jobs on the line, our heads on the block if we don't find those papers. That's what the PPS said at yesterday's committee meeting.'

'Cumberland, Sophia, Garth.'

'Ah-hah!' Charlie touches the side of his nose and winks with appalling conspiratorial bonhomie. He already looks a lot better, has lost most of his gaolbird patina: his clothes, shabby though they are, have been washed and pressed by Deirdre, he has had his favourite lunch – steak and oyster pie washed down with a quart of Guinness – and is now looking forward to Victoria sponge, dusted with powdered sugar, with raspberry jam in the middle, accompanied by clotted cream and a dish or two of best Darjeeling. His cheeks have taken on a delicate blush from the food and the heat of the fire, his hair, now freed from grease and lice, is almost white but still hangs long, almost to his shoulders. It is a transformation on a par with the one that turned South West Wind Esquire into the King of the Golden River in young Mr Ruskin's fairy tale of that name.

Cargill's tea is beef: weak beef tea with a slice of French toast.

'Put you on to that, have they? How did that come up, I wonder. That's the way with evil things. Like bodies in the water they can lie below the surface for weeks, but one day they'll break the surface, revealing all.'

'The Duke's . . . the Duke of Wellington's private papers I believe.'

'Ah-ha! And my name . . . my name was connected?'

'I believe so.'

'Ah, the Dook, God bless him, was never one to refuse credit where credit was due.'

Cargill takes the plunge.

'You performed a service on this occasion?'

'The usual. And with even less regret than usual. Not that I ever felt any. Always for my country, Mr Cargill. Right or wrong. There is no higher service is there?'

Somewhat clumsily, he detaches a corner of sponge with the prongs of the Sheffield plate silver cake fork (Mappin Bros.), dips it in the cream on the side of his Real Old Willow Pattern plate, and masticates with abundant satisfaction. This gives Cargill time to reflect momentarily on what he has worked out since his interview with the PUS. Cumberland, if not a sausage, Sophia, if not the delectable heroine of his favourite novel, could have been siblings, the children of George the Third. Neither was assassinated. Ernest Cumberland, Duke of Cumberland, later King of Hanover, died of natural causes in 1851. Which leaves Garth.

'Garth?' he suggests.

'The same. Captain Thomas Garth. Simple matter. Caught up with him in a hotel on the rue Git-le-Cœur in Paris, dreadful dump, more a dosshouse than anything else, run by an old harridan called Madame Rachou who was even shorter in stature than I am. Beats me how even a half-pay captain with no prospects could sink so low, but by then he was well on the way to becoming an opium addict. In fact I had to do a fair bit of burrowing around to find him. Anyway, all I had to do, once I had found him, was walk in, check that the dreaming wretch on the bed really was the hit, and do the business.'

'The business?'

'A ball from my old friend Spinks and Pottle, in one ear and out the other. Then I pulled his papers from under his mattress and scarpered.'

Cargill feels a wave of dizziness, not in the least connected with his churning stomach, which is in fact settling somewhat since the sudden evacuation of his bowels he was forced to make in the public lavatories (almost the first of their kind) on Waterloo station.

'And the Duke of Wellington asked you to do this?'

'Of course not. But he let it be known that in his opinion the world would be a safer place if no longer graced by the presence of Captain Garth.'

'Ah!'

There is a lonely note in the exclamation, much like that that might creep into the utterance of a small boy who is lost but is not ready to admit it. Charlie hears it, leans sideways and places his blue and white cup and saucer on the occasional table at his side, and bends forward. Cargill catches a whiff of his own eau de Cologne.

'You have no idea of what I am a-talking about, have you?'

'I suppose not.'

'Right then.'

Charlie wriggles his scrawny buttocks forwards on to the edge of the leather chair, Cargill's chair, and, dropping his voice to a hoarse whisper, begins.

'It's commonly believed, or anyway it was twenty years and more ago, that back a further twenty years or so before that the Princess Sophia got her leg over a royal equerry called Garth, later General Garth. One way of ensuring promotion, eh, Mr

327

Cargill? And was in due course of time delivered of a boy, the future Captain Garth, whose quietus became a charge on my conscience. Or rather not.'

He wheezes with laughter, wipes spittle, Victoria sponge and cream from his wet lips, and continues.

'But that promotion arose not from what you might think he done, did, but rather, if you catch my drift, for covering for what another had done. And who was that, you are now desperate to ask. And since you have already linked their names you might dare to hazard a guess. But you need the devil's courage to go down that road, eh, Mr Cargill?'

The eyes glitter in the encroaching gloom, but Cargill is loth to interrupt the flow by getting to his feet to turn up the gas.

'You're right to feel the chill that betokens the presence of the utmost evil. Yes. The father of the Princess Sophia's bastard was none other than her own brother, the Royal Dook of Cumberland, Prince Ernest Augustus, later, on our gracious Queen's accession to our throne, King of Hanover, on account their German laws won't allow a lady to succeed. He raped her. Sophia I mean. Not Victoria. At least twice, she said. And maybe she liked it and asked him back for more. Who knows? Naturally the mists of time as well as a curtain of dark secrecy have fallen between us and those distant events. And all this, the said General Garth committed to paper. For 'twas he, you see, who carried the can for the Royal and Noble Dook. A lawyer got a sight of these papers after the demise of the General by when they were in the possession of his supposed son, Thomas Garth, the Captain, who was, if all is to be believed, not, as everyone accepted, the son of the General and the Princess, but rather the son of the Princess and the Prince! Said lawyer referred matter to the Prince Regent's Attorney General who now put in a demand for these papers. They were duly passed over, and eventually, on Prinny's death (by then George the Fourth) went to the Dook in his capacity as Chief Executor of what was private in the royal estate. However . . .'

328

and again came the tap on the nose, 'it was generally believed that the bastard Captain, in whose blood ran a double dose of royalty, had had them copied and certified as copies. And it was understood that he intended to make or repair his fortune with them . . .'

At last he leans back and his shoulders begin to shake with, Cargill is distressed to realise, spasms, convulsions of silent but uncontrollable laughter.

'And these copies . . . these copies were among the papers you took from under the Captain's mattress?' Cargill asked. 'So where are they now? Oh my God!'

At last the full significance of his superior's enquiry into progress in the search for Charlie's papers comes home to him with bowel-watering force.

'The cache you have hidden somewhere? Part of your old-age insurance plan? Oh my God!'

Charlie continues to shake, but now manages to insert into the movement a repeated and exaggerated nodding of his head, the meaning of which is unmistakable.

Charlie makes Cargill's front room, the parlour he calls it, his station, his HQ, the nerve centre of his operation. He has moved, or rather re-angled, the big leather chair so he can see up and down the Portsmouth Road with the stoop of the house in the corner of his vision and an extensive view of the common beyond it. He sits there through most of the cold grey February days with a rug across his knees, the coals of the fire to his side and slightly behind him, and a cup of chocolate, tea or, later in the day, hot toddy, beside him. He reads Mr Cargill's paper once it has been delivered, but always with an eye on the world beyond the windowpane.

Sitting there, what he most enjoys is how the prison cold slowly leaks out of his toes, the small of his back, and, eventually, even the very marrow of his bones. It is a dank, deep, miserable graveyardy sort of a chill, the prison cold, and does not shift easily.

329

Deirdre, operating from the half-basement below, administers to his wants, answers when he pulls the bell sash, and brings him whatever he calls for. He sees little of Mrs Cargill, Emily, little that is to say to speak to. But he hears the tinkle and boom of her Broadwood as she picks, no, *digs* her way through nocturnes, waltzes and mazurkas; he marks her footstep on the stairs and the click of the door latch and then the sight of her as, dressed in a hat with a dark feather, a fur jacket, a waisted dress with a tiny bustle and buttoned-up ankle boots, she hoists her umbrella and under full sail crosses the road to be subsumed between the black-trunked chestnuts into the fog of a London Peculiar. She returns at five minutes to four, just as the darkness begins to close in and the lamplighter is going about his duty, and often as she fumbles the key out of her reticule she glances in at him, in her husband's smoking jacket and tasselled round pillbox hat, and sometimes a knowing little smile hovers briefly on her lips before she pulls her eyebrows together in a frown that either registers irritation at the way the key sticks, or self-admonishment at her indiscretion.

Charlie is no fool, at least not with regard to the ways of the world, and an early hint he gives Deirdre, who no doubt passes it on to Emily, that nothing will possibly tempt him to impart to Mr Cargill a history of her mistress's goings and comings contributes, he feels sure, to the readiness of Deirdre's ministrations.

And so it is in the angle of the bay window that he is sitting when he receives the first caller he has had, on his fifth day, a Friday, at number eight Waterloo Villas, and gets a clear view of him standing on the stoop, waiting for Deirdre to answer the bell.

He does not like what he sees.

The man is round but not fat, is neatly dressed in a low-crowned hat, and a good coat but not in the latest fashion. He looks about him, at the park, at the road, at the Guildford stage just passing, with a sort of unpresuming authority that does not lay claim to what he sees but seems to suggest that he will not readily let it out of his sight. The door behind him opens, he turns, and glances in at the window, in at Charlie. His smile is open and frank, and yet Charlie shivers with a presentiment that he has not yet felt the prison chill for the last time. A moment later and Deirdre is showing the visitor through the parlour door, taking his hat, his gloves, which are woollen and functional, and his stick.

'Mr Boylan,' she says, 'we have here a Mr Bucket, come to call on yous.'

40

Charlie's worst forebodings are proved accurate.

'I am Inspector Bucket of the Detective,' says Mr Bucket in a confidential voice, 'and this is my authority.' And he produces the tip of his convenient little staff from his breast pocket.* He then takes a turn or two around the room, pausing to look at an engraving of Bath Abbey and to pick up a tiny china jug painted with blue flowers.

'Delft and genu-yne, I shouldn't wonder,' he says. 'Your host, or possibly the mistress of the house, is a person of taste.'

The most open of smiles floods his face like sunshine as he moves the upright chair from the corner and brings it into the window embrasure where he sits on it so his knees are close to Charlie's though not, of course, in any danger of actually touching them.

'Boylan,' he says. 'An Irish name, I believe. The person who showed me in is Irish I would say, from her manner of speech.'

---

* I have not been able to ascertain the precise nature of this 'staff' but I imagine it was an object only an official detective of the Metropolitan would be expected to carry. J. R.

'I am not Irish, sir, and Boylan is a name I use when I choose to.'

'If not Boylan, then Bosham. Am I not right? No harm in it, no harm in it at all . . .' and here the smile fades somewhat as though a nasty grey cloud has passed across the sun's visage, and the cheery voice becomes a touch harsher, 'unless you use the change of name for purposes of deception. And, come to think of it, Mr Whatsyourname, I'm damned if I can guess at a circumstance where a cove might wish to use more than one moniker without he was practising a deception.'

Not only is the voice suddenly less cheerful and accommodating but these last remarks are accompanied by a waving and stabbing motion of Mr Bucket's rather fat right forefinger, a digit Charlie is about to get to know all too well, for Mr Bucket uses it to admonish, probe and rebuke with equal ease.

'And, if I may revert to what is known as the Irish Question, may I say that I look on one person of Irish extraction with no more suspicion than I would any other cove, but where three are gathered together I am led to suspect conspiracy. Two together I keep an open mind about. This is not mere prejudice, Mr Boylan, but the result of experience, many years' experience, in the force.'

Charlie pulls himself together, clears his throat.

'Mr Bucket, I should be obliged if you could tell me the purpose of your visit.'

'Well, upon my word, Mr Boylan, spoken direct and to the point like a real gentleman.'

Has he pressed down too obviously on the word 'real'? Enough to make Charlie think he might have done, not quite enough to justify taking sensible umbrage.

'I'll come to the nub then, shall I?'

Charlie nods and waits with a slight quickening of his pulse and a touch of that chill in the pit of his stomach. He is not unaware that in a long life, much of it spent clearing the shit from beneath the feet of the great and the good, there have been incidents when he may have gone beyond the call of duty, stepped over the mark, and left himself vulnerable to the attentions of an overassiduous detective.

'Not, then, to beat about the bush, I'll be direct. It is understood at the Home Office, who are our masters, those of us who work out of Scotland Yard almost opposite, that you might have knowledge of the whereabouts of a bundle or cache of papers, that could include some over which you have no proprietary rights.'

He cocks an eye at Boylan and that finger comes into play again.

'Now, I am not going to dispute the case with you, Mr Boylan, for we know it to be true. What I am commissioned to find out is not whether this is the case or not; that is, as the new scientists we have around us say, a given. What I mean to get from you is a clear indication of where this cache may be found.'

Charlie needs a moment to collect himself. He gives the bell sash a pull and waits. Deirdre is prompt, as prompt as if she has been waiting in the hallway for just such a call. Possibly, so Mr Bucket thinks, for his was, by training, a suspicious nature, with her ear to the door.

'You'll join me in a cup of tea, Mr Bucket? Of course you will. Deirdre, tea for the two of us please, and a plate of the Nice biscuits?'

The pause thus engineered gives him time to come up with a prevaricatory stratagem.

'Mr Bucket, I imagine you already know that I too have served the Home Office with some distinction for a very long time. Early in my career I was advised by a colleague, a Mr Guy de Bourgeois, never to throw away paper. Not any paper. Not a bus ticket or a tailor's bill even. Charlie, he used to say to me, Charlie, you never know, you never know. Hang on to the paper.'

What it was Bourgeois was sure Charlie would never know is not something Charlie is about to divulge. However, he continues: 'And the result, Mr Bucket, is that I have collected so much paper I have had to split it up and put it in different

334

places. Is your name really "Bucket"? You'll forgive me if I am curious as to its origin.'

Caught off guard the Inspector begins a tedious exposition about Huguenot forebears called 'Bouquet' but breaks it off before he is well under way.

'Humbug, Boylan, it won't do, y'know.' And his finger stabs the air only inches from Charlie's nose. 'Our information is that there is one cache and one only and you will be so good as to tell me where it is. Now I have here,' the finger curls to a fist which plunges into Mr Bucket's capacious side pocket, and comes up with a sheet of fine paper which Charlie can see carries the VR monogram at its head, a dash of red sealing wax at its foot, and some fine black copperplate between the two, 'a properly drawn magistrate's warrant for your arrest for obstructing a policeman in the course of his duty. Which I shall execute forthwith.'

'Ah,' says Boylan. 'Our tea. Deirdre, will you pour for us?'

Bucket sighs, leans back and waits, but with the warrant clearly displayed upon his knee.

Now a very curious thing occurs during the ceremony that follows, and curious things, as we have already noticed, always catch the Inspector's attention. Deirdre is about to offer him the Real Old Willow Pattern sugar bowl when she turns suddenly pale, pulls it away from him, and rushes out of the room. She is back in no time, still holding the small receptacle on her palm, but this time she offers it to Bucket with a servile smile. Bucket duly stirs a heaped spoonful into his tea and smiles across at Boylan.

'The papers, Boylan. Where are they?'

Boylan, who has had time to give the matter some thought, smiles back.

'They may be found, sir, in Bognor. In the roof of a fisherman's cottage. The address is number four, Steyne Street. I took a room there in thirty-one, shortly before I left for the Americas. And, as far as I know, my papers are still there. My departure was somewhat hurried and unexpected and I had neither time nor means to take them with me.'

Mr Bucket beams. ''S truth, Boylan?'

'God's truth, Mr Bucket.'

And at that moment upstairs, for she has slipped in un-noticed, Emily Cargill begins to play. The 'Funeral March'.

'The mistress?' Mr Bucket asks. 'She has a fine touch. A fine touch. Boom, boom, b-boom, tum-t-tum, tum, tum. Last time I heard that was the Duke's funeral. Wonderful occasion. Grandeur and sorrow flowering on one tree.' His eye becomes misty, he dabs it with a huge handkerchief, then becomes brusque and practical again.

'Bless my heart, but she is very musical, aint she? Has the gift, I'd say.'

'I'd say so,' Charlie replies, a touch warily, wondering where this is leading.

'I have a friend, do y'see, who is looking for a second-hand wiolinceller, of a good tone, and I do wonder if, being as musi-cal as she is, whether she might not know where one could be found. At a reasonable price, you understand.'

Bognor, not yet blessed with a railway, though one has been proposed, takes a day and a half to reach since there is no direct connection. Bucket has to take the Portsmouth stage, and stop over at Petersfield, before taking a second coach through Chichester to the coast. Bognor he finds to be a dismal place centred round the country home of the Hothams which stands a hundred yards or so from the sea. A little to the west a grand terrace of houses and hotels for the gentry is going up, with bathing machines already in place on the shingle in front of them, the thought being to rival the sea-bathing at Littlehampton and Worthing, which, of course, Bognor never will. The shore is swept with an icy wind, which Bucket tries to persuade himself is bracing.

A further hundred yards or so bring him to the tiny hamlet which was all that was there before Hotham, one of Nelson's captains, built his house out of prize money. It consists of little more than a double row of fishermen's cottages hardly enough to justify the title of 'street'. The whole place is tiny and shabby and has no reason to exist but to sell fish to the surrounding farmers and farm labourers when there is enough money available to buy them, or barter them for bread when there is not. To the east lies the far more substantial village of Felpham, where Billy Blake resided for a year or two, and to the west lie Aldwick and Pagham.

Number four, Steyne Street, is empty. The plank door is rotting at the edges, the shutters have fallen from the two windows, one on each floor. A neighbour, who is busy smoking haddock in his chimney, tells Mr Bucket that Widow Parfrement is in the Felpham Union, that Master Parfrement was lost at sea some five years since. Bucket decides not to stand on ceremony, kicks in the front door of number four, and picks his way through clinging cobwebs and over cracked flags to the ladder that goes to the top of the hovel. Next to the ladder, on a shelf by a bottle about which a ghost of gin still lingers, there is a stub of candle and a box of lucifers, with two sticks unused. The ladder's rungs surprise him by remaining solid and soon he is poking about in the roof, prodding and pushing aside a pile of rotten fishing nets.

There are no papers, and no signs that there ever were any.

Another day and a half take him back to Scotland Yard where startling news awaits him.

This time two uniformed constables accompany him to number eight, Waterloo Villas. Again the tall, gaunt Irish woman opens the door. At a sign from Bucket one of the constables moves forward and immediately fastens the iron bracelets on her wrists.

'Hang on, mister, what d'blazes d'yer tink yer at?'

'You'll see. Now where's Boylan?'

'In hell, I hope, if all diss has onyting to do wi' him.'

But he is just coming down the stairs, wearing Cargill's quilted dressing gown and a bobbled nightcap. On seeing Bucket below and the constables behind him, he turns through one hundred and eighty degrees, and attempts to scamper back the way he came. He misses his footing and slides down, feet first, on his stomach, to arrive at Bucket's feet. He turns over, looks up at Bucket who appears the more hellish as a puff of London Peculiar, laden with sulphur, comes in through the open door behind him and swirls briefly about his head. He stoops, grasps Charlie's wrists, first one and then the other, fastens on the second pair. He adjusts them.

'How do you find them? Are they comfortable? If not, say so, for I wish to make things as pleasant as is consistent with my duty.'

Charlie looks up at him; a deeply pleading look swims in his eye.

'No papers, Mr Bucket? Now surely we needn't be surprised at that. Not after twenty years.'

'It's not on account of the papers I'm here, Charlie. It's my duty to inform you that any observations you make will be liable to be used against you. Therefore, Charlie, be careful what you say. You don't happen to have heard of murder, do you? Hopefully, I should say . . . murder attempted?'

'Mr Bucket, what the devil are you talking about?' Still on the floor, looking up at his tormentor.

'Murder most foul, as indeed it always is, Charlie. Mr Cargill is at present in St Thomas's hospital possibly dying, but hopefully on the road to recovery, from arsenical poisoning. His loving and musically talented wife is at his bedside and it is she who has indicated that you and Deirdre Doyle here has colluded in this crime.'

Charlie continues to plead.

'Not Pentonville, again, Mr Bucket.'

'No,' replies the Officer of the Law, 'Millbank. It'll be handier for the investigation.'

Behind him Deirdre Doyle finds her tongue at last.

'The fockin' bitch,' she cries. 'The fockin', fockin' bitch.'

'Language,' Mr Bucket remarks, and leads the little procession down the steps to where the horses stamp and steam in front of a closed and windowless Metropolitan Police Black Maria.

41

It is not the wheels of justice that grind slowly so much as those of the Circumlocution Office, to give a generic name to that endless maze of departments that include the Home Office, the Secret Service, branches of the Foreign Office, the Treasury, all those organs of government whose business it is to interfere as subtly as may be into every corner of our lives, recording, in the days of which we speak, in its ledgers all transactions and movements that its functionaries might deem of interest to the State and granting or withholding our right to blow up the House of Commons or blow our own noses. Now, of course, they use computers.

Consequently, turning a contingent but unrelated event to its advantage to enmesh Charlie Boylan in the matter of the possible poisoning of Thomas Cargill, the office has made it possible for the poor man to be held, on this occasion, with some legality, appearing monthly before magistrates who routinely deny him bail, before returning him to his cell in Millbank.

A nasty February shifts to a stormy March, through to an unusually warm and stuffy April, and the first hot night of the year, the sort of fine steaming night which turns the slaughter-houses, the unwholesome trades, the sewerage, bad water and burial grounds to account, and gives the Registrar of Deaths (another branch of the Circumlocution Office) plenty to do the next day. This is the night Charlie at last receives a visitor, the first since young Mr Guppy pronounced himself unable to do anything for him in a legal sort of a way until the most material witness in his case, Mrs Emily Cargill, can be found. She was last seen back at the end of February, boarding the Dover packet in the company of a young, good-looking man believed to be an American teacher of the pianoforte. Though the note she left, addressed to her still very sick husband, stated she was in the company of one of her Newport (Mon.) cousins.

'I am here,' the tall, saturnine sergeant, with a strong melancholic cast to his features, announces, once the turnkey has locked him in and departed, 'in an entirely unofficial capacity, for purposes not at all connected with the poisoning of Mr Thomas Cargill.'

'How is the poor fellow? He is hardly ever out of my mind. I think I even dream of him.' Charlie's face lights up with a glow that combines with a skill one would normally expect only on the physiognomy of an experienced Thespian, anxiety, sympathy, and a warm delight in his acquaintanceship with a suffering friend.

'Much better, I understand. The doses of arsenic he was receiving were not large and administered only when he drank tea or coffee. But all this we know you to be already aware of. His system is almost purged of the evil substance and time and a careful regimen are all that are needed to bring him back to health.'

'He remains at St Thomas's?'

'No. He has been granted leave of absence to convalesce at his mother's house in Orpington.'

'Well, that is a relief.' Charlie leans back against the whitewashed wall, which is all the headrest there is for his plank bed, and looks around. 'He is better lodged than I. This place is even worse than Pentonville. Apart from being larger, the largest in the country I believe, it is plagued with the damp that rises from the river. A damp that froze on the walls when I first came here and is now no doubt laden with the cholera. It was built, I understand, on Benthamist principles. The governor, something of a gentleman and a serendipidist, informed me that the great philanthropist and philosopher was responsible for its design on utilitarian lines. Bentham even invested his own money in its construction, thereby establishing a template for subsequent structures with a similar purpose, among them Pentonville. You could call it a privately financed initiative, and since the motive of most crime is redistribution of the wealth of the very rich, it would seem to have been an investment both sound and fair.'

But this has lost the sergeant who has not come to Millbank to discuss the reform of prison building or the merits of using private money to finance public works. He pulls up the single wooden chair – as yet there is no table – and sits by the plank bed, facing Charlie, but not so close as to be bothered by the prison staleness which has long since once again impregnated Charlie's clothes and skin. He gives a little cough, leans forward.

'Am I to understand, Mr Boylan, from your concern for Mr Cargill's health, that you continue to protest your innocence in the matter of his attempted murder?'

Now they are so close together, Charlie finds himself more than a little disconcerted by his visitor's appearance and manner. The sergeant, not a young man, is miserably lean, dressed in decent black with a white cravat. His face is as sharp as a hatchet, the skin as yellow and dry and withered as an autumn leaf. And his eyes, of a steely light grey, have a very disconcerting trick of looking at you as if their owner knows that you would not, whatever, tell the truth, the whole truth and nothing but the truth. Such, at any rate, are Charlie's thoughts as he turns his own eyes to a close study of the man's hands whose long, lanky fingers are hooked like claws.

'Why should I want to kill him? He was giving me lodging, food, warmth, comfort. He even lent me his clothes. Besides, did you not just say that you are here on an entirely different matter?'

The sergeant ignores this last sally, but digs, like a surgeon, into murkier depths.

'But he was engaged in investigating your past. A past, which on your own admission, included murder and many other less serious crimes.'

'I did nothing for which your superiors at the Home Office did not signify their approval, and later gratitude. My only complaint is that they have not been as forthcoming as justice would demand with the dibs.'

The sergeant, detective sergeant Boylan presumes him to be, since he is un-uniformed, waves this to one side.

'Deirdre Doyle was your accomplice. She procured the arsenic. You formed a liaison with her—'

'Oh come on, Sergeant . . . what's your name?'

'Cuff.'

'Sergeant Cuff. Why not Mr Bucket? I thought he was in charge of my case.'

'At the moment Mr Bucket is otherwise engaged. The murder of an important man of law.'

Charlie feels put out. A case more important than his own, on which the fate of nations may rest? However, he swallows his pride and returns to the subject in hand, his relations with Miss Deirdre Doyle.

'A liaison with Miss Doyle? On two separate occasions I spent an hour or so in her bed. But at my age, and having suffered the privations I have been forced to bear, I am afraid I was able to do very little for her that she could not manage on her own. And the bed being hardly any bigger than this one and her attic room in February almost as cold, she decided I might as well not attend her there again.'

The melancholic sergeant frowns at what he takes to be an allusion to practices he'd really rather not think about; murder and theft are more his line.

'At all events,' he hurries on, partly to conceal his confusion, 'you can see that the case against you and Miss Doyle is watertight. Attempted murder is still a hanging matter.'

Charlie, as we know, has seen enough hangings to know what this means. And he's not even sure that removing the process to the privacy of an indoor shed, as is now the case with all but the most newsworthy of executions, is an improvement. The solemn silence of the crowd, the knowledge that one is the chief actor on the stage, the opportunity for a last word of penitence or defiance . . . all these must have gone some way towards mitigating the less pleasant aspects for the central character . . . at all events he feels a sudden sick chill more penetrating and horrid than the prison cold. Yet he senses a glimmer of hope.

'First,' he asserts, 'I must be tried. I will have a brief who will ask me germane questions. Such as . . . how did I know Mr Cargill, why was I at his house, why indeed had he made so many visits to me at Pentonville . . . These and my answers could cause some embarrassment.'

Cuff sighs, places his palms on his serge-clad knees.

'You cannot believe that any such consideration is in the minds of any of my superiors, whose only concern is that justice should be done, justice tempered with clemency.'

Quite clearly he is now rehearsing what he has been told to say, but being a man of obvious intelligence and mature years is doing it in as natural and reasonable a way as can be desired. 'In which last respect, I am to advise you that although the Penal Servitude Act is shortly to be debated there is still time for the authorities to make a special case in, um, your case, and substitute deportation for the supreme penalty.'

But Charlie has had enough. The bushes have been thoroughly beaten, it is time the pheasants, crows, whatever that shelter within it, reveal themselves.

'Van Diemen's Land in exchange for what?' he cries.

Cuff is now abrupt. 'Your papers. The cache of papers you have hidden away.'

Charlie, aware that the nub has at last been reached and that it indeed has little to do with Mr Cargill's indisposition, now feels a strange sensation spreading from the furthermost of his extremities, his toes to be precise, and slowly climbing to his knees. Can it be hope?

'Ah,' he murmurs. Then, 'Ah' again. Then: 'I'm not sure I can recall precisely where they are. But I might be induced to remember.'

Cuff has been prepared for this.

'And the office of Her Majesty's Attorney General might be prepared to instruct immediately the solicitors to the Metropolitan Police to proceed with your prosecution as the perpetrator of an attempted murder.'

So many ps to mind, but as yet no qs. Cuff's tongue does not stumble.

'And a *quid pro quo*,' here come the qs, 'is proposed?' Charlie suggests.

'As I said: Van Diemen's Land.'

'I shall want better than that. I shall want a free and unconditional pardon.'

Cuff allows himself a melancholic smile, stands. 'It's gone eleven, my time is up.'

He pulls down his jacket, smooths his trousers as if to brush from them every mote of prison dust that might have contaminated them, retrieves his tall black hat from the bed, and with a sort of half salute takes his leave. At the door he turns. 'The papers, Boylan. Or an accurate indication of where they might be found.'

'Cuff? Fuck off.'

The Circumlocution Office is like an octopus with many tentacles. Like many, many octopodes with many, many tentacles. If a left hand may not know what a right hand is doing, how goes it when there are a hundred left hands and a hundred right hands? It should be no surprise then to the reader to learn that a Mr Smiley in one department might order one approach to the problem of Boylan's papers, while in another cubbyhole or offshoot of Whitehall a Mr Brotherhood develops and puts into execution an entirely different *modum operandi*.

42

'Where am I?' asks Charlie, a week later.

He is looking out through a tall casement, not on to faery lands forlorn but a view as like as you will find in the English countryside. The furthest horizon is bounded with steep hills crowned with heather, with outcrops of a bluish rock, some of which are rounded into huge boulders and split by frost. Two of these on the skyline resemble a reclining woman, but severed in half at the waist so a tall man could walk between her upper and lower parts.

Beneath her the hillside, scarred with a quicksilver line of tumbling water, drops into plantations of mixed trees, cunningly placed so one may nod to the other across a lake that reflects them. A cackle of crows wheels above one of them. A white diminutive pantheon lends interest to one bank, a Gothick grotto to the other. On this side of the lake are rolling lawns, close-cropped by fallow deer kept by a virtually invisible ha-ha from the formal garden beneath his window. Wallflowers and tulips are marshalled in its flowerbeds. Charlie, without attempting to peer round the drapes that have just been opened by a flunkey in tailed coat and striped trousers, senses that his

345

window must be on a third floor, just off the centre of a splendidly decorated portico.

The only thing that mars the experience is the sensation of nausea that afflicts him, and a sick headache that seems to go with it.

The old man, who is wearing white kid gloves, places a cup and saucer of papery thinness and a silver-domed toast warmer on an occasional table.

'If sir wishes a more substantial breakfast, he has only to pull the bell handle by the door, though I have been advised that a light repast would suit sir's condition better than the full English.' His voice is like a cracked bell, his accent coloured with a sort of northern twang Charlie has not heard for thirty years. He continues: 'You are, sir, a guest at Pemberley, in the county of Derbyshire.'

A chord is struck. Pentrich.

'Not far then,' Charlie remarks, 'from Chatsworth.'

'We are honoured, sir, that his grace the Duke of Devonshire's land marches with ours at about five miles to the east of us.'

And the old man, having glanced around the room, checking that all is as it should be, departs. The only jarring note that is struck is the turning of the key in the lock on the outside. Charlie is a prisoner still, but in a far better situation than he was at Millbank.

How did he get here? He has confused recollections of returning to near consciousness, of being off-loaded from a hansom cab at a railway station, possibly the new terminus at King's Cross, of being half-carried, half-persuaded to walk along a platform, of two personages sitting opposite him in a first class railway carriage who rather ostentatiously displayed newfangled pistols with revolving chambers stuck in their belts beneath their coats. Then Morpheus, possibly morphine, overtook him again and, lulled by the motion of the train and the sulphurous fumes that occasionally blew in through a window left open an inch or two, by the rattle and rhythm of

346

the permanent way, he had sunk back into a deep slumber. He had not come properly to from a drugged sleep until he woke with the sick headache in the valanced bed that now stands behind him.

He hesitates for a moment over the steaming cup of fragrant orange tea and then says to himself 'they would hardly have brought me all this way to murder me', and drinks a little. The cup that cheers but does not inebriate. Orange Pekoe. And quality too.

'I had, I suppose, better bring you up to steam with your situation.'

A robust, smoothly clad, but large and rather domineering figure looks down at Charlie. A wry grin briefly crosses a healthily russet face.

'You are a prisoner, but this is no ordinary prison,' he continues.

'Indeed not, sir,' Charlie replies briskly though with a slight lisp, the last effect of the drugs he has been given still lingering in his bloodstream, 'the best it has been my fortune to be incarcerated in.'

'The fact is, it is what we call a Safe House. A place where we may hide for a time such persons as we . . . want to hide. Safely. You may wish to know why we want to hide you.'

Charlie advises the man who looms over him like a benign Jove that he is all ears.

'Quite so. We, that is the particular branch of the Foreign Office which I represent, have been interested for some time in your past. There are two sources, there were I should say, two sources available to us. One was the cache of papers your solicitor Mr Guppy took from your rooms. Since he has indicated that he will resort to the law to keep them, claiming they are material to your defence in the case of the attempted murder of Mr Cargill, we must turn to the other – your account of your past as transmitted to Mr Cargill. He, poor chap, transcribed your verbal recollections and filed those you wrote and these

347

we have in our possession. However, they are of course incomplete. Basically, what we want is an account of your activities from the point where you left off. Especially in so far as they relate to places and events beyond these, ah, shores. But not necessarily. Anything which relates to national security is grist to our mill. You worked for the Home Office as, not to put too fine a point on it, as a spy—'

'Assassin too. I was licensed.'

'Er . . . so you say. Now, we at the Foreign Office run a similarly clandestine operation. Its main concerns are in the further reaches of the Empire – for instance on the North-West frontier of India, Afghanistan particularly is proving to be a thorn in our flesh as the Russians attempt to extend their influence in the area – or among the Dutch settlers in the Cape of Good Hope. But recently we have been interesting ourselves in the activities of the Fenians in Ireland, which we have always considered to be our patch. The Home Office of course prefers to think of Ireland as home ground so in this respect there is some rivalry between us, not to say bad feeling . . .'

The benign gentleman now takes a quick turn round the room and comes back to look down on Charlie . . .

'In short we need you to complete the story that you began for Mr Cargill. On paper. In writing. Should you demur I would remind you that you have been charged with attempted murder. Or indeed, we might just drop you in one of the quarries that scar the hills you can see from your window.'

Until now one corner of Charlie's mind has been reflecting that you get a better class of civil servant in the foreign service than you do in the Home Office. Now he is not so sure. He sighs, looks at his lumpy knuckles, reflects on how his knees hurt when put under pressure, and how his breathing fails him if he has to make an effort. He also remembers the really very unpleasant nature of the cells in Pentonville and Millbank. Here he is warm, hopes to be well fed. He looks up. That the gaze that meets his watery eyes is tinged with scorn does not in the least bother him.

348

'Where shall I start?'

'Where you left off.'

'That was thirty years ago. Nearly thirty-one. The drowning of that poet chappie. Shelley.'

The gentleman from the Foreign Office sighs.

'Then that is where you had better start again.'

Charlie grins. This will take some time. In such surroundings he is prepared to take all the time in the world.

'Pen? Paper?'

'They shall be brought. Ah. I see our landlord is up earlier than usual.' The robust gentleman is now standing by the window, looking down and out. 'Perhaps he has caught wind of the fact that we have a new inma— . . . guest. He's deuced curious about our comings and goings, to the extent that we sometimes wonder if he aint employed by the other side.'

The Russians? The French? No, the Home Office.

'Landlord? You rent this place?'

He joins the man, who has now in his mind lost status having dropped from owner to tenant in a sentence, though he rocks a little unsteadily as he gets to his feet. The landlord in question is walking along the edge of the ha-ha with a couple of flat-haired black retrievers in tow and a hunting gun under his arm. But his gaze is fixed on the façade of his house, possibly on the very window where Charlie and the gentleman from the Foreign Office are observing him. He is tall, his grizzled hair is visible for he wears no hat, he is dressed for the country in high walking boots and a long brown, caped but lightweight coat with large pockets, which say 'poacher' rather than landowner.

'A Mr Darcy,' the man from the Foreign Office continues. 'Lives in the west wing now. Once a very wealthy man but lost a packet when the negroes created all that trouble in Jamaica back in thirty-four. Before that happened he married beneath him, that is to say his wife came from a family who were almost poor, she being one of five sisters. It was a marriage of the heart, which means of course that they soon tired of each other.

349

It has been said he beat her. She now lives in Bath with her sister, the widow of Colonel Wickham who, you may recall, made a fortune in India. If he should try to get in touch with you, be discreet and report to me anything that passes between you, would you? I might add he is a bit touched. Eccentric. That sort of thing. Right?' He comes back into the room leaving Charlie stranded by the window. 'By the way, my name is Elliott. With two ts. Not that I suppose you will ever have cause to write it down.'

He goes, leaving behind a whiff of expensive cologne on the air and the sound of the key turning in the lock. Charlie turns back to the window. Mr Darcy is indeed behaving very oddly. He is divesting himself of all his clothes. When he is quite naked he dives into the lake and comes up with his head and shoulders festooned with fleshy lily-pads and their succulent stalks. His dogs bark at him. This is not, Charlie decides, the behaviour of a real gentleman, however unfortunate or touched.

Charlie sits at the table and waits through a long ten minutes; then the door opens again and the flunkey reappears, bearing paper, inkpot, pens and a blotter.

In his best copperplate Charlie inscribes a heading.

Memo prepared at Mr Eliott's request by Mr Charles Boylan, begun this twentieth day of April 1853. And he underlines it with a flourishing squiggle.

43

Having achieved what I had set out to do at Leghorn (Livorno) and witnessed the last rites from behind a sand dune at Viareggio, I went to Rome where I sought out Mr Bourgeois at an address he had given me. He duly paid me the fifty guineas he had promised me though only after some irritable discussion during which he asserted that the *Don Juan* had gone down simply as the result of the incompetence of its crew.*

Leigh Hunt and Lord Byron remained to be done.

'Oh, I don't think so, Charlie,' the cadaverous Mr Bourgeois replied when I suggested that Hunt should not present much of a problem if I could only get him away from the Byron entourage for an hour or so. 'Our masters feel that *The Liberal* will not come to much with Shelley gone. Not only would he have written with far more conviction and force than either of the others, Byron's talent after all does not go much beyond versifying, which no one takes seriously, it is also the case that he was much taken with Shelley and it was Shelley's involvement

---

* Was he paid or wasn't he? (see page 318). We'll never know. J. R.

351

in the enterprise that attracted him to it. No, the word out now is that his lordship will be off to Greece: he is more interested in the insurgence of Greek brigands than the indigence of Nottingham stockingers, or Lancashire mill-workers. Once he's gone, and with Shelley gone already, *The Liberal* will die. If it's not stillborn in the first place.'

There was more to it than that. Not only did I not get paid for what I had been commissioned to do, there was no work to take its place. The thing of it was that for a year or two events took an upturn in England. There were three or four good harvests, people started buying and consuming the products of the manufactories again, trade improved and dissent, let alone the possibility of revolution, simply became a less interesting project than it had been.

On top of all that there was the new broom of Sir Robert at the Home Office, setting up a proper police force and so forth, which there was never any chance I would be employed in, not even the un-uniformed branch, and so one way and another, just as workers were being hired elsewhere, I was laid off. For eight years to be precise. It now occurs to me that with my fluency in several languages I might well have found employment with your worships at the Foreign Office instead, but there you go, Mr Eliott, that was an opportunity neither party took up.

I made shift. I always do. I returned to Pau for a time where I set up as a teacher of languages and continued to write the memoirs of the early part of my life, which I dedicated, with no thought of reward, and indeed received none, to his grace the Duke of Wellington, and for a time was employed again as a kitchen porter by Captain Branwater. He, poor fellow, was taken off by an ague in, as I recall, the winter of twenty-nine: the climate of the south-west of France is by no means as healthy as it is generally believed to be. It gets a lot of rain, and, inland, which Pau is, snow as well, yet being south these cold and inclement patches are often followed by spells of the humid warmth that breeds illness.

Whatever, the Captain was taken off and, as is so often the case, was discovered to have been in debt. The apartment on the boulevard des Pyrénées was cleared and sold up and with the contents went my memoirs. I had been keeping them in a wicker basket of which I had fond memories, for it was the one the Captain had used to carry his changes of clothes on our campaigns in the Peninsula.

By late October or early November, I forget the exact date, but it was 1830 right enough, I had made my way back to London. My first port of call, after renting a room in a newish house in Kennington, was the Home Office. Just as I had on my very first visit I made my way to the mews and found them still to be supervised by a man called Sam, whose other name or names I never discovered. He was now of course some fifteen years older than when I had first been introduced by him into those hallowed halls, but recognisably the same man – and he remembered me.

'Long time no see, Mr Boylan,' he cried, pausing in his duties of shifting horse-shit from the cobbles with a large broom. 'Vot can I do for you?'

'Take me to Mr Stafford, of course,' I replied, as cheerily as I might. 'Who else?'

'Pass-vord?' says he, leaning on his broom handle.

'"Who pays the piper?"' I ventured.

'Bless you, sir, that vent out some five years back, but seeing as who you are,' and having seen the half-sovereign I was rolling between the knuckles of my left hand, 'I'll see vot I can do.'

It cost me that half, and also an hour's wait in the corridor outside Room 101, before old John Stafford came rumbling and wheezing down the corridor having just come from Bow Street where he still maintained his cover as Clerk to the Magistrates' Court. Sir Robert had offered him the post of Chief to the new constabulary but he'd turned it down on the grounds that he already knew his way around, being the government's Spy-Master and it was too late to teach an old dog new tricks. He had aged in the time, the white streak in his hair no longer visible since all of his hair was now white.

'Bless me, Boylan, I thought we'd seen the last of you,' he grumbled, as he opened the door and went through, leaving me to follow him. 'They told me you were here. No business to let you in, but now you are, what do you want?'

'Employment, Mr Stafford. And my arrears for being on your books these eight years and not a penny paid me.'

'Books be damned. Your sort don't appear in no books.' He hummed and hawed, wandered about his room as if it were new to him and he a stranger in it, then came back at me. 'Swing,' he barked. 'Heard of Swing, have you? Captain Swing?'

I thought for a moment. I knew a fair bit about Swing, but didn't want to let on too readily how much.

'There was talk on the Dover packet, and then on the stage we passed a burning rick and one of the travellers said it was Swing. Another said it was French revolutionaries, come to spread the revolutionary disease, not Swing. And a third reckoned they're one and the same.'

'Frenchies be damned. Fact is you turned up just now could be sort of heaven sent. You've not been seen around for a few years, it's a part of the country you haven't been active in, and the plain fact of it is since none of the nobs agree as to what it's all about, we need to know a bit more. It's already spread from Kent to Sussex and into Hampshire. Get down to Hampshire and find out.'

Just like that. He continued.

'The Prime Minister says it's just the scum of the country folk aping what happens in the village next door and that's how it spreads. Sir Robert says it's organised and there has to be a leader or at least a cabal. I'm with him on that. The Prime Minister says leave it to the justices and the gentry – they'll sort it. Sir Robert wants the army in. In short they're at logger-heads. So the Duke says—'

'The Duke,' I asked, 'being the Duke of Wellington?'

'Yes, the Duke. The Prime Minister.'

'You mean his grace is Prime Minister?'

'Where have you been these last two and a half years?'

I realised I'd overdone the pretence of ignorance.

'France, Italy, Spain, Portugal, Poland . . . but of course I

354

know he's Prime Minister. I just thought he'd be on the side of those who want to call out the army.'

'Not at all. God bless his grace, he'll do anything to avoid a civil war. That's why he gave in on the Catholic Bill. And why, once he's seen it trimmed to nothing, he'll withdraw his opposition to Reform. But that's beside the point. What he says, and I've just come from Number Ten, not that he lives there but he comes in from Number One most mornings, is what he always says. We don't know enough of what's going on on the other side of the hill. Indeed he's off now, back to Stratfield Saye. If there's trouble there, that's where he feels he should be. And then he'll go on to Winchester, the county town. He don't expect to be PM longer than the end of the month, the Reformers will have him out, but he is Lord-Lieutenant of Hampshire, and that, he reckons, is where his duty lies. So there we are, Boylan. The Duke goes to Hampshire and you get down there too but on the other side of the hill. Five sovs a week plus expenses, and don't even think about asking for back pay, you won't get it.'

'Guineas,' said I. 'And a month up front.'

'Done,' said he.

So, after one or two very minor preparations, such as getting my pistol, the Spinks and Pottle, serviced by young Mr Spinks, the old one having fallen off the perch as they say, from his new workshop in the Burlington Arcade, and a fresh supply of cartridges and percussion caps, and a new hat and a pair of good shoes, the ones I had on being down to their uppers, I returned a day later to Southwark and boarded the Winchester mail coach, alighting in the November dusk at the Red Lion Inn, Alresford, some six miles short of Winchester, the same day.

It being almost dark and a damp fog descending over the town, I decided to remain indoors. After dining off venison patty and apple pie with a jug of local winter ale, I removed myself to the snug, took the corner settle, and lit up my pipe, ready to eavesdrop on the local gossip. I did not have to wait long. Four or five men gathered at the counter, and since they all had their own pewter mugs I took it that they were all regulars, not passing through, it being a staging inn.

'Specials or no, I shall be boarding up my shop windows,' cried one, wiping his mouth first on the back of a rosy but soft, no labourer he, hand. 'I gotta new genelman's saddle on display and I aint risking losing that.'

'But they baint be cummin into town, 'taint shopkeepers they'm after,' said another, who from the amount of leather he had on by way of leggings and patches I took to be a gamekeeper or maybe a tenant farmer. 'It's the barn of unthrashed grain and the thrashing machine they'm after. They got nothing against shopkeepers.'

A third, an older man with a touch of authority about him, now spoke up.

'Thrashing machines be blowed,' he grunted. 'What they want is better wages, and for them with families, I'd say why not. Take a good few off the parish if they earned a bob or two more a week, and make my job easier.'

'That's all very well, master overseer,' from which I understood Mr Authority was the local dispenser of the poor law, 'but I can't afford to pay more wages than I am,' Mr Leather came back at him, 'not 'less the landlord drop the rent.'

'Aye and the parson his tithes. What's a parson want three thousand a year for, I ask, what's a parson want that sort of money for?'

'Now that be Wesleyan talk, George, so stow it . . .'

' 'Taint Wesleyan to ask why Parson out at they Worthys, King's Worthy, Abbot's and Martyr Worthy, gets tithes from three parishes.'

From which I guessed that perhaps the Worthys would be the scenes of Swingish activity and I resolved to head in their direction the next morning.

I make no secret of it, Mr Eliott, but I've never been a great man for walking nor for riding a horse, but I hired a nag, a mare, a dull sort of orange colour she was, called Lady, from the

356

ostler at the Red Lion, promising to bring her back in a week and putting down ten pounds as a deposit, which was twice what she was worth. I expended more energy on kicking her flanks and whipping her buttocks with a hazel switch I pulled out of a hedge for the purpose, than I would have done had I chosen after all to leg it. Still, I made an early start, before sun up, and was just over halfway to Martyr Worthy when I truly ran, well, ambled, right into it.

First sign I had of it, as Lady paused to tear at the last of some traveller's joy draped like washing over a hedge, was a column of white smoke rising into the misty air the other side of the slow rise we were climbing, and the sound of distant shouts, a dog barking and then the bang of a fowling piece. The shouts turned to guffaws and as I came on to the ridge which the track followed I heard a distinct shout of: 'It's only birdshot, you silly moo.'

So there, the other side of a small meadow, was a thatched farmhouse, an oast house, a hayrick burning, well a sort of black smoulder rather than a proper fire on account of the wet, with maybe fifty labourers in round soft hats and smocks, and a farmer booted like the one in the snug the night before, busily ramming more shot down the barrel of his fowling piece while his dog leapt about him trying to lick his face 'stead of driving off the rioters. One of these had his breeches down and his smock up and was craning his head round over his shoulder to see what damage the farmer's shot had done to his upper right buttock.

I and Lady stayed where we were, with a good view, in good hearing range, but out of reach of birdshot. Presently there were more shouts and more labourers, who had been scouting round the outhouses, came running back.

'We've found 'im,' they shouted. 'Ol' Gabby here had hid him in the oast house under his hops!'

And there followed a ratchety squeaking sort of a noise, and round the corner of the house they came, from the oast house that lay behind it, dragging what looked like a big metal drum or barrel, with crossed iron beams on top and a system of gears below, which was what I took to be a thrashing machine that could be powered by four horses walking in a circle. It seemed the heads of corn were churned about in the barrel until the grain fell to the bottom leaving the chaff on top, when it was emptied and the process begun again. If you've ever seen men flailing, *swinging* away with strips of leather on a thrashing floor, you'd know this was a better way of doing it. Nevertheless the men all crowded round now with big hammers, saws and so forth and began to smash it. They seemed to be enjoying themselves the way most of us do when breaking something up.

'Here, give Farmer Gabriel his axe, let 'm have a go,' and blow me, Mr Eliott, if the farmer didn't do just that.

'Silly fucker was always jamming up,' he cried.

Pardon the language, but I know you want as truthful an account as I gave Mr Stafford. What's more, the farmer wasn't fussed about his ricks neither, being as they were insured with the Norwich Union.

When they were done his wife came out and gave them all some fresh baked cob loaves and a jug of cider and when they'd finished these they all came across the meadow through the gate, touched the rims of their hats at me, assuming I suppose from the cut of my clothes and the fact I was on a horse, albeit a pretty strange one, that I was gentry or a servant to the gentry. They set off along the ridge above the river, and I followed a hundred yards or so behind, reining in, which was never a problem with Lady, whenever they came to a halt.

This they did at every cottage and cabin they passed, hoicking out all of the labouring sort they came across to join them, and demanding charity in the form of coin or food at the farms, desisting from rick burning and machine smashing where gold was forthcoming. Their message was simple: we are all ground under by taxes, tithes and rents, there were people earning thirty or forty thousand pound a year off taxes, and tithes were an abhorrence. Many agreed with all this, and not a few joined in with them, especially when the message was got across that if the farmers raised the wages, they, that is the mob, would put an end to tithes.

44

'What do you know of the condition of the English farm labourer?'

'I believe him to be a strong, well-set-up sort of chap, who can work hard, does well for himself, eats roast beef, drinks too much and too often, and is inclined to trade too much on being free-born and owned by no man.'

'Your description fits the tenant farmers in the more prosperous parts of the country. It has nothing to do with the labourers they employ, who are, for the most part, paupers. It is on the latter that all the burdens of tithes, taxation and rent eventually fall . . .'

This from James Thomas Cooper, a leader of the mob, though by no means Captain Swing himself.

'Swing?' he has already declared to me. 'He's a myth, a legend, invented like Ned Ludd to scare the bosses.'

He was a tall, dark man, with deep-set eyes, and a lantern or coffin-shaped face. His hands were enormous. He was well spoken in a Hampshire-ish sort of a way, and well read too, in a Thomas Paine-ish or Richard Carlile fashion. Cooper continued, as we climbed St Catherine's Hill out of Winchester, not emotional or angry, but speaking slowly and carefully as if what he had to say was the clearest sense and could stand or fall by that alone.

'If the harvest is bad it is the labourer for whom the price of wheat may mean the difference between starvation and survival. As you know, at such times the price is kept high by the Corn Laws that prevent the import of grain at a price the foreign producers would happily settle for. Meanwhile, the labourer's main means of subsistence in hard times have been stolen away from him by the enclosures of common land to which is now added the use of machinery, particularly the thrashing machine, corn-reaper and binder. His only safety net is the parish and the local overseer, but what is looked on as a charity by all who pay rates, rather than a duty, brings small comfort. The more people on the parish, the higher the rates are set. The ratepayers reimburse themselves by setting wages ever lower, and rents higher and by agitating to have the poor rate set lower. And of course if the labourer is to claim the poor rate, he cannot move to find work elsewhere for the rate is only paid to those born and bred in the parish. We will not stop at burning ricks. It is not just a vicious circle we are trapped in, but a net of interlocking circles.'

Brought about of course by overpopulation as the good Doctor Malthus has pointed out, but by now I was sufficiently aware of Cooper's point of view to suspect that he would not take kindly to such an argument.

We moved on slowly north through that country for the next two days, burning ricks and smashing machines; round about the middle of November it would have been, and construing Mr Stafford's instructions, as I always did, I kept my eyes and ears open to what was happening around us.

It became clear to me that, although we knocked up labourers from dawn to dusk from their cots and cabins, who most willingly joined us, and some tenant farmers too, the crowd never exceeded a couple of hundred at most, for as we moved on we lost as many as we gained. I soon cottoned on to the way it worked. There was a nucleus of five men to a dozen who came maybe twenty or thirty miles before dropping out and going back to their homes. The others went five or ten miles, keeping in the background until they were in an area where they reckoned not to be known, then they became active at burning and breaking, before turning back. Hardly any lasted from one day to the next, it being chill and damp, and no one wanting to sleep rough, and most had never been out of their own countries in their lives, so once they found the beer tasted different or the bacon was cured in a way that seemed strange and the people around spoke a different sort of a tongue they wanted home.

Cooper and I, and a young lad called Henry Cook, yet another as thin as a rake and with an angry tearful look about him as if he had been crossed in love, he was only eighteen, and three more like us, including an elderly ex-sailor with a heavy limp called Dan Pitt from the west side of the county, were the only ones who pressed on into more distant places and it soon became clear that word of our little party went ahead and we formed a knot or magnet to attract the next lot of rioters. Mostly we bedded down in ale houses and the like, occasionally did well in a coaching house, sometimes broke into a hay barn for the night, and occasionally slept in a labourer's cot, especially if the local ale house keeper had had wind of us or was warned by his local Justice to turn away anyone who answered our description.

Yet not often did we bed with the poorest. The labourers rarely had more than two rooms beneath a low roof, often just a hurdle or piece of sacking making two tiny spaces out of one small one. Once or twice the family moved out into a barn or shed where they had formerly kept a pig or a cow, but, with the commons gone, it was no longer possible to feed such livestock; a chicken or two or some ducks if there was a pond were all they had, and their sheds were left empty if not burnt for firewood long since, fuel being another commodity denied by the enclosures. I recall one such family of shiftless yokels who yet kept a skeletal cat that was too weak to catch the rats, and a dog with suppurating sores. In the back room, beyond the dividing hurdle, there was a bed with six children in it, one dead, again evidence of the truth of Dr Malthus's best calculations.

And every morning, before dawn, the word would have got out and there'd be five or six, sometimes more, waiting to show us the way to the worst of the local grinders of the faces of the poor, namely the tenant farmers, the parsons and the landowners. And as we moved off, others would gather around us until we were back to a couple of hundred, many with hay forks and the like, and one or two with fowling pieces.

In living memory it was the case that labourers had been contracted by a farmer for a month, a harvest, a season, a few weeks, often at the hiring fairs, which had long since disappeared. Even in slack times, when harvest was in and ploughing done they were given hedging and ditching to do or even, especially in the downlands, collecting and carting off the flint cores that strewed the ground no matter how often they were cleared, as if some malevolent spirit lay beneath the furrows and pushed them up, and all this done to keep them loyal to their hirer, and fit and fed for the seasonal work when it came round again. But all that was gone now, what with the machines and overpopulation and the men returned from the wars, and the pressures the landlords put on their tenants. Well, that was the view of the likes of Cooper, but it seemed to me a man with a good pair of shoes could always take to the road and find work somewhere.

And, as we went, those that ran in front of us left handouts nailed to gateposts and doors where no one was found to answer our call:

This is to inform you what you have to undergo, gentelmen if providing you dont pull down your machines and rise the poor man's wages, the maried men give tow and six pence a day, the singel tow shilling or we will burn down your barns and you in them, from Capt. Swing.

Soon the county was throbbing, no other word for it, troops of breakers and arsonists going off in every direction. We kept on the move but never shifting more than a league a day and always leaving news of where we could be found. During this week or so one party, constantly renewing itself in the way I have described, was increased yet further by the labourers of Arundel, Bersted, Bognor and Felpham, then moved west in such considerable numbers, over a thousand it was said, and gained promises from justices and landowners alike in the market at Chichester for better wages and steady employment. And the like was happening, and increasing all the time, reaching to Ringwood on the Dorset border. But never more than a few hundred at one time in one place.

Another factor was subsistence. How could a force of say ten thousand or even as few as five be fed and kept together in November save by plundering the barns and slaughtering the flocks of those whose land they marched through and turning against themselves the very people to whom they should look for support and to increase their numbers?

45

And then, in the midst of all, the government fell. For some it was like falling through a door one had been pulling instead of pushing. I forget just why, some stuff about the Civil List, but really to avoid a more notable defeat on Parliamentary Reform, due to be debated the next day. Now many believed that this would lead to real reform, universal suffrage and such like nonsense, and that all the ills Swing was striving to remedy by rebellion and destruction, fire and machine breaking, would be solved peaceably by talk in a Parliament of the People. In short, many were about ready to go home.

But others had a greater sense of reality and did not see it like that. The burning and breaking went on through the rest of November and indeed into the New Year, but more sporadically and involving ever fewer numbers, not out of lack of conviction but, as is so often the case in England, because of hunger, the rain, the snow, the dragoons . . . and the public houses. And not least because of a Special Commission of magistrates and judges set up to tour the area and get those the dragoons had arrested off to the gallows or Van Diemen's Land as expeditiously as possible. More of that anon, except to say there were those who likened the Commission to Judge Jeffreys' Bloody Assizes which some recalled their grandparents talking of.

Meanwhile, two or three incidents remain in my mind. The first direct effect of the fall of the government was that the Duke was reminded that, though the guidance of the nation was no longer in his charge, that of the county he was Lord-Lieutenant of was. And that county was Hampshire although his seat at Stratfield Saye was close to the Berkshire and Surrey borders. A few days before he resigned I and a handful of those closest to Cooper had gone that far north, I now riding on a donkey on account Cooper got tired of the way I could not keep up on foot being small in stature. We were heading for Reading, where it was hoped we could raise a mob, and on the very day the government fell, though of course we didn't know of it until a day later, broke into Stratfield Saye church and set fire to his grace's pew. It seems a small and silly thing now, but I did have it in mind that Old Nosey still owed me sixpence. Anyway, being old and seasoned oak it failed to catch properly and no harm was done.

We took the opportunity to have a look at his new house, and found it nothing like as grand a place as we had expected. It was small, well, half the size of Chatsworth or Pemberley, brick-built not faced with stone, and a bare two storeys high. We, that is the dozen or so of us as had tried to fire the church, peered in through the downstairs windows and found the rooms cosy enough but not large. Altogether a very poor sort of a thing compared with Blenheim. And there was a notice too in one of the windows that read: *Those desirous of seeing the Interior of the House are requested to ring at the door of entrance and to express their desire. It is wished that the practice of stopping on the paved walk to look in at the windows should be discontinued.*

Quite frankly there was nothing there to attract the viewer other than such as would pamper the curiosity of the idle.

Well, trust Old Nosey, he had the answer to the whole affair and, if all Lord-Lieutenants had followed suit, Swing would have been over before it was scarce begun. Freed of his prime ministerial duties he wrote to all the gentry, landowners and magistrates of the county, many of whom were carousing and whoring at the outset of the London Season, and demanded they should return to their seats. Once home they were to put their backsides on their horses, get together all their servants, retainers, grooms, huntsmen, gamekeepers with horse whips, pistols, fowling pieces and what they could get, and attack the mobs, seizing those who did not disperse quickly enough, and locking them up.

It did very well. If there's one thing marks out your southern labourers from your northern workmen it's deference. Your southerner'll cheat and abuse a tenant farmer who treats him unfairly. He'll mob a parson who is greedy over tithes. He fears and hates a mounted soldier and will cut his throat in the dark if he can get away with it. But show him a booted and belted knight, or preferably a lordship, and he'll tug his forelock, bend his knee, and go home happy as a child with a new top, especially if he's given a sixpence and told what a good boy he is.

I saw it happen, with these two eyes. We were still in the neighbourhood of Stratfield Saye, breaking up a winnowing machine with the smoke of a couple of ricks blowing about us and the rich fruity smell of rotting apples from the orchard on the other side of the farm in our nostrils and the unpicked blackberries mildewed in the brambles. There were about a hundred of us, more having come up on our report that soldiers seemed pretty thin on the ground. The first we heard of them, from a quarter of a mile off, was that high squeaky toowooot, toowooot, the view halloo they call it, raspberried through their stupid little hunting horns, and then the yapping of the dogs which were a touch confused since they were used to being set on foxes not men.

Over the hill, past a hanger of beeches and on to the floor of the bottom they came, about twenty of them, and the Duke up front or almost, in his black coat and high hat and his nose like a beacon of fire from the cold and maybe the port wine he'd had when they met, careering along towards us. By the time they reached us we were down to about eighty, the rest running for the woods and thickets with the foxhounds snapping at their heels.

But three-quarters of us stayed put (as far as I was concerned

I saw no future in trotting off on my moke with giant hunters in pursuit), and blow me, with pitchforks, a pike or two and a couple of arquebuses, we formed a square. Front rank of ten on one knee, the other rank behind standing, making each side twenty strong. Old Cooper knew what he was up to and had drilled his mates accordingly. Waterloo, you see. Well, that's what I thought and I wasn't the only one.

Whatever the rest of the hunt thought, the Duke knew the game was up as far as putting us to flight was concerned. His raggle-taggle of toffs was not about to achieve what the Imperial Cavalry had failed to do. He reined in, touched the brim of his hat.

'Sergeant Cropper, if I'm not mistaken.'

'Your honour?'

'Grenadier company of the thirty-second?'

'Correct, your honour.'

'Never forget a face. All right, Cropper, tell your men to form fours, stand easy and we'll say no more. Oh, and here's a sovereign, buy them all a drink at the nearest ale house, will you?'

And of course the silly bastard did as he was told. Deference, you see? And we marched off, in due order, forks and pikes shouldered, to the nearest hostelry. But those who were chased into the thickets by the hounds were taken to Reading gaol and no doubt are now scraping an even poorer living in Van Diemen's Land. Meanwhile his grace caught my eye as we marched off in front of him, he upright in the saddle, crop raised to touch the brim of his topper in salute, the men whistling 'See, the Conquering Hero Comes' from *Judas Maccabaeus* by his favourite composer, caught my eye, as I say, and gave me a conspiratorial wink. He knew whose side of the hill I was on.

'Hey, Cooper,' one of the men called out, once we were clear of the Duke and his troop of swells. 'You was never in the thirty-second, nor was you at Waterloo. You was in the Hampshires and at the burning of Washington, I reckon.'

'That's right,' our sergeant answered, 'but I'm not about to argue with the likes of the Duke, now am I?

367

'Say what you like,' he added, when we got to the ale house and all were settled with their ale and cider, 'if all took care of their tenants and those who work their farms as well as he does his, there'd be less cause for complaint throughout the land. He wouldn't let his agent enclose a common on his estate, you know? And now,' he concluded, 'which way is it back to Micheldever and The Grange at Northington?'

We were already heading back to Winchester, and in discussion with men like Cook who came from Micheldever it had come up that on our way was the seat of one of the worst families for extorting every last penny from their tenants as they could get their hands on. Young Henry Cook was especially strong against them since he'd suffered at a remove or two from their cupidity, his family having lost much of its natural support in the enclosure of commons in the neighbourhood. Moreover, the nest of brothers who now ran the place demanded far more from their tenants than their tenants could reasonably pay, and they in turn took it out of their labourers' wages. So it was decided we should take a small detour and pay a visit to The Grange at Northington.

The road took us through rolling downs-like countryside, sometimes shut in by the steep turfy sides of a bottom, sometimes running along a chalky crest which gave us huge vistas right the way across the river plain above Southampton to the Water beyond. You could say, along with Bishop Heber, every prospect pleases, only man is vile, so that is what I did, at which point to the east of us, parkland opened up with a huge building, much like an ancient Greek temple, a colonnaded palace, one of the biggest I've ever seen, filling a rise with sombre plantations of timber, planted where commons had been since before the Conqueror. Cooper completed the quotation.

> 'In vain with lavish kindness,
> The gifts of God are strown
> The heathen in his blindness
> Bows down to wood and stone.' ﹡

This great building seemed to grow in stature as we got nearer. The drive passed between lodges and through iron gates twenty feet high, tipped with gold, and then meandered between beeches, and we were forced by the situation to look up at it as if we were mortals gazing in awe on the palaces of the gods on Mount Olympus. Cooper paused again, took breath.

'This really is monstrous,' he declared, his voice low but hard, sharp and cold, like a steel knife. 'This is obscene. Who owns it?'

'Lutheran manufacturers from Bremen started it,' an older man, the Dan Pitt I mentioned earlier, who had come over from a village further west, where he worked as a forester, now filled in, limping along as he did so for he'd had his hip broken by a flying piece of timber below decks at Trafalgar. 'The old man spoke like a Prooshian till the day he died. But then his sons took over, they became bankers, ran the East India as I've heard. Baring their name is, but one of them married an American woman, Bingham, so it's a Bingham Baring runs this place while his brothers do the banking.'

' 'Ow do you know all that, Dan Pitt, when you doos be livin' in a dump like Thorney Hill?' cried one of the men walking with him.

'Ol' Dan knows everything there is to know,' another replied. 'Every night Ol' Nick himself come and whisper the latest noos in his ear, aint that right, Dan, you ol' sorcerer?'

'All bankers,' Dan commented, 'are richer 'n Greesus.'

'And waiting for us by the look of it.'

For stretched all along the high raised stone parterre in front of those gross stark Doric columns there emerged from between them maybe thirty or forty liveried servants, footmen, groundsmen, gamekeepers, gardeners, and most armed with guns, and in the middle a big, red-faced man, wearing morning clothes but with a gold chain about his neck such as some Justices wear, about thirty years old I'd say he was.

'That's him,' said Cook. 'Bingham Baring.'

'Um, he looks like he means business,' a small fellow called

Joe Green, who was next to me, muttered. I looked behind us. About sixty with the usual hay forks and such like. And in front of us not gentlemen farmers on hunters but the lackeys of the really rich armed to the teeth.

'We mean no harm,' said Cooper. 'Do you have that petition ready, Henry?'

'Aye, that oi doos.'

For that was the point of our visit. The idea was to hand in a petition asking the Barings to reduce their rents so the farmers could pay their men a pound a week. They stood silent, waiting for us. We got off our beasts, those of us who had them, and moved forward to the foot of the wide flight of steps, bordered with urns, that climbed to the parterre. Cooper took the papers the petition was prepared on.

'Mr Baring,' he began, his voice strong and clear. 'We come in no spirit of ill will, or out of a desire to cause you or your people harm, but simply to present this petition which is an appeal from the people hereabouts who request only to be able to work for a wage they can live on . . .'

Bingham Baring ignored him. Looking out over his head at his rolling parkland and the sheep safely grazing across what had once been commons, though not within living memory, he raised his voice.

'By the powers invested in me as a Justice of the Peace in the county of Hampshire, I hereby declare the Riot Act read. Constables, do your duty.'

And all along the line above us we heard, like the rattle of an urchin's stick along railings, the clicking of flintlocks and percussion hammers pulled back and round a corner, from where they had been hidden from us, came fifty or so uniformed Specials, with truncheons and cuffs at the ready. Suddenly it was clear they had no intention simply to turn us away; what they were after was us, bodies and souls, and Winchester prison scarce five miles away.

I felt a sudden movement behind me, my side was jarred by his elbow as he burst through, I smelled the sweat on him and something more rank, and there went young Henry Cook, charging up the steps, and then went James Cooper too in pursuit of him.

'The fucking bastard,' yelled Cook, then screamed: 'THE FUCKING, FUCKING BASTARD, let me knock his hat off!'

'Come back you stupid idjit,' shouted Joe Green, but all to no avail. Cook got to the top and indeed knocked off Bingham Baring's hat. Cooper tried to stop him but was barged in the back by a constable, so he stumbled head first into Bingham Baring's stomach, and as he did so a pistol fell to the ground and went off. Fortunately the ball glanced off the boot of a second Special, breaking his toe but doing no further harm.

'Yes, Mr Eliott, it was a Spinks and Pottle, primed and cocked.' Intrigued by the possibility that Charlie has had more of a hand in all this than he was initially admitting to, Elliott has come to his room and quizzed him about it. And asked him to make a correction in another matter too.

'Elliott with two ts *as well as* two ls. How very grand,' Charlie smirked. 'I'll get it right from now on.'

'Only three hangings came out of the whole Swing affair,' Charlie resumed, out loud. 'Fines, prison, deportation yes, but only three hangings. It was all that was needed. The rest thus condemned were commuted. Two of those Swingers who swung were Cooper and Cook. James Cooper and Henry Cook – for the attempted murder of Bingham Baring JP. I was there at Winchester gaol on the fifteenth of January 1831, and saw with my own eyes the black flag go up when the President of the Immortals, whose earthly home might well be The Grange, Northington, ceased his sport with Henry Cook. He's buried in Micheldever churchyard, and you know what they say, Mr Elliott? That when it snows on his grave the snow never settles.'

371

46

A messenger in a dark cloak returned old Spinks and Pottle, wrapped in an oiled cloth, a week after the trial. We were sitting in an ale house on the Furlong by Ringwood Market, just by the Quaker Meeting House, having us a cheese buttee and a pint of Ringwood ale, watching the lads coming in from all over, ready to march up to Fordingbridge in the afternoon. Two thousand of them there had been the day before, it was said, and there had been a bit of a tussle when the police and Specials came in but we saw them off. That was the only time the other Hunt, old Orator Hunt, turned up, still on his white horse with his white hat. He gave us a speech but he was careful not to incite us to anything that might have put a noose round his neck or bought him a ticket to Van Diemen's Land.

Anyway, this messenger with his dark cloak and big floppy Napoleon-style hat came across to me and clunked the package down on the trestle table in front of us.

'Magistrates have seen it, an affidavit was sworn, that'll be enough for the judge when he comes.'

And off he went again.

Now I don't know who this fool was, or why he gave me back

my little stinger in this fashion, but he'd fucked me all right. Dropped me right in the shit. Because the next thing was that Dan Pitt, nosey bastard as he was, reached over and unwrapped it before I could and there it sat on the table, gleaming in the December sunlight. A sort of silence settled over our little group, then he leant across to me, close, so I could smell the apple he'd been eating, one of those new Granny Smith's it was, and he murmured: 'That's the gun they say dropped out of Cooper's belt. He'll hang on account of that.'

'Old James Cooper never had no pistol,' Joe Green chipped in.

Well, I reckoned it was time to be off. I slipped the offensive weapon in my belt, told them I was going for a piss, went round the back of the ale house, got on my donkey and headed out on the Southampton road before taking a detour which took me back north via Romsey and Winchester. And that was the end of Captain Swing for me, Mr Elliott, though not of occupation commissioned by Mr Stafford.

By now we were in 1831, and in the midst of the agitation that led to the Reform Bill. Well, Mr Elliott, you'll recall reform for the great mass of reformers meant a vote for everybody, even women, and a new election every year, and a fat chance they had of getting it; but for the Industrialists, the Manufacturers, the Mill- and Mine-Owners it meant an end to rotten boroughs and the creation of new seats for the new big towns. However, there were those among the latter groupings who leaned towards people like Mr Robert Owen, just the year before returned from America, and such as Messrs Cobbett, Carlile and even Orator Hunt, all of whom seemed inclined towards enfranchising the Common People, with the ultimate aim of a distribution of wealth which bore some correlation to a person's contribution towards creating it. Not many, to be sure, but Stafford instructed me to move in certain circles in the North and North-West particularly and identify just how serious a danger they presented to those who lawfully and right-fully owned land or stocks. The Unitarians of Liverpool particularly were drawing the attention of his superiors. He mentioned the Rathbones, merchants and ship-owners, drifting from their Quaker backgrounds into Unitarian beliefs, or non-beliefs. He had a file on the head of the family, prepared for Lord Castlereagh I believe, which said of William Rathbone: 'He is dangerous, but has done nothing as yet . . .'

But Elliott is bored with the Rathbones, and looks up at Charlie from the desk where he has been reading what Charlie has just written, and drops a bombshell.

'Charlie,' he says, 'I think, indeed I am almost certain, we have been put to a lot of trouble and some expense as a result of a misunderstanding. I'm beginning to think we may have to eat humble pie and send you back to Millbank, where you belong.'

Outside mad Darcy's fowling piece bangs away and his dogs yap. Charlie recalls that, albeit confined as he has been so far to one room, such is all this comfortable place has in common with a cell in Millbank. A rumbling in the central heating system adds confirmation. Desperately he trawls his brain for a sprat even that might please Elliott.

'I was abroad, Mr Elliott, in foreign parts, for seventeen years.'

He emphasises the word 'foreign'. Elliott sighs.

'The Americas, I believe.'

'The republics of Texas and California, both before and after their incorporation in the United States. And then through the Rockies, across the prairies to New York.'

'America is of no interest to us at all. France, yes. Prussia, certainly and the states belonging to the Zollverein. Russia most definitely and the Ottoman Empire. India even. China, of course, though less so since we've tidied up that opium business. Japan. But America no, certainly not North America. The only significance America has had since the 1812 war has been their readiness, for reasons best known to themselves, to take the surplus population of Erin off our hands. I'm sorry

Boylan, but of all places in the world you chose the wrong one as far as Her Majesty's Foreign Office is concerned. Wrong place at the wrong time, old boy.'

He sighs, looks down at Charlie who is now almost collapsed in the silk upholstered upright chair that is in the corner by the window. Does a tremor of sympathy for the ageing hairy dwarfish wreck in front of him tickle his diaphragm? Certainly not.

His podgy, well-scrubbed hand is on the ormolu door handle. 'I'll set the wheels in motion that'll get you back to Millbank. May take a day or two.'

Charlie, alone again, and desolated by the Millbank threat, falls into a reverie, punctuated only by the distant popping of Darcy's gun and the barking of his dogs.

Maggie-May. She'd let him down, betrayed him in a way. It had been going well until she offered to help him.

But before that, before he set out on the mission that ultimately took him to the New World, he'd travelled as far north as Liverpool, changing his cover to suit the circumstances he found himself in. He'd got himself into Greenbank on the outskirts of the city, the country residence, just built, of the Rathbone family, persuading old William Rathbone that he was an active proselyte of the cause of Slave Emancipation and also that he could instruct the children of the household in drawing.

The former had been easier to maintain than the latter, especially when Sir John Gladstone and his family were invited to dinner, including young William, named after Sir John's friend. Differences between the families had arisen which this dinner party had been planned to heal. It had not been a happy occasion. The Gladstones were Evangelical, the Rathbones only a whisker away from being Deists. Over that, they agreed to differ. Slavery was a different matter: a large part of the Gladstone fortune depended on Demerara sugar grown, harvested and processed by their slaves. Piecemeal emancipation was their solution, proceeding hand in hand with a programme of education for the negroes; the Rathbones could see no point in delaying. Charlie won their approval by stoutly affirming that if education was considered a prerequisite of emancipation then one might as well put the English working man back in his Norman chains and start giving him lessons.

However, it was but a week before his inability to do more in the artistic line than copy crudely an already crude rendering of a scene or a portrait became apparent, and that the children of the family were better at it than he. He was given five sovs and asked to leave. Nevertheless, he was able to report to Mr Stafford that while the Rathbones and many of their circle of merchants, ship insurers and the like, were drifting from religion to apostasy, and were concerned beyond reason to improve the circumstances of their workers' lives (recently they had shocked their associates by closing their offices at seven in the evening so their clerks could enjoy a fuller home life), they remained great respecters of the sanctity of property, both in land and stocks.

Moving south he managed to penetrate the Wedgwood set who were also known to be very hot for Reform, possibly asking for more than the Whigs in Parliament thought allowable, but found them more intellectually curious than politically minded. Again he felt he had stumbled into a nest of near atheism, and extreme rationalism, but not so much as would preclude one of their connections, whom he was to meet later, from considering the priesthood as a career. Or at any rate as a way of getting an income (from tithes at that) to support his obsession for hunting beetles and collecting fossils. All were in a considerable state over Reform, Earl Grey having introduced his Whiggish Bill at the beginning of March with the intent of staving off demands for greater reforms. For Charlie the time was marked by a meeting which was to have far greater significance in his life than either reform or revolution could have had.

Armed with a letter of introduction from William Rathbone,

376

he got himself invited to a *soirée* at The Mount, a newish house not far from Shrewsbury, the property of a prosperous doctor called Robert Darwin, the son of Erasmus, who had married one of the Wedgwood girls. The occasion, though social, had a serious purpose: to discuss reform and what should be done should the Bill before Parliament fail on account of the opposition of the Tories led by the Duke. All present were hot for Reform to the extent of giving seats to the new industrial towns, doing away with the rotten boroughs and extending the franchise to the middle classes, though all feared the revolution that would come if such as Robert Carlile had their way and universal adult suffrage became the goal.

And almost immediately, as he moved through the gathering of professional men, inventors, tyros of the new sciences, and manufacturers, he was struck by the presence of a tall and beautiful young lady, whose face initially put him in mind of Botticelli's *Primavera* which he had seen in Florence nine years earlier, but whose manner and way of speech persuaded him he had known her in the flesh in the past. But it was she who placed him – not surprisingly considering his stature and general appearance.

'Mr Boylan, is it not?' she murmured to him, coming at him from behind and placing her left hand on his arm. With her other she held a tea cup and saucer of classical design, one of Josiah Wedgwood's he assumed, as if it were a shield.

'You have the advantage of me,' he replied, adopting, almost to the manner born, the style of an Austenite gentleman.

'Kate Bramshaw.'

And instantly he remembered her and the bevy of misses who had picked him up on his way north and taken him to Nottingham and disaster some ten years earlier, a bevy led and protected by an heiress on the run from cruel, greedy and ruthless relations, a bevy which had included Maggie-May, the waif he had found and to some extent taken care of during his first stint as a Home Office spy whose cover was potboy at the Three Tuns, Islington. His past flooded back and the awareness, too, that if Miss Bramshaw now chose to reveal it it would blow his cover among these Wedgwoods and Darwins. He need not have worried. Miss Bramshaw had no desire for her past as the leader of a group of female mountebanks and petty thieves to be aired in the salon of Dr Robert Darwin. However, she was not averse to sharing a confidential tête-à-tête on a handy ottoman during which she told him how she and her erstwhile companions had fared in the decade that had passed. She had survived into her majority and her inheritance and was now a well-to-do landowner with property in Shropshire as well as the Bramshaw seat in Sissinghurst in Kent. Three farms in Devon she had sold, since they were too far away for her to look after properly. She busied herself with good works such as prison reform and emancipation, and had thus become accepted in the circle in which she was now moving.

'And the other . . . girls? How have they got on?'

She bent her head towards him and looked round to make sure no Wedgwoods or Darwins were eavesdropping.

'They have all done very well,' she replied in a low voice, almost a whisper. She wore on a velvet ribbon an intaglio, black and white, of a classical female head, Athene perhaps, which rested at his eye level on her breastbone. It almost hypnotised him, but he managed to keep his mind on what she was saying. 'Tess is on the Continent, in Leipzig, where she actually has a position playing flute in the Linen Hall Orchestra; Tiger Lily has gone to America, to San Francisco, a small port on the west coast, where she runs a lodging house . . . ,' she took a deep breath, causing the Athene to swim an inch or so towards him, producing a swooning sensation, 'but it is Margaret-May who has done best. She is now Lady Danby, wife of Sir George Danby, of Plympton Hall in Devon. He is in the Consular Service in India, but out of fear of the malaria he remains in Devon . . .'

At this moment Robert Darwin, a huge man, grossly overweight, and exuding bonhomie and exuberance, loomed over them.

378

'Miss Bramshaw,' he boomed, 'do come and meet my daughters. I would introduce you to my sons, Erasmus and Charles, but, drawn by the excitement of recent events, they have elected to stay in Erasmus's London lodgings . . .'

A day or two later Charlie, ours, not Darwin, steered clear of Derby and Nottingham, fearful he might stumble again on any who might recognise him. Passing between Birmingham and Coventry his moke cast a shoe, and hearing, by fortunate coincidence, the dum-de-de-dum-dum of a farrier's hammer on shoe and anvil, he turned off the road he was on and found himself at Arbury Farm, then managed by a Mr Robert Evans for the local landowner, a Mr Francis Newdigate. He paused here for three days, taking a spare room above the porch of the main house, beneath the thatch and above the rambler roses that were now in bloom, and worked away with the enigmatic machine Captain Quex had given him so long ago, preparing an encrypted report for Mr Stafford. It was a tediously slow business but necessary: many of the people he had been, um, investigating were prominent public figures, Members of Parliament, even Justices. Supposing an open report had fallen into the wrong hands and *The Times* got hold of it . . .

A knock at the door while he was at it, late the second afternoon, and the solemn face of the land agent's daughter peered, perhaps a touch myopically, round the doorjamb.

'Mother sent me,' she said 'to see if you want a biscuit and a cup of tea.'

'That would be nice,' Charlie replied, and waited, pen poised, for her to go. But she came into the room.

'You writing, then?'

Looking over his shoulder, she pushed her dark brown hair off her face and behind her ears so she could better see what he was up to. She was, he supposed, about twelve years old, gawky, thin and with a strong middle England accent.

'It's all numbers,' she exclaimed, looking at the sheets his pen

379

had, like a long-legged fly, already tracked over. 'You interested in the mathematicks, then?'

Not wishing to be lured into an explanation of what he was really doing, he agreed that he was.

'Me too. Do you know Fermat's Problem?' With a sly little wriggle she slipped between table and his knees and sat on them. 'That's mathematicks but generally expressed by the algebraic method which is all letters.' She wriggled, put an arm round his neck. He felt her breath on his cheek and caught the tang of blackcurrants on it. 'I prefer letters. I might write a novel one day. But it will be a romantic one. About Italy, Florence at the time of the Medicis. Life round here is far too boring. Far too boring for a good story.'

A door slammed below. She eased herself off him, leaving him in a state of embarrassment she had been well aware of creating, and which necessitated the adjustment of his coat-tail over his lap.

'Does he want his tea or not?' her mother called. She had a cough, possibly, Charlie thought, consumptive. 'Mary Ann, did you hear me? Does he want his tea or not?' Then, 'Mary Ann? Your dad says to tell you he just heard in the village that the peers have thrown out Reform and there is likely to be revolution or a General Election. It will be up to King Billy which.'

Now, why has that stuck in his mind after twenty-one years?

In Oxford he put his encryptions in the post and picked up a packet. Ten pounds in the new notes and an instruction to continue into the south-west, which had not pleased him, since it would take him back into Swing country. However, a hurried postscript had been added, *en clair* as they say, calling him back to London from where he was sent to Paris to deal with the despicable Captain Garth. Recalling all this now in his comfortable cell in Pemberley, he gives no thought to the body in the bed, but dwells in his mind with some satisfaction on the bundle of papers he pulled from under it, papers which his friend and protector, the solicitor Mr Guppy, has taken from his lodging and hidden. Perhaps, if he is really to be returned to Millbank to stand trial for attempted or actual murder, this will be the time, along with other depositions, to deploy them. It is a matter though that will have to be handled with some care. The bastards at the top will not be scrupulous about the means they use to conceal from the great English public an incestuous affair between such close relations of our dear Queen.

On his return from Paris he was sent west again, the far west. The target was a confederacy of fishermen, smugglers and the like with cells from Exmouth to Plymouth, who were said to be communicating with the French across the Channel. Just how far they represented the sort of political threat Mr Stafford's office usually concerned itself with was unclear, but Charlie's instructions were to seek out a schoolteacher, a customs officer and a local landowner in a small way, who were said to be involved. It turned out to be nothing at all to do with the French, but a conspiracy to form a Union of Fishermen and Associated Trades. There was a lot of talk of unions, associations and so forth across the region at this time which was not satisfactorily dealt with until three years later when those of Tolpuddle were exampled and deported.

By when, Charlie muses, still in his upright chair with the demesnes of Pemberley stretching beyond his window, I was extremely miserable somewhere in the South Atlantic, maybe in the Malvinas Islands, which, just the January before, had been taken from the Argentinians and called the Falklands. But not as miserable as I shall be if I'm carted back to Millbank.

Was it on my way to the West (the West indeed) that time that I met a man, old but hale, plump and cheery, with a red face and big labourer's hands, but well dressed, on the back of a great big bay who, some five miles north of Salisbury, declared himself lost and would I direct him? He was close to the hill of

381

Old Sarum, and at a junction of two roads, both of which led to the city, hidden by the ridge of a down.

They kept company for a half-mile.

'How do you get on?' he asked Charlie.

Charlie replied: 'Not too well, really.'

He asked why not: the harvest had been good had it not.

'Well,' said Charlie, 'they make it bad for poor people.'

'They!' he cried. 'Who are "they" then?'

Well, not for anyone would Charlie blaspheme against the gentry, so he said nothing. The old man rambled on, as if crazed, about it being the Accursed Hill, by which he seemed to mean Old Sarum, that lay behind the evils of the times. He chose the turn that would take him up to the top of his Accursed Hill, while Charlie pushed on, but round the west of the city taking the road to Shaston or Shaftesbury where he caught the mail coach to Plymouth. Was the mad old man Will Cobbett himself, out on a Rural Ride? Blest if Charlie knew.

Plymouth was a fucking disaster. Don't really want to think about that. Problem right now is, how do I persuade fat bastard Elliott to keep me here rather than sending me back like one of these new mail-order packages as not required, surplus to requirements. Continental foreign he wants. Continental foreign he'll have. And he picks up his pen, dips it in the inkwell, and yet again begins to scribble.

Part VI

AN END AND A BEGINNING

The end is where we start from.

T. S. Eliot, 'East Coker'

47

He'd had dealings with them twice. They had frightened him so badly that he had bottled up the memory, sworn to himself to keep the whole matter to himself. But that had been nearly two years ago, back in fifty-one, and Charlie rarely kept any promise for that long, and least of all the ones he made to himself. He'd tell Mr Elliott all about it, well, not *all* about it but enough to stir the man's interest into keeping him safe, safe in this safe house. In fact, in Pemberley, with its apparent isolation, its quality of self-containment, its civilised views over a tamed landscape, the central heating and the regular meals, Charlie felt safer than he had ever felt and he wanted it to go on for ever. If that meant telling Mr Elliott about Chancellor Wurmwolt then so be it.

So, we skip a mere twenty years to late February or early March 1851. The first approach came from a big, manly, bearded creature who slipped on to the bench next to him at an ale house cum brothel on the river near Limehouse. Charlie was making a pint of small stretch and stretch before returning to the roach-infested room which, for a month or so, he had been forced to call home while he looked about, waiting for something to turn up.

'Boylan? Herr Boylan? To make your acquaintance I am pleased. Schumacher.' And his new acquaintance, thus revealing by his name and form of address that he was of the Teutonic persuasion, thrust a large red hand under his chin. Charlie took it, much in the way you might put your own hand into a bag, not knowing what to expect. Surprisingly the Prussian's grip was soft, flabby, moist. 'Boylan the spy and occasional assassin you are being?'

There was no answer to that. Charlie waited. A drab wench passed with a tray and Schumacher caught her elbow, quite roughly.

'Another beer for my friend.'

'Actually I'd rather have a large brandy and a pasty.' Charlie was never slow about opportunities of this sort, and especially when he had not eaten properly for two days.

'Well, why not? Since Chancellor Wurmwolt, how do you say? in the chair is sitting.'

Schumacher gave the order and then turned, shifting his weight on to the buttock nearest to Charlie and contriving to swivel his body like a large gun in one of the new turrets that were beginning to appear as part of port defences, so, if his podgy knees, clad in heavy tweed, had not got in the way, his whole body would have been facing Charlie. He offered up a large slow wink that closed one bloodshot rheumy eye.

'Repeat after me if you would . . . number ten, Chesham Square.'

'Number ten, Chesham Square.'

'Chancellor Wurmwolt.'

'Chancellor Wurmwolt.'

'On Chancellor Wurmwolt at ten of the clock, tomorrow morning, at number ten, Chesham Square, you will be pleased to call. And so goodbye my friend.'

And Schumacher, if that really was his name and Charlie doubted it, stood, gave his shoulder a prolonged but soft squeeze, clapped a low rounded hat of hard felt (the sort which, once it became fashionable in London a decade later, was called a billycock or bowler) on his head, slapped a sovereign down on the table, and almost danced through the crowd the way large men sometimes can. In a moment he had disappeared, like a genie back into his lamp, obscured by the tobacco smoke and then hidden by the ratty curtain that hung over the door that opened on to the street. Charlie was wondering whether to go or stay when the drab wench appeared in front of him with a tin tray.

'One large brandy and a pasty,' she said. 'Enjoy.' Then, picking up the gold Schumacher had left, 'Aint you got anything smaller?'

Enjoy it he did, although the meat in the pasty was gristly and overpeppered, and the brandy caramel-flavoured industrial spirit. Moreover, the waiting girl never came back with his change. Nevertheless, he took it to be a propitious beginning to whatever lay ahead.

Belgravia was not a part of London Charlie was overfamiliar with, and although the first brash flush of splendour that came when the marshes were drained and Thomas Cubitt, the speculative builder, developed the area some twenty years earlier, had worn off, he found himself almost daunted. The polished knockers on the front doors were larger than any he had seen before and stretched as far as the eye could reach, the clean windows shone with a dark opaque lustre, the swift flow of hansoms whispered on tarmac. During his long absence from the Wen there had been many changes, many improvements, and the extravagance and luxury of what had happened to Knightsbridge were among the things that most bewildered him. In the old days terraces of town houses of some magnificence enclosed a Mayfair square (Grosvenor, say, or Hanover) and were backed by humbler mews, thus forming islands among the smaller dwellings and they were, for all their imposing size, built in the brown drab brick of the London Brick Company:

here all were stuccoed to resemble carved white alabaster and looked like nothing so much as pillared palaces set in rows. Nevertheless, it seemed the Olympian occupants still needed nourishment other than nectar and ambrosia for a milk cart rattled noisily across the distant perspective and a butcher boy, driving with the noble recklessness of an Olympic charioteer, dashed round a corner sitting high above a pair of red wheels.

A guilty-looking cat, a mangy specimen with a torn ear, its tail a proud panache, trotted in front of him for a moment before diving through railings into a basement area, and won Charlie's sympathy. He felt a kinship, knew, he thought, how it felt.

Number ten, Chesham Square, was guarded by a thick police constable, whose physiognomy looked a stranger to every emotion. He ignored Charlie as he climbed the five steps into the colonnaded porch, one of whose acanthine pillars was decorated with a rococo coat of arms in cast and enamelled bronze. The sound emitted by the lion's head knocker was laden with doom and answered by a liveried porter in a red waistcoat and knee breeches.

'Chancellor Wurmwolt? Boylan's my name. I have an appointment.'

'Please this way to come,' and the porter took Charlie's hat between a white kid-gloved finger and thumb, much as if he were a surgeon removing an organ distressed by cancer and useless. He led him past the foot of a marble staircase and along a corridor which, though splendid with gilt-framed paintings, crimson silk wall-hangings and black marble flooring, yet had an air of use, of work about it, rather than display or ceremony. Almost immediately, however, he took a sharp turn through a much smaller door, set in a corner beneath a second and less grand flight of stairs, and descended a short flight of steps into a basement corridor. This boasted only a single gaslight and a threadbare brown runner. Another door opened into a small office lined with cabinets that almost enclosed a large desk. Dressed in black, bald-headed, with drooping dark grey whiskers, half-hidden behind a pile of papers, Privy Councillor Wurmwolt, Chancelier d'Ambassade, peered up at him myopically. The flunkey withdrew.

Wurmwolt exchanged one pair of pince-nez for another. He made no sign of greeting, but neither did Charlie. The latter simply altered the outline of his shoulders and back to suggest unobtrusive deference. Wurmwolt shifted some paper and, with a definite cold tightening of his chest Charlie recognised a sheet in his own handwriting. But he couldn't make out when it dated from. Was it from the reports he had made to Stafford some twenty odd years earlier? Or from a batch he had hidden away as insurance? And, whichever, how had they ended up here? The question remained unasked and unanswered. Wurmwolt sighed, with every appearance of mental and physical exhaustion.

'We are,' and his voice was a hoarse whisper, 'not very satisfied with the attitude of the police here.'

Charlie's shoulders contrived a shrug though they barely moved.

'Every country has its own police,' he suggested.

Wurmwolt felt no need to comment on this aperçu. He went on: 'What is desired is the occurrence of something definite to stimulate their vigilance.'

Charlie waited.

'The vigilance of the police, the general leniency of the judicial procedure here, the utter absence of all repressive measures . . .'

And here Charlie realised just how far things had changed. If pressed he would have said that his life's work had been dedicated, at least up to 1831, in contributing, however humbly, to repressive measures. These things though, he would have conceded, are relative.

'. . . are a scandal to Europe. What is wished for just now is an event which will stimulate what passes for authority in this country into efficient proscription of all dangerous groupings and societies and if necessary the arrest, permanent or only for

389

the duration of the opening festivities, of all the many European dissidents at present making an asylum, here in London, from the laws of their own countries.'

'Ah yes. The opening festivities.'

Wurmwolt looked up sharply, detecting a hint of doubt behind Charlie's affirmation.

'I refer of course to the first of May.'

'Ah yes, of course. The first of May.'

'The day set for the opening of the Great International Exhibition.'

A pause ensued during which Wurmwolt peered through his pince-nez, then over them, then through them again.

'You are,' he added, 'even smaller, and even less prepossessing than I had been led to expect.'

Through a life which already exceeded by getting on for a decade the life expectancy of European males, Charlie had learnt to suppress his reaction to such comments. Equally Wurmwolt was unconcerned that he might have caused offence.

'You recall,' and his white, wrinkled fingers laced themselves above his pile of papers, Charlie's papers, 'the extremely unpleasant affair involving Field Marshal Baron von Haynau. Six months ago.'

'Name rings a bell,' Charlie replied cheerfully.

'The Field Marshal gained a reputation for efficiency in suppressing workers' revolts in Hungary and Italy. On a visit to this country he made a tour of London as the guest of Barclay and Perkins's Brewery. The carters employed by the brewery threw a hay bale at him, and pelted him with horse droppings. He escaped on to the quay where lightermen and coal-heavers chased him, and tore his clothes and pulled his moustache. He hid in a large bin provided for the collection of refuse.'

'Ah, yes. I do believe I recall reading an account of the incident in one of the newspapers. Er, wasn't there a celebratory rally afterwards in the Farringdon Hall?'

Charlie knew this for a fact. He'd been there, hoping to earn a few shillings by reporting back to the Home Office the names of those prominent in the Workers' Movement who had attended.

'That is the case. Among the speakers was a Herr Frederick Engels. And this leads me to why you are here.'

And high time, thought Charlie.

'The diplomatic corps, and other invited representatives of most European states, will be there. On the first of May. Among them there will be gentlemen who will bring with them a similar false reputation to that which attached itself to Baron von Haynau . . .'

Known, Charlie now recalled, as the Hyena, on account of the way he tortured ringleaders and flogged their wives.

'. . . some of them from the state one of whose accredited representatives I am honoured to be, some from that of Herr Engels. What I wish to ensure is that there will be no possibility of a similar fate befalling them as was suffered by—'

'The Field Marshal?'

'Precisely.'

Again the pause, while Wurmwolt made adjustments to his pince-nez. Then he sighed again, and took a long slow look at Charlie, as if weighing up the propriety and indeed expedience of going the distance with him.

'*Faute de mieux*,' he muttered, then raising his voice, but not by much, 'what we have in mind is a bomb. Small but loud, and it must be clearly apparent that it has been placed and detonated by known asylum seekers from my country. The aim being to ensure that they are all rounded up and detained until the visitors have returned home. We envisage that the detonation should take place within the Crystal Palace itself. We understand that the "Hallelujah Chorus" is to be performed by massed choirs and orchestras, accompanied by two organs, early in the proceedings. If the explosion takes place during this it will not be noticed except by the authorities and a general public panic will be avoided.'

Charlie, puzzled, frowned.

'Would it not be better to arrange for all this to take place before the opening?'

'No. The particular targets that might inspire a similar outrage as that which befell the baron are due to arrive only the day after. They are, however, to remain guests of your Queen and the British government for a further month or so during which they will frequently appear in public. They, are, after all, related to your Queen's husband, the Prince. Which brings me to the other reason for choosing the first of May. Maximum effect, that is maximum effect on what pass for the forces of Order and Security in this country, will only be achieved if your Queen and her Consort are present and are perceived to have been in some danger, however slight.'

Oh shit, thought Charlie. Am I up to this? Can I do it?

'You will be given every assistance. You will be paid one hundred pounds.'

I can do it.

48

Springtime in Park Lane and thereabouts. The elms, limes and chestnuts should have been in brilliant new leaf, the chestnuts with their candles just bursting into life, but the wind tore through, creating an autumn-like season of whirling branchlets and petals, flattening the tulips, shredding the wallflowers. Cherry blossom, natural English and ornamental Japanese, span in clouds like confetti. Azaleas and rhododendrons, wishing they were back in the Himalayas, tightened their sepals and sat it out. The ducks on the Serpentine, the male ones anyway, which should have been burnished with testosterone, and raping the females with the assiduity of a Goth or a Tartar, huddled in the reeds or in the lee of the skiffs that remained upside down on the sloping lakeside. Spume raced off the water and across the grass. The wind turned umbrellas inside out, plucked top hats, while curtains of grey muslin rain swept through everything in their path. And amidst it all, above it all, as airily as the phantom *Flying Dutchman*, the serried arches and the vast vault of the semicircular transept sailed like a fairy palace.

Everybody said that: Fairy Palace, and then, by common

consent, Crystal Palace. It was a wonder, the eighth the world had seen. It lay like a mist upon the earth. It merged into the elements that surrounded it with its giant elm tree and sparrows inside which at first you thought must be reflections. It reflected and enhanced the weather too: its pearly greyness when it rained held an effulgence rain never had and its brightness in the rare fits of sunshine in a very wet April outshone the sun itself. And occasionally, just occasionally, when the conditions were right, it blazed at sunset like a furnace.

Of course, any endeavour which breaks the bounds and allows Human Imagination, itself the most wonderful thing in the Universe, to give substance and material reality to the most airy and fairy of its dreams, will always attract the dark speculations of killjoys. The *Morning Chronicle* laid out the dangers others had foreseen with relish, including those arising from 'a large accumulation of respectable foreign gentlemen dispersed throughout the hotels and lodgings of the metropolis' which 'suggested a fear of the black fever or the sweating sickness . . .' while 'a considerable number of intelligent persons firmly believe in the existence of a conspiracy on the part of all the revolutionists and Socialists in Europe to seize our metropolis and destroy our constitution'.

Clearly Chancellor Wurmwolt was one of this intelligentsia which harboured these fears; but they were felt as well and as strongly by all who suspect mischief when Johnny Foreigner comes together in any great number.

Divine retribution was also in some people's minds. The normally tolerably rational *Manchester Guardian* argued, in measured if oxymoronic periods, 'There was a wise superstition among the Ancients that a man who was eminently successful was tempting the immortal gods and would be overtaken by some dire misfortune unless he averted the doom by sacrifice and self-abasement . . . The Christian view of it was expressed in the general desire for some form of religious service, and its celebration accordingly by the Primate of the English Church.'

Ironic, therefore, that Charlie's explosion was planned to take place during the performance of the 'Hallelujah Chorus'.

In preparation for which, round about St George's Day, he made his way across Hyde Park from Constitution Hill towards his target, pushing against the wind, one hand pressing down on his battered hat, the other thrust into the pocket of a coat that was far too big for him and billowed soggily around his shins. He was accompanied by the large and gingery Schumacher and they were accredited by passes which declared them to be representatives of exhibitors. Busily, officiously, they pushed through the crowd, always large in spite of the weather, which now gathered daily to witness the completion of the Palace and the installation of the exhibits.

Turnstiles clanged, belted constables vetted them, they were in, and into a different climate, a different world. It was warm and humid for the ventilation had to be kept low to avoid gusting draughts from the storm outside. There was a background rattle and whistle of rain and wind, but muted and all but drowned by the bustle, the toing and froing, the noise: the clang of iron, the clump of wood as crates were dropped, the screech as they were dragged, the smashing and splintering as they were opened; the shouted orders, the objections bellowed in answer, the cursing at the misplaced stroke of a hammer, the cheers as a particularly large and recalcitrant exhibit was finally rocked into its predestined place; the song of saws, the scream of metal cutters, the chimes of clashing girders.

And then there were the smells. Instead of the freshness of wind and rain, the dustiness of all the fabrics you could think of from jute and kapok to cotton and silk, the spiciness of strange woods and indeed comestibles, the rancid sweat of the workers and the pomades used by their bosses; new wood and old wood, hot metal and oil and, occasionally, when the wind span round an opened entrance or exit, the sulphurous fumes of smouldering coke and coal and the hot smell of steam from the giant exterior boiler house which provided power for many of the machines inside. It all added up to a fever, a rapture, an ecstasy of expectation that filled the head with a manic lightness and the chest with the aching hollow of dread anxiety: will we be, can we be, surely we never will be ready in time. We must be.

But it was the size of the place that got to Charlie. One thousand, eight hundred and fifty-one feet long, they said. Four hundred and eight feet wide, enclosing nineteen acres, six times the area of St Paul's. Four thousand tons of iron, nine hundred thousand feet of glass, two hundred and two miles of sash bars to hold it all together. And surely higher than any building nearer than the towers of the Abbey? If not, the lightness of the glass made it seem so. The vistas were immense, the vault above the transept as high as the sky. The workers seemed like ants infesting a greenhouse.

And the stuff! The clocks, the statues, the fountains, the thrones and cabinets, the chests and carpets, the hangings, the gallery of stained glass on the top floor, the flowers, the flowers and more flowers and plants and shrubs and trees. The jewels . . . even the Koh-i-noor itself, lit from beneath by gas. And the machinery and all the things machinery can make from railway engines to intricately woven fabrics, machine-made copies of Gothick altarpieces to pen-nibs. Huge things, some too big to go inside, like a pillar carved from one block of Cornish granite over forty feet high, and small things like the penknife made in Sheffield,* whose eighty curving blades were opened out so it looked like a sea anemone from another planet . . . it went on and on and on. You could not name a type of man- or machine-made object in the world but it had its example here.

'Between Austria and Russia are we to be found,' cried Schumacher, weaving through porters and warehousemen,

---

* It can still be seen in the Metalwork Collection in the Sheffield Millennium Galleries. J. R.

carpenters, painters and decorators, giving the Koh-i-noor no more than a glance, and leaving Charlie, whose mouth inevitably dried then filled at the sight (which, to tell the truth, was a touch uninspiring since it had been badly cut at a hundred and eighty-six carats – a year later it was recut to the way it is now at a hundred and nine carats and much more sparkly), hanging behind.

The French galleries of course went on for ever, showing mounds of swanky stuff from Gobelin tapestries to calculating machines; the Belgian was relatively dull but rational; the Austrian seemed to be mostly made up of very grand, very ornate furniture (that was Charlie's impression, who was again matching Schumacher stride for stride); and here they were in the Zollverein, the customs union of German States, one of which employed Wurmwolt, Schumacher and now Charlie. In their particular exhibit there were sausage-making machines, cheeses, sporting guns, cuckoo clocks and an entire wall filled with the tanks, brass piping glowing like gold, gas-heaters and the rest, with sacks of hops and malted barley, that added up to the very modern model of a functioning brewery producing the beer for which the Principality was most famous. Including barrels, of course.

'One of those will do nicely,' Charlie murmured.

'With what filled? Gunpowder?'

'I think *filled* would be a touch more than we need. Isn't this just meant to be a demonstration, a matter of giving everyone a bit of a fright? A small charge, with perhaps some small amount of incendiary material, say straw soaked in naphtha, and placed near one of those extinguishers. We don't want to set the whole caboodle on fire or create a blast strong enough to break all the glass.' He looked up and around him. Glass everywhere. 'Though it would be rather fun.'

'Caboodle? What is caboodle?'

Charlie gave that a miss. It was a word he'd picked up in America.

They were now standing side by side, hands behind their

backs, for all the world like a couple of gents discussing how the arrangement of the display in front of them might be improved.

'Socialists, or anarchists, must responsible be made to seem.'

'Home-grown? Or at any rate German?'

'I am thinking so. And also that this is not the right place for the barrel to be exploded I am also thinking.'

'Why not?'

Schumacher looked around. 'At the end of a cul-de-sac we are standing. Maybe it is going off and no one is being here to see it. Or be exploded with it.'

That was fairly precisely why Charlie favoured the position they were in.

'We can hardly move one of your barrels to another part of the exhibition.'

'But I am thinking we can.'

Charlie sighed but prepared himself to listen politely. In political assassination, just as in everything else in an increasingly commercial world, the customer is always right. Nevertheless, he added one or two refinements to Schumacher's improvised plan as they made their way back to the Crystal Fountain and the elm tree that marked the centre of the whole edifice at the point where the vaulted transept crossed the main hall.

As they approached it they became aware of a veil of near silence spreading out like the circle emanating from a stone dropped in a pool, while further off, from the crowd outside, a spatter of hurrays and huzzas died away in the wind. Inside men doffed (no other word will do) their hats and caps and the few women around curtsied and pulled back, forming a circle that left Charlie in its very front row. A small group moved down the aisle from the main entrance, coming to rest in the middle.

The centre of the group was a small woman of very considerable beauty, about thirty years old or a little more, wearing a long fur-trimmed coat over a spreading crimson dress with a star on her breast and a small tiara on her head which was framed in the lowered hood of the coat. Her dark but glossy hair was centrally parted and drawn back from her heart-shaped face. The best feature among several good ones was her dark eyes, the lids almost but not quite heavy, not unlike those of the Virgin in Velasquez's *Immaculate Conception*. They looked around her, serious, attentive, taking note. On one side of her a tall moustachioed man in Field Marshal's uniform, almost her equal in good looks, supported her elbow. On the other, a smaller man, who always looked taller than he was, wearing a formal frock coat with long grey very slightly flared trousers, stooped attentively towards her, his abundant but short-cut white hair stirred by a draught. Behind them three or four ladies also in outdoor clothes hovered, though the attention of one of them was partially directed towards a chubby but good-looking baby boy almost a year old, sitting up in the basket-work perambulator that was in her charge.

The attention of the baby, bright as a beam of sunlight, was suddenly caught by a movement above and beyond them. His little fist shot up and he crowed with delight and pleasure.

They all heard the clack of wings and then, gliding in a wide circle, its wings up and tilted in a 'v', the pigeon came in a long slow, arcing glide, right over Charlie, before flapping its wings again and swooping up into the branches of the elm. Cr, cr, crooo, it went, and Charlie, his face reddening, lifted his hand and touched the smear of white lime that had landed on his head.

Queen Victoria's eyes met his across the space between them, and a glimmer of a slightly naughty smile briefly lit those eyes, and then her brows drew together in a frown.

The elderly, no, really rather old, gent next to her lifted the proud prow of his unmistakable nose.

Mindful perhaps that on this occasion he was not only the Commander-in-Chief of her armies but also the Ranger of her Parks, and it was in that role that he was present (though he was also godfather to the little boy, christened Arthur after him), he cleared his throat.

'Try sparrow hawks, ma'am.'

A week later, Charlie wrote, just two days before the opening, I bumped into the old man. We were both on our way back from the Crystal Palace where he had been checking out that the mere presence of tethered sparrow hawks up near the roof had indeed frightened the sparrows and pigeons out of the place. I had been looking into where the barrel of gunpowder was to go, the purpose being to achieve maximum effect with minimum loss of life.

We arrived on the pavement of Hyde Park opposite Apsley House (Number One, London) almost together. It was raining, and the road was full with fast moving cabs and omnibuses. He looked around, the gaze of his slightly clouded eyes passing over my head, although it was obvious that the stoop I had noted the week before was more apparent than ever. Nevertheless I raised my forearm and, after a moment's hesitation, he took it and we crossed together.

'I thank you, sir,' he said.

I felt touched and honoured. 'My Lord,' I said, 'I have passed a long and eventful life; but never did I hope to reach the day when I might be of some assistance to the greatest man that ever lived.'

'Don't be a damned fool,' he replied. Then, 'Owe you sixpence, don't I?'

But again his pocket was empty of change.

May the first, 1851: the first birthday of Prince Arthur, the eighty-second birthday of the old man who lived at Number One, London, when he wasn't at Stratfield Saye or Walmer Castle, the day the Great Exhibition of the Industry of All Nations opened, was the first day of spring that year, the first truly fine, balmy promising day after a cold winter and a wet, stormy April. There were flags everywhere. The crowds began to gather shortly

400

after dawn: by midday there were three hundred thousand lining the short route from Buckingham Palace, up Constitution Hill, on to Rotten Row and so to the main entrance to the Crystal Palace. They were on the lamp-posts and up the trees.

Thirty thousand had tickets that got them inside, and there were maybe a couple of thousand or so more who did not need tickets: functionaries, exhibitors, cleaners, mechanics, musicians, singers in the massed choirs, two organists, a couple of conductors, the diplomatic corps, the exhibition's Royal Commissioners including Joseph Paxton, who had once been the Duke of Devonshire's under-gardener at Chatsworth where he had designed and built a large greenhouse. There were guards, of a sort, the Yeomen of the Tower in full rig, with highly polished halberds, and a few Peelers who seemed to be acting more as stewards than as guards, directing people to areas where there were still places and bawling out, every now and then, 'Children and Ladies to the front, if you please'. If there was any other security at all, it had a very low profile indeed. The only military apparent, apart from bands, were the Royal Horse Artillery out in the Park, waiting with their guns for the moment when they would fire, towards the end of the proceedings, a royal and martial salute.

At eleven thirty the greatest and the best in the land began to line up in serried rows at the front of the eastern transept. Those whose position gave them the right to wear a ceremonial uniform wore it (the military, judges, bishops and so forth); the rest were in evening dress. The Duke got a special cheer. At twelve precisely the Royal Party entered through the northern doors and passed through the Coalbrookdale Gates.* A band played 'Rule, Britannia!' and there were several fanfares. The men, inside and outside the Palace, took off their hats, all except the Beefeaters who saluted and Charlie who had just put on the round pillbox of an embroidered cap which he preferred

---

* They can still be seen in Hyde Park. J. R.

not to take off again since it completed his disguise as a Chinese mandarin.

Her Majesty, your fashion correspondent reported the next day, was in pink watered silk brocaded with silver and wore a tiara of diamonds and feathers. Her husband was in full-dress Field Marshal's uniform and their eldest son, the Prince of Wales, was in Highland rig, the lot. His eldest sister, the Princess Royal (in fact older than he, the first child of the royal couple) wore two skirts of Nottingham lace and a chaplet of roses.

There was a podium with a throne and, as Queen Victoria moved towards it, the National Anthem was sung by the choirs of the Chapel Royal, St Paul's Cathedral, Westminster Abbey, St George's Windsor, the Royal Academy of Music and many others, accompanied by two organs, an orchestra, and no doubt a band or two. It shattered the air, the ears, the pride of Johnny Foreigner, the fears of the doubting Thomases, but not the glass – though it did, some said, who stood near the outer walls, vibrate just a touch alarmingly. All remained rooted to the ground through all five verses, six with the first repeated at the end – all except Charlie.

> *O Lord our God arise*
> *Scatter her enemies*
> *And make them fall;*
> *Confound their politics,*
> *Frustrate their knavish tricks,*
> *On thee our hopes we fix,*
> *God save us all!*
>
> *Thy choicest gifts in store*
> *On her be pleased to pour,*
> *Long may she reign;*
> *May she defend our laws*
> *And ever give us cause*
> *To sing with heart and voice,*
> *God save the Queen!*

Not in this land alone,
But be God's mercies known,
From shore to shore!
Lord, make the nations see,
That men should brothers be
And form one family,
The wide world over.

From every latent foe,
From the assassins' blow,
God save the Queen!
O'er her thine arm extend,
For Britain's sake defend,
Our mother, prince, and friend,
God save the Queen . . .

Charlie used the hiatus to slip away from the exhibition space of the German statelet he had been employed by and where he had hidden himself behind a giant cheese press in order to change into his hired oriental gear.

The Queen sat on the throne. It was a moment that placed her and her country at the head of everything. The foreign representatives were reduced to the level of subjects. It was a moment that had for Britain the significance the fall of the Berlin Wall was to have for the United States. Great before, Britain was now indisputably the greatest and would remain so for forty-six years, until Her Majesty's Diamond Jubilee. Forty-six years? Not a lot, but now, a hundred years on, History moves even more quickly. New empires founded on the exploitation of their masses, and those of their colonies and clients, will rise and fall before our new century is done.

Meanwhile, back in 1851, Prince Albert began his speech. It was long, too long, which was just as well for Charlie – if he was to get everything in place before the scheduled performance of the 'Hallelujah Chorus'.

49

Charlie's gear had been hired from a theatrical costumier in Carnaby Street and had last been used four months earlier by the actor playing the Grand Vizier of Peking in the Drury Lane pantomime of *Aladdin*. For comic effect the Grand Vizier is often played by a dwarf, or at least by an actor of as small a stature as one can find – which was why Charlie had chosen it. It was also convenient that with the late Opium War still an unpleasant memory in the minds of the proud Chinese that country was just about the only one of any significance in the world that had not responded to the invitations to attend the opening.

The costume consisted of the aforementioned round hat which had a pigtail attached that almost reached Charlie's waist, two long moustaches that touched his collarbones, a green silk jerkin with long wide sleeves, embroidered with gold dragons, white pantaloons, and slippers jewelled with glass that looked like so many boiled sweets. Before putting on this attire he had of course painted his face a pasty yellow, and indicated oriental eyes with upward and outward slanting eyeliner. This disguise was meant to look like a disguise: the effect aimed for by him and Schumacher was of a European, preferably a mid-European, dressed as a Chinaman. In this they failed: among several hundred foreigners from all races and cultures, encouraged by the Prince to wear their national dress, a man appearing as a Chinaman was naturally taken to be a Chinaman. Charlie's height even added to the illusion, for are not all yellow folk known to be smaller than the White Man?

This was only the last, or last but one contrivance, that was to lead up to the outrage they had planned. On April the twenty-ninth, Schumacher had declared that the barrels in the brewery exhibit looked dull. They must be taken out and painted red. There were five of them. Six came back the next day and the sixth was simply and casually placed further down the main thoroughfare exactly on the dividing line between the Russian and American displays. Neither country wanted to risk offending the other by asking its neighbour to move it, and, as Charlie had foreseen, the barrel remained where it was.

Apart from two features the American display was judged to be a disappointment: there were typewriters, sewing machines, candle- and brick-making machines. Even the mechanised harvesters were less than impressive. Few who saw them appreciated the significance of telegraphs, new signalling technology for trains, and the large display of India rubber-ware from Charles Goodyear. The two features that did attract attention, and particularly Charlie's, who would have been only too happy to see them blown to smithereens, were Colt's revolving pistols and rifles, mass-produced by Robbins and Lawrence, and a tea service made entirely from solid Californian gold. Both gold and guns reminded him of experiences he preferred to forget.

But this is by the way. With the barrel in place on the border between Russia and America, Charlie now had only two tasks left to carry out. One was to place, as surreptitiously as possible, a wallet close to the barrel in a situation where it would certainly be found and could conceivably have been dropped by accident. It contained identification that showed its owner to be from Frankfort (sic), and a member of the German Workers' Educational Society. It also contained a receipt for the purchase of gunpowder. The second task was to light the short but slow-burning fuse that protruded from the back of the barrel at exactly the right moment to make a small but impressive explosion which would coincide with the climax of the 'Hallelujah Chorus'.

Charlie was just about to perform the first task when it occurred to him to check the contents of the wallet. To his dismay he found it also contained a receipt from the Carnaby Street costumier for a Chinaman's costume and, since it was he himself who had hired the costume and he knew how easily his stature and hairiness could be remembered and identified, he realised he was possibly being set up. Confused, not knowing how to handle his situation, he dropped the wallet into the deep and capacious pocket that hung from the sleeve of his tunic. Then he pulled it out again and had another look at the gunpowder receipt. The amount of gunpowder bought, '50kg', meant nothing to him at all but the price, ten pounds, seemed excessive. Well, he thought, an English supplier of the commodity was taking advantage of a foreigner and overcharging him.

It remained for him to light the fuse. Glancing at a cuckoo clock just visible in the Austrian exhibit, he waited until the minute hand reached the eight, then fished a box of Swan wax vestas from his other sleeve.

At this point in time the general public, the ordinary ticket holders, had not been admitted and would not be admitted until the Royal Party, the Greatest and the Best, and the Diplomatic Corps had completed their tour following the opening ceremony. And consequently the explosion would probably not harm anyone at all in the almost deserted aisles, but would simply give any bystanders, and ultimately the authorities, the nasty shock and warning which was Chancellor Wurmwold's objective. But what Wurmwold had not allowed for was the fact that the very lack of crowds would render Charlie's presence conspicuous and his actions suspicious.

He hung around the barrel for a couple of minutes under the gaze of a Cossack on one side and an American Red Indian Chief with an Irish accent on the other, both dressed in their full and appropriate costumes and accoutrements, the booted Cossack in furs with an intimidating scimitar-like sabre, the Red Indian in huge goose-quilled war bonnet, buckskinned, with Bowie knife and tomahawk. They watched him with growing intentness until at length the Indian Chief came up behind him, and stooped so his large chin almost rested on Charlie's shoulder.

'OK Mr Chinkee, whoi don't you just piss off the now?'

Charlie was ready to do what he always did when faced with failure: give up. He had been paid twenty pounds in advance, and that would have to do. But at this moment he sensed a presence behind him and felt a tap on his shoulder. The burly, gingery Schumacher had joined them.

'Charlie, the operation I'll be seeing to. As the gentleman you has instructed, please to do. Piss off.'

He held out a hand to the Irish-American who put in it a second box of vestas. Charlie needed no further encouragement. He set off up the wide aisle, at a brisk pace, almost a trot, towards the central cross-over beneath the vaulted transept. There were soon more people about, but not many more, for he was moving in reverse up the path the Royal Party would take and it had been kept clear. Presently the dull murmur of a rather high-pitched but male voice in front of him became more distinguishable, but there was nothing in it that threatened and he continued. He could clearly see the splendid Crystal Fountain and beyond it a crowd of closely packed people in top hats or ceremonial fancy dress, but he could not see to the left or to the right, to the podium on one side and the massed choirs on the other.

The voice, Teutonically accented, rose towards a peroration.

'It is our heartfelt prayer that this undertaking, which has for its end the promotion of all branches of human industry and the strengthening of the bonds of peace and friendship among

407

all the nations of the earth, may, by the blessing of Divine Providence, conduce to the welfare of your Majesty's people, and be long remembered among the brightest circumstances of your Majesty's peaceful and happy reign.'

There followed a brief and possibly relieved spatter of applause. Neither his audience nor Prince Albert himself can be blamed for not foreseeing that the Indian Mutiny and the Crimean War were just round the corner. Though it should be said that such events cast long shadows in front of them, and are generally predicted by those who have nothing to lose by saying so.

Another voice took over before the coughing and impatient shuffling of feet could get a hold, the sonorous only too imitable rise and fall of the Anglican Church at prayer which inevitably and always disrobes its words of all content and meaning.

'And *now* let us bow our *heads* in prayer. Almighty and *ever*-laahstin' Gawd, who hast of thine *in*-finite mercy granted thy servants the gifts of . . .' and so on to 'Our Father Witchart . . . Amen, and may the blessing of he, him and the other one . . . be with you and remain with you . . .'

And CRASH! At last. Hallelujah! Haaaallelujah! Hal-lel-oo-ya, hal-lel-oo-ya, hal-e-eh—looya! Foooor, the, Lord, God, Omni-i-ipotent reigneth . . .

With his eye on the massed Greatest and Best to his right, and keeping the fountain, which, when all is said and done, looked like nothing so much as a tall and elegant cakestand, between him and them, Charlie scampered into the open space.

For ever. And Ever. Hallelujah. Hallelujah.

Some people, at the back of a transept or too far down one of the aisles, complained later that they had not been able to hear it properly, others that its parts came microseconds apart, bounced off the glass walls. But Charlie got it full and quadrophonic. He turned his back on it, hands on ears and . . . bowed. Again she smiled, indeed she had to hide behind a glittering feathered fan a not quite successful struggle with the giggles, while graciously she very slightly inclined her head back at him.

Who was he? What was to be done with him? He stood aside as the Royal Procession moved off, and the Ambassadors fell in behind. The trouble was no one could be sure that he was not what he might just be taken to be – an actual representative of the Dragon Throne, accredited by invitation but not expected owing to some bureaucratic muddle.

The Examiner summed up the dilemma and its solution in its report the following day.

> This live importation of the Celestial Empire managed to render himself extremely conspicuous, and one could not help admiring his perfect composure and nonchalance of manner. He talked with nobody, yet he seemed perfectly at home, and on the most friendly terms with all. A most amusing advantage was taken of his appearance, for, when the procession was formed, the diplomatic body had no Chinese representative, and our stray Celestial Friend was quietly impounded and made to march in the rear of the ambassadors. He submitted to this arrangement with the same calm indifference which marked the whole course of his proceedings . . . His behaviour was that of a 'citizen of the world' . . .

In the rear of the Ambassadors. The one nearest to Charlie, possibly not the actual ambassador, but a *chargé* or whatever, had the pointed beard and well-trimmed moustaches that suggested a continental, possibly even a Frenchman. And Charlie realised he might be able to enlighten him concerning a nagging doubt that had begun to bother him. He took hold of the diplomat's elbow and gave it a tug.

'*Combien,*' he asked, '*de livres sont-ils dans cinquante kay gees?*'

The diplomat shrugged him off impatiently. Charlie fished out the wallet, extracted the gunpowder receipt, returned the wallet to his sleeve, and prodded the receipt with his forefinger.

'*Combien?*' he tried again.

The diplomat, still striving to keep up with the crowd in front of him, puffed his cheeks, blew out a raspberry through pursed lips, shrugged, and said, speaking slowly as if to an idiot: '*Beaucoup. Très beaucoup. Assez pour une explosion très, très grande. Boum!*'

'Oh shit,' said Charlie.

He walked on tiptoe, tried to peer above the massed and for the most part hatted and headdressed heads in front of him, dodged to the side to get a better view, climbed on to a huge glazed pot decorated with Japanese calligraphy containing a giant fern, and, as it began to topple, saw that any possibility of getting to the front of the procession was out of the question. He turned and ran, cutting corners, skidding to take ninety degree turns, heaved himself up a spiral stair on to the floor above, scampered down long aisles past bewildered exhibitors of all nations, tumbled down another flight, and came finally to the Russian and American spaces just as the procession came into view, returning to the main aisle, after sampling the delights of Hornsby and Sons' steam-driven ploughs.

Sure enough the fuse had been lit. A tiny curl, a thread of blue smoke spiralled up into the still air above the barrel. There was about an inch to go. Using thumb and forefinger Charlie tried to snuff it out, but, no, it refused to extinguish. He wet his digits and tried again. All he achieved was a sudden stab of pain. He got a tighter grip, fighting back the smart, refusing to acknowledge to himself the whiff of burning flesh and pulled. No, it wouldn't budge. He looked up over his shoulder. The Russian Cossack looked down at him.

Hauling in breath like sacks of coal, Charlie gasped: 'Gunpowder. Full of gunpowder. Fuse. Burning . . .'

'Holy Mary, Mother of God!' But in Russian, of course.

'Absolutely. But can't you do something?'

A quarter of an inch remained.

The Cossack drew his sabre as Charlie glanced over his shoulder. His Queen, her Consort, and all the rest were thirty

410

yards away. With a shrug that dismissed any doubts as to the political correctness of what he was about to do, the Cossack ran the razor-sharp edge of his huge blade down the side of the barrel and sliced off the last burning shreds of the fuse. Charlie, with his back to him, and his hands in his sleeves, bowed, and bowed and bowed again as the Queen, her Consort, her Children, and all the Greatest and Best of the land, including the Duke, who gave him a sharp look, passed slowly by.

'Fyodor Pavlovich Karamazov it was who saved the Queen's life. And the existence of the Crystal Palace and the Great Exhibition itself. Not you.'

Elliott turns from the window, spreads his coat-tails, and sits on the castellated top of the radiator.

'Chancellor Wurmwold was sent packing,' he goes on, 'although of course he had no part in filling the barrel with powder. All he wanted was the minor contrivance he had planned. Schumacher was the villain. He had anarchist connections. And the Red Indian was, of course, a Fenian accomplice. You yourself were very lucky to escape prosecution on a number of counts.'

'If I had lit the fuse, as I had been paid to do, if I had set off the bomb . . .'

'Oh, come on, Charlie. You can hardly claim to be a hero for failing to commit a crime. Every honest citizen in the country could say as much of himself.'

'But Mr Elliott, I am not an honest citizen—'

'That is indeed the case.' The man from the Secret Service hoists himself up again, leaves the window and the comfort of the central heating, looks down on Charlie and adds, 'Which is why you are on your way back to Millbank,' he glanced at his watch, 'an hour from now. We have received a telegraph. Brought up from the station. Poor Cargill suffered a relapse and is expected to die.'

411

50

It all went wrong, Charlie reflects, after Elliott has left him to watch the gathering dusk, when Maggie-May put me on that bloody boat. Slumped in his chair, with the light thickening outside over the lawns, the lake, and the Derbyshire moors beyond, and the crows making wing to the rooky wood, his inner sight goes back twenty years once more. Back from Paris, the order had been repeated: Go West. Plymouth, Ho! Since there seemed to be some urgency about the matter and anyway he had sold Frankie, his moke, to a horse-meat butcher whose customers, he said, wouldn't know the difference if she were fricassee-ed up with a lot of onion or put in a pie, the final stage of his journey, as we have seen, was in the mail coach from Shaftesbury to Plymouth.

It should have arrived on the evening of the second night; however, a snowdrift held it up for an hour and the coachmen refused to continue after dark on a road that skirted Dartmoor, so they pulled into the coaching inn at Plympton, ten miles or so short of their destination. He recalled that Kate Bramshaw had told him that this was where Maggie-May had fetched up and that she was now Lady Danby of Plympton Hall, no less. In

412

the morning he left the coach to continue on its way to Plymouth, made enquiries and was presently walking up a gravelled drive. The early snow, which had delayed the coach the day before, had almost entirely melted, leaving banks and drifts only where the sun had not reached it. In front of him there stood a pleasant villa, two storeys only, but with dormer windows in the roof, and a verandah running along a frontage closed in with wrought-iron arches. There was a balcony above, the curlicues of which provided support for rambling roses, now over. The front door, set between two Doric pillars, with three steps leading up to them and a shoe scraper shaped like the silhouette of a sausage dog beneath the brass bell pull, was in the side of the house, opening on to a cobbled space with stables behind.

He pulled the bell, heard its distant jangle. Two minutes later the door was opened by a large but old butler. He must have been in his sixties, and must once have been over six feet tall. Now his shoulders were rounded in a hunch over an enormous portmanteau of a stomach cased in a striped vest beneath a shabby coat whose buttons on one side would never make the acquaintance again of the buttonholes on the other.

'Well?' His voice was rough, hoarse.

'Is her ladyship at home?'

'Depends who to.'

'To whom. Charlie Boylan.'

'I'll see.'

The door closed. This time the wait extended to six minutes and its opening was preceded by the wheezing grunts of the butler on the other side. The round trip of a hundred yards or so had cost him dearly.

'Her ladyship will see you. In the rose garden.'

He remained where he was like a beached whale, blocking Charlie's access.

'How should I get there then?' he asked, a touch plaintively, after another minute had ticked by.

'Through the door between the stables and the house. Brick

wall far side of the lawn. Another gate. That's the rose garden.'
Each period was marked by breaths dragged in over shingle.

For all she was now twenty-four years old, and she had only
been about thirteen when he had last met her on the road to
Nottingham, Charlie felt sure he would have recognised the
darker red of her hair, the wicked smile in her blue eyes, her
freckles and her rosebud mouth. She stood at the end of a short
mossy avenue of rose bushes, framed by a pergola, in front of a
small grey statue copied from the Medici Venus. She was wearing a sky-blue dress, full but simple, with lace at the cuffs and
hem, and an Indian shawl, reds and browns, that went with her
hair. As soon as she saw him she set down the trug she was carrying in one hand and the pruning shears she had in the other,
took off her leather gloves and dropped them in the trug, and
ran like the tomboy she had always been, down the mossy flags
and into his arms.

'Charlie!' she cried. 'It's really you!'

Her chin was level now with the top of his head. She kissed
it.

'You've got a bald patch,' she said, pulling away. 'Did you
know that? Not really bald but getting thin. How did you find
me? What took you so long?'

Although it was early in December, it was also, yet again,
one of those occasional warm afternoons you can get, even
into December. There was a wall with an espaliered peach tree
against it and a stone seat in front of it which she took him to,
and there, sitting side by side with her holding one of his hands
with both of hers in her lap, she told him her story. And as she
did so the sun slowly sank until the bare twigs of an ancient
apple tree stood out, silhouetted against it.

Among the properties Kate Bramshaw had inherited on
reaching her majority, or rather come into, for they were already
hers, was a parcel of farms down there in the West Country,
right under the lowering brow of the moor. It being against her
principles to own farms and land where she could not personally
oversee on an almost daily basis the welfare of her tenants and

414

their labourers, she decided to sell them, and it also being against her principles to pass these people from her care to that of a landlord she had never met, she had come down to Plympton to vet the sale. And Maggie had come with her.

Sir George Danby, who had recently inherited his baronetcy, had immediately presented himself as a suitable candidate. He was a considerate landlord, that was clear, for the tenants of the largest of the three farms he owned lived in higher style than he did, and to ensure that her tenants came into his care Kate let him have her farms for half the going price.

'Let better people than I,' she asserted, 'lay themselves open to the temptations that come with accumulated surplus capital.'

During the negotiations it became clear that George was a man of the highest integrity, a gentleman of the old school, and though no Whig or reformer a man of conscience and sensibility. And at the time he was barely forty-five years old, a mere quarter of a century older than Maggie.

He had remained a bachelor and something of a melancholic, following the horrors he had witnessed at Waterloo, but he had only to see Maggie-May dance and sing as Kate had taught her to, and laugh in the way Nature intended, for him to be restored to the best of spirits. And for two years or so this had been the case. However, there was a fly in the ointment. Let Maggie-May tell you in her own words, just as she told Charlie on that mossy seat against the spreading if constrained branches of the peach tree.

'Frankly, Charlie, he couldn't get it up. Know what I mean? Technically, that is to say officially, I'm a virgin yet.'

Deprived of the fruitful joys of a full married life the relationship withered like a worm-infested apple on the bough. Lengthy silences grew by day between them that could last a day. At night she did what she could to stimulate him, but made no headway, and he soon became disgusted by the knowingness of her advances. It came as a relief to both of them when he entered the Consular Service and took up an appointment that suited his age and rank in India. After a hopeless night spent in one last attempt to impregnate his wife, he rode to Plymouth where a cutter took him out to the transport hove to off the Hoe especially for him, leaving Maggie-May to fend for herself alone apart from an agent who managed the farms and a sister-in-law, Sophie, Lady Tarrant St Giles, who lived in Dorset and came over with her husband every month or so to make sure that everything was all right.

'In other words, Charlie, to count the silver teaspoons, check the family pictures are still on the walls, and make sure I don't have a Don Juan in or under the bed. Jesus, Charlie, you don't know how bored I've been. Now tell me what you've been up to, and what brings you to Devon. Nothing good, I'll be bound.'

Supposing her views to march with those of her dearest friend Kate Bramshaw, it was clear to Charlie that she would not be pleased to hear that he was on his way to Plymouth for a spot of Union busting, the plan being to use the fact he was a stranger in town to infiltrate the Union of Fishermen and Associated Trades and in due course of time peach on them. On the spur of the moment all he could think of was emigration. Fallen on hard times he was, he said, going to try his luck in the Americas and hoped to save himself a pound or two on the fare by taking ship at Plymouth rather than London or Southampton. He had had a horse and enough money he thought to get him to Plymouth but the money, apart from what he had on one side to pay for his berth, had run out, back at Exeter the horse had cast a shoe which he could not afford to replace . . .

'I don't believe a word of it,' Maggie-May carolled, 'but I'm sure you can stay with me a week or so and cheer me up. I'll not hear any different.'

And he agreed he could.

What followed was the happiest time Charlie had during the course of what you are reading, perhaps the happiest time of his life. It didn't last, of course. How could it?

For the rest of that evening they remained constrained by a

certain formality and unfamiliarity. At supper he sat on the far side of the large oval table they dined off, a candelabra turning the polished mahogany into a pool of darkness between them, a small wood fire in the simple marble fireplace, decorated with just two fluted pilasters on either side, warming Charlie's thigh. Plumpstead the butler served a brace of pheasants each, hen and cock, just as they should be, gift of one of the tenants, and a damson tart sweetened with clotted cream. They drank a bottle of ordinary claret. Then, although they got quite high with their reminiscences of Islington and Nottingham, they each took their own candles upstairs where Maggie-May kissed Charlie quite chastely on the cheek, before going to their separate rooms.

The next day remained fine after a heavy frost and they spent most of it out of doors.

'I'll show you what I have,' Maggie cried, once they were in the yard after an Anglo-Indian breakfast of saffron-flavoured kedgeree, 'the extent of my kingdom. Lady Muck, I am, Charlie, you'd better believe it,' and she pinned a veil over her face beneath her feathered hat and buttoned up her mirror-shining black boots beneath her red velvet riding habit. She rode a fine black hunter, a gelding called Satan. There was no pony available for Charlie so the stable boy was sent down to the parsonage to borrow the parson's donkey.

Until the sun melted it the frost crackled in the shin-high grass beneath their animals' hooves, their nostrils plumed steam into the sharp air in front of their faces. The hedgerows smelt dank and fruity with rotting hips and haws, and on the edge of a hanger of oaks they found big ceps like penny-buns, but turning them over found they were fly eaten and maggoty. Rooks cackled above them, and pheasants scampered across the paths they took. High above them to the north, mist gathered over the Moor, but once they were following the line of the first of its escarpments they could see the sea below them, ten miles or so away like a burnished and chased shield beneath the sun. Over to the west a smog of coal smoke from chimneys and steamboats, as yet there were no trains, hung above Plymouth. On the way down a shepherd with thirty ewes, not yet noticeably pregnant, saluted her ladyship by raising his crook, and at the furthest point from Plympton Hall they dined in the Danby Arms off a local vinney cheese, white bread and the landlord's own ale.

Everywhere they went Maggie-May was her ladyship, even though she insisted on having pickled onions with her cheese, and if Charlie got some odd looks especially from those who took him for a lackey and were puzzled when Maggie-May treated him like friend, well, that just added to his pleasure. As she said, as an ostler at the inn reluctantly helped Charlie back on to the parson's donkey, 'If I'm a lady, then my friends are gents.'

That evening Maggie-May taught him *bézique*, a French card game not yet common in England, which she had been taught by a French cardsharp who had travelled with the girls towards the end of their career together – until Tess and Maggie-May quarrelled over him at which point Kate had thrown him out. They drank most of a bottle of Napoleon cognac she had Plumpstead bring up from the cellar. He tried to object but was scolded for it; nevertheless, he finished the bottle in his pantry later that night.

'You know, Charlie, you came in the nick of time,' she said with quiet firmness as she shuffled the double pack with twos to sixes taken out. 'They were slowly wearing me down, the two of them, Plumpstead and Grimpen—'

'Grimpen?'

'Housekeeper. You'll meet her though she keeps a low profile. It's always "Yes, your ladyship, but Sir George likes it done this way", or "We've never had one of them; I'm not sure Sir George would approve", that sort of thing, all the time. I tried to stand up for myself, but well, you know me, daughter of a regimental washerwoman and whore I don't doubt, and where I come from, in spite of Kate giving me a bit of polish. Your glass is empty.'

418

And she topped them both up.

'The object of the game,' she explained to Charlie, once the stopper was back on the decanter, 'is to get both Jacks of Diamonds and both Queens of Spades in one bed, or hand, and declare them.' Then she went coy and added, 'I think we should alter the rules and make it the Jack of Spades and the Queen of Diamonds being as you're so dark and I'm so flash. Anyway, once they're together, that's *bézique* and that's what you're meant to call out, when you have them.'

Poor Charlie, who had learnt the game in Spain decades earlier where it's called Besico or Little Kiss, was hard put not to win all the time, especially as Maggie-May continued to hit the Napoleon. At last she threw down a hand halfway through.

'Bugger this for a waste of fucking time,' she cried, somewhat ambiguously, 'let's go to bed.'

On the landing, she held on to his hand and pulled him into the master bedroom.

Twenty minutes later she shouted '*Bézique*' rather loudly, loud enough for sour Miss Grimpen, who slept in the attic room above, to hear.

How could Maggie, how could she? I hear you ask. But remember the Charlie you have most often had described to you was the Charlie of 1853 and this was taking place in 1831. All right, he was small (though above average in certain matters), dark and very hairy, but, as they say, *vive la différence.* She, though strong, was soft-skinned, creamy with that creaminess only redheads have, with small pink nipples like cherries and long feet which she loved to run over his body so the soles could feel his furriness. In short the differences made all the difference and they revelled in them.

Miss Grimpen, as thin and gawky as Mr Plumpstead was fat and soft, watched Charlie with a spiteful eye. She had it always in mind that if she could rid Plympton Hall of the present Lady Danby she had only to serve the master when he returned in as humble and efficient and hard-working a way as possible for it to become not an improbability that he would leave her a substantial bequest. She had a formidable ally in his sister, Lady Tarrant St Giles, who could not abide Maggie and had lived in terror, unaware of her brother's disability, that she would one day present them all with a son and heir to the Danby estates. However, Grimpen knew that a blunt accusation of adultery, even backed by the soggy evidence of Mr Plumpstead, would not be enough and could easily result in her own dismissal. Whatever her origins, Lady Danby was now gentry, and the gentry are always believed in preference to their servants. *In flagrante delicto* was what was needed; nothing less would do.

She plotted. She had Charlie followed when he and Maggie went into Plymouth for a day, followed by her own bastard son who had been brought up by her sister who was married to the village schoolmaster. Lady Danby went shopping, as she usually did, but Boylan took himself off to the docks, to a tiny pub at the back of the fishing harbour, behind the big wholesale market where the catch was sold off. There, according to her son, who was as sharp as his mum and nobody's fool, Charlie joined in with others preaching bloody revolution and a fair price for cod before returning to town and, after reuniting with his inamorata, Plympton Hall.

That's a start, Grimpen thought, but not enough. Nothing for it but a trip across the county to Tarrant Royal and a proper confabulation with Lady Tarrant St Giles. She invented a sick aunt in Shaftesbury and asked for a week. Maggie was very happy indeed to let her go.

For the lovers, on their side, Plumpstead remained a problem but Charlie soon found the butler was happy to be locked in his room with a bottle of brandy every evening from seven o'clock, by when the other servants, who all lived in the village, had gone home.

They now had a whale of a time. They ate and drank what they liked. They took their clothes off and when they weren't naked played dressing up like a couple of kids. They chased each other, played hide-and-seek. Mostly Maggie was an empress, getting herself up with everything gaudy and bright they could find from brocade curtains to the family heirlooms, while Charlie played a monkey, a monster, a devil. But sometimes they swapped round and he was King of the Jungle and she the missionary sent to convert him, but the conversion always went awry, usually with her on her hands and knees with her dress round her waist and him coming at her from behind. Yes, they fucked. They fucked all they could and when they couldn't they found ways of simulating fucking which had their own charms and delights.

They were not tidy people. After three days the two main floors of the Hall looked like a brothel after a heavy night, the morning after of a Roman feast. Plumpstead tried to tidy up the empty bottles, the stripped carcases of more pheasants, a hare, and a couple of guinea fowl, spilt cream, scattered garments, the debris caused by a crab-apple-throwing fight, the strewn bedding and the rest, but after two or three minutes he tended to fall over and go to sleep. Perhaps it was just as well that three days was as long as it all lasted.

Miss Grimpen, accompanied by Sir Fred and Sophie Tarrant St Giles and a posse of huntsmen, whippers-in and even a constable or two, arrived in the village on the evening of the third day, and picked up a startling account of what was going on at the Hall – for, needless to say, Grimpen's bastard son had been keeping a surreptitious eye on it all, peeping through windows, and watching the upstairs from the top of a handy mulberry tree.

Sir Fred, who had not aged well and had to get his carriage out for the journey, whose cheeks were now as tight as a drum, as round as an inflated bladder or one of Mr Goodyear's balloons, and as red as the flag of revolution, whose stomach preceded him by a foot or more, was all for stopping at the Danby Arms for the night, but Sophie would have none of it and Miss Grimpen did not advise it.

'Word'll get to them we're here, be sure of it,' she hissed, and her dark snake eyes darted round the entrance hall to the inn and the suddenly quiet bar beyond.

421

'Damnme, if they don' hear us coming,' grunted Sir Fred, thinking of his carriage.

'We'll walk the last half-mile,' his wife commanded.

'Walk, damnme? Half a mile? The last time I walked half a mile was at Waterloo!'

In the end they left him in the carriage. The two women did indeed walk, accompanied by four men from the Tarrant Royal Hunt and two constables, all with pistols primed and loaded. Grimpen took them round the back of the house and let them in by the tradesman's door. They climbed the back stairs. They crept along the landing, ignoring Plumpstead's huge snores that rolled down from above. Grimpen opened the door of the master bedroom and such was her shock she fainted clear away into Sophie's arms, who in turn fell back against a constable. His pistol went off and shattered a small candle holder on the wall hung with five crystal droplets. All of which gave Charlie, encouraged indeed urged by Maggie-May, time to extract his fingers from her arse and exit through the window and down the cast-iron trellis to the rose bed fourteen feet below.

Why had Grimpen been so shattered by what she saw?

The master bed faced the mistress dressing table which was surmounted by a very large and on the whole unclouded Venetian mirror whose gilded frame was in the rococo style. In it she saw reflected her ladyship's freckled face, wreathed with a blissful smile for a brief second before consternation took over. Her breasts swung above Charlie's shoulders and neck which she had encircled with her plump white arms. Grimpen's eyes tracked from the mirror to the back of Maggie's head *en clair*, across her shoulders down to her spread buttocks. Charlie had his dick up her cunt and three fingers in her arse, and, as above, she looked as happy as Larry.

'You know, Charlie,' Elliott remarks as he turns the pages of Charlie's account of these events, 'I'm really not too sure about you.'

422

They are still in Charlie's room at Pemberley, but waiting for the trap that will take them to Chesterfield station.

'Undoubtedly you had an agendum beyond merely telling the truth when you wrote most of these memoirs,' and he taps the pile of papers he has in front of him, rescued, for the most part, Charlie assumes, from poor Cargill's office.

'I have always endeavoured to give satisfaction in what I have written,' he replies, a touch stiffly since no one likes to be accused of telling porkies, 'and I cannot believe that the rather superior people who have read my memoirs would be satisfied by anything less than the truth.'

'Charlie, don't come the pompous ass with me, it won't wash.'

'Then you'd better tell me just what it is you are getting at.'

Elliott, elbow on the arm of one of the two chairs, chews his knuckle for a moment, then points an admonitory finger at Charlie, which puts him in mind of Mr Bucket.

'Charlie, you are a rogue. A liar, a cheat.'

'I do my best to get by, Mr Elliott.'

'And the main aim,' Elliott continues, ignoring this last interjection, 'of these memoirs is to present yourself as a threat to the establishment by claiming to have done all sorts of really rather nasty things at the behest of the great and the good.'

'The greatest and the best, Mr Elliott.'

'In the hope that they will stuff your mouth with gold to keep you quiet.'

'A modest competence is all I require. To see me through what is left of an already protracted old age.'

'Just as you say, Charlie. But I wonder. Sometimes I wonder.'

423

51

Clickety-clack, clickety-clack, clear of Chesterfield with its bent spire the train rackets on towards London. Elliott sits opposite Charlie, knees almost touching.

'And what happened next?' he asks.

'I hid out with the fishermen unionists for a week or two, through Christmas, then that bastard Grimpen lad found me. He had the constables after me straightaway, he and Sir Fred, and the rest, but Maggie-May got to me first and saved me. With the help of the fishermen who knew what boats were in the harbour, where they were headed for, and when they were likely to sail.'

'So you were actually saved by the men you had been employed to betray.'

'I suppose you could put it like that. But in fact I believe the vicissitudes of the next seventeen years were far worse than anything I could have expected at home. After all a horse-whipping, which is what Sir Fred was promising, is soon forgotten and Stafford would have seen me through any charge that I had consorted with Trades Unionists and Association members.'

'So what happened?'

'Maggie-May and the fishermen rushed me down the quay at Barnpool till we found a Royal Navy brig of ten guns that they said was due to sail the next day, and the Blue Peter at her fore-peak indicated this was so—'

'Bound for the Americas?'

'Eventually. But I have to say it was by a somewhat round-about route.'

'And you didn't get back until forty-eight?'

'That's right.'

Clickety-clack, clickety-clack. Elliott gives it all a bit more thought.

'Ironic really, isn't it?' he asks, eventually. 'You went to so much trouble to convince us all that you had killed all these people, on our instructions, in order to persuade us that we should give you a pension . . .'

'A modest pension.'

'A modest pension, and now these very accounts of yours will be available to the prosecution when you are tried for the murder of Cargill. What you have told us, and written down, could hang you, you know? Most juries will say bugger Cargill, we should do him for the rest.'

For a moment or two Charlie lets the motion of the train swing him from side to side.

'But you're not going to let—'

'And the real irony is that—'

They both speak at once.

'Go on,' says Charlie, giving way.

'And the real irony is that you didn't actually do any of them, did you?'

Charlie shrugs, looks out of the window. Elliott looks at his tired profile, the lank hair, the slightly hooked nose, the hollow cheeks, but concedes he looks better than when he arrived at Pemberley. There is a sensitivity there he has begun to recognise, a humour too. He knows this ageing man might never have done an honest day's work in his life, but he suspects he probably wouldn't hurt a fly either. This time a moment of compassion really does take him by surprise.

'The gunsmith at Spa Fields, the man Glew on the way to Pentrich, it's hardly likely you got away with shooting them without being spotted.'

'There were those in Nottingham believed I had,' muttered Charlie, remembering the beating he'd been given at the Goose Fair.

'There was no broken window at St Peter's Fields, I've checked that, and no one found the stab wound you say you gave the constable in Cato Street. And as for the Shelley business . . . well, all I can say is that Lady Jane Shelley says that her mother-in-law, Mary Wollstonecraft Godwin Shelley, never mentioned the presence of anyone like you at Lerici, and she went over those last weeks almost obsessively, again and again.'

Charlie falls silent, chews his lip, then turns back to Elliott.

'They all would, wouldn't they?' he offers. 'I mean where murder's concerned you keep quiet if you can.'

This is so nonsensical that Elliott turns away with a sort of mild disgust at Charlie's apparent obtuseness.

'And Captain Garth,' he concludes, 'the French coroner was satisfied that he died of opium and alcohol addiction. If there was a hole in his head he didn't see it. However, you are right about one thing in that particular case.'

'I'm glad to hear it.' There is more relief than sarcasm, Elliott is amused to note, in Charlie's reply.

'His papers, including the certified copy of Princess Sophia's and General Garth's statements, were missing from under his mattress. And I do have to say it is a matter of some concern, to both my superiors and poor Mr Cargill's, that they are found. You might yet manage to pull off a deal. We'll see . . . once you're safely back in Millbank.'

'There you go then, squire.' A certain smugness is apparent on Charlie's face as he looks out of the window and grins at his own reflection.

*

426

They're already out of the Derbyshire hills. The dull rolling fields and hedges slip by, almost all arable and pastoral, orchards grubbed out, commons enclosed. Coal pits with their lifting gear and slag heaps are more and more a feature too as they get further south, since Tyneside can no longer produce enough to fuel the Industrial Revolution. Yet in a hundred years and a decade or two it'll all be over. Even the slag will have gone.

'Who are you really, Charlie? You're not Boylan, are you? He was killed at Waterloo. He looked a bit like you. And you took his name to conceal the fact you'd started the day on the wrong side, that's it, isn't it?'

'I was christened Charles.'

'Joseph Charles Edward, yes?'

But Charlie won't be drawn on that one. He thinks through what Elliott has been saying. He must be after something, something Charlie has not yet given him. And not just the Garth papers. There may be hope yet if he can fathom out what.

'The Great Exhibition wasn't the only time I worked for a German state, you know?'

'Tell me, Charlie. Tell me.'

This time it was the Frankfort lot. They paid me a pound a day, a rural labourer's weekly wage, to keep an eye on twenty-eight Dean Street. It didn't last long. I was just filling a gap left when one of their salaried employees died of cholera which he probably caught drinking from the fountain in Soho Square.

The family I was asked to spy on were even more hard up than I. They had a son, six years old or thereabouts, called, I later learnt, Edgar. He was known all through the area as a scrounger and on occasion a thief. I saw him nick some bread rolls off a baker's tray. The baker caught him and was hollering for the constable but the situation was saved when one of the family's regular callers, a German too but a prosperous businessman who came down from Manchester every now and then to visit his friends, appeared in the street and paid for the

427

buns. Young Edgar was a pert, jolly, clever sort of a lad, but he had a nasty cough which was familiar to those who lived in Soho and they didn't reckon he'd last more than a year or so.

Anyway, where was I? Yes, I kept an eye on the house for a couple of weeks in November, this is November last year I'm talking about, and in a way it was through them I got to see the greatest event of the era, even more stirring than the opening of the Exhibition the year before. Less than six months ago, Mr Elliott, so you can guess what I am referring to, but it's a mark of how low I was at the time, that I didn't even know that it was happening, or at any rate which was the chosen day. The thing of it was I felt rather bad about the whole affair. Still do. Why? I'll tell you.

I really was very hard up at the time. I'm talking about September now, end of August, not November, by when I was getting that daily sov from the Frankforters. Before that I was on my beam ends as the sailors say and I know what they mean. We were on our beam ends a couple of times going round the Horn. And I couldn't think of any shift other than to make my way to Sissinghurst with a view to putting the bite on Kate Bramshaw. But when I got there I was told she'd sold up and gone to India or some such place to help out with the famine. That's the trouble with these charitable types, eh, Mr Elliott, always ready to help the starving heathen, when there's white men dying on their doorsteps.

I was brought up in Spain, as you seem to be aware, and my knowledge of the geographicals of England is not complete. I knew I was in the county of Kent; I knew Walmer and Walmer Castle are in Kent and on the coast though to the east of Sissinghurst, so I took the road to Ashford and then Folkestone then headed up towards Deal. Of course it turned out to be a lot further than I had supposed. Why was I heading in that direction? Miss Bramshaw gone, I reckoned my old friend, the one who owed me a tanner, was the next best bet. It was a lot further than I expected. I scrumped taties and apples and, though I rarely had the means to cook the former, kept body and soul together. I've been in worse straits in California and Nevada and learnt a thing or two from the Natives I lived with in a place called Yosemite and on the banks of Lake Tahoe about how to survive in a wilderness. And Kent being no wilderness, though it has constables and gamekeepers, I managed, though always conscious of winter coming on and the fact I'd need a regular berth before long, and so was able to keep out of the Union or gaol as a vagrant.

And a regular berth is what I hoped for from Walmer Castle and the old gent who spent the back end of his summers there. Yes, I know this has got nothing to do with the Frankforters, but we've time enough before we reach King's Cross, haven't we? That was just Derby we stopped at.

Never forget a face, he always said. And he always gave a sov to any old rogue that wore the Peninsular medal. Not that I had one, though I was well due to it. And as I've said: he owed me a tanner.

Of course once I got there, there was no getting in or getting near him. But I'd sent him letters in the past and always he answered, though not to any useful effect. However, I thought it worth a try, and then, once the pencil was in my hand and a scrap of paper I'd filched beneath it, I thought to myself how writing to him in my own character had never done much good, so why not try another? I represented myself as a religious man and took on the appropriate tone telling him I was a Messenger of the Lord and would deliver His Message the next morning, a Monday, at Walmer Castle. Well, that Monday was the thirteenth, and the next day, the Tuesday, he was dead!* Almost it seemed to me I'd wished the old man's demise upon him!

* One of the last letters Wellington wrote was to Lady Salisbury, telling her he had had a letter from a madman who claimed to be a messenger of the Lord who would indeed deliver the Lord's Message. So we must assume that at least on this occasion Charlie is not lying. J. R.

Anyway, as you very well know, they embalmed the poor man and kept him for two months before putting him in the crypt of St Paul's and by then I was in Dean Street keeping an eye on behalf of the Frankforters.

Of course I'd seen the black bunting go up everywhere, and I knew there was a lying-in-state at the Chelsea Hospital, in the Great Hall, but I stayed away. And on the morning of the funeral itself I was standing in the boarded-up doorway of the house almost opposite number twenty-eight, as per usual, with my coat collar turned up against the rain, and was quickly aware that all was very quiet, none of the shops or pubs open, very few people about and those that were hurrying down towards the Trafalgar Square and bit by bit it dawned on me that this must be the day. There were muffled bells tolling, the nearest was St Martin's, and some way off, in one of the parks I suppose, a minute gun was being fired.

I was just beginning to feel a sort of regret that I was rooted as it were to the spot and would miss the big occasion when the door facing me opened and on the stoop there was the prosperous looking gent from Manchester, all done up to the nines in full black mourning, with a black silk scarf round the base of his topper and a black cane with a silver top and, coming out with him the two kids of the household, my friend Edgar and his sister, three years or so older; they all called her Jennychen. Pretty little girl she was, most attractive. Their dad, big man with a huge mop of silvering black hair, huge brows, big black beard like a pirate, in his waistcoat and shirtsleeves with a pen stuck behind his ear like a bank clerk, was inside the door, wishing them a good day of it. So it was clear he was staying behind to get on with his scribbling. He was a journalist, I'd learnt, writing for a New York newspaper, as well as being a socialist or anarchist or whatever. Which is why the Frankforters wanted an eye kept on him. And while he was working his friend was taking the children . . . well, to see the funeral, obviously. So I felt I had my excuse, and followed them.

430

It occurs to me now to wonder why he was so poor if he was a newspaperman. I mean, like the Spanish say of lawyers, who ever saw a dead donkey or a poor journalist?

We were early. We would not have seen a thing if we had not been. The crowd was already four or five deep and the windows filling up, and a couple of hundred on the raised plinth of the column.* Our prosperous Teutonic Mancunian succeeded in getting us into the portico of the National Gallery, but those already there occupied, as tight as may be, the gaps between the columns, so we headed to the east side and got on to the lower steps of St Martin's which wasn't bad at all as it gave us an uninterrupted view right down the Mall. Jennychen stood in front of her guardian whom both kids called 'Uncle Fred', and so shall I from now on, while Edgar, sharp as ever, winkled himself through the crowd, slipping like a sheet of paper through gaps where no gaps were, and got himself to the very front next to a Special, one of thousands who lined the route.

We still had a couple of hours to wait before the first of the bands reached the plaza during which the crowd became more and more dense until it was like a sea of black on either side of a causeway, and every window, every roof, every tree was filled with black too, black hats both tall or, on the women, confected out of piles of black velvet above white faces.

And there were all sorts in there, believe me. Gents and their ladies, working men, shopkeepers, barrow boys and costermongers, and still after thirty-five years a good sprinkling of the old men who had fought with him, wearing one or both of the medals, the medals I should have had by rights. They were the ones that cried, even more than the women.

But there was a fair sprinkling of foreigners and colonials too. Hindoos, Arabs and Blackies, for had he not made the French

---

* The lions arrived fifteen years later and, see below, there was no Admiralty Arch interrupting the view up the Mall. J. R.

give up the Slave Trade, and had he not spoke for emancipation? In short, there was a unity of disparate parts there, a readiness to forget conflicting interests, an acknowledgement we all belonged to something bigger than we could fully understand. A brotherhood, Mr Elliott? An Empire? Well, whatever. I flatter myself I have made my contribution one way or another in its creation.

There was intermittent sunshine out of a cloud-filled sky and occasional squalls, enough to make some attempt to put up umbrellas which their neighbours then made them pull down. There was a constant susurration of speech, rising and falling, even occasional bursts of laughter or song, especially from those who remembered the old ones like 'The British Grenadiers', and 'Rule, Britannia!', and even, a touch ironically, for he'd fallen victim to the one enemy none can defeat, 'See, the Conquering Hero Comes'; but then, as the first band wheeled in slow march into the Mall, a half-mile away, and began its slow advance towards us, the silence spread in front of it like a dark wave.

Behind the first bands came the coaches, most of them open, filled with the highest dignitaries of the land, the nobility, the Commons, the bishops and archbishops, the Lord High Chancellor, the Lord Chief Justice and all the other justices in their wigs and robes, and then bands again and more bands. The 'Funeral March' by Chopin, and the 'Funeral March' of Beethoven and most often the dead march from *Saul* by his favourite, George Handel. He liked a good tune, did the Duke. Next came the heralds in their splendour, and all those more closely connected to the Deceased than those who had gone before, including Prince Albert himself in a coach and six (the Queen maintaining the protocol that says the Monarch attends funerals of family only, though there were those who said an exception should have been made), and a Lord carrying the Duke's baton, the first a British Field Marshal ever carried. And then. At last. The Funeral Car, and the second duke, on his own, trailing a long black velvet gown.

The car was beyond everything. How big was it? Twenty-one feet long by twelve feet wide, made out of moulded bronze, decorated with a hundred allegorical figures, a great moving pyramid or Juggernaut weighing eighteen tons and pulled by twelve giant carthorses decked with nodding black plumes that did not disguise the fact that they could only have been borrowed from a brewery. The coffin on the top looked tiny.

And there, right in front of us but maybe two or three hundred yards away, while it still had a third of the Mall to go, it stuck, stuck in the mud where a gas main or whatever had been recently laid or repaired and sixty stout men from the crowd were called for to get the thing moving again.

It made no difference to the occasion. Indeed it added to it, for now the Common People had had a hand in it. As indeed was right – for had he not admitted himself that it was with the scum of the earth he had conquered Europe? And one and a half million of them had turned up to see him buried.*

Across the bottom of Trafalgar Square it all came and off came all the hats in front of it, person by person, in a concerted flowing movement that was strange and moving to see, like a huge flock of black birds rising and settling, so I wished I had a hat too I could have lifted as the old man went by. And then came his horse, not Copenhagen, who had died some fifteen or more years earlier, but a black beast he'd hunted on and ridden on state occasions, led by his groom and with his own boots, yes, those boots, hung reversed from the saddle, a sight that brought a long strange whisper from the crowd as if at last they fully realised they'd never see him again in Rotten Row, or riding to the State Opening of Parliament or at the Trooping of the Colour.

* Still, I believe, the largest crowd that has ever appeared on the streets of London to witness a state event. J. R.

> *Let the long long procession go,*
> *And let the sorrowing crowd about it grow,*
> *And let the mournful martial music blow;*
> *The last great Englishman is low.*

And Edgar is lost, and not long after Jennychen too who breaks free from Uncle Fred's hand and wiggles through the crowd like an eel or a baby dolphin, looking for him. Uncle Fred is distraught, as well he might be. He pushes through the slowly turning tide of the crowd calling their names, and 'Has anyone seen a small boy?', or 'Has anyone seen his sister?' He pushes along the Strand one way then back to the Square again, and there I leave him, alternately wringing his hands and waving his hat in the hope the missing children might see it above the crowd.

He is, I know, reputed to be a clever man, but like all clever men lacks sense. We are what, a scant half-mile from Dean Street? Those kids know where they live, especially streetwise Edgar. I slip away and get back to my doorway just ahead of them. I slip out as they turn the corner and by the time they have reached the door I am between them and holding their reluctant hands. Edgar bangs the knocker and their father, our bearded friend who looks more like a Moor than ever, stands in front of us.

'Herr Marx,' I say, 'your children were lost—'

'We were NOT,' cries Edgar.

'—but I recognised them and here they are.'

He looks down at us, shrugs, his hand goes to his pocket, he sighs, for it's more than he can afford, and he gives me . . . sixpence. A tanner.

I have it still, Mr Elliott. It's a pretty coin, don't you think? The young Queen on one side with her hair pulled back beneath her crown and a spray of oak leaves on the other. True silver, all through.

52

Charlie pauses on the steps of the prison while Elliott pays off the cab that has brought them from King's Cross. Make a dash for it? I should co-co. A necklace of lit globes lines the new embankment diminishing towards the bend and the big square tower at the west end of the Palace of Westminster. The tide is out, the mudflats glisten like the skin of a porpoise, the shit-coloured sullen river flows as slow as lava between. A snot-coloured mist begins to rise above it for although it is April the effluent that flows in from the sewers is warmer than the river water. Voices, those of the trusties allowed to leave their cells for Evensong, for it is a Sunday, are raised behind him in raucous unison.

> *All things bright and beautiful*
> *All creatures great and small*
> *All things wise and wonderful*
> *The Lord God made them all.*
>
> *Each little flower that opens*
> *Each little bird that sings*

He made their glowing colours
He made their tiny wings.

Elliott comes up the steps, takes his elbow.

'Right then. In we go.'

Charlie sniffs, pulls away his arm, wipes his nose on his sleeve.

They go through the formalities at the gatehouse, Elliott signing papers, forms in triplicate, Charlie asserting that he is indeed Charles Boylan and adding a signature to that effect. Two screws form up on either side of him, one carrying a lamp, the other the inevitably huge bunch of keys.

'Well. This is it. For the time being.' Elliott offers a hand for Charlie to shake. 'The papers, Charlie. Tell us where they are and we might get you out of here, yet.'

'Fuck off,' says Charlie.

They lead him away. Footsteps echo stonily, iron clangs behind him. Elliott turns away and sings to himself, joining in with the congregation.

The rich man in his castle
The poor man at his gate
He made them high and lowly
And ordered their estate.

All things bright and beautiful . . .

On the steps again the view he sees is very different from the one Charlie experienced. Sunset. A big sky laced with high cloud, liquid gold, white gold above, a wonderful confusion of vermilions, crimsons, violets and purples lower down, last gleaming reflections on the opalescent waters, a lozenge-shaped red buoy on the mud. Evening it might be but it's a dawn song comes into his mind:

The lark's on the wing
The snail's on the thorn

God's in his heaven –
All's right with the world!

That night Charlie Boylan, aka Joseph Charles Edward Bosham, is back in his cell, sitting at the table they had brought him, knowing that the following day he will be arraigned before the magistrates and formally charged with the attempted, or actual, murder of Thomas Cargill. Since he is innocent, he is not unduly bothered, though he supposes the process may be long and bothersome. Meanwhile, Elliott, hoping perhaps that he might be induced to record where the Garth (and other) papers might be, has arranged for him to have paper and a pen. He pulls them towards him, adjusts the position of his candle, blows on his fingers. He lifts his head and hears again the thunder of the surf and sees the sails, hull down, drop beneath the horizon, and, with a sigh, he dips his pen once more. The nib scratches and a tiny spray of ink, which he brushes dry with his threadbare sleeve, flicks across the page.

Since the Voyage of the Beagle has been fully and well described by the Scientist on board, Mr Charles Darwin, in his extended account published in 1839, I will not endeavour to surpass his efforts but begin the next part of my tale on the day I was inadvertently marooned on the larger of the Galapagos Islands . . .

THE LAST ENGLISH KING

Julian Rathbone

In 1066, a 'jumped-up little Norman and his bunch of
psychopaths' cross the water and alter the course of
English history. Three years later and Walt, King Harold's
only surviving bodyguard, is still emotionally and
physically scarred by the loss of his king and country.
Wandering through Asia Minor, headed vaguely for the
Holy Land, he tells his extraordinary story.

'Embroidering fact with fiction, rather as the makers of
the Bayeux tapestry did, Rathbone has Walt expand
on the confessions of Edward the Confessor, on the
megalomaniac notions of Canute's descendants the
ambitions of the Saxon thanes, and the savage empire
building of William the Conqueror . . . powerful'
Sunday Telegraph

'Fascinating' *Guardian*

'There are scenes of such solidity that no reader will
easily forget them' *The Times*

'Gripping . . . a rattling good story, told in strong, clear
prose . . . unforgettable' *Spectator*

'A considered and passionate evocation of the
past . . . hugely enjoyable'
Andrew Miller, author of *Ingenious Pain*

Abacus
0 349 10943 5

KINGS OF ALBION

Julian Rathbone

'In 1460, during the War of the Roses, the Lancastrians and Yorkists are busy chopping each other into little pieces and, during time out, amusing themselves with a game called "footie", which involves kicking an inflated bladder around a field. Into this unlikely idyll walks a bunch of tourists from the East who have come to search for a missing kinsman. In no time at all, they are horrified by the weather and confused by a series of appalling European idiosyncrasies (in particular, the fact that the Emperor of the Romans lives in Germany and the Christian High Priest in Rome). Julian Rathbone's follow up to the bestselling *The Last English King* is a hugely enjoyable ramble into a most gruesome period of history' *The Times*

'Although *Kings of Albion* is packed with jokes it is a serious book . . . The Wars of the Roses never seemed so strange – or so real . . . whether describing a journey through London by boat or country fields in winter, so strange to an oriental eye, Rathbone has evoked the sights and smells of fifteenth-century England . . . the result is a historical novel of charm and intelligence' *Sunday Telegraph*

'A superb adventure story. The battle scenes combine excitement with an overwhelming squalor, and there are moments of real tragedy and pathos' *Independent*

Abacus
0 349 11385 8

Now you can order superb titles directly from Abacus